About the Authors

A *New York Times* bestselling author, **Christine Rimmer** has written over ninety contemporary romances for Mills & Boon. Christine has won the *Romantic Times* BOOKreviews Reviewers Choice Award and has been nominated six times for the RITA® Award. She lives in Oregon with her family. Visit Christine at http://www. christinerimmer.com

USA TODAY bestselling author **Catherine Mann** has books in print in more than twenty countries with Mills & Boon Desire, Heroes, HQN and other imprints. A six-time RITA® finalist, she has won both a RITA® and Romantic Times Reviewer's Choice Award. Mother of , Catherine lives in South Carolina where she joys kayaking, hiking with her dog and volunteering animal rescue. FMI, visit: catherinemann.com

The day **Maggie Cox** saw the film version of *Wuthering Heights,* was the day she became hooked on romance. From that day onwards she spent a lot of time dreaming up her own romances, hoping that one day she might become published. Now that her dream is being realised, she wakes up every morning and counts her blessings. She is married to a gorgeous man, and is the mother of two wonderful sons. Her other passions in life – besides her family and reading/writing – are ic and films.

Mavericks

Mavericks: Her Secret Maverick

CHRISTINE RIMMER

CATHERINE MANN

MAGGIE COX

MILLS & BOON

First Published in Great Britain 2020
By Mills & Boon, an imprint of HarperCollins*Publishers*
1 London Bridge Street, London, SE1 9GF

MAVERICKS: HER SECRET MAVERICK © 2020 Harlequin Books S.A.

Marooned with the Maverick © 2013 Harlequin Books S.A.
An Inconvenient Affair © 2012 Catherine Mann
A Rule Worth Breaking © 2014 Maggie Cox

Special thanks and acknowledgement to Christine Rimmer for her contribution to the *Montana Mavericks: Rust Creek Cowboys* continuity.

ISBN: 978-0-263-28176-7

MIX
Paper from
responsible sources
FSC™ C007454

FSC
www.fsc.org

This book is produced from independently certified FSC™ paper to ensure responsible forest management.

For more information visit: www.harpercollins.co.uk/green

Printed and bound in Spain
by CPI, Barcelona

MAROONED WITH THE MAVERICK

CHRISTINE RIMMER

For my dad.
I love you, Dad.
And miss you so much!

Chapter One

At 2:10 in the afternoon on the Fourth of July, Collin Traub glanced out the great room window of his house on Falls Mountain and could not believe what he saw in the town down below.

He stopped stock-still and swore under his breath. How could the situation have gotten so bad so fast? He probably should have been keeping an eye on it.

But he'd been busy, his mind on work. And it was later than usual when he stopped for lunch and came upstairs.

To *this*.

He could kick his own ass for not paying more attention. It had to be about the wettest day on record in Rust Creek Falls, Montana. The rain had been coming down in buckets since yesterday morning. And Rust Creek, which ran northeast to southwest through the center of town, had been steadily rising.

Collin had told himself it was no big deal. The creek

had good, high levees on either side, levees that had held without a break for more than a hundred years. He'd never doubted that they would hold for another hundred.

And yet somehow, impossibly, sections of the levee on the south bank were crumbling. Through the thick, steady veil of rain that streamed down the windows, he watched it happen.

The levee just...dissolved, sending foaming, silvery swaths of water pouring through more than one breach. It was a lot of water and it was flowing fast and furious onto the lower-elevation south side of town.

People were going to lose their homes. Or worse.

And the water wouldn't be stopping on the edge of town, either. South of town lay Rust Creek Falls Valley, a fertile, rolling landscape of small farms and ranches—and any number of smaller creeks and streams that would no doubt also be overflowing their banks.

The Triple T, his family's ranch, was down there in the path of all that water.

He grabbed the phone off the table.

Deader than a hammer.

He dug his cell from his pocket. No signal.

The useless cell still clutched in his hand, Collin grabbed his hat and his keys and headed out into the downpour.

It was a hell of a ride down the mountain.

One-third of the way down, the road skirted close to the falls for which the mountain was named. The roar was deafening, and the pounding silver width of the falling water was twice what he was used to seeing. He made it past without incident. But if the rain kept on like this, the road could easily be washed out. He'd have himself a real adventure getting back home.

But now was not the time to worry over coming back.

He needed to get down there and do what he could to help. He focused his mind on that, keeping his boot light on the brake, giving the steering wheel a workout, as he dodged his 4x4 F-150 around mudslides and uprooted trees, with the rain coming down so thick and fast he could hardly see through the windshield. Now and then, lightning lit up the gray sky and thunder boomed out, the sound echoing off in the distance, over the valley below.

Lightning could be damned dangerous on a mountain thick with tall trees. But with the rain coming down like the end of the world and everything drenched and dripping, a lightning strike causing a forest fire was probably the last thing he needed to get anxious over today.

Water. Rivers of it. That was the problem.

There were way too many spots where the streams and overflowing ditches had shed their contents across the narrow, twisty mountain road. He was lucky to make it through a few of those spots. But he did it.

Fifteen endless minutes after sliding in behind the wheel, he reached Sawmill Street on the north edge of town. He debated: go right to North Main and see what he could do in town, or go left over the Sawmill Street Bridge, skirt the east side of town and make tracks for the Triple T.

The rest of his family was three hundred miles away for the holiday, down in Thunder Canyon attending a wedding and a reunion. That made him the only Traub around.

His obligation to the family holdings won out. He swung left and crossed the Sawmill Street Bridge, which was still several feet above the raging water. With a little luck and the Almighty in a generous mood, that bridge might hold.

The Triple T was southeast of town, so he turned south at Falls Street until he caught sight of the miniature lake that had formed at Commercial and Falls. He saw a couple of swamped vehicles, but they were empty. He swung left

again. Having been raised in the valley, he knew every rutted dirt road like he knew the face he saw when he looked
in the mirror to shave. Collin used that knowledge now,
taking the higher roads, the ones less likely to be flooded
in the troughs and dips, working his way steadily toward
the ranch.

About a mile from the long driveway that led to the
barns and houses on the Triple T, he crested a rise and,
through the heavy curtain of pouring rain, saw another
vehicle on the road ahead of him: a red Subaru Forester
moving at a dead crawl.

He knew that Subaru. And he knew who was behind
the wheel: Willa Christensen, the kindergarten teacher.

In spite of everything, the pounding, relentless rain and
the flooded road and the pretty-damned-imminent danger, Collin grinned. Since a certain evening a little more
than four years before, Willa had been running away from
him—and no, he hadn't been chasing her.

Yeah, he had something of a reputation. People called
him a skirt chaser, a player, the Traub family bad boy. But
come on. He had better things to do with his time than
sniff around after a woman who wanted nothing to do with
him. And since that night four years ago, Willa took off
like a shot whenever she saw him coming. Collin found
her frantic efforts to get away from him pretty comical, if
the truth were known.

His grin faded. She shouldn't be out in this mess. The
way she drove—so cautious, like some nervous old lady—
she was way too likely to misjudge a flooded spot, to get
all flustered and stomp the brake and end up trapped in the
waters that swamped the low sections of the road.

He knew where she was headed. The turnoff to the
Christensen Ranch wasn't far past the one to the Triple T.

But the way she was handling her vehicle, he didn't like her odds for getting there in one piece.

Collin readjusted his priorities, skipping the turn to the Triple T, staying on her tail.

The rain came down harder—if that was possible. He had the wipers on high, beating fast and hard across the windshield. *Thwack thwack thwack thwack.* Even on high, they could hardly keep up with the sheer volume of water falling out of the gunmetal-gray sky.

Lightning flashed, a jagged spear of it striking a twisted oak on a rise up ahead. The red Subaru in front of him lurched to a stop as the old oak crashed to the ground, smoke trailing up in a shower of sparks. Thunder boomed across the valley as the Subaru inched forward once again.

Every dip in the road held a churning miniflood. Each time Willa drove that little red station wagon down into a trough, Collin held his breath, sure she wouldn't make it through the swirling waters streaming across the road. But each time, she surprised him. She drove steadily forward at a safe, even crawl. And each time, the swirling water had to surrender her to higher ground. He went through in her wake, gritting his teeth, letting out a long breath of relief when he made it clear, too.

The sick ball of dread in his gut tightened to a knot when she suddenly hit the gas—no doubt because she'd finally realized that he was the guy in the pickup behind her. Instead of taking it slow and steady as she had been, watching the bad spots on the streaming, rutted road in front of her, suddenly she was all about getting the hell away from him.

"Damn it, Willa," he muttered under his breath, as if she might actually hear him. "Slow the hell down…." He leaned on the horn to get her to ease off the accelerator and watch the next dip. It looked pretty deep down there.

But the honking only seemed to freak her out all the more. She must have lead-footed it right to the floorboards. The Forester shot forward—and then took a nosedive into the water rushing across the low spot in the road.

It was bad. Deeper than he'd realized. As the vehicle leveled out, she was up to her side windows in churning brown floodwater.

And going nowhere. She'd swamped it.

Collin hit the brakes. The pickup came to a stop several feet above the flood. He shoved it into Park, turned off the engine, kicked down the parking brake and jumped out, hitting the rain-slick road at a run. Instantly drenched to the skin, with the rain beating down like it wanted to flatten him, he reached the churning water and waded in.

The Subaru was already drifting, picked up by the current and, half-floating, pushed toward the lower side of the road. The water was too high to see the danger there, but Collin knew that the bank at that spot dropped off into a ditch. A deep ditch. If the Subaru went over the edge, he'd have a hell of a time getting Willa out before she drowned.

She'd been raised in the valley, too. She knew what waited at the edge of the road. Inside the station wagon, she was working the door latch, trying to get it to open. She shouted something at him and beat on the window.

He kept slogging toward her, though the water seemed to grab at him, to drag him back. It was like those dreams you have where you have to get somewhere fast and suddenly your legs are made of lead. It seemed to be getting deeper, the pull of the swirling current more powerful, second by second.

Half stumbling, half swimming, while the Subaru slowly rotated away from him as it drifted ever closer to the shoulder and the ditch beyond, Collin bent at the knees and launched himself at the driver's door.

He made it. His fingers closed around the door handle. He used it to pull his feet under him again.

"You push, I'll pull!" he yelled good and loud.

She just kept pounding on the window, her brown eyes wide with fright.

He hollered even louder than before, "Push, Willa! Count of three."

She must have heard him, must have finally understood. Because she pressed her lips together and nodded, her dark, pulled-back hair coming loose, the soft curls bouncing around her fear-white cheeks. She put her shoulder into the door.

"One, two, three!" He pulled. She pushed. The door didn't budge.

"Again! One, two, three!"

The miracle happened. The Subaru rotated just enough that the current caught the door as he yanked the handle and she threw her shoulder against it. The damn thing came open with such force it knocked him over.

He went under. The door hit him in the side of the head. Not all that hard. But still.

Trying to be a hero? Not the most fun he'd ever had.

Somehow, he managed to get his waterlogged boots under him and pushed himself upright, breaking the surface in time to see his hat spinning away on the current and Willa flailing, still inside the Subaru as the water poured in on her through the now-open driver's door.

Wonderful.

He went for her, diving through the open door, grabbing for her and catching her arm. He heard her scream—or she tried to. The water cut off most of the high-pitched sound. It kept pouring in, beating at them as it filled the cab.

They had to get out and get out now.

He pulled on her arm until he'd turned her, faceup, and

then he caught her in a headlock. Okay, it wasn't delicate. It wasn't nice and it sure wasn't gentle. But with his arm around her neck, at least he could turn and throw himself out the door. She grabbed his arm in both her hands, but by then, she seemed to have caught on to what he was trying to do. She wasn't fighting him anymore. She was only holding on as tight as he was.

He squirmed around to face the open door. The water shoved him back, but at least the rotation of the vehicle kept the door from swinging shut and trapping them inside. He got his free hand on the door frame, knees bent, boots braced on the side of the seat. Another hard push and they were out just as the Subaru went over the bank into the ditch.

The weight of the vehicle going under sucked at them, but Willa slipped free of his hold and started swimming. Since she seemed to be making it on her own steam, he concentrated on doing the same.

Side by side, they swam for the place where the road rose up out of the ditch. His boots touched ground. Beside him, she found her footing, too—for an instant. Then she staggered and went under.

He grabbed her again, hauling her up, getting one arm around her waist. Lightning tore another hole in the sky and thunder boomed as he half carried, half dragged her up and out of the racing water.

She coughed and sputtered, but she kept her feet moving. The woman had grit. He had to give her that. He kept hold of her, half-supporting her, urging her to the high side of the road and up the hill far enough that they were well above the water and reasonably safe.

They collapsed side by side onto the streaming ground as the rain continued to beat down on them, hard and heavy, never ending. She turned over, got up on her hands and knees and started hacking and coughing, spitting up water. He dragged in one long, hungry breath after another and pounded her back for her, helping her clear her airways so she could breathe. When she was finally doing more breathing than hacking, he fell back on the ground and concentrated on catching his own breath.

Lucky for him, he just happened to turn his head and glance in the direction of his truck about then. The water *had* risen. Considerably. It was maybe two feet from his front wheels now.

He turned to the waterlogged woman gasping beside him. "Stay here. Do not move. I'll be right back."

Swearing low and with feeling, he lurched upright and beat feet on a parallel track with the road. When he got even with his truck, he half ran, half slid down the hill, raced around the rear of the pickup and hauled himself up into the cab. The key was still in the ignition—and the water was lapping around his front wheel wells by then.

He turned it over, released the brake, put it in Reverse and backed to the top of the last rise. Once there, he slammed it in Park again and jumped out to see how things looked behind him.

Not good. The road was flooded in the previous trough. Water in front of him, water behind. The truck was going nowhere until the water receded.

Fair enough. He got back in and parked on the shoulder. Taking his keys with him that time, he left the truck and locked it up.

Then he looked for Willa.

She was gone.

Chapter Two

A moment later, Collin spotted her.

She was on her feet and slogging up the long slope of the hill. He knew then where she was headed. There was a big, weathered, rambling structure way at the top—the Christensen barn.

"Willa, what the hell?" he yelled good and loud. "Hold on a minute!"

She didn't pause, she didn't turn. Her hair plastered to her head, and her little white T-shirt and snug jeans covered with mud and debris, she just kept on putting one boot in front of the other, heading up that hill.

He was powerfully tempted to let her go.

But who knew what trouble she'd get herself into next? If something happened to her, he'd end up with a guilty conscience for leaving her all by her lonesome. Plus, well, he didn't have a lot of options himself, at the moment. The floodwaters were all around.

And it might be July, but the rain was a cold rain and the

wind was up, too. He needed shelter to wait out the storm and the barn had walls and a roof. It was better than nothing. Willa was going to have to get over her aversion to him, at least until there was somewhere else he could go.

With a grunt of resignation, he climbed the hill after her, tucking his head down, putting one foot in front of the other, as the water streamed over him and his boots made sucking sounds with each step he took.

He caught up to her maybe twenty yards from the barn. She must have heard the sloshing of his boots at last.

She stopped, her arms wrapped around herself to control the shivers that racked her, and whirled to confront him. "Collin." She tipped her head up and drew her slim shoulders back. Water ran down her cheeks, into her wide mouth and over her chin.

He could see her nipples, hard as rocks, right through her T-shirt and her bra. "What, Willa?"

"Thank you for saving my life."

"Hey." He swiped water off his nose. Not that it did any good. "No problem. Can we move it along? It's pretty damn wet out here. I'd like to get in that barn."

She gripped her arms tighter around herself. "I would like for you to go away and leave me alone."

"Oh, you would, would you?"

"Yes. Please."

He raised his arms out wide, indicating all of it—the never-ending storm, the floodwaters surrounding them, the cold wind and the flash of bright lightning that lit up the sky again right at that moment. The thunder rumbled. He waited for the sound to die away. "Exactly where do you suggest I go, Willa?"

She flung out a hand. "What about your truck?"

He folded his arms across his chest and simply looked at her.

Her shoulders sagged and she let out a low cry. "Oh,

fine. All right. You can come in the barn. Just…fine. Okay." And she turned around again and continued walking.

He fell in behind her.

The barn loomed ahead. When they reached it, she undid the latch and slipped in. He went in after her, pulling the door to, latching it from within.

The barn had another door on the far wall. Someone must have left the latch undone, because that door stood wide-open. It was probably not a bad thing in this situation. The Christensen livestock needed more than a run-in shed on a day like today and the animals had found what they needed through that wide-open door.

The rambling space was wall-to-wall critters. There were cattle, goats, some chickens and several cooing pigeons. Carping blackbirds perched in the rafters. A couple of pigs snorted beneath one of the two windows and somewhere nearby a barn cat hissed and then yowled.

A dog barked. Collin spotted a muddy white Labrador retriever. The dog was headed for Willa.

She let out a happy little cry. "Buster! There you are!" She dropped to a crouch and opened her arms. The dog reared up and put his front paws on her shoulders. Whining with excitement, he licked her face with his sloppy pink tongue. "You are such a bad, bad dog," she crooned in a tone that communicated no criticism whatsoever. "Hey, now. Eww." She turned her head away from Buster's slobbery attentions and saw Collin watching her.

"Nice dog." He'd had a great dog named Libby who'd died the winter before. She'd been sixteen, with him since he was eleven and she was an ugly pup, the runt of the litter wanted by no one—but him.

"Down, Buster." She rose again and tried to brush the mud and water off her soaking wet shirt and muddy jeans.

It did zero good. "Technically, he's my dog," she explained, "but he's always loved it here on the ranch, so he lives here more than with me. He was supposed to be staying with me in town, though, while my parents and Gage are in Livingston for the big rodeo." Gage Christensen, her brother, was the town sheriff. "That dog just will not stay put. He keeps running off to get back here." A shiver went through her. She wrapped her arms around herself again.

"You're freezing," he said. It came out sounding like an accusation, though he didn't mean it that way.

"I am fine." She shivered some more. Her hair was plastered on her cheeks and down her neck. She swiped at a soggy hunk of it, shoving it back behind her ear. "Just fine." She scowled at him.

Whoa. For a minute there, she'd almost seemed friendly—but then she must have remembered that she hated his ass. She turned her back on him and started weaving her way through the crush of horses and cattle. The Lab followed her, panting happily, wagging his muddy tail.

It should have been warmer in there, with all the steaming, milling livestock. But it really wasn't. How could it be, with that far door wide-open and both of them soaking wet? He slapped the bony butt of a little red heifer who'd backed in too close. She let out a cranky "moo," and ambled away—not far, though. There wasn't really anywhere to go.

He found a hay bale against the wall and sat on it as he pondered what he ought to do to make things a little more comfortable. He hesitated to go over and shut the other door. The smell of wet livestock and manure would get pretty strong if he did that.

As he considered what to do next, he watched the dripping brown-haired woman who had spent the past four years avoiding him and now happened to be stuck with him until the rain ended and the floodwaters receded.

Willa was keeping busy shivering and ignoring him, wandering from steer to goat to barn cat to bay mare, petting them all and talking to them low and soft, as though she had a personal relationship with each and every four-legged creature on her family's place. And maybe she did.

She'd always been a fanciful type, even way back when they were kids. He knew this from actual observation.

Collin had run wild as a kid. He was the youngest, sixth of six boys, and his mom was worn-out by the time he came along. She didn't have the energy to keep after him. He went where he wanted and came home when he felt like it. He wandered far and wide. Often, he found himself on Christensen land. Now and then, he'd run into Willa. She would be singing little songs to herself, or making crowns out of wildflowers, or reading fairy-tale books.

She'd never seemed to like him much, even then. Once she'd yelled at him to stop spying on her.

He hadn't been spying. A kid wasn't spying just because he stretched out in the tall grass and watched a neighbor girl talking to herself as she walked her big-haired brunette Barbie doll around in a circle.

Collin tried to get more comfortable on the hay bale. He scooted to the wall, leaned his head back against the rough boards, closed his eyes and tried not to think how cold he was, tried not to wish he'd grabbed a snack to take with him when he'd run out of the house. His stomach grumbled. He ignored it.

It would have been nice if he could drop off to sleep for a little and forget everything. But no such luck. He would just start to doze when a fit of shivering would snap him awake and he would realize anew that they were smack-dab in the middle of one hell of a disaster. He hoped that no one in town had drowned, that the hands and the animals on the Triple T were safe. He couldn't help wondering how much of both the town or his family's ranch would be left standing when the floodwaters receded.

And how much of the state was affected? What about Thunder Canyon, where his family had gone? Were they underwater, too?

Eventually, he gave up trying to sleep and opened his eyes. Willa stood at the window that faced southwest, the one not far from where two spotted pigs were snorting over an upturned bucket of feed. With the white Lab at her feet, she stared out through the endless curtain of the rain. He rubbed his arms to try and warm up a little and knew she must be staring at her parents' place. The Christensen house was about level with the barn, on high ground, atop the next hill over.

He knew he was asking for more rejection to try and talk to her, but he was just tired and dejected enough to do it anyway. "The house should be safe," he said. He didn't mention her brother Gage's house, which was down the slope of the hill behind her parents' place. It wouldn't be visible from Willa's vantage point, which was just as well. As Collin remembered, it was a ways down the hill and probably already below the rising waterline.

She surprised him by replying. "Yes. I can see it. It's okay, for now...." She sounded strange, he thought. Kind of dreamy and far away. She had a few scratches on her arms. And a bruise on her cheekbone. But like him, no serious injuries. They'd been very fortunate. So far. She added, "It's all so unbelievable, don't you think? Like maybe this isn't even actually happening. Maybe I'm just dreaming it."

"Sorry, Willa." He meant that. He *was* sorry. "I think it's really happening."

She sent him a glance. For once, her mouth didn't pinch

up at the sight of him. "I lost my phone." A shiver went through her and her teeth chattered together. "Do you happen to have yours with you?"

"It's in my truck, I think. But there must be towers down. I was getting no signal when I tried using it at a little after two."

Willa sighed and turned back to the window. "Life is so…fragile, really, isn't it? I mean, you go along, doing what you need to do, thinking you're taking care of business, that you're in control. But you're not in control, not really." Outside, lightning flared. Thunder rolled out. "Anything could happen," she said. "It could rain and rain and never stop…." Her lips looked kind of blue, he thought.

He really needed to come up with a way to warm her up a little. Rising, he began to work his way around the barn, looking for a blanket or a tarp or something.

Willa kept talking. "Oh, Collin. I keep thinking of the children in my class last year. And the ones in our summer school program. I can just close my eyes and see each one of their sweet, smiling faces. I hope they're all safe and dry. Our school, the elementary school? It's on the south side of town. That's not good news. And my house is on the south side, too…."

He pushed a goat out of the way as he came to a spot where the wall jogged at a ninety-degree angle. Around that corner was a door. He opened it. "Willa, there's a tack room here."

She sighed again. "Yes. That's right. And a feed room over there." She put out a hand in the general direction of the other shut door farther down the wall. And then she started in again, about life and the flood and the safety of her friends, her neighbors and her students.

Collin took a look around the tack room. There were the usual rows of hooks holding ropes and bridles and bits. He was a saddle maker by trade and he grinned at the sight of one of his own saddles racked nice and neat, lined up with several others on the wall. There was a window. And another door, allowing outside access.

The floor in there was wood, not mixed clay and sand as it was out in the main part of the barn. And the walls were paneled in pine.

And then he saw the stack of saddle blankets atop a big cedar storage trunk. He went over and grabbed one. Shooing out the goat that had followed him in there, he shut the door and made his way through the milling animals to Willa.

She didn't even flinch when he wrapped the blanket around her. "Thank you."

He took her by the shoulders. "Come on. Let's go...." She went where he guided her, back through the cattle and horses and goats, with the dog right behind them. He let the dog in the tack room with them, and then shut the door to keep the rest of the animals out. There were a few hay bales. He sat her down on one and knelt in front of her.

She frowned down at him. "What are you doing?"

He held her gaze. "Don't get freaky on me, okay?"

She looked at him in that pinched, suspicious way again. "Why not?"

"You need to get out of those wet clothes. There are plenty of blankets. You can wrap yourself up in them and get dry."

"But...my clothes won't dry."

"It doesn't matter. Right now, *you* need to get dry."

She considered that idea—and shook her head. "I'll take off my boots and socks. I'll be all right."

He decided not to argue with her. "Fine. You need help?"

"No, thank you." All prim and proper and so polite. "I'll manage."

"Are you thirsty?"

She gaped at him. "Thirsty?" And then she let out a wild little laugh. "In this?" She stuck out a hand toward the water streaming down the lone window.

"Are you?"

And she frowned again. "Well, yes. Now that you mention it, I suppose I am."

He rose. "I'll see if I can find some clean containers in the barn. We can catch some of the rainwater, so we won't get dehydrated."

She blinked up at him. "Yes. That makes sense. I'll help." She started to rise.

He took her shoulders again and gently pushed her back down. "Get out of your boots and shoes—and wrap this around your feet." He held out another blanket.

She took it, her gaze colliding with his. Holding. "What about you?"

"Let me see about setting out containers for water. Then I'll grab a few blankets and try and warm up a little, too."

Half an hour later, he had his boots and socks off. They'd pushed four hay bales together and spread a blanket over them. Side by side, wrapped in more blankets, they passed a bucket of water back and forth.

When they'd both drunk their fill, there was still plenty left in the bucket. He set it on the floor, where Buster promptly stuck his nose in it and started lapping. "You don't happen to have a nice T-bone handy, do you, Willa?"

She chuckled. There wasn't a lot of humor in the sound, but he took heart that at least she wasn't staring blindly into space anymore. "Plenty on the hoof right outside that door." She pointed her thumb over her shoulder at the door that led into the barn.

He scooted back to the wall for something to lean against. "Not that hungry yet."

"I didn't think so." She scooted back, too, settling alongside him, and then spent a moment readjusting the blanket she'd wrapped around her feet. "There." She leaned back and let out a long breath. "I believe I am actually beginning to thaw out."

"That was the plan." Outside, the rain kept falling. The sky remained that same dim gray it had been all day. "Got any idea what time it is?"

"I don't know. Six, maybe? Seven?" She sounded... softer. A little sleepy. That was good. Rest wouldn't hurt either of them. "Won't be dark for hours yet...."

He was feeling kind of drowsy, too, now that he wasn't chilled to the bone anymore and most of the adrenaline rush from the various near-death events of the day had faded a little. He let his eyelids droop shut.

But then she spoke again. "It's really very strange, Collin, being here with you like this."

He grunted. "This whole day has been pretty strange."

"Yes, it has. And scary. And awful. But, well, that's not what I meant."

He knew exactly what she meant. And why was it women always had to dig up stuff that was better left alone? He kept nice and quiet and hoped she wasn't going there.

But she was. "Maybe this is a good chance to clear the air a little between us."

"The air is plenty clear from where I'm sitting."

"Well, Collin, for me, it's just not."

"Willa, I—"

"No. Wait. I would like a chance to say what's on my mind."

He didn't let out a groan of protest, but he wanted to.

And she kept right on. "It was very...humiliating for me, that night at the Ace in the Hole." The Ace was on Sawmill Street. It was the only bar in town. People went there to forget their troubles and usually only ended up creating a whole new set of them. "It was my first time there, did you know? My twenty-first birthday." She sounded all sad and wistful.

He'd known. "I think you mentioned that at the time, yeah."

"Derek had just dumped me for a Delta Gamma." Straight-arrow Derek Andrews was her high school sweetheart. They'd graduated the same year and headed off to the University of Idaho together. "Collin, did you *hear* me?"

"Every word," he muttered.

"Did you *know* it was over between me and Derek?"

"Well, Willa, I kinda had a feeling something might have gone wrong with your love life, yeah."

"You led me on," she accused. "You know that you did." He'd seen her coming a mile away. Good-girl Willa Christensen, out to find a bad boy just for the night. "And then you..." Her voice got all wobbly. "You turned me down flat."

"Come on, Willa. It wasn't a good idea. You know that as well as I do."

"Then why did you dance with me all those times? Why did you flirt with me and buy me two beers? You acted like you were interested. More than interested. And then, when I tried to kiss you, you laughed at me. You said I wasn't your type. You said I should go home and behave myself."

He'd had some crazy idea at the time that he was doing her a favor, keeping her from doing something she wouldn't be happy about later. But with Willa, no good deed of his ever went unpunished. And was she going to start crying? He hated it when a woman started crying.

She sniffled in her blankets, a small, lost little sound. "I still can't believe I did that—made a pass at *you*. I mean, you never liked me and I never cared much for you and we both know that." That wasn't true—not on his part anyway. Far from it. But he wasn't in the mood to dispute the point at the moment. He only wanted her not to start crying—and he thought maybe he was getting his wish when she squirmed in her blankets and grumbled, "Everyone knows how you are. You'll sleep with anyone—except *me,* apparently."

Mad. Now she was getting mad. As far as he was concerned, mad was good. Mad was great. Anything but weepy worked for him.

She huffed, "I just don't know what got into me that night."

He couldn't resist. "Well, Willa, we both know it wasn't me."

She made another huffing sound. "Oh, you think you're so funny. And you're not. You're very annoying and you always have been."

"Always?" he taunted.

"Always," she humphed.

He scoffed at her. "How would you know a thing about me the last four years? Since that night at the Ace, all I see is the backside of you. I come in a room—and you turn tail and run."

"And why shouldn't I? You are a complete tool and you never cared about anything or anyone in your whole life but yourself."

"Which is girl talk for 'You didn't sleep with me,'" he said in his slowest, laziest, most insolent tone.

"You are not the least bit clever, you know that?"

"You don't think so, huh?"

"No, I do not. And it just so happens that I'm *glad* we never hooked up that night. You're the last person in the world I should ever be sleeping with."

He tried not to grin. "No argument there. Because I'm not having sex with you no matter how hard you beg me."

"Oh, please. I mean just, simply, *please.*" She sat up straight then. Dragging her blankets along with her, she scooted to the edge of the hay bales, as far from him as she could get without swinging her bare feet to the floor. Once there, she snapped, "You do not have worry. I want nothing to do with you."

He freed a hand from his blankets and made a show of wiping his brow—even though she wasn't looking at him. "Whew."

"In case you didn't know, it just so happens that I have a fiancé, thank you very much."

"A fiancé?" That *was* news to Collin. The information bothered him. A lot—and that it bothered him bugged him to no end.

"Yes," she said. "Well. Sort of."

"Willa, get real. You do or you don't."

"His name is Dane Everhart and he's an assistant coach at the University of Colorado. We met at UI. We've been dating on and off for three years. Dane loves me and knows I'm the one for him and wants only to marry me and, er, give me the world."

"Hold on just a minute. Answer the question. You're saying you're engaged?"

She fiddled with her blankets and refused to turn around and look at him. "Well, no. Not exactly. But I *could* be. I promised to give Dane an answer by the end of the summer."

He stared at the back of her head. Her hair was a tangle

of wild, muddy curls from her dip in the floodwaters. It should have looked like crap. But it didn't. It looked like she'd been having crazy good sex with someone—and then fallen asleep all loose and soft and satisfied.

And why the hell was he thinking about sex right now? Was he losing his mind? Probably. A few hours trapped in a barn with Willa Christensen could do that to a man, could drive him clean out of his head.

He sat up, too, then, and sneered, "You're in love with this guy, and you're not going to see him until *September?*"

"So? What's wrong with that?"

"Well, I mean, if you're in *love* with him, how can you *stand* to be apart from him? How can *he* stand to be away from you?"

"You wouldn't understand."

"Are you in love with him, Willa?"

She squared her slim shoulders. "I just *told* you that you wouldn't understand."

"That's right. I wouldn't. If I loved a woman, I'd want her with me. Where I could touch her and be with her and hold her all night long."

Willa gasped. She tried to hide the small, sharp sound, but he heard it. "Oh, please. As if you know anything about being in love, Collin Traub."

"I said if I *was* in love."

"Well. Humph. As it happens, Dane has gone to Australia until the end of the month. He gets only a short summer break before practice begins again. And do you know how he's spending his limited free time? I will tell you how he's spending it. At a special sports camp. He's helping Australian children learn about American football. Because he's a good man, a man who *cares* about other people. That's how he is. That's *who* he is…"

There was more. Lots more.

Collin let her heated words wash over him. The point, as far as he saw it, was that she hadn't answered the main question. She hadn't come out and said, "Yes. I'm in love with Dane Everhart."

He felt absurdly satisfied with what she *hadn't* said. She could rant all night about the wonderfulness of this Dane character while talking trash about *him*. At least she was acting like the Willa he'd always known. At least she was full of fire and vinegar and not shaking with cold, shock and fear anymore.

Collin smiled to himself, settled back against the wall and closed his eyes.

Chapter Three

Willa felt Collin's presence behind her acutely.

But she didn't turn to him. She sat on the edge of the pushed-together hay bales and stared resolutely out the tack room's one window as waves of never-ending rain flowed down the glass.

She finished what she had to say about Dane. "It just so happens that Dane would have liked to have taken me with him. But he was going to be very busy with the Australian children and I had things I could be doing here at home. We have summer school at Rust Creek Falls Elementary, in case you didn't know and I…" Her voice trailed off.

Collin hadn't said a word for a couple of minutes, maybe more. Had he fallen *asleep,* for heaven's sake?

She wouldn't put it past him. He was such an exasperating, impossible man. Always had been. And no doubt always would be.

So why am I starting to feel ashamed of myself?

Willa's cheeks were flaming. She tucked her chin down into the scratchy saddle blanket he'd wrapped around her. At least he couldn't see her embarrassment at her own behavior—not as long as she didn't turn and face him.

Which she was not going to do right now, thank you very much.

Stretched out on the floor by the hay bales, Buster huffed out a long sigh. Willa bent down and scratched him on the head. His tail bounced happily against the rough plank floor.

She gathered her blankets close again. All right, she probably shouldn't have gone off on Collin like that. No matter how humiliating her history with the guy, he'd been there when she desperately needed him. He'd saved her life a few hours ago, at no small risk to himself.

Plus, well, she hadn't really been honest while she was getting all up in his face just now, had she? She hadn't bothered to mention that she had serious reservations about her and Dane. Dane was the greatest guy in the world and he did want to marry her, very much. But Rust Creek Falls was her home and he wasn't about to give up his wonderful career at CU. And more important than geography, Dane somehow didn't quite *feel* like her guy.

Whatever her guy *should* feel like. She wasn't sure. She just had a certain intuition that Dane wasn't it.

And worse than her doubts about her future with an ideal man like Dane, well, there was that longtime *thing* she'd had for Collin—oh, not anymore. Of course not. That night at the Ace in the Hole had put an end to her ridiculous schoolgirl crush on the town bad boy. But before that night she used to fantasize about him now and then.

Or maybe even more often than now and then.

She used to wonder what it would be like if bad-boy Collin were to kiss her. Or do more than kiss her...

Not that it mattered now. None of her past silliness over Collin mattered to anyone. It had been a fantasy, that was all. *Her* fantasy. He'd never been the least interested in her. He'd made that painfully clear on the night he led her on and then laughed in her face.

And really, after all that had happened today, her four-year grudge against him for not having sex with her was beginning to seem nothing short of petty. She really needed to let the past go. She needed to be…a bigger person than she'd been so far about this. She needed to be a *better* person.

And she needed to start doing that now.

Willa cleared her throat. "Um. Collin?"

He shifted a little, back there against the wall. "What now, Willa?" His voice was scratchy and deep. Lazy. What was it about him? He just always made her think of wrinkled sheets and forbidden passion.

In a purely impersonal, objective way, of course.

"I, um, well…"

"Come on. Spit it out."

She made herself say it. "I'm sorry, okay?" She hauled her blanket-wrapped legs back up on the hay bales and wiggled around until she was facing him again. He lay sprawled under his blankets, his head propped against the wall, his eyes shut, his eyelashes black as coal, thicker than any girl's, his full mouth lax and lazy, just like his voice had been, the shadow of a beard on his cheeks. A curl of that impossibly thick black hair of his hung over his forehead. She clutched her blankets tighter to keep from reaching out and smoothing it back. "I shouldn't have jumped all over you like that. I shouldn't have called you a tool. That was…small-minded and mean-spirited of me, especially after all you've done for me today."

He didn't say anything for a minute. And he didn't open

his eyes. Again, she wondered if he'd dropped off to sleep and she had to resist the urge to reach out and shake him. But then those bad-boy lips curved upward in a slow smile. "So you don't think I'm a tool, then?"

"Um. No. No, of course not. I shouldn't have said that. I'm sorry. I am."

"And you think maybe you could stop racing off like your hair's on fire every time you see me coming?"

A fresh wave of embarrassment had her cheeks flaming all over again. But what did it matter? He couldn't see her blush. His eyes were shut. Also, she truly wanted to make amends. "Ahem. Yes. Fair enough. I will do that. I will stop avoiding you."

"Well, all right then. I accept your apology." He patted the empty space beside him. "Stretch out. Try and get some sleep. I'm thinking we're going to be busy when the rain stops and the water goes down."

His words brought reality crashing back down on her. She hung her head. "Oh, Collin. It seems like it's never going to stop. I know my brother's house is already underwater. And what if it just keeps rising, what if we—?"

"Shh." He reached out and clasped her arm through the thick wool of the blanket. His grip was strong. Sure. It made her so very glad that he was here with her, that she wasn't huddled in the family barn all alone, waiting out the endless storm. "Don't go there." His voice was calm and firm. "There's no point."

She lifted her head. His eyes were open now, steady on hers. Shamelessly, she pleaded, "Tell me that we're going to be okay, that Rust Creek Falls will be okay, that we'll make it through this, come back better and stronger than ever."

He didn't even hesitate. He told her what she needed to hear. "We will. Just watch. Now come here. Come on…" He lifted the blanket that covered him.

She didn't think twice. She went down into the shelter of his offered arm, resting her head on his shoulder. He was so warm and big and solid. He smelled of mud and man, which at that moment she found wonderfully reassuring. He fiddled with the blankets, smoothing them over both of them.

Willa smiled to herself. All those crazy teenage dreams she'd had about him. And here she was, damp and dirty, bruised and scratched up, lying practically on top of him, grateful beyond measure to share a pile of saddle blankets with him. The world seemed to have gone crazy in the space of a day. But right now, in Collin's arms, she felt safe.

Protected.

She closed her eyes. "I didn't realize until now how tired I am...."

He touched her hair, gently. Lightly. "Rest, then."

She started to answer him, but then she found she didn't have the energy to make a sound. Sleep closed over her. She surrendered to it with a grateful sigh.

When she woke, the light was different.

Sun. It was sun slanting in the window—and the window faced east. That meant it had to be morning, didn't it? Also...

She was lying on a man. Collin. He had both arms wrapped around her and his cheek against her dirty, snarled hair. Her head was on his shoulder, one arm tucked in against her side.

Her other arm rested on Collin, which was perfectly acceptable, given the circumstances. But the hand that was attached to that arm? That hand was exactly where it shouldn't be.

And where it shouldn't be was hard.

Blinking, not quite putting it all together as reality

yet, Willa lifted her head from his shoulder and blearily squinted at the morning light. Outside, faintly, she could hear birds singing.

Without moving her hand away from his very definite, very thick and large hardness, she looked down at him. Because, seriously. Could this actually be happening?

It was.

And he was awake. He gazed up at her with the strangest, laziest, *sexiest* expression. "Mornin'."

She puffed out her cheeks as she blew out a slow breath. And then, with great care, she removed her hand from his private parts and whispered, "The sun's out."

He nodded. "The rain's stopped. It stopped hours ago." He was playing along with her, pretending the contact between her hand and his fly had not occurred. Which was great. Perfect. Wonderful of him.

She backed off him onto her knees, dragging the blankets with her, and shoved her hair out of her eyes. "You, uh, should have woken me."

"Uh-uh." He reached out and clasped her shoulder, a companionable, reassuring sort of gesture that made tears clog her throat. She swallowed them down. And he said, "You needed your sleep and so did I. I woke up in the middle of the night and it was quiet. I knew the rain had finally stopped. I thought about getting up, but then I just closed my eyes and went back to sleep."

Buster was up, making whining noises, scratching at the door that led outside. "I should let him out...." He took his hand from her shoulder. She wished he hadn't, that he would touch her again, hold on tight and never, ever let go. But he didn't. And she pushed the blankets aside, swung her legs over the edge of the hay bales and stood up. Barefoot, she went and pulled the door open. Buster went out and she scolded, "Don't run off, now." And then she lingered in the open doorway, staring up at the sky. Blue as a newborn baby's eyes. She glanced back over her shoulder at Collin.

He was sitting up, bare feet on the floor. He had a case of bed head every bit as bad as hers, and he was kind of hunched over, his elbows on his knees. "Come on," he said gruffly. "Put your boots on," He raked his fingers back through all that thick, every-which-way hair. "We'll see if the water's gone down enough that we can get across the ravine to your folks' house."

They put on their damp socks and boots and pulled open the door that led into the main part of the barn.

"Needs a good mucking out in here," Collin said. Did it ever. Most of the animals had wandered off, out into the morning sunshine, leaving a whole lot of fresh manure behind. "You supposed to be taking care of the place all by your lonesome while your folks and your brother are off at the rodeo?"

She shook her head and named off the neighbors who'd agreed to look after things and feed the stock until the family returned. "But I'm guessing they probably all have their own problems about now." At least it was summer and grazing was good. The animals wouldn't starve if left to their own devices for a few days.

Instead of slogging through the mess on the barn floor to one of the outer doors, they ducked back into the tack room and went out through the exterior door there. Buster was waiting for them, sitting right outside the door, acting as though he'd actually listened when she told him not to wander off.

Willa scratched his head and called him a good dog and tried to tell herself that the jittery feeling in her stomach was because she hadn't eaten since lunch the day before—

not rising dread at the prospect of how bad the damage was behind the barn on the next rise over, and along the roads that crisscrossed the valley. And in town…

"It's a beautiful day," she said, tipping her head up again to the clear sky. "You'd almost think yesterday never even happened."

"Hey."

She lowered her gaze to him. Even with his hair sticking up on one side and a smudge of dirt at his temple, he still looked like every well-behaved girl's naughty, forbidden fantasy. "Hmm?"

His dark eyes searched hers. "You okay?"

And she nodded and forced her mouth to form a smile.

On the other side of the barn, the two pigs from the night before were rooting around near the water trough. A rooster stood on a section of busted-down fence and crowed as Willa stared across the ravine at her parents' house.

The house was untouched by the flood, though the water had gotten halfway up the front walk that was lined with her mother's prized roses. Her dad's minitractor lay on its side at the base of that walk. And a couple of steers had somehow gotten through the fence and were snacking on the vegetable garden in the side yard.

Below, in the ravine, the water had receded, leaving debris strewn down the sides of the hill and up the one on which the house sat. There were tree trunks and lawn chairs down there, boulders and a bicycle, a shade umbrella and any number of other items that looked bizarre, scary and all wrong, soggy and busted up, trailing across the pasture. Willa turned her eyes away, toward the road.

And saw her red Subaru. It had drifted past the ditch and lay on its side in the pasture there. It was covered in mud.

"Guess I'll be needing a new car." She tried to sound philosophical about it, but knew that she didn't exactly succeed.

"Come on," he said. "Let's go check out the house. Watch where you put your feet in that ravine."

Buster and the two pigs followed them down there. They picked their way with care through all the soggy junk and knotted tree roots. It was going to be quite a job, cleaning up. And she knew that all the other ranches in the valley had to be in a similar state, if not worse. Her family still had a barn and the house, at least. And as far as she could see, there were no animals or—God forbid—people lying broken amid the wreckage down there.

When they reached the house, they skirted the downed tractor and went up the front steps. She'd lost her keys. They were probably still stuck in the ignition of her poor Subaru. But her mom had left a house key where she always did, in the mouth of the ceramic frog by the porch swing.

They went inside. The power and phone were both out, but still, it all looked just as it had the last time she'd been there, the white refrigerator covered with those silly smiling-flower magnets her mother liked, some of them holding reminders to pick up this or that at the store. There were also pictures of her and her brother and a few recipes her mom was meaning to try. In the living room, the remote sat on the magazine table by her dad's recliner and her mother's knitting bag waited in its usual place at the end of the fat blue sofa.

Her childhood home. Intact. It seemed a miracle to her right then. And she wanted to cry all over again—with a desperate, hot sort of joy.

Collin turned on the water in the kitchen. It ran clear,

but they both knew that the flood could have caused contamination of any wells in its path.

She said, "We have wells for the stock. But for this house and Gage's place, we have a water tank that taps an underground spring higher up on this hill. The floodwaters wouldn't have reached that far. So the water here, in the house, is safe."

"That's good. A lot of valley wells are going to need disinfecting. Any source of clean water is great news."

She nodded. "And in town, they get water from above the falls. So they should be all right, too, shouldn't they, at least on the north side of the creek?" He shrugged. She knew what he was thinking. Who could say what they would find in town? And what about his family's place? "I know you probably want to head over to the Triple T...."

"Yeah. But let's check out your brother's house first, and then see about getting something to eat."

Gage's house. She realized she didn't want to go there.

But she did it anyway. And she was glad, again, for Collin's presence at her side. The house was locked up. They looked in the windows. It was bad. The waterline went three feet up the walls, but the moisture had wicked higher still in ugly, muddy little spikes. Gage's furniture was beyond saving, soggy and stained, the stuffing popping out.

"Can we get to the propane tank?" Collin asked. "Better to be safe than sorry when it comes to a possible gas leak." She showed him the way. They were able to turn it off from outside. Then he said, "Come on. There's nothing more we can do here right now."

They went back to her parents' house and found plenty to eat in the pantry. She filled Buster's food bowl and the hungry dog quickly emptied it. After the meal, she took the perishables out of the fridge and put them in a bucket in the front yard. The two pigs went right to work on the treat.

By then it was still early, a little after seven. Collin suggested they make use of the safe water source and take showers before they left. There was just no way to guess the next time they'd have a chance to clean up a little. As at Gage's place, the tank was heated by propane, so they even had hot water.

Willa chose from some of her own old clothes that her mom had stored for her in a box under the stairs. She got clean jeans, a fresh T-shirt and a pair of worn but sturdy lace-up work boots to wear. For Collin, she found an ancient purple Jimi Hendrix Experience shirt that belonged to her dad, a pair of her dad's boots that were a pretty decent fit, and some trusty bib overalls. She also gave him a towel, a toothbrush, shave cream and a disposable razor. He took the guest bathroom. She used the master bath, and she made it quick.

Still, as she stood before the steamy bathroom mirror wrapped in one of her mother's fluffy towels, combing the tangles out of her wet hair, she couldn't help but think that Collin was just down the hall in the other bathroom, possibly naked.

Or if he wasn't by now, he *had* been a few minutes ago.

She caught her lower lip between her teeth and glared at her own reflection. "Get your mind off Collin naked," she told her steamy image in an angry whisper. "Seriously. You should get help, Willa Christensen."

And that struck her as funny, for some reason. The idea that she needed counseling over Collin Traub. She laughed. And then she pulled herself together and pinned her still-wet hair into a knot at the back of her head.

A few minutes later, they were out in the kitchen again, deciding what to take with them when they left.

She didn't tell him so, but he looked sexy even in overalls. He'd used the razor she'd given him and his dark stubble was gone, his hair still wet, but minus the dried mud from the flood.

Before they left, they filled a couple of gallon-size plastic containers with water. She stuffed a backpack with a few personal items. Her mom had a key to Willa's house in town and she took that, since hers was lost somewhere in her mud-filled car. She also grabbed a leash and a plastic container of food for Buster. She would have grabbed her dad's first aid kit, but Collin said he had one in his pickup.

"You want to wade out to your car?" Collin asked her. "See if maybe we can find your purse or your keys?"

It was way out there in the middle of that muddy field. And it didn't look promising to her. "We just got dry boots," she reminded him. "Let it go."

Collin didn't argue. She figured he was probably anxious to get to the Triple T.

They locked up the house again and headed for his truck, which waited at the top of the road where he'd left it. Buster hopped in the back and they climbed in the cab.

His cell was stuck in one of the cup holders. He tried it. "Still no signal."

Willa hooked her seat belt. He started the engine, pulled a U-turn and off they went.

It took them over an hour to get to the Triple T. The roads were washed out in several places and they had to find a way around the trouble spots. There was soggy, broken stuff strewn randomly wherever the water had risen, not to mention swamped, abandoned vehicles. Willa tried to take heart that they were all only *things*.

Collin played the truck's radio for news. Roads and bridges were out everywhere. Any number of small towns on the western side of the state from Butte north had sustained serious damage. A third of the state had been designated a disaster area and there were constant warnings—about staying off the roads as much as possible, about exercising caution in flooded buildings, about the danger of snakes and the hazards of rats. About steering clear of downed power lines.

At the Triple T, all the buildings were above the water-line and undamaged, but there would still be one heck of a cleanup to deal with. The hands who'd been taking care of the place were there and safe. Willa told them how to get into her parents' house to get fresh water for the next day or so, until they could disinfect the wells. They said they would check the stock for her as soon as they'd dealt with the animals on the Triple T.

Once Collin seemed satisfied that the hands had things under control, he said, "We should get going, go on into town."

She caught his arm before they got in the cab.

He stopped and turned to look at her. "Yeah?" His skin was so warm under her hand. Smooth flesh, hard muscles beneath. She felt suddenly shy with him and jerked her hand away. He frowned. "What's the matter?"

"I, well, I was just thinking that I'll bet you really want to go back up the mountain to check on things at your place. You could just drop me off when we get to Falls Street and I can hitch a ride in."

He stuck his fists into the front pockets of her dad's overalls and tipped his head to the side. "What the hell, Willa? I'm not leaving you alone on the street."

His words warmed her. But still. She really did need to stop taking advantage of his kindness to her.

Kindness.

Incredible. She'd been so busy judging him as a heart-less, undisciplined sex maniac for all these years, she'd never had a clue what a softy he really was. She shook her head. "Oh, come on now. It's Rust Creek Falls. We both know I'll be perfectly safe."

"We don't know what's going on since last night. And I don't want you wandering around alone."

"Collin, I would hardly *wander.* And I know everyone in town, so I won't by any stretch of the imagination be alone."

"I'm coming with you. I want to be with you when you check on your house." He said the words in a cautious tone. They both knew where her house was: directly in the path of the water. She was already resigned to the fact that it had to be flooded and was hoping that at least some of her clothing and furniture might be salvageable.

"Honestly, I can handle it. I was pretty shell-shocked yesterday, I know. But I'm over that. I'm ready to face whatever comes. You don't have to worry about me."

He was scowling now. "Why are you trying to get rid of me?"

She fell back a step. "But I'm not. I just thought…"

He caught her arm with his calloused hand. It felt so good, his touch. And his grip was so strong. "What?" he demanded. "You thought what?"

She looked up at him, at his smoldering dark eyes and those lips that seemed like they were made for kissing a woman and she wondered what he would do if *she* kissed *him.* The idea made her feel both embarrassed and giddy. She almost giggled.

"Willa," he demanded. "What is going on with you all of a sudden?"

Now she was thinking about earlier that morning. About waking up with her hand where it shouldn't have been—about how he'd been turned on.

Get real, Willa. Just because he became aroused didn't

mean he was dying to have sex with her in particular. It was simple biology, and she needed to remember that.

And if he wanted to keep on being kind to her, well, maybe she'd just let him. Maybe she'd just go right on taking advantage of Collin Traub and enjoying every minute of it. "Nothing is 'going on' with me. I just wanted to make sure I wasn't taking advantage of you."

"You're not."

"So…you don't mind going into town, then?"

"It's not about minding. It's what I planned to do. People will need help. They'll need every able-bodied man."

"And woman," she reminded him.

"Right." He had the good sense to agree.

She pressed her lips together to keep from grinning up at him like some addled fool and said, "Well, fair enough, then. I was just, um, checking."

He seemed to realize suddenly that he was gripping her arm—and let go. "Checking." Now he looked suspicious.

She put on her most innocent expression. "Uh-huh. Nothing wrong with checking, making sure you're okay with what's going on."

"If I'm not okay, you'll know it."

"Well, then, I'll stop checking."

"Good. Can we go now?"

She had that silly urge to grin again. Must be the stress of all she'd been through since yesterday. Yeah. Right. That must be it.

The trip into Rust Creek Falls was as booby-trapped with obstacles as the ride to the Triple T had been.

There was the smell of smoke in the air. It wasn't just from wood fires in stoves and fireplaces. They heard the sirens, saw the roiling smoke in the distance. On the south side of town, some homes had caught fire. Willa prayed her house wasn't one of them—and then she put her house out of her mind and prayed that no lives were endangered by the fires.

Other travelers were on the road by then, most of whom they recognized. Everyone seemed to have somewhere important to go. People waved and honked, but nobody pulled over to talk about what they'd been through or exchange information about the disaster. Collin had the radio on. All the way there, they listened to advice on how to deal with the aftermath of the Great Independence Day Flood.

When they finally got to Falls Street on the southeastern edge of town, they had to circle around and take other roads farther east and then work their way back in. It was nothing but mud, pools of water, swamped, abandoned vehicles and way too much debris south of the creek. The buildings they saw before they turned east were still standing, but bore the telltale signs of water damage within.

Eventually, they reached Sawmill Street and turned west again. The water level was way down from flood stage and the bridge appeared intact. Collin pulled the pickup to the shoulder before they crossed it. They both got out to have a look, to make sure that crossing would be safe. Buster jumped out to follow them.

But then a couple of pickups came rolling across from the town side. Behind the wheel of the second truck was a rancher they both recognized, Hank Garmond. Hank owned a nice little spread at the southwestern edge of the valley.

He pulled to a stop. "Willa. Collin. I see you're both in one piece and still breathing. Could be worse, eh? I'm headin' back to my place. We still got a house, but we lost the barn and sheds. Haven't started counting cattle yet. I just stopped in at Crawford's to try and get a few supplies to tide us over." Crawford's General Store, on North

Main, was a town landmark. The store sold everything from basic foodstuffs to farm supplies, hardware and clothing. "Shelves are already lookin' pretty bare in there."

Collin asked, "How bad is it?"

"In town? Power's out, and all the phones. North of the creek is okay, from what I heard. No flooding, the water supply unaffected. South is not lookin' good. Commercial Street Bridge is washed out. There's damage to the Main Street Bridge. People are bypassing it. We still got this bridge though." He pointed a thumb back over his shoulder. "Praise the Lord for small favors." *Very small favors,* Willa couldn't help thinking. True, it was pretty much what she and Collin had thought it would be, but somehow, to hear Hank confirm their suspicions made it all the more horribly real. "And then there's what happened to Hunter McGee." Hunter McGee was the mayor.

"What?" Willa demanded.

"Tree fell on that old SUV of his. So happened he was in the SUV at the time."

Willa respected Mayor McGee. He was a born leader, a real booster of education and had planned and promoted several school-related fund-raising events. "My Lord," she cried. "Was he hurt?"

"The tree fell on the hood. Not a scratch on him." Hank resettled his hat on his head and Willa felt relief. But then Hank added, "Must have scared the you-know-what right out of him. He had a heart attack."

Willa put her hand over her mouth. "Oh, no…"

"Oh, yeah. It was over real quick for Mayor McGee."

"Over?" Willa's heart sank. "You—you mean he's…?"

Hank nodded. An SUV and another pickup came across the bridge. The occupants waved as they drove by. Hank said somberly, "They took him to Emmet's house. Emmet pronounced him DOA." Emmet dePaulo, a nurse-practitioner, ran the town clinic. "Clinic's flooded, in case you were wondering."

Willa and Collin exchanged grim glances. They weren't surprised. The clinic was south of Main. "Emmet and a couple of his neighbors waded in there and saved what equipment and supplies they could first thing this morning. Luckily, Emmet had a lot of his medical stuff stored on the second floor and the water didn't make it that high. He's set up an emergency clinic at his house, for now."

"They got the volunteer fire guys out on search and rescue?" Collin asked.

Hank shrugged. "Can't say. I ain't heard of anybody dead, hurt bad or stranded…'ceptin' Mayor McGee, I mean. Rest his soul. But I did hear that some county trucks brought in salvage-and-rescue equipment and sandbags yesterday before the levee broke. This morning, the town council put together an emergency crew to patch up the places where the water got through. So that's taken care of for now. And you can just have a look at the creek. Water level's back to normal range."

Collin gave a humorless chuckle. "Yeah, one good thing about breaks in the levee. They tend to bring the water level way down."

"That they do," Hank concurred. "Plus, there's no rain in the forecast for at least the next week. So we're unlikely to have a repeat of what happened yesterday—oh, and the town council called a meeting at noon in the town hall to talk cleanup and such. Wish I could be there, but I got way too much cleanup of my own out at my place and I need to get after it. Bought the bleach I needed, at least. I can disinfect my well." Hank tipped his hat.

"You stay safe and take it slow on the road, Hank," Collin said.

"Will do. You keep the faith, now." The rancher rolled on by.

Collin put his arm around her. "You're lookin' kind of stricken, Willa."

She leaned into him, because she could. She needed someone to lean on at that moment. And Collin was so solid. So warm. So very much alive. "I'd been letting myself hope that at least no one had died—and I really liked Mayor McGee."

"I hear you. Hunter was a good man and this town could sure use him about now." He pulled her a little closer in the shelter of his arm and turned them both back to the pickup, Buster at their heels. The dog jumped in back again and they got in the cab.

As they drove across the bridge, Willa tried not to dread what might be waiting for them on the other side.

Chapter Four

It didn't look so awfully bad, Willa told herself as they drove along Sawmill Street. In fact, there on the northern edge of town, things seemed almost normal. Willa spotted a couple of downed trees and some flattened fences, but nothing like the devastation they'd witnessed coming in.

When they turned onto Main Street going south, they saw that the Crawford store parking lot was packed, people going in—and coming out mostly empty-handed. She supposed she shouldn't be all that surprised. It wouldn't take long to clear out the shelves of emergency supplies if everyone in town and most of the valley's ranchers showed up all at once and grabbed whatever they could fit in a cart.

The Community Church had its doors wide open. People sat on the steps there or stood out under the trees in front. Most of them looked confused. And lost.

"Shouldn't the Red Cross be showing up any minute?" she asked hopefully. "And what about FEMA and the National Guard?"

Collin grunted. "With a lot of the state in this condition, the phones out and the roads blocked, we'll be real lucky if a few supply trucks get to us in the next day or two." And then he swore low. "Isn't that the mayor's SUV?"

The old brown 4x4 was half in, half out of the town hall parking lot. It had definitely come out the loser in the encounter with the downed elm tree. The tree lay square across what was left of the hood. The driver's door gaped open. A couple of boys in their early teens were peering in the windows.

"That's just too sad," Willa said low. "You'd think they'd want it off the street."

"Damn right." Collin muttered. "A sight like that is not encouraging." He hit the brake—and then swung a U-turn in front of the library, pulling in at the curb.

"Collin!" Willa cried, surprised. "What in the...?"

He shouted out the window at the two boys. "Hey, you two. Get over here."

Both boys froze. They wore guilty expressions. But then they put on their best tough-guy scowls and sauntered to Collin's side of the truck. They were the older brothers of a couple of Willa's former students and when they spotted her in the passenger seat, they dropped some of the attitude and mumbled in unison, "'Lo, Ms. Christensen."

She gave them both a slow nod.

One of them raked his shaggy hair off his forehead and met Collin's eyes. "Yeah?"

As he'd already done several times in the past eighteen hours or so, Collin surprised her. He knew their names. "Jesse. Franklin. Show a little respect, huh?"

Jesse, who was fourteen if Willa remembered correctly, cleared his throat. "We are, Mr. Traub." *Mr. Traub.* So strange. To hear anybody call the youngest, wildest Traub *mister.* But then again, well, the Traubs were pillars of the

Rust Creek Falls community. Some of that probably rubbed off, even on the family bad boy—especially to a couple of impressionable teenagers.

Franklin, who was thirteen, added, "We were just, you know, checkin' things out."

Collin leaned out the window and suggested in a just-between-us-men kind of voice, "You two could make yourselves useful, do this town a real big favor…."

The two boys perked up considerably. "Well, yeah. Sure," said Jesse.

"How?" asked Franklin.

"Head on up to the garage. See if Clovis has a tow truck he can spare." Clovis Hart had owned and run the garage and gas station at Sawmill and North Buckskin for as long as Willa could remember. "Tell him the mayor's SUV is still sitting in the middle of Main Street with a tree trunk buried in its hood and lots of folks would appreciate it if Clovis could tow it away."

The boys shared a wide-eyed look. And then Franklin said, "Yeah. We could do that."

"You want me to take you up there?"

"Naw," said Jesse, puffing out his skinny chest. "We can handle it ourselves."

"Good enough, then. Thanks, boys—and tell Clovis he probably ought to bring a chain saw for that tree."

"We will." The two took off up Main at a run.

"That was well done," Willa said, and didn't even bother to try and hide the admiration in her voice.

Collin grunted. "Maybe, but do you think they'll make it happen?"

"You know, I kind of do. They're good kids. And this is a way for them to help. And you know Clovis."

"Yes, I do. Clovis Hart respected Hunter McGee and he won't like it that the car Hunter died in is sitting on

Main with the hood smashed in for everyone to stare and point at."

She glanced toward the dashboard clock. It was 10:45 a.m. "So what do we do now?"

"I was thinking we could go and see how your house made out...."

She glanced over her shoulder, out the back window, past a happily panting Buster, at the Main Street Bridge. Someone had put a row of orange traffic cones in front of it to warn people off trying to use it. And one of her brother's deputies was standing, arms folded, in front of the pedestrian walk that spanned one side. "It doesn't look like they're letting folks cross the bridge."

Connor glanced over his shoulder, too. "We could try heading back to the Sawmill Street Bridge, then going on foot along the top of the levee until we get to your street."

"That could be dangerous...I mean, with the breaks in the levee and all. We would have to go carefully, and we don't know what we'll find if we manage to get to my house. It could take hours and we would miss the noon meeting Hank mentioned. I do think we should go to that."

Collin faced front again, his big shoulders slumping, and stared broodingly out the windshield back the way they had come. "You know who'll be running that meeting now Hunter's gone, don't you?"

She did. "Nathan Crawford." Nathan was in his early thirties, a member of the town council. Everyone expected him to be mayor himself someday. He and Collin had never liked each other. It was as if the two had been born to be enemies. Nathan was as handsome and dynamic as Collin was brooding and magnetic. Collin had always been a rebel and Nathan considered himself a community leader.

Rumor had it that five or six years back, Nathan's girlfriend, Anita, had gone out on him—with Collin. Word was Anita had told Collin that she and Nathan were through. But apparently, she'd failed to inform Nathan of that fact. There'd been a fight, a nasty one, between the two men. Some claimed Collin had won, others insisted Nathan had come out the victor. After that, the two had hated each other more than ever.

Plus, there was the old rivalry between their two families. Nathan was a Crawford to the core. The Crawfords not only owned the general store, they were also as influential in the community as the Traubs. And for as long as anyone could remember, Crawfords and Traubs had been at odds. Willa didn't really know the origin of the feud, but it seemed to be bred in the bone now between the town's two most important families. Traubs didn't think much of Crawfords. And the Crawfords returned the favor.

She spoke gently, but with firmness. "I really think it's important that everyone who can possibly be there attends that meeting."

He put his arm along the back of the seat and touched her shoulder, a gentle brush of a touch. She felt that touch acutely. His dark eyes sought hers—and held them. "So you want to go to the meeting first and then decide what to do about getting to your place?"

She smiled at him. "I do. Yes." Right then, a Rust Creek Garage tow truck came rumbling toward them down the street.

"I've got a chain saw in my toolbox in the back." Collin got out to give Clovis a hand.

At ten past two that afternoon the town hall meeting was still going on.

Collin sat next to Willa and wished he was anywhere but there. He was getting hungry, for one thing. And he figured the rest of the crowd had to be hungry, too.

The big multipurpose meeting room was packed. They had a generator for the lights, but there was no air-conditioning, never had been in the town hall. As a rule, it didn't get that hot in Rust Creek Falls. But with all the bodies packed in that room, it was hot now.

Tired, frightened, stressed-out townsfolk had taken every chair. More people stood at the back or along the side walls. There were children, too. People didn't want to let their kids out of their sight at a time like this. And kids got restless when forced to sit or stand in one place for too long.

Babies were wailing and small voices kept asking, "Daddy, when can we go?" and "Mommy, is this over yet?"

There were a lot of big talkers in town and every one of them was insisting on being heard. Plus, that jerk Nathan sat up there on the hall stage with the other useless members of the council and kept banging the mayor's big hand-carved oak gavel for order.

All right, it was true. A lot of people thought the world of Nathan Crawford. And maybe, if Collin were being fair about it, he'd admit that Nathan had a few good qualities. However, when it came to most Crawfords, and Nathan in particular, Collin just plain didn't feel like being fair.

Nathan had the council in his pocket, naturally. They all looked at him like he was wearing a damn halo or something, like he was the one sent down from heaven to single-handedly fix everything that had gone so completely wrong since the day before.

"Everyone, your attention!" Nathan boomed in that smooth baritone that made people think he knew what he was talking about. "We all have to work together here. As I've said before, though phone, internet and TV are temporarily out of commission, we have the radio system at the sheriff's office and we are in communication with

DES—that is the state office of Disaster and Emergency Services. They are well aware of what is going on in Rust Creek Falls and the valley. And, unfortunately, in far too many other communities in western Montana. The good news, however, is that everything is under control and moving along."

Somebody in the crowd made a rude noise.

Nathan banged the mayor's gavel some more. "If we could all just be patient for a little bit longer, we will get these teams firmed up, so we can all get going on the cleanup right away."

Collin knew he should keep his mouth shut. His plan had been to get through the meeting, help Willa deal with the probable ruin of her home and then pitch in wherever he was needed. But Nathan and the council had their priorities turned around. And while there were plenty of people willing to go on and on about the difficulty of the situation and how much they wanted to help, nobody else seemed ready to tell the council they were putting the cart before the horse.

He got to his feet. Beside him, Willa startled and looked up at him, wide-eyed. She did amuse him, the way she always looked so worried about what he might do next. He sent her a glance that he meant to be reassuring. Her eyes only got wider. So much for soothing her. He faced front and waded in.

"I'm sorry. Nobody's speaking up about the real issue here and so I suppose I'm going to have to be the one. Nathan, cleanup is not the issue yet," he said good and loud. "First, we need to get teams into the flooded areas and see who needs help there. We need search and rescue and we needed it hours ago."

A chorus of agreement rose from the crowd. Apparently,

others thought there should be a rescue effort. It was only that no one had been willing to stand up and say it out loud.

Nathan banged his gavel. He looked at Collin the way he always did: as though he'd just crawled out from under a rock. "Order. Please, everyone. I already explained. We have the volunteer firefighters out searching for trapped or injured survivors."

"One team, you're saying? With how many men on it?"

Nathan didn't answer either question. Instead, he went right on with his argument. "Those men are trained for this and know what they're doing. We don't think it's a big problem. No one has reported anyone missing."

"And how're you going to know if someone's missing?" Collin demanded. "People can't call. The phones are out. There can't be more than a third of the people in the valley here at this meeting or hanging around Main Street. Where are the rest of them? Trying to clean up what's theirs? Off to Livingston for the rodeo, or down in Thunder Canyon with the rest of my family? Or trapped on the upper floors of their houses, wondering why no one's come looking for them?"

"But we *are* looking. And I honestly do not believe—"

Collin didn't even let him get started. "And you didn't answer my first question. How many men are out on search and rescue, Nathan?"

Others spoke up then. "Yeah! How many?" someone demanded.

"Not enough, that's how many!" answered another.

Nathan's face had gone a deep shade of red. "People, please. Order!"

Collin stuck his hands into the pockets of Wayne Christensen's overalls and waited for Nathan to stop pounding that gavel. Once he did, Collin answered the question himself. "I'm guessing about nine. Nine men to cover the whole of this town and the valley. Have I got that right?"

"Nine strong, able men who are trained in effective search and rescue," Nathan insisted, his face even redder than before.

Collin kept after him. "It doesn't matter how good they are. Nine men are not enough. We need to put every able-bodied adult on the search until we've made a circuit of all the homes and ranches in town and in the valley. It shouldn't take more than the rest of today and tomorrow, if we get a move on. After that, we can change our focus to salvage and cleanup."

Down the row from him and Willa, one of the Crawford men called out, "Sit down and shut up, why don't you, Traub? Let them that knows what they're doing make the decisions here."

"Yeah," said another voice. "We don't need the likes of *you* tellin' us what to do first."

And that was when Willa shot to her feet beside him. At first, Collin thought she would grab his arm and beg him to stay out of it.

But it turned out he'd misjudged her. "I feel I must add my voice to Collin's," she said in that prim schoolmarm way of hers that never failed to get him kind of hot. "We have no idea how many people might be trapped in their homes or their barns. There are bound to be collapsed buildings. People could be buried in the rubble, praying they'll be rescued before it's too late. We've already lost Mayor McGee."

"Bless his soul," said a woman's voice.

"Amen," said another.

Willa wasn't finished. "Search and rescue is the first job. And we need to give it everything. We can't afford to lose one more precious life in Rust Creek Falls or the valley."

And Collin added his voice to hers. "We've got to save our *people* before we worry about our property."

The room erupted in whistles and applause. People shouted, "By God, he's right!" and "Search and rescue!" and "Collin's said it!" and "Listen to the schoolteacher!"

By the time the clapping finally stopped, even Nathan had seen the writing on the wall. He did what he had to do and went along. "The council, as always, seeks to understand and take action according to the wishes of our citizens. We will call in the nine trained men and reassign them as team leaders."

Willa leaned close and asked softly, "Call? The phones are out…."

He whispered back, "They'll have handheld radios—walkie-talkies."

"Oh. Right…"

Nathan was still talking. "For today and tomorrow—and as long as is needed—those nine leaders will head the teams in our search-and-rescue efforts. Volunteers, seek out a leader. Marjorie?"

Marjorie Hanke, the council member to Nathan's right, stood, picked up a pointer and smacked it against the map of the county that hung behind the council table. The map had already been divided into sections for the proposed cleanup teams. "Team one, section one—and so on," Marjorie announced. "We've been fortunate in that rubber boots, heavy rubber gloves and necessary tools have already been trucked in and will be provided to each of you. Please wear the boots and gloves at all times when searching in mud or standing water. Be on careful lookout, everyone, for vermin of all persuasions. Floods bring out the rats and displace the snakes. Thank you, Nathan." With a nod, she set down the pointer and took her seat again.

Nathan wrapped it up. At last. "Getting around in the flood areas isn't easy, but we are able to truck in supplies from Kalispell for those in need. The Ladies Auxiliary of the Community Church has set out a meal on the church lawn while we've been busy with our meeting here. If everyone will file outside in an orderly manner, Pastor Alderson will lead us in a prayer, after which we will share a late lunch. By then, your team leaders will have returned—and the search for missing survivors can commence."

Chapter Five

Buster, leashed to a railing outside the town hall, whined and wiggled in greeting when Willa went to collect him. She took a minute to pet him and praise him for being such a good dog.

Collin got her pack from his pickup for her and then he walked across the street to the church at her side. When her friend and fellow teacher, Paige Dalton, waved and called her name, Willa quickly looked away and pretended she didn't hear.

No, it wasn't nice of her to treat a friend that way. But she wanted a few more minutes with Collin. Soon, he would be off with one of the search teams. And then he would probably want to go up the mountain, to check on his house. There would be no reason, once he left with the searchers, for them to be together anymore. The time had come when they would go their separate ways.

She would always be grateful to him—for saving her

life in the flood, for helping her make it through those awful first hours trapped in the barn. But she felt a bit wistful, too. For most of that day, it had almost seemed as though she and Collin were a team, ready and able to do what needed doing, fully capable, between them, of handling whatever challenges might arise. It had been a strangely heady feeling.

She wished she didn't feel so sad suddenly. But already, she was looking back longingly on the afternoon and evening before, and at the morning just passed. In retrospect now, it seemed hard to believe that she'd held a grudge against him for four long years. Her recent ill will toward him seemed something from another lifetime—from someone *else's* lifetime. She simply didn't have it in her to feel bitterness toward him now.

Now, she could almost view the flood and its immediate aftermath as some sort of lovely, exciting adventure story come to life, an adventure starring the two of them— which was way too self-absorbed of her and she knew it. This was no adventure story. This was a bona fide real-life disaster. People she cared about were losing everything.

Including herself, if you came right down to it. She wasn't holding out a lot of hope for the condition of her house. And what about all of her stuff? She had so many treasures—her favorite velvet sofa pillow, the fairy-tale books she'd collected since childhood, that spindly inlaid table she proudly displayed in the front hall...

The list was endless. What would be left of the things that she loved?

She ordered herself not to go there. Her belongings might be precious to her, but they *were* only things and she needed to remember that now.

At least she had flood insurance, as did Gage, thank God. Whatever condition her house might be in, there would eventually be money to repair or rebuild. Many people in town and in the valley couldn't afford flood insurance. They could end up with nothing.

Collin nudged her arm. "You're wrinkling up your forehead. What's the matter?"

She tugged on Buster's leash as he dawdled, sniffing at the curb. "Just worrying, I guess."

"Stop." He gave her one of those sexy bad-boy grins of his. "We're going to get fed. It's something to be happy about."

At the church, the ladies auxiliary had been busy. They'd set up rows of tables out on the lawn. And they'd even thought of people's pets. Thelma, Hunter McGee's mother, gave her a bowl of water for Buster and a couple of dog biscuits. The older woman looked pale, Willa thought, and her eyes were swollen and red-rimmed.

Willa wrapped her in a hug and whispered, "He will be greatly missed."

Thelma sniffed and forced a brave smile. "We must soldier on," she said, and bent to give Buster a pat on the head.

Everyone remained standing while the pastor said a short prayer. He praised the stalwart heart and fine leadership of their lost mayor and asked that the people of Rust Creek Falls might find the strength they needed to endure this difficult time. At the last, he blessed the food.

"Amen," they all said softly, in unison.

It wasn't a fancy meal, but when you're hungry, the simplest food can be so satisfying. They had chicken salad sandwiches, chips, apples, oatmeal cookies and all the water they could drink. Collin sat next to her. They didn't talk. They were too busy filling their empty stomachs.

The volunteer firemen started coming in, muddy and looking tired. They washed up in the church restrooms and grabbed sandwiches, which they ate standing up. People rose from the tables and surrounded them, eager to join their teams.

Collin leaned close to her. He smelled faintly of her dad's shaving cream, which made her smile. He muttered, "I meant what I said before. Finish eating and we'll find a way to get to your house. I can join a team after that."

She set down her cup of water. "Thank you, but no. You said it yourself in the town hall just now. The search for survivors has to come first."

He looked at her, a probing sort of look. That dark lock of hair had fallen over his forehead again the way it tended to do. More than ever, she wanted to smooth it back.

But she didn't. Instead, she took a bite of her cookie and downed her last sip of water.

"You sure?" He looked doubtful.

"I am, yes. First things first."

Willa assumed she would end up watching the little ones while their mothers and fathers went out on the search-and-rescue teams. People knew she was good with their kids and trusted her with them.

While Collin went to join a search team, she asked Mrs. McGee about pitching in with child care. Thelma told her to check in with the church nursery. The older woman also volunteered to look after Buster for the rest of the day.

"He's a nice dog," Thelma said, her tone bright and cheerful, endless sadness in her eyes. "Taking care of him will be no trouble at all."

Willa thanked her, gave her another quick hug and ran up the steps into the church, headed for the nursery in back.

Paige caught up with her in the sanctuary. "Willa. I've been so worried about you. The whole south side is flooded. Your house, is it…?"

"I don't know. I haven't been there since it happened. I left to check on the ranch and track Buster down before the levee broke. On the way, my car got swamped."

"Oh, my Lord. But you got out all right…."

"Thanks to Collin Traub." Willa brought her friend up to speed on how Collin had saved her from the flood. "My car's a total loss. And we ended up waiting out the rest of the storm in the barn."

"I don't know what to say. It's awful. But I'm so glad you're okay."

"Yeah. Still breathing and all in one piece—and the barn and my parents' house are fine."

Paige asked hopefully. "Gage's place?"

Willa bit her lip and shook her head. "Bad."

"Oh, Willa." Paige held out her arms.

Willa went into them and held on tight. "It's all so scary…"

"Oh, I know, I know." Paige pulled back, took Willa by the shoulders and gazed at her through solemn, worried brown eyes. "Collin, huh?" she asked gently.

Willa wasn't surprised at her friend's cryptic question. Paige was one of the few people in town who knew about that awful night at the Ace in the Hole *and* about Willa's longtime crush on the Traub bad boy. Willa had told her friend everything on one of those Friday nights they shared now then—just the two of them, watching a romantic comedy on DVD, a big bowl of popcorn between them. Paige could keep a secret. She would never tell a soul.

Willa realized it was time to admit that she'd let injured pride cloud her judgment in a very big way. "I was all wrong about him." There was no one else nearby, but she kept her voice low just in case. "I mean, so what if he turned me down once? It's not that big of a deal. He's a good guy, someone anyone would want at their back in a crisis."

"Well, I can see that, but still…" Paige let the sentence die unfinished.

Willa reminded her friend, "Paige, seriously. The man saved my life yesterday and he was right there, sticking by me all night and this morning, too, when we had to face all the damage."

Paige put up both hands. "All right. He's a hero. You've convinced me." And then she shrugged. "I'm not surprised, really. I always believed there was a good guy underneath all that swagger." Like Willa, Paige knew the Traub family well. She'd even been in love with a Traub once—Collin's brother Sutter. It hadn't worked out for them. Now Sutter owned a stable in the Seattle area. He didn't come home often, and when he did, he never stayed long. "So…" Paige hesitated.

Willa tried not to roll her eyes. "Go ahead."

"Are you and Collin together now?"

Together. With Collin. The thought made her cheeks grow warm. She hastened to clarify, "No. It's not like that. He helped me out when I needed a hand, that's all. He helped me a lot and I'm grateful to him."

"Right." Paige gave her a knowing look. "And there *is* still Dane to consider."

Willa felt instantly guilty. She hadn't given Dane Everhart a thought since last night, when she'd made a big show of throwing the poor guy in Collin's face. "I told you. I really don't think it's going anywhere with Dane—and yes, when he proposed marriage, I should have said no right then and there. But Dane is so sure that he and I are a good match. And he's so charming and confident and… I don't know. We get along, but it's never been anything romantic."

Her friend said softly, "But Dane would like it to be."

Willa gulped and nodded. "It's so completely...*Dane*, to decide to marry me and refuse to take no for an answer. But in the end, he'll have to face facts. He's just not the guy for me."

Page coaxed, "But Collin is?"

"No. Really. Come on, Paige. I said it was nothing like that with Collin."

"But you *always* liked him—and not in that friends-only way that you seem to feel about Dane."

Willa lowered her voice even more. "It was a crush that I had on Collin, a teenage crush, that's all—and stop looking at me like that."

"Like what?"

"Like you think I'm lying to myself."

"Did I say that?" Now Paige was looking way too innocent.

"You didn't have to. And you've got it all wrong. It's just that Collin and I have patched up our differences and we're on good terms now." Okay, she'd spent the previous night in his arms, but only because it had helped them keep warm. And she wasn't even going to *think* about that moment in the morning when they first woke up. Uh-uh. She was just wiping that moment clean out of her head.

"So you and Collin are friends, then?"

Friends? With Collin? It kind of felt that way, but maybe it was just the flood and all they'd been through since yesterday. She had to be careful not to read too much into it. He was off helping with the rescue effort now. When he returned, there would be no reason for him to seek her out. Their future contact with each other would be casual: saying hi when they passed each other on the street, stopping to chat now and then when they ran into each other at the store or the doughnut shop. "I don't know. We're... friendly, okay? We're getting along."

Paige's soft mouth tipped up in that warm smile that always made Willa so glad to be *her* friend. She chuckled. "Honey, you sound confused."

Why not just admit it? "Okay. Yeah. I am, a little..."

"You come and stay at my house tonight." Paige lived on North Pine, well north of the flooded area. "We'll have a nice glass of wine and I'll set you straight."

Willa laughed, too. "Uh-oh."

"Seriously. I want you staying with me as long as you need to. And don't you dare go out and stay at the ranch alone now. You need to be with a friend."

Willa felt suddenly misty-eyed. "Thanks, Paige."

Paige leaned closer. "And I have to say, I like it that Collin stood up in the meeting and got everyone to see that we need to put all our effort on searching for survivors first."

"Yes—and that reminds me. Are you helping with child care? I was just going to the nursery to see if they need me."

Paige caught her arm again. "I guess you didn't hear. The older ladies are taking care of the kids. Women our age in good shape, they want pitching in with the rescue effort. Come on. We'll get ourselves on a team."

Three people were rescued that day: two disabled shut-ins marooned upstairs in their flooded houses, and a rancher, Barton Derby, who lived alone and whose barn had collapsed on top of him. The team leaders kept in communication on their handheld radios and passed on the news when someone was found.

Barton Derby had compound fractures to both legs and had to be taken to the hospital in Kalispell, a long drive with so many of the roads badly damaged or still flooded. The word was that Derby survived the trip without incident.

The two shut-ins were physically unhurt, just very hungry and frantic over the damage to their homes. Willa and Paige's team leader told them that Thelma McGee, who owned a big house on Cedar Street, had taken them both to stay with her until other arrangements could be made.

For Willa and Paige's team, the triumphs were small. They pulled two foundering heifers from a pond, contacted old Barrett Smith, the local vet, to treat an injured horse and brought a frightened cat down from up a tree. Mostly, though, they made the circuit of the houses and outbuildings in their section of the search map and found the owners in residence doing their best to deal with the thousand and one challenges the flood had dumped in their laps.

The teams began returning to Main Street at dusk. The phones and electricity were still out, but there was food in the church multiuse room for anyone who needed it. Makeshift dormitories had been set up in the town hall and Masonic Hall for those who had nowhere else to go.

Paige came with Willa to the church, where they ate with their team by the light of kerosene and battery-powered lanterns. Once they had food in their stomachs, she nudged Willa. "Come on. Let's go to my place and get some rest…"

Willa hesitated. She would have loved a shower and to settle into that nice, big bed in Paige's guest room. But somehow, she couldn't do it. "I think I'll just get a cot in the town hall."

"Willa. Why? I want you to come and stay with me."

"And I love you for that. But I just can't…" It seemed important right then to stick with the other people who had been dispossessed. She wanted to stay close to the center of things, at least for the first night or two, until the search for survivors was finished and she could be certain that everyone in town and in the valley was safe and whole, with food in their bellies.

"You're sure?" Paige brushed her arm, a companionable touch.

Willa nodded. "Yeah. It just…feels right, to stay with the others for now."

So Paige gave her a hug and promised to be back for breakfast before the search began again in the morning. Then she asked around to see who needed lodging. She took Buck and Bella McAnder and their two little girls home with her. The McAnders lived a few houses down from Willa, on South Broomtail Road. All over the north side of town, people were doing that, taking in families who lived south of the creek.

So far, Collin had yet to appear for dinner. Once Paige was gone, Willa checked out the team sign-up sheets that were posted on the wall right there in the church multiuse room. He'd joined Team Three, headed by Jerry Dobbs. It was the team that had rescued Barton Derby.

Team Three came in a few minutes later. Collin wasn't with them. She knew she ought to leave it alone. If he'd been injured in the search, she would have heard about it. There was nothing to worry over.

But then, well, she just *had* to know for sure that everything was okay with him. She approached Jerry Dobbs and asked if he knew where Collin might be.

"A real asset to our team, that Collin," Jerry said. "Without him, we might not have gotten Bart out from under his barn. People can't help but get scared around piles of unstable materials. Some held back, afraid to pitch in. Or worse, some were *too* brave and not careful enough. Collin reassured the scared ones and kept an eye on the chance-takers. The man's a born leader, levelheaded and calm and encouraging to others in a crisis. Plus, he's in top shape and light on his feet."

Willa didn't especially like the sound of all that. Had Collin put himself in danger to get Barton out? It would be just like him, after all. "Yes," she said, and tried to sound cheerful. "Collin Traub has no fear."

Jerry nodded. "And I think he mentioned something about stopping over at the Triple T to see how they were getting along out there."

She should have known. Of course he would have to go see how the hands at the family ranch were managing. She thanked Jerry, shouldered the pack she'd been dragging around with her all afternoon and walked over to Thelma's to get Buster.

By then, Thelma had a houseful of visitors. She'd made room not only for the two rescued shut-ins, but also for a couple of young families who owned houses on the south side of the creek.

"I'll be over at the church for breakfast tomorrow," Thelma said, as Buster sat on the step, cheerfully panting, cocking one ear and then the other, glancing from Thelma to Willa and back again. "I'll be happy to take Buster then. He's been a comfort, I have to tell you. He likes to stick close to me, but he's not in the way."

"He's a good dog," Willa said fondly. Buster made an eager little whining sound in response. "Just don't let him out unsupervised or you never know where he'll head off to."

"I won't," Thelma promised. "I'll keep him close."

Willa thanked her again and said good-night.

In the town hall, the generator was still going strong. It seemed so bright in there compared to the lantern light at Thelma's and in the church. The chairs in the meeting room had been folded up and stacked against the walls.

Rows of narrow cots waited for her and about fifty other people whose houses were in the still-restricted area south of the creek. She was a little anxious that Buster might not be allowed in. But it wasn't a problem. Marjorie Hanke, the councilwoman assigned to supervise sleeping arrangements in the hall, told her that as long as he behaved himself he could sleep beside Willa's cot.

Collin wasn't there. Disappointment tried to drag her down, which was ridiculous. The man had his own life, after all. He had things he needed to do. He could be staying at the Triple T for the night, or over at the church getting something to eat, or possibly bedding down in the other makeshift dormitory in the Masonic Hall. He might even have headed up the mountain to his house.

She truly hoped he hadn't been foolish enough to do that. Not in the dark. After the storm, there was no telling what condition that road would be in.

It was very annoying. He was so unpredictable. A person hardly knew what he might do next.

And really, she needed to stop thinking about him. She needed to be grateful that he'd saved her life and glad that she'd gotten past her issues with him—and let it go at that.

She leashed Buster to a leg of the cot and took her turn in the bathroom, washing up as best she could in the sink. Marjorie was passing out baggies containing personal grooming supplies to those without, but Willa had her own. She'd raided her mother's medicine cabinet for soap, deodorant and a toothbrush, and she'd also thought to grab an old pair of lightweight pink sweatpants, flip-flops and a clean T-shirt from the box under the stairs.

Back in the meeting room, people were settling in, getting as comfortable as possible for the night. When everyone had finished in the restrooms, Marjorie turned off all the lights, save one. She left it on low, for a night-light.

Willa lay back, stared at the dark ceiling overhead and felt certain she'd be awake half the night, worrying about her parents and Gage, who were probably going nuts, wondering what was happening at home. She knew she would end up lying there, eyes wide-open, obsessing over the extent of the damage of her house. She was positive that she would have to firmly remind herself not to get all worked up over the tragic death of the mayor, and not to think about Collin, who surely would not have been so foolish as to head up the mountain in the dark of night.

But strangely, within minutes of zipping up her borrowed sleeping bag, her eyes had drifted shut. With a sigh, she turned on her side, tucked her hand under her cheek, and let sleep steal all her worries away.

The double doors to the town hall meeting room were shut when Collin arrived. He eased through them soundlessly.

Marjorie Hanke, in a cot by the door, sat up and pointed to an empty one a few feet away. Collin whispered a thank-you and tiptoed to the unoccupied cot. It wasn't that far from the door, which was great. He had a big plastic bag full of stuff for Willa and a pack for himself. Both of those, he stowed under the cot.

A couple of rows over, he heard a low, familiar whine. A tail thumped the floor: Buster. So Willa *was* sleeping here. He considered going over there and making sure she was all right.

But come on. His creeping close and peering down at her wouldn't help her in the least.

Uh-uh. If he went to her, he wouldn't be doing it because she needed him right now. It would be because he wanted to see her, plain and simple. In the space of one night and the morning after, he'd found it all too easy to get used to having her around. All too easy to wish she might *stay* around.

He liked her.

Always had, though he knew she used to think he didn't.

Maybe he liked her too much. He needed to keep a rein on himself because he knew that nothing was going to come of his liking Willa Christensen more than he should. She was a nice girl. She had a college-graduate Mr. Good-Guy boyfriend off in Australia, a boyfriend who'd asked her to marry him.

There was no way Collin fit into that picture.

Someone coughed. A cot squeaked as someone else turned over. At the other end of the room near the stage, somebody was snoring. Collin should shuck off his boots, stretch out on the cot and try to get a little sleep. Morning would come way before he was ready for it.

Too bad he didn't feel all that much like sleeping. He moved silently back to the doors and slipped through again. Swiftly, he crossed the dark front hall and let himself out into the cool of the night.

On the steps, he sat down, drew his legs up and wrapped his arms around his knees. It was a clear night, a sliver of the waning moon hanging above the distant mountains way across the valley. He stared up at that moon and tried not to think about the woman sleeping in the dark hall behind him, tried not to think about that morning, when he'd woken up with her soft, pretty little hand on his fly. A bad, bad idea, to think about that. Thinking about that would only get him all worked up all over again.

He heard a faint sound at his back, the squeak of heavy hinges as the door opened behind him. Buster nuzzled his shoulder. He threw an arm over the dog and scratched him behind the ear as the door squeaked shut. The latch clicked.

Willa. He could feel her, hovering there behind him in

front of the door. He was way too glad she'd come out to find him.

"Go back to bed, Willa," he said lazily, not turning to look at her, keeping his gaze front, on that sliver of moon. "How many times do I have to tell you? I'm not having sex with you."

Willa laughed, a low, slightly husky sound, one that seemed to skim the surface of his skin, raising goose bumps as it went. Raising more than goose bumps if he was going to be honest about it. He drew his knees up a little tighter so she wouldn't see how she affected him.

"You are impossible," she said in a voice as low and husky and full of good humor as her laugh.

He shrugged. "So I've been told."

And then she came and sat on his other side, so he was sandwiched between her and her dog. It wasn't a bad place to be. Not bad at all.

She said, "Buster's happy to see you. He woke me up when you came in."

"Sorry."

She leaned toward him a little, nudging him with her shoulder in a way that felt downright companionable. "Don't be."

He stroked the dog's big white head. "He's a great guy." The dog turned, tongue lolling, and gazed at him adoringly. "And so good lookin'."

Willa chuckled again. "Oh, yes, he is."

He still hadn't looked at her. Mostly because when he did, he knew he wouldn't want to look away. "What about you, Willa? You happy to see me, too?"

"I am," she answered in a near whisper. "Yes." She was quiet. He could feel the warmth of her along his side. She smelled of soap and toothpaste—and something else. Something that was simply Willa. Kind of green and fresh and a little bit lemony. Who knew the smell of soap and lemons could get a man worked up? She spoke again. "I was kind of worried you'd tried to go up the mountain to your place."

"Not in the dark."

"Good."

"I went to the Triple T. They got the wells disinfected and are hoping to be using the water by tomorrow or Sunday. Most of the stock survived. And they're busy with cleanup. I stopped in at Clay's house and borrowed a few things—clean jeans and boots, a couple of shirts." Third-born of his five brothers, Clay had recently married. He lived down in Thunder Canyon now, but he still owned a house on the Triple T. "Then I went over to your family's place, just to see if things were okay there."

"You didn't have to do that."

"Willa. I wanted to."

A silence from her, then, "Thank you."

"I used the guest-room shower again. And I left your dad's clothes in the hamper. Hope you don't mind."

"I don't mind at all. How was it there?"

"Better."

"Really?"

"Yeah. The neighbors and the hands from the Triple T had been there. The pigs are back in their pen and the chickens are in the coop. Looked like they even made a start on the cleanup."

"That's good," she said. "Really good. I'm grateful."

He did look at her then. She was staring out toward the moon, the curve of her cheek so smooth in the dim light, her pretty lips slightly parted. She wore a different T-shirt from the one she'd had on earlier, pink sweatpants with white trim and a worn-down pair of flip-flops.

She kept her gaze on the moon, and that was fine with

him. Gave him more time to look at her. He took in everything about her. Her toenails were painted. In the dark, it was hard to be sure of the exact color. Maybe purple. Like plums. He stared at them for a time. When he looked up, she was watching him. "Did you get something to eat?"

He nodded. "I had some stew at the Triple T."

Those cute dimples of hers tucked themselves in at the sides of her mouth as she smiled. "Jerry Dobbs says you're a natural leader, that they might not have saved Bart Derby if not for you."

"Well. You know Jerry, heavy on the 'go, team, go.'"

"I think you're being modest, Collin." Her big brown eyes gleamed at him.

He felt an odd little pinch, a heated tightness in his chest. Also, in his borrowed jeans. "Modest? Me? Not a chance."

Buster got up and wandered down the steps to lift his leg on a tree trunk. When he started sniffing the ground, moving toward the street, Willa called to him. "Buster. Come." He came right back and plopped down where he'd been before.

Collin said, "I filled a bag with clothes from that box under the stairs at your folks' house, in case you need them. I left it back in the hall, under my cot. I brought jeans and shirts and underwear, too." There had been little lace panties and a bra and several pair of socks. "Not that I noticed the underwear or anything…"

"As I recall, it was pretty frayed, that underwear. But I'm grateful to have it at this point." She groaned, lowered her head and put her hand over her eyes. "I can't believe I'm sitting here discussing my old underwear with you."

"Hey." It was his turn to bump her shoulder with his. "What are friends for?"

She looked up and into his eyes, all earnest and hopeful, suddenly. "We are, aren't we? Friends, I mean."

He wanted to kiss her. But he knew that would be a very bad idea. "You want to be my friend, Willa?" His voice sounded a little rough, a little too hungry.

But she didn't look away. "I do, yes. Very much."

That pinch in his chest got even tighter. It was a good feeling, really. In a scary sort of way. "Well, all right then. Friends." He offered his hand. It seemed the thing to do.

Her lower lip quivered a little as she took it. Her palm was smooth and cool in his. He never wanted to let go. "You better watch it," she warned. "I'll start thinking that you're a really nice guy."

"I'm not." He kept catching himself staring at that mouth of hers. It looked so soft. Wide. Full. He said, "I'm wild and undisciplined. I have an attitude and I'll never settle down. Ask anyone. Ask my own mother. She'll give you an earful."

"Are you trying to scare me, Collin Traub? Because it's not working."

He took his hand back. Safer that way. "Never say I didn't warn you."

She gave him a look from the corner of her eye. "I'm onto you now. You're a good guy."

"See? Now I've got you fooled."

"No, you don't. And I'm glad that we're friends. Just be straight with me and we'll get along fine."

"I am being straight." Well, more or less. He didn't really want to be her friend. Or at least, not *only* her friend. He wanted to be *more* than her friend. But sometimes a man never got what he wanted. He understood that, always had. Sweet Willa Christensen was not for the likes of him. But right now, he just needed to look out for her, take care of her a little. Make sure she got through this hard time all right. He added, "And I've been thinking."

"About what?"

"The things that need doing."

She braced an elbow on her knee and dropped her chin in her hand. "Such as?"

"I'm guessing we'll finish up the search for survivors by around noon tomorrow. Meet me at the church when your team comes in. One way or another, we're going to get to your house tomorrow."

Her smooth brow furrowed. "What if they won't let us into the area?"

"You worry too much. They'll let us in. They pretty much have to."

"Not if they don't think it's safe."

"At some point, people are just going to go in anyway. The whole town has pitched in, put their own problems aside to search for survivors. It's not right to expect them to wait forever to get to their homes. Nathan and the rest of them have to take that into account or they'll have trouble on their hands."

"Collin…"

"Your face is all scrunched up again. Relax."

"It's only that I feel kind of bad, to keep on taking advantage of you like this."

"Don't," he commanded gruffly.

She just couldn't let it go. "But I know you need to get up to *your* place."

"My place is fine."

"But you can't be sure."

"Willa. We're going to your house and we're going tomorrow."

"I'm only saying that you don't have to—"

He put up a hand. "I know I don't have to. And you don't

have to worry. It's pretty much impossible to take advantage of me. If I say I'll do a thing, it's because I *want* to do it." And when it came to the woman beside him, well, what he wanted was to do whatever she needed. He added, just to make himself sound tough and uncompromising, "I don't do anything because I think I *have* to. Life is too damn short for that."

Chapter Six

It all went as Collin had predicted, which only made Willa more aware of how completely she had once underestimated him. He understood so much, really. About people. About the way things worked.

The nine teams searched for four hours the next day, covering the rest of the valley and the flooded area south of the creek in town. They found a couple of stranded pets and more cattle that had to be pulled from muddy ponds, but no people in need of rescue.

Willa's team was out at the far western reaches of the valley. They finished up the search of their section by a little past noon and returned to town, where everyone had gathered at the church for the midday meal. Willa sat with Paige and the rest of their team.

Collin sat at another table, his team around him. He glanced up and saw her and gave her a nod that she took to mean he still intended to take her to her house.

Her heart kind of stuttered in her chest and then re-commenced beating a little too fast. Partly because trading meaningful glances with Collin excited her more than it should. And partly because it was happening at last: she would see her house again. She sent a little prayer to heaven that it wouldn't be too bad.

While they ate, Nathan Crawford got up and gave a speech. He thanked everyone for the great job they were doing. He praised Rust Creek Garage for having plenty of gas to share with the searchers and the foresight to own a generator so that the pumps were still working. He said that state and county workers were on the job around-the-clock, trying to get services back online and roads and bridges repaired.

He advised, "If you have family members who were out of town for the holiday and you're wondering why they haven't returned—please don't be overly concerned. The governor has declared a state of emergency and asked that people try and stay off the roads, many of which are badly damaged. Bridges are out all over the western half of the state. It's just going to take a while to get all our services back up and running and for people to get back home."

Nathan also reminded them that the next phase was cleanup. "I hope many of you will pitch in with the community effort, that you'll donate your time if you can spare some. But we're suspending our teams for the rest of the day and all day Sunday so that everyone can handle personal business. Those who live south of the creek will have a chance to visit their homes." The floodwaters had sufficiently receded, he added, and gas and water mains to the damaged areas had been shut off for the time being. The town council realized that people had to be allowed back in to begin to assess the condition of their property.

"Please use the Sawmill Street Bridge only. Follow the newly posted signs for the safest route to your property."

Next, he got to the hazards, which were many. "Please, please, be extra careful about entering buildings. Proceed with caution. If you see a downed wire or pole, keep clear and remember to report it." He reminded them all to wear boots and gloves and watch out for dangerous animals displaced by the flood. "Also, take note. Any buildings roped off with yellow tape have already been determined to be unsafe for entry. We've done our best to personally warn all of you whose houses are in that condition, but the priority until now has been rescuing the stranded. There are assuredly buildings that should have been roped off but haven't yet. Please. Don't approach any houses that are taped off. Search-and-Rescue Team One reports that our elementary school is badly damaged and possibly structurally unsound. So, also, we ask that you stay away from the school and the school grounds."

Willa's heart sank at that news. Beside her, Paige made a low sound of distress. Were they going to lose the school?

That would hit hard. If they had to rebuild, how long would it take? They only had two months until the start of the next school year.

Nathan ended by saying that dinner would be served at six and thanking the charitable organizations that had come through with donations of food and supplies. Then Pastor Alderson got up and invited them all to a brief Sunday service after breakfast the next morning, a service that would include a final farewell to Mayor McGee.

A funeral. Willa sighed. Lately, life was just packed with sad and difficult events. But then again, it was important to give people a chance to pay their respects and to grieve.

She glanced toward Collin again. But he'd already left

his table. She thought of last night, of sitting out on the front steps of the town hall with him. That had been so nice. Just the two of them and Buster, alone under the sliver of moon.

She almost wished she could go back there now, just run away from reality and all the everyday grimness of surviving the worst flood in the history of Rust Creek Falls. Run away and sit out under the moon with Collin, forever.

Even if they were just friends.

"You ready, Willa?" His voice, behind her. A little thrill pulsed through her.

Beside her, Paige frowned. "Ready for what?"

She pushed back her folding chair and gathered up the remains of her meal to carry to the trash and recycle stations. "Collin's taking me to see my house."

Paige looked at Collin. He gazed coolly back at her. "How are you, Collin?"

"Just fine, Paige. You?"

"Wonderful," Paige said in a tone that could have meant anything. She turned her gaze to Willa. "Shall I come with you?"

Willa shook her head.

"Are you certain?"

"Yes. But thank you. I'll be fine."

"You be careful."

"I will. Don't worry."

They got into Collin's truck and he paused before he started the engine. "Where's Buster?"

"Thelma's keeping an eye on him."

"Good. Safer for him if stays at Thelma's until this is done."

She nodded her agreement and he pulled the truck out into the flow of traffic, most of which was going where they were going. Her neighbors were as eager as she was to see firsthand how their homes had fared.

They followed the signs across the Sawmill Street Bridge, down Falls Street and then west on Commercial. They had to move at a crawl, even though road crews had already been hard at work. Fallen trees, utility poles and flooded vehicles had been cleared from the roadway. But the streets themselves were badly damaged, the pavement erupted and broken apart in places, pools of standing water and puddles of mud everywhere, some as big as ponds. The buildings that lined the street had not fared well. Some were partially collapsed and roped off with yellow tape. Yards were still cluttered with household items and who knew what all.

Fires had taken out a whole row of houses on South Pine. A few of them were burned all the way to the ground.

At Main, they passed the elementary school. It was still standing, at least, though sections of the roof had fallen in. There was no way to tell from the street how bad the damage might be.

For Willa personally, the moment of truth came much too soon. They turned onto South Broomtail and pulled to a stop at what was left of the curb in front of her one-story bungalow.

She had to stifle a gasp of dismay at what she saw. Like all the other yards on the street, hers was a mess, strewn with a bunch of mud-caked stuff she couldn't even identify. The roof on one side of her front porch sagged alarmingly. The porch itself was empty. Her white wicker chairs and cute little spray-painted metal folding tables topped with potted geraniums were nowhere to be seen. And the cosmos and columbines, the boxwood hedge and the rows of mums and Shasta daisies she'd so lovingly planted along her front walk? If they were still there, she couldn't recognize them under the layer of mud and trash.

Collin reached over and took her hand. She wove her fingers good and tight with his. It helped—his warm, strong grip, the calloused flesh of his palm pressed to hers. The contact centered her down, reminded her again that she *could* get through this, that she wasn't alone.

He said, "You can wait for the insurance people, let them tell you what can be saved. I can turn this truck around and get us the hell outta here. You don't have to try and go in there."

She gripped his hand tighter. "What was that you said last night? About not wasting any part of your life doing what you think you *have* to do?"

"So don't. We'll go." He tried to pull his hand from hers.

She held on. "I mean, I *want* to go in. I...need to go in, Collin."

"Look at that porch roof. It could be dangerous. Someone on one of the county crews should have roped it off."

"I'm going in."

"Willa, it's not safe."

She hitched up her chin and stared straight in his eyes. "I have to. I do. I don't agree with what you said last night. Some things, well, a person does just *have* to do."

Collin tried to think of a way to talk her out of it. But she had that look—so solemn and determined. When Willa got that look, there was no changing her mind.

Maybe he could bargain with her a little. "Just let me go in first, okay? Let me make sure that it's safe."

She still had his hand in a death grip. "Great idea. You can get killed instead of me."

"Willa. I'm not going to get killed—and if you think

that it's too dangerous, well, why are we even talking about going in?"

"It was a figure of speech, that's all. I'm sure it's all right. We can go in together. But you're not leading the way. I won't have it. Do you understand?"

In spite of the very real danger in the situation, he wanted to smile. "You know you sound like an angry schoolmarm, don't you?"

"Well, I *am* an angry schoolmarm. And you'd better not cross me right now, Collin Traub."

He put on his most solemn expression. "No, ma'am. I wouldn't dare."

She let go of his hand and he wished that she hadn't. "Here." She passed him his heavy black rubber gloves. He put them on and she put on hers. They were both still wearing their waterproof search-and-rescue boots. "All right," she said. "Let's get it over with."

They got out and picked their way through the piles of broken, muddy junk in the yard. The smell was pretty bad—like spoiled food and smelly socks and other things he decided not to concentrate too hard on.

"Look," she said, and pointed. "One of my wicker porch chairs. Right there—and look over there. Isn't that a slow cooker?"

He only shrugged. The things she pointed to were unrecognizable to him.

The mud-caked porch creaked in an ominous way when they went up the steps. But it held. One front window was busted out, the other crisscrossed with cracks.

She reached for the door—and then she dropped her hand and laughed. "The key…"

For a moment, he knew relief. She'd forgotten the key. Good. But then she reached into her pocket and came out with it. She stuck it in the lock and gave it a turn.

The door swung inward.

It wasn't anything he hadn't expected. Mud everywhere and water wicking halfway up the walls. The same rotting, moldy smell as in the yard.

They went through the small entry hall and into the living room, where he doubted that any of the furniture could be saved. The large picture window on the side wall had cracked from corner to corner. The fireplace was full of mud.

"My grandmother's clock," Willa said in a tone of hope and wonder. It was on the mantel, a brass carriage clock, untouched. She went over to it, and gathered it into her arms. "It's an antique. A mercury pendulum clock." She glanced up and met his eyes. Hers were suspiciously misty. "Hey. It's *something....*"

They moved on, first to the kitchen and then down the short hallway to the bedrooms and the single bath. It was bad, all of it, every room full of mud. There wasn't much worth saving.

But there were some pictures on the walls that were good as new, and some stuff in the kitchen, dishes and such in the higher-up cabinets. And the things on the counter, too: a red toaster, cutting boards, some glass figurines on the windowsill. He suggested that they try and see if they could scare up some boxes to put the stuff in.

Willa shook her head. "And put the boxes where?"

He wanted to offer his house, but he hadn't made it up the mountain yet, and he knew she'd only argue that she couldn't impose on him. He thought of Paige. He didn't like what had gone down with Paige and his brother Sutter, but he knew Paige was a good woman at heart and a true friend to Willa. She would store Willa's stuff for her in a heartbeat. But then Willa would only give him some other excuse as to why that wouldn't work. "We'll haul them out to your parents' place. How's that?"

She clutched the brass clock like a lifeline and said primly, "That would take the rest of the day. And they are just *things,* after all."

"They're *your* things. And you need to get them out of here." He asked gently, "And what else are we gonna do with the rest of the day?"

"Other people might need our help and we should—"

He didn't let her get rolling. "Need our help doing what? Saving *their* things? We're doing this. Deal with it."

Her lower lip was trembling and her eyes were more than misty now. "I can't... I don't..." He felt a tightness in his chest at seeing her cry. She sniffed and turned her head away. "Oh, this is ridiculous. I have so much to be grateful for. There is no point in my crying over this. My crying will not change a thing...." A tight little sob escaped her.

"Come on. Come here." He reached out his rubber-gloved hands and pulled her close. "It's all right."

"No. No, it's not. I loved this house. I loved my little red Subaru."

"I know," he soothed. "I understand."

"I...I keep telling myself how it doesn't matter, that what matters is I'm alive and in one piece and so is most everyone else in town. But then I think of my...my treasures. My fairy-tale books, my favorite velvet pillow...I want them back, Collin. I want my *things* back."

"Shh, now. I know you do. There's nothing wrong with that. It's natural. Don't be so hard on yourself...."

"Oh, I am being such a big baby...." Sobs shook her slim frame.

He held her. He stroked her back. She curved into him, fitting against him as though she was made to be in his arms. For that moment, he forgot about everything. It all just…receded: her ruined house, the smell of mud and mildew, her grandmother's clock poking into his belly. There was only the woman in his arms. He held her and rested his cheek on her soft hair and waited.

Eventually, she pulled back enough to gaze up at him. Her nose was red and her eyes were puffy and she was so beautiful that his chest got tight all over again. He wished that…

But no. It was never happening. He wasn't going there. No way.

She sniffed. "Well. This is embarrassing."

He took her lightly by the upper arms. "You okay now?"

She sniffed again. "My nose is red, isn't it?"

"Your nose is beautiful."

"Liar."

It all seemed…strange and scary, suddenly. For a moment there…no. *Uh-uh. Not going there,* he reminded himself for the second time. He put on a big, fake smile and asked, "What do you say we go find those boxes?"

It took the rest of the day to scare up the crates and boxes, pack up what was salvageable and drive it out to the Christensen place. Her dad had a storage area off his work shed. They put it all in there.

By then, it was past time for the community meal back in town. They'd planned ahead and brought clean clothes with them so they could take advantage of the chance for hot showers. As before, he took the hall bath and she took the one off her parents' room.

She came out of her parents' bathroom, her brown hair still wet, smoothed back into a knot at the nape of her neck, smelling like flowers and rain and lemons, better than any woman he'd ever known.

And he'd known a lot of them—well, not in the past

couple of years. After he hit twenty-five or so, all that chasing around had begun to seem kind of pointless. But back when he was younger, he'd lived up to his rep as a player. Then he'd been out to have himself a good time every night of the week.

And not one other woman back in the day had ever smelled as good as Willa did right then.

They raided the pantry. As they ate canned stew, crackers and peaches, Willa said how happy she was with the cleanup around the ranch.

"They've done a lot," she said, "in just a couple of days."

Her car was still out there on its side in the pasture and probably would be until she could call her insurance guy or the FEMA people and have it towed away, but the animals were back in their proper pastures and pens. The neighbors were making sure the stock got fed.

They headed back to town at a little after eight, stopping off at the Triple T for a few minutes on the way, just to check on things. In Rust Creek Falls, they went to Thelma's to get Buster, and then they returned to the town hall for the night. There were several empty cots. Some people had found neighbors to stay with and some had gone to live with out-of-town relatives for a while.

Marjorie Hanke turned out the lights at eleven. Collin still felt wide-awake, so he got up and went outside to sit on the steps under the sliver of moon.

What do you know? He wasn't out there five minutes before Buster was nudging up against him on one side and Willa was dropping to the steps on the other.

He almost teased her about how he wasn't having sex with her. But no. Sex seemed a little dangerous to speak of now, something he couldn't afford to joke about.

And then she kind of leaned against him and said,

"Aren't you going to tell me to keep my hot little hands to myself?"

There was nothing he would like better than her hot little hands all over him. However, that was not going to happen, as he knew damn well and kept constantly reminding himself.

He kept it light, meeting her eyes, teasing, "I know I can count on you to do the right thing."

She didn't reply. There was one of those moments. They looked at each other and neither looked away. He would only have to lean in a few inches to capture that mouth of hers, to feel her lips against his.

Finally.

At last.

But he didn't. Apparently, he had some small amount of self-control left.

He thought of the boyfriend, the one who had asked her to marry him. He reminded himself that it was only an accident of fate that had her sitting next to him on the town hall steps at a quarter of midnight on July 6. And somehow, he managed to turn his head and stare at the moon again.

She said, very softly, "Remember when we were kids? You used to spy on me...."

He chuckled. "I had a lot of free time on my hands. And I never thought of it as spying."

"You would watch me when I had no idea you were there. That's spying, Collin Traub. I would look up—and there you would be, staring at me."

He gave her a grin. "You're getting mad about it all over again."

She frowned—and then her brow smoothed out. "You're right. I am. And that's silly. It was years ago. It's like that night at the Ace in the Hole. Better to just let it go." She tipped her head sideways and studied him. "You were so different from your brothers...."

"Yeah, well. My mom was tired when I came along. She had five boys already. Boys are exhausting. They need discipline and supervision. Mom did a good job of that with the rest of them. But she kind of gave up on me. I ran wild."

"I remember," she said wryly.

He elaborated with some pride, "I broke every rule and climbed every fence and spied on you when I knew it would freak you out. I also used to like to tease the bulls."

"Well, that's just plain asking for it."

"Yeah, it is. I guess I had an angel on my shoulder, though. Because somehow, every time I got in the pasture with one of the bulls and danced around shouting and waving my arms, I managed to jump the fence before I got gored."

She was shaking her head. "What were you thinking?"

"That it was fun! I mean, I liked it, being known as big trouble just waiting to happen. I got blamed for everything, sometimes for things I didn't even do. And it kind of got to be a point of pride for me that not a day went by I didn't get grief for some crazy, dumb-ass behavior or other."

She was looking at him again, her eyes shining brighter than the stars in the clear night sky overhead. "So you became known as the family troublemaker, the one no one could ever depend on."

"Because I *am* the family troublemaker that no one could depend on."

"But you're not," she argued. "Just look at you lately, standing up for what's right in the town meeting, getting a couple of kids to make sure the mayor's car was towed off Main Street the day after he died, saving Barton Derby from under the wreckage of his barn...."

"My *team* saved Bart Derby, the mayor's car was not a big thing—and you stood up in that meeting, too."

"What about rescuing me when I would have drowned, and then looking after me during the storm? And what about afterwards, too? What about today, at my house, when you held me while I cried and promised me it was going to be all right?"

"It was what you needed to hear right then."

"Exactly. Honestly, Collin. I don't know what I would have done without you since the flood." She'd better stop looking at him like that. If she didn't, well, he was going to grab her and plant one on her.

"Don't make a big thing out of it, okay?" he heard himself mutter.

"But it *is* a big thing."

"No, it's not...."

"Yes, it is!" She got that bossy schoolteacher look. "And that does it. I'm not sitting still while you minimize all the good you've done. I'm going to tell you how I see it."

"Uh-oh."

"You listen to me, now...."

He tried not to groan. "What will you do if I don't?"

She put her hand on his arm, apparently to hold him there by force. He felt that touch from the top of his head to the tips of his toes—and everywhere in between. "You are a born leader, Collin. This town is going to need a new mayor and I keep thinking that you could be the right man for that job."

Mayor? She thought he should be *mayor?* He couldn't help it. He threw back his head and laughed out loud. "Willa, okay. We're friends now and everything. But you don't know what you're talking about."

"Oh, yes, I do. I am onto you, in a big way."

He grunted. "No, you're not. You're making something out of nothing."

She pursed up her mouth at him. "When you're finished blowing me off, you just tell me. And then I will share my insights with you."

There were a whole bunch of sarcastic comebacks to that one. But for some unknown reason, he didn't use any of them. Probably because he did kind of want to hear what she had to say. "Okay, fair enough. Hit me with it."

"I will. Ahem. So you grew up a wild child, undependable. And as it so often happens in a small town like ours, people get it in their heads what a person is like and that's it, that's just the way it is. No one ever thinks to look at that person differently, to take a chance on depending on him, to expect more than misbehavior. There's a local perception and no one ever tests it. The perception becomes the reality."

"Took psychology at UI, did you, Willa?"

She gave him her sweetest smile. "And I'm not even at the good part yet…. Where was I? Oh, yes. So in the meantime, you're keeping busy fulfilling everyone's low expectations of you. And, as you said yourself, you find that not having anyone expect much of you is actually kind of fun. Because you can do what you want. You're not stuck like all your brothers, bearing up under the weight of everyone's high estimation of your sterling character. You actually have the freedom to live exactly as you please and you never have to worry about letting anyone down."

He could easily become annoyed with her. "Think you got me all figured out, don't you, Willa?"

She didn't back off. "To a degree, yes. You are adventurous and bold, with no desire to settle down. So naturally, in your teens, you become the town heartbreaker.

You do a lot of experimenting with women. Because, as you said, it's fun."

He'd heard about enough. "Come on. You're getting into dangerous territory here. You know that, right? Next you'll be digging up that night at the Ace again, getting all up in my face for not taking you up on what you were offering."

She put her hand on his arm again. He wanted to jerk away—and also to grab her and kiss her senseless. "No. Honestly. I'm over that." And then she smiled. So sweet and open, that smile. He realized that he definitely wanted to kiss her more than he wanted to get away from her. "Even if I am probably the only woman you ever turned down."

He almost told her that wasn't true, but then she'd just say he was bragging. "Seriously. Where are you going with this?"

She tipped her head to the side, frowning a little the way she did when she was thinking something over. "Hmm. I guess I'm just trying to make you see that being defined by other people's low expectations of you isn't really working for you anymore."

"And you know this, how?"

"I'm not blind, you know. I've been around you a lot the past few days. And what has been a tragedy for Rust Creek Falls has brought out the best in you. After all that's happened and all the good you've done—all the good you *will* do in the coming days, you're not going to be able to go back."

"Go back where?"

"To the way things were before the levee broke."

"Believe it or not, I happen to like the way things were."

"Maybe you did. Before. But it won't be enough for you now."

"You have no idea what's enough for me, Willa." He

ached to reach for her. Reach for her and pull her close and kiss her until her head spun and she let him do whatever he wanted with her, until he finally got a taste of what she'd been tempting him with since before he was even old enough to know what temptation was.

She just wouldn't stop. "You've started to expect more of yourself and that is a wonderful thing. Why can't you admit that?"

It was the tipping point. He couldn't stop himself. He reached out and grabbed her by the shoulders good and tight. And then he growled at her with all the frustrated heat and hunger he was trying so hard to deny. "I don't need you telling me how I feel or where I'm going."

She blinked at him and her big eyes got bigger and her mouth looked so soft and surprised he only wanted to cover it with his and stick his tongue inside. "But, Collin. I was only—"

"*Don't,* all right? Just don't." With great care, he straightened his arms, pushing her away from him. Then he let her go.

"Collin, I..."

He stood up. That was pretty damn stupid. He was as hard as a teenage kid caught thumbing through *Playboy.* All she had to do was look and she would see it.

Too bad. He wasn't hanging around to watch her reaction. He mounted the top step, hauled the door wide and went in, pulling it firmly shut behind him.

Chapter Seven

Willa had trouble getting to sleep that night. She felt awful. She knew that she'd gone too far. Yes, she did honestly believe she'd only told Collin the truth about himself.

And really, not a thing she'd said to him had been bad. Some men wouldn't mind being called a born leader. Some men would be pleased to hear how wonderful they were.

But not Collin, apparently.

And all right, well, maybe she'd laid it on a bit heavy. She'd turned her inner schoolmarm loose on him—and not the good, patient, understanding and gentle schoolmarm.

The other one. The bossy one who knew what was good for you and was bound to tell you all about yourself whether you wanted to hear it or not.

Had she wrecked their new friendship?

Oh, she did hope not. Because she really, really liked being his friend. She liked it more than she should, probably. With a guy like Collin, well, a girl could get really confused as to where she stood with him.

On the floor by her cot, Buster whined in his sleep. She reached her hand down to him, ran her fingers over the smooth, warm crown of his big head. He woke enough to press his wet nose against her palm and then settled back to sleep with a sweet chuffing sound.

She thought of all the good things Collin had done for her since the flood, of the way he'd held her that afternoon, so tenderly, so kindly, in the muddy ruin that had once been her home.

No. He was a real friend to her now. Too good a friend for her to lose him just because she'd presumed to lecture him about his life.

In the morning, she would apologize. And everything would be all right.

He wasn't there for the community breakfast in the morning and he didn't come to the church service after the meal.

Willa sat with Paige and wished he was there. She worried that he *wasn't* there because she had pushed his buttons and made it necessary, somehow, for him to prove what a tough, bad guy he was—too bad to show up for Sunday services and give Willa a chance to say she was sorry.

The choir sang of sweet comfort and the pastor quoted inspirational sections of scripture, verses meant to be uplifting in hard times. He gave a sermon on sacrifice and the meaning of community. He talked about how the Lord was with them and that each and every one of them was proving their worth and their goodness by their deeds in this time of trial.

And finally, when the sermon was over, Pastor Alderson led them in a prayer for Mayor McGee and the service became a farewell for Thelma's only son.

People stepped up with vases full of flowers, picked wild or from their own gardens. The choir sang the songs that Hunter had liked best, a couple of country-and-western love songs, "Red River Valley," a Bob Dylan ballad and some other songs Willa hadn't heard before.

It was during one of those other songs that she sensed movement at the end of the pew. She glanced that way.

Collin.

He wore clean jeans and a white shirt and his face was smooth from a recent shave. Had he made it up to his house on the mountain, then? He caught her eye, just for a moment. He didn't smile. But he wasn't scowling, either. She could have stared at him forever.

But she didn't. She forced her eyes front again while he made his way along the pew toward her. He muttered soft apologies as their neighbors slid their legs to the side, giving room for him to pass. Shelby Jenkins, a friend who sometimes worked as a substitute teacher at the elementary school, was sitting on her left.

She heard Collin whisper, "S'cuse me, Shelby…"

Shelby slid over and he took the empty space next to Willa. He smelled of soap and aftershave and her heart just lifted up when he settled in beside her. She couldn't even look at him right then, there were so many strange and powerful emotions chasing themselves around inside her. She had a dopey smile on her face, she just knew it, a totally inappropriate expression for a funeral.

He did that thing—that thing they'd started when they sat out on the town hall steps in the evening—leaning to the side in her direction, nudging her so gently with his shoulder.

She had to press her lips together to keep from letting out a silly squeak of pure joy. Because he wasn't all that mad at her, after all, evidently.

Because now she knew that everything between them would be all right.

The service continued. Pastor Alderson invited folks to stand and a say a word or two, to speak their testimony on the life of Hunter McGee.

In the front pew, Thelma stood first. Her voice only shook a little as she spoke of how proud she was to be Hunter's mom, as she told a little story about his boyhood, about his dreams for Rust Creek Falls, about how his one true love had died too young and he'd never known the joy of fatherhood, but he had loved Rust Creek Falls. It had meant the world to him that the people of his town had elected him their mayor.

When Thelma was finished, others stood, one at a time, taking turns, telling about growing up with Hunter, about the many ways that he'd helped them or made their lives richer, somehow. Each of the town council members took a turn, with Nathan Crawford going first. Willa had thought she might speak, but then it turned out that the things she would have shared were already said. She felt content to let it be.

The testimonies went on for over an hour. Until finally, one of the older Daltons sat back down after speaking of how Hunter had pitched in to help repair the Masonic Hall. There was a silence in the chapel. Willa thought that the sharing was done.

But then Collin shifted at her side. She blinked and looked over at him as he rose to his feet. He looked a little nervous, she thought, and so very handsome and dear.

Everyone turned and watched him expectantly. As a rule, Collin Traub didn't speak out in public, but Willa knew they all had to be remembering his impassioned arguments in the town hall the other day and eager to hear whatever he might contribute now.

Collin cleared his throat. "I just want to say that Hunter McGee was a man we all thought of as a friend. He had a way about him. He was wise and he was patient, too. But he had a killer sense of humor and that gleam in his eye that let you know he didn't judge you and he wanted only the best for you, no matter how big a troublemaker you might happen to be." Collin paused then, and glanced around with an abashed sort of expression.

People grinned and a few even chuckled.

Collin continued, "Somehow, Hunter always managed to get to the heart of an issue without ever choosing sides. He had a rare sort of fairness in him and a willingness to help. Yes, he's gone to a better place now. But at the same time, it seems to me that he's still here with us in spirit, that he's working beside us now, in this tough time when we need men like him the most. We haven't really lost him." Collin fisted his hand and laid it against his heart. "He's right here." He raised his hand and touched his temple. "And he's in here, too, in all of us. We can remember all he showed us about how to live and work together. And we can be grateful that we have his fine example to carry us forward as we work side by side to rebuild this town."

Collin sat back down.

There was a silence. Somebody murmured, "Oh, yeah."

And someone else said, "Tell it, Collin."

Several more "Oh, yeahs" and one or two "Praise Gods" followed.

Collin turned and looked at Willa, which was when she realized she was staring at him. He gave her a scowl, mouthed, *What?*

She only shrugged and faced front again and tried not to feel smug that he had just proved the truth in what she'd said to him the night before.

* * *

Outside after the service, Thelma embraced Collin and laid her hand gently on the side of his face. "Such a fine young man," she told him softly. And then she raised her lacy handkerchief to dab at her wet eyes.

A couple of the Dalton men clasped his shoulder as they filed out of the chapel. Willa observed all this and tried really hard not to feel too self-righteous about the things she'd said the night before. He really was a born leader, but what he did with that talent had to be of his own choosing.

Paige touched her arm. "I'd ask you to come sit with me for lunch, but I have a feeling you've got plans."

Willa gave her a hug and they parted. Buster whined at her, eager to be released from the iron bench where she'd leashed him. She went over and got him, crouching to pet him and make a fuss over him for being so good during the long church service.

"Rumor has it the church ladies are serving pizza for lunch today," Collin said from behind her.

Buster whined and wagged his tail in greeting and Willa's heart seemed to do a sort of forward roll under her breastbone. She asked, without turning, "Does the rumor mention pepperoni?"

"Yeah. Pepperoni and sausage, too." He dropped to a crouch at her side. Buster wiggled closer to him and head-butted his hand. Collin scratched the dog behind both ears and Buster lolled his tongue in doggy bliss.

Willa felt terribly shy suddenly. She stared at his hands as he petted her dog. "I, um, should walk Buster first...."

"Hey."

Her throat had a big lump in it. She gulped it down and made herself meet those low-lidded black eyes. "Hmm?"

"We okay, you and me?"

She remembered that she was going to apologize. "I lectured you. I shouldn't have done that. I'm sorry."

"You got nothing to be sorry for." His voice was low and more than a little rough. The sound of it sent a warm, lovely shiver running underneath her skin. He added, "You got a right to your opinion."

"But, well, you did get mad."

He smiled then, one of those slow smiles of his, the kind that used to make all the girls back in high school sigh and fan themselves. "So then, *I'm* sorry. I had no right at all to jump all over you for telling the truth as you see it." He kept on looking at her, a deep look that made her whole body feel sensitized, excited. Wonderfully alive. "Forgive me?"

That lump was back in her throat again. She gulped a second time to clear it. "I do. And yes. We're okay."

"Whew."

She felt her mouth tremble into a smile that answered his. "Did you go up to your house, then?"

"No. I'm hoping I'll get to that tomorrow. This morning, I went out to the Triple T and had breakfast with the hands. They got the wells in working order, so I had a shower, too." He swept upward and she stood, too. "Let's walk this dog," he said.

"Good idea."

"The park? We can let him run."

"Perfect."

After lunch, the governor dropped in—literally—in a helicopter.

The chopper landed in the middle of Main Street and the governor emerged, waving and smiling, trailed by a guy in a FEMA vest and another, more muscular fellow in dark glasses. Waving as he went, the governor ran up and stood on the town hall steps, where the town council members waited. He shook hands with each of them.

And then he gave a little speech—more of a pep talk, really. He said the same things Nathan was always saying: that road crews and the power and telephone companies were working around-the-clock to get the roads open and services back online. He asked everyone to sit tight until services were restored and, whenever possible, to stay in the Rust Creek Falls Valley until the roads were declared safe for travel.

He praised their spirit of independence, their ability to roll up their sleeves and do for themselves. Since the good people of Rust Creek Falls seemed to be managing better than most in the stricken areas, he could see that the Red Cross and the National Guard wouldn't be needed there—not at that point anyway.

After the governor spoke, the FEMA guy talked about the services FEMA offered and the progress of the cleanup. And then, with more smiling and waving, the three visitors ran back and boarded the helicopter and off they went.

Collin leaned close and said in her ear, "Wasn't that inspiring?" She gave him a look and left it at that. And then he said, "I was thinking we could try and see what we can salvage from Gage's house."

She wanted to grab him and hug him—for being so generous, for thinking of her poor brother, who had to be worried sick about now and was no doubt moving heaven and earth to get back to town. "Yes. Please. Let's do that."

The church ladies had several boxes they could spare. So she and Collin put them in the back of his pickup and headed for the ranch, where they worked until after five packing up things at Gage's and putting them with Willa's boxes in her father's work shed.

They made it back to town in time for dinner at the

church. As they ate beans and rice with ham, Nathan got up and proudly announced that cell phone service was restored. He reminded them of the places that had generators where they might charge their batteries. People applauded the news—and then hurried off to find the phones they'd stopped carrying around with them for the past three days.

In the pickup, Collin called his mother first. Willa had run out with him and ended up sitting in the passenger seat beside him as he nodded and listened, and seemed to be having trouble getting a word in edgewise. He kept trying to tell his mom what had happened there at home, but Ellie Traub had never been the quiet type. As soon as he started talking, she would get going again and he ended up mostly saying, "Yeah. Okay. All right. That's good, Mom. Really..."

When he finally said goodbye, he reported to Willa that his mom, his dad and his brothers were fine. "They got the rain down there in Thunder Canyon," he said, "but flooding was minimal. Mom says they're willing to wait a few more days until the governor gives the go-ahead. But if the okay doesn't come soon, they're heading for home." He added that the people of Thunder Canyon were already talking about ways to help Rust Creek Falls with flood cleanup and the rebuilding that would follow.

And then he handed her the phone. "Go on. Call your folks."

Again, she had a really strong urge to hug him. But instead she started dialing.

Lavinia Christensen cried when Willa said hello. "We've been calling and calling," she sobbed. And then she wanted to know why Willa wasn't calling from her own cell.

Willa explained that she'd lost it in the flood. "This is Collin's cell."

Her mother sniffled. "Collin *Traub?*"

"Yes." She cast Collin a warm glance. "He's been great to me, Mom. Wonderful." Collin sent her one of those *knock-it-off* looks when he heard her praising him. She pretended not to notice.

Her mom was kind of sputtering. "Well, I, ahem. The Traubs are good people."

"They certainly are—and if you need to reach me, just call this number. Collin will make sure I get back to you until I can get a phone of my own."

"I…I will. Yes. Of course."

Willa assured her mom that she was all right and that the ranch house was fine and so was the barn. She said that most of the stock had survived the flood and the neighbors had all pitched in to keep the animals fed and to clean up the mess. Her mom cried some more when she heard the bad news about Willa's house and Gage's place.

It turned out her folks were still in Livingston, waiting for news that the roads were clear. Gage, however, had set out for home.

When Willa called him, she had to explain all over again that he should call her on Collin's phone for the time being. He started quizzing her about Collin.

She cut him short. "What about you? Where are you now?"

He said he'd been held up three times so far with washed-out bridges and roads, but he wasn't giving up and had spent each night since the flood in a different town. Willa got teary eyed then and told him about the condition of his house—and hers. Her brother said he loved her and not to cry and he would be there as soon as he could. He said he'd visited the sheriff's stations in the towns where he'd stayed and used their radio systems to contact his office. So he'd known that she was all right and he'd been told of the death of Hunter McGee.

When he mentioned Mayor McGee, Willa started crying all over again. She'd been dry-eyed at the funeral, but there was something about her brother's voice. She could tell that the mayor's death had hit him hard. Collin hauled a box of tissues from the glove box and passed it to her. She grabbed one and wiped at her streaming eyes.

When she hung up with Gage, she gave the phone back to Collin. He turned on the pickup so he could hook up his car charger and then, with the phone plugged in, he called a couple of his brothers in Thunder Canyon and then his brother Sutter, in Washington State.

When he hung up, he said in a tone that dared her to argue, "I think a lot of Sutter. He's a damn good man."

Willa only nodded. There were people in town who didn't approve of the stand Sutter had taken when their older brother Forrest went off to fight in Iraq. And then there was the way he'd broken Paige's heart. But still. Willa had always liked Sutter and if he and Collin were on good terms, well, that was just fine with her.

Collin narrowed those almost-black eyes at her and his full mouth curved down at the corners. "You got something on your mind, Willa, you ought to just go ahead and say it."

Willa answered sweetly, "You love your brother. There is nothing wrong with that."

That evening, the number of citizens requiring emergency shelter was a third what it had been the first night. FEMA had brought in some trailers that day for people to stay in temporarily. And more people had either left town to stay with relatives or moved in with friends. A lucky few had discovered that the damage to their homes wasn't bad enough to keep them from moving back in.

Willa and Collin stayed in the town hall again that

night. After the lights were out, she took Buster and went to join Collin under the stars.

"Been waiting for you," he said when she dropped down beside him.

A little thrill shivered through her at his words and she had to remind herself not to be an idiot. It wasn't a man-woman kind of thing between them. They were friends. Good friends, amazingly. But that was all. He wasn't interested in her in *that* way and he never had been.

She wrapped her arms around her knees and rested her chin on them. "Are you still planning to go up the mountain tomorrow?"

"Yeah. In the afternoon. It should be fine up there. The generator automatically kicks in when the power goes out, so what's in the fridge and the freezer stays cold. I've got a freezer full of food I'll bring down and donate to the church kitchen."

She stared at him, thinking how smoking hot he was—because, hey, even if they were just friends, there was no law that said a girl couldn't look. She could get lost in those eyes of his. And even in the darkness, his hair had a shine to it. And it was so thick.

That night four years ago, at the Ace in the Hole, before he laughed at her and told her to get lost, they'd danced to a couple of slow numbers together. She remembered so clearly the feel of his hard, hot shoulder beneath her hand. His lips had looked soft and dangerous, both at once. And the scent of him: incomparable, a heady mix of aftershave, man and something temptingly wild. The rush of blood through her veins had been dizzying. And she would never forget her powerful desire to slide her fingers upward, over the hot flesh of his neck and into that thick, crow-black hair of his.

He asked, "Do I have dirt on my nose?"

She chuckled, the sound surprisingly husky to her own ears. "No. Why?"

He held her gaze as though he never planned to look away. "You're staring at me."

Right. She supposed that she was. She went on staring and told him way too dreamily, "Buster and I are going with you."

"Going with me where?"

"Up to your house tomorrow."

Those thick inky brows drew together. "It's not a good idea."

Too bad. He wasn't talking her out of it. But for now, she played along. "Why not?"

"The road up there is bound to be a mess. It could be dangerous."

"All the more reason you shouldn't go alone."

"You're going to protect me, are you?"

She braced her chin on her hand. "I am. Absolutely. You're a big, tough guy and all, I know. But even tough guys sometimes need a little help."

The way he was looking at her now, she could almost imagine that he did think of her *that* way. Which probably meant she was being an idiot again. But so what? There were a lot worse things than being an idiot. A girl could live her whole life without ever getting her fingers into Collin's black hair. That would be sad. Immeasurably so.

Now he was looking stern. "It's not a good idea."

"You already said that."

"I'll probably end up staying up there overnight."

"So? I'll take the sleeping bag from my cot. It will be fine."

He seemed a little insulted. "I have a guest room—and believe it or not, it has a bed in it, complete with sheets and blankets and pillows."

"Wonderful. So it's settled."

He wasn't going for it. "I told you. You need to stay here."

"We'll see...."

"I mean it, Willa. You are not going up the mountain with me."

The next morning, Collin rejoined his team.

Before he left to help with cleanup down in the area around the flooded clinic, Willa told him that she and Paige and some of the other teachers had been asked to reconvene summer school. Since the day would be a clear one, they would hold their classes in Rust Creek Falls Park. On rainy days, classes would be hosted by some of the parents—and a few of the teachers, as well.

When he came in for lunch in the church, he returned a call from his mom, one from his brother Clay and another from Sutter. Then he made calls to a few top CT Saddles customers. He apologized for the fact that he would be filling their orders late. They'd all heard about the flood and told him not to worry, to stay safe and take his time.

Willa wasn't there at the church for lunch. He ignored the little curl of disappointment in his chest when he didn't see her. Every day he was with her, it got easier to let himself think that there was more going on between them than friendship.

There wasn't. Once things got back to normal, her bigshot boyfriend would show up. She would realize what that other guy could offer her and she would end up with his ring on her finger. Which was the way it should be. Willa deserved the best.

Dolly Tabor, one of his teammates on the rescue-turned-cleanup crew, had kids in summer school. She mentioned that the church ladies were delivering the school lunches to the park.

So, great, he thought. Willa was having lunch with the kids in the park.

He asked Dolly, real casual-like, when summer school would be over for the day. Dolly said at three.

Collin made his plans accordingly. He knew Willa and he knew her ways. She thought she was going up the mountain with him. And there was more than one good reason why he couldn't let that happen. For one thing, the trip up there was likely to be hazardous. He wasn't putting Willa in danger. And then, if they ended up stuck at his place for the night, well, that would present a whole other kind of danger.

It was one thing to be alone with her for an hour out on the town hall steps at night, or while they worked side by side hauling stuff out of her brother's flooded house. It was another thing altogether to spend the night with her at his place, just the two of them, alone on Falls Mountain.

Uh-uh. That would be asking for the kind of trouble they weren't going to get into together. He had to face reality here. He'd done what he could to help her through the worst of it after the flood. Her family would be back in town any day now. From what she'd said about Gage working his way north, her brother could be home already.

Collin needed to start getting a little distance from her. He had to stop spending so much time with her, had to give up those nighttime talks out on the town hall steps. He needed to stop kidding himself that it was innocent, that they were just hanging out, joking around a little before turning in.

It wasn't innocent—not for him anyway. Every night it got harder to keep his hands to himself. If he didn't get some distance, he would end up making a move on her.

He knew she really wanted to be his friend and all that. But he wanted more than friendship and where was that going to go? He liked his relationships with women to be simple—and short.

Nothing with Willa was simple. So he would put an end to it, make sure it never even had a chance to get started. She would be hurt and probably angry with him for taking off up the mountain without a word to her. But too bad.

It was for the best.

He got Jerry Dobbs aside and said he was heading up to his place. Jerry clapped him on the back and told him to be careful on the road up there.

Across the street at the town hall, he collected the plastic bag full of clothes and personal items he'd left under his cot. Marjorie Hanke was there, so he told her he wouldn't be needing the cot anymore.

And that was it. He was free to get the hell outta town.

He shouldered the bag and headed for his truck in the parking lot in the back, feeling more down than he should have, wishing things could be different and calling himself ten kinds of fool to want a thing he was never going to have—and wouldn't know what to do with anyway.

He almost tripped over his own boots when he caught sight of Willa. She was leaning against his rear wheel well, Buster on one side, her bag of stuff and backpack on the other.

Chapter Eight

She had her arms folded across her middle and her head tipped to the side. The early-afternoon sun brought out bronze highlights in her coffee-colored hair. She gave him a slow once-over. "I knew it."

He glared at her, trying his best to look pissed off. "You knew what?"

"You were just going to sneak away without even telling me. That's not very nice, Collin."

"I did tell you. I told you last night."

She tightened her arms around herself and pressed her lips together. "And I told you that I was going with you." She pushed off the wheel well and stood up straight. "So here I am."

His bag of clothes rustled as he let it slide to the pavement. He was actively ignoring the rapid beating of his heart, the ridiculous surge of happiness that was blasting all through him.

She really did want to go with him. She wasn't letting him get away without a fight.

But so what? He needed to focus on the goal: to get her to give up this insanity and go back to the park. "No. It's a bad idea. And aren't you supposed to be over at the park teaching summer school?"

"Shelby Jenkins is helping out. She took over for me."

"But you—"

"I'm going, Collin. Don't mess with me on this."

How in hell could he do the right thing if she kept pushing him to screw up? A voice in the back of his mind kept chanting, *She wants to come, she wants to come.* And the bad-acting idiot inside him kept whispering, *Man, if it's what she wants, why not?*

He ground his teeth together. "I wasn't planning to come back until tomorrow."

"That's okay. I've got my stuff. And you've got a guest room. It's all good."

"I thought you had summer school."

"I told you, Shelby's helping out. I explained to her that I was going up the mountain with you and we might not make it back until later tomorrow. She'll take my kids for me. I'm covered."

"Get real, Willa. You go up the mountain with me and spend the night, the whole town will be talking when you come back down. The Traub bad boy and the kindergarten teacher. I can hear them all now."

She laughed. Like it was funny. He watched the dimples flash in her pink cheeks and he thought about licking them. "I'm sure they're already talking. We've practically been joined at the hip since the flood. And in case you've forgotten, we spent a whole night together in my dad's barn and the world didn't come to an end."

In case he'd forgotten? He would never forget. Especially not what had happened in the morning. His fly. Her hand. Sitting there on the edge of that hay bale, willing the humiliating bulge in his pants to go down. He strove for calmness and reasonableness. "We had no choice then. It was the barn or drowning. This—you and me, up the mountain together? That's a clear choice."

Her mouth had pinched up tight. "What is going on with you? Suddenly you're acting like it's 1955 or something. Like you're worried about my reputation, which is excellent and unimpeachable, thank you very much."

Unimpeachable? She really did talk like a schoolteacher sometimes. Which got him hot. Real hot. But he wasn't going to think about that. "It's a very small town, Willa. People here are conservative. You know that as well as I do."

She just wouldn't back down. "You're making way too much of this. Everyone in town knows me and respects me. No one has—or will—judge me for being your friend." In her excitement, she unfolded her arms and waved them around. "In fact, Crawfords aside, this town happens to think the world of *you,* in case you haven't been paying attention."

"That doesn't mean they won't gossip."

"Oh, please. You never cared about people talking before."

"I care now."

"I don't believe you. Here's the way I see it. If you really don't want me along, if you're sick of having me around and you want to get rid of me, that's one thing. If you just *have* to have a little time to yourself, well, okay. I can accept that. But all this other stuff you've been handing me about my reputation and how it's 'a bad idea,' how I should be over at the park instead of with you, well, you can just stop that, Collin Traub. You can just...get a little bit straight with me. Please." And with that, she blew out a hard breath and flopped back against the wheel well again, folding her arms across her chest once more.

"Crap, Willa." He folded his own arms. He told himself that this argument was over and he'd won it. Because she'd just given him the out that he needed. He only had to say he didn't want her with him, that he preferred to be alone. He only had to lie to her.

Which he had no problem doing, under the circumstances. After all, it was for her own good.

Buster whined and stared up at him hopefully. And Willa simply waited.

He opened his mouth and said, "Fine. Get in the truck."

Willa had always loved the drive up Falls Mountain. It was paved only a part of the way up, but when the pavement ran out, the dirt surface was well tended and the ride reasonably smooth—or at least, it always had been until the flood.

The narrow road proceeded in a series of switchbacks under the tall evergreens. Now and then a switchback would lead out onto a rocky point before doubling back. You could park your vehicle and stroll to the edge and gaze out over the whole of the Rust Creek Falls Valley below, a beautiful sight that never failed to steal her breath away.

And then, two-thirds of the way to the summit, you would round a sharp turn—and see the falls up ahead, hear their splendid, endless roar. The air would turn misty and the sun would slip through the spaces between the trees and light up the falling water with a million pinpricks of shining light.

This trip, however, wasn't so much about the scenery. This was about getting safely to Collin's place and dealing with whatever obstacles the big storm might have left in its wake.

As they set out, you could cut the tension between them with a knife. He was pretty steamed at her. He seethed where he sat, strong hands viselike on the wheel, staring out the windshield with fierce concentration, never once glancing in her direction.

And frankly, well, she was annoyed with him, too. She only wanted to help. And he could have gotten rid of her just by honestly saying he didn't want her around.

But no. It had to be all about protecting her good name. Please. She wasn't buying that silliness and he should give her more credit than to imagine she would.

So she spent the first part of the ride until the pavement ran out keeping very quiet, not pushing her luck with him. Buster was in the back and they'd taken their bags of stuff up front with them. She had them both on her side, his on the floor, hers tucked in next to her with her pack against the console. She leaned on the door armrest and stared intently out at the trees and the occasional glimpses of blue Montana sky and told herself that when they got to his place, they would talk it out.

She was so busy staring out her side window she didn't see the first downed tree until he stopped the truck.

"This'll take a while," he said sourly. "Hope you brought a book or maybe a little knitting." He leaned on his door and got out.

Oh, for crying out loud. As if she hadn't helped her father and brother clear any number of fallen trees off the ranch in her lifetime. She'd come ready to work. She had on her old lace-up work boots from the box at her mother's. Her jeans were sturdy and her sleeves were long. She dug around in her plastic bag until she found the pair of work gloves she'd borrowed from Thelma.

Collin's chain saw roared out as she left the truck. Buster was already down from the bed and sniffing around on the side of the road. He would probably take off if she didn't put him on his leash, but he looked so happy and free, she didn't have the heart to tie him up.

So she decided to leave him free, but keep an eye on him. If he started ranging too far, she'd call him back.

She went to join Collin at the fallen tree.

Willa hauled and Collin expertly stripped the branches from the log, then cut the log into sections. When he was done with the saw, he helped her drag off the brush.

As they cleared the brush, he finally started speaking to her again.

"I hate to waste firewood," he said. "But I've got more than enough up at my place."

They left the stove-size logs and the cleanest parts of the branches stacked on the side of the road for anyone in need to collect. It wasn't that big of a tree. In an hour, they had the roadway clear.

She took off her gloves. With her sleeve, she wiped sweat from her brow. And then she remembered to check on the dog. Wouldn't you know? "Buster's run off again."

He put two fingers between his lips and let loose with a whistle so high and piercing, she put her hands over her ears. As soon as he stopped, Buster came bounding out of the trees. He ran straight to Collin and dropped to his haunches in front of him.

"Good dog," Collin said. "Stay."

Willa blinked in admiration. "Wow."

"I used to call Libby that way. Never failed."

She remembered his dog. A sweet-natured brown-spotted white mutt that followed him everywhere. "What happened to Libby?"

"Lost her last winter. She was pretty old."

"I'm sorry. She always seemed so devoted to you."

"Yeah. I guess she was." He made a low, thoughtful sound. "I still miss her. Now and then I think I see her out of the corner of my eye. I forget for a split second that she's gone and I turn to call her to me…."

Willa was nodding, thinking of Mr. Puffy, the barn kitten she'd claimed as her own when she was five. Puffs had become a house cat and lived to be seventeen. "Oh, I know the feeling. It's like they're still with you, somehow, even though you know that they're gone…."

"That's right." He regarded her for a moment that seemed to stretch out into forever. He didn't seem angry anymore and she realized that neither was she.

"Thirsty?" he asked at last.

At her nod, he turned and started walking, pausing only to signal her with a wave of his powerful arm.

"Come on, Buster." She fell in behind him.

A trail took off below the road. They followed it, pine needles crunching under their feet, Buster taking up the rear.

Maybe two hundred yards later, they came to a ditch full of rushing, clear water. They both got down on their bellies to drink. Buster tried to join them, but she shooed him downstream a ways.

It was so good, that water. Fresh and cold and perfect. When they'd both drunk their fill, they scrambled upright and returned to the pickup. They got in, Buster hopped in the back and off they went.

After that, it was stop and go. There were three more downed trees to clear and any number of rutted, rough places scattered with rock, where instant streams had formed during the storm, destroying the road surface, dragging debris. Often they would have to get out and clear away the biggest of the boulders. It was dusty, thirsty work. But there were plenty of ditches to drink from once the road was passable again.

At one of the outlook points, they found that the road had fallen away at the edge of the cliff. It was just wide enough for the pickup to proceed. Twice on that narrow spot, she felt the back wheel on her side slip over the edge.

But Collin had done a lot of driving on narrow, treacherous mountain roads. He knew when to change gears and when to hit the gas. Both times, there was only a split second of falling and then the truck gained purchase again and they went on.

They didn't reach the falls until a little after seven. More than two hours of daylight remained to them, so they stopped the truck. Buster following behind them, they walked close to admire the view.

"It was twice as wide when I came down on the Fourth," he told her, as they stared at the wall of shining water.

"So beautiful." She stood near the edge, looking over, entranced by the plumes of mist that rose from the rocks below. A prayerful kind of feeling came over her. It happened every time she visited the falls.

When they turned for the truck, he said, "It's not that far now." He put down the gate long enough for Buster to hop in the back again. Then he joined her in the cab.

Around the next sharp curve another tree lay, uprooted, across the road. They got out and got to work. By the time that one was out of the way and he was starting up the truck again, it was nine-thirty and the sky was steadily darkening.

He sent her a glance across the console. "We're there in five minutes, barring more crap in the road."

She grinned. "I will pray for an absence of crap."

"Good thinking." He started to shift into gear—and

then stopped. "I would be sleeping in this truck tonight, three fallen trees back, if not for you."

"If more crap happens, you could still end up sleeping in this truck."

He arched a brow. "That was a thank-you."

She felt hugely gratified. "Well, all right. You're welcome."

"And an apology."

"Which is accepted."

They did that thing, the eye-contact thing. The moment stretched out. Finally, he said, "I'm glad you're with me."

"That is so nice to hear." She said it softly, a little bit breathlessly. "Because I'm glad to be with you."

They shared another endless glance. The world seemed a fine place, exciting, a place where anything might happen. A place where a girl's lifelong forbidden fantasies might just come true.

Friends, she reminded herself. *We are friends and that's all.*

But the way he was looking at her, well, a girl could definitely get ideas.

"We should get going," he said.

"Yeah," she whispered, as though there was some kind of secret they were sharing.

He buckled his seat belt and put it in gear.

The headlights were on, the powerful twin beams cutting the thickening shadows. Everything looked clear up ahead. The road was very steep, though, there at the last. Gravel spun out from under the tires as they kept losing traction. But Collin held it in low, with an even pressure on the gas. They climbed steadily upward, almost there.

"One more switchback," he said. The sharp turn loomed ahead. Tires spinning, gravel flying, the truck slipping to one side and then the other, Collin guided them around it.

They'd made it without having to sleep in the cab. Through the tall, thick trees, she could see the shadowed form of his house up ahead. A light shone in the window, one he must have left on when he raced down the mountain four days ago, a light that still burned because he had a generator.

Lights that wouldn't be turned off promptly at 11:00 p.m. How wonderful. She had a couple of bestsellers she'd borrowed from Paige in the bottom of her bag. Why, she might read late into the night if she felt like it. She might blow-dry her hair—well, if only she'd thought to scare up a blow-dryer.

And not only would there be light that was hers to control, she would sleep on a real bed, in a real bedroom, without all those other people nearby snoring or mumbling in their sleep....

The truck slid, snapping her back to reality, and she felt a stomach-turning lurch as the rear wheels lost contact with the road. Collin swore under his breath.

The truck—and the world—hung suspended by two front wheels.

It was bad. She knew it. She tasted copper in her suddenly dry mouth. Her heart boomed, the sound a roar in her ears.

It took her a second or two to realize what had happened. As they came around the turn, the road had collapsed on the cliff side, just dropped off and fallen away under the back wheels.

"Oh, dear Lord," she whispered, and nothing more. Words were lost to her.

The truck was sliding backward, the bed dropping, dragging. They were going to go over the cliff, tail first....

But Collin hit the gas then. The front wheels grabbed

and held. Praise heaven for four-wheel drive. He eased the throttle even higher.

The truck lurched again, jumping forward this time, grabbing at the road. The front wheels had good purchase. Gravel flew every which way, grinding grooves in the dirt, but they did move forward. The truck leveled out as the rear wheels reached the road again.

He had done it. He had all four tires on solid ground again. She heard him suck in a long breath and realized that she was doing the same thing.

"We're okay," she whispered, as though to say it too loudly would somehow send them rolling backward over the cliff once more.

But then she glanced through the rear window. Buster wasn't there.

Chapter Nine

"Collin, Buster's gone!"

Collin hit the brake as Willa's door flew open. "Willa. Wait…" But she didn't wait. She was out the door before the truck came to a full stop. "Be careful at the cliff edge!" he shouted.

Not that she heard him. She was already out and running back to that last almost-deadly turn.

He slammed it in Park, turned off the engine, and shoved in the parking brake, grabbing a flashlight from the glove box before he jumped out and ran after her. "Stay back from the edge, damn it, Willa!"

She was already there, craning to see over, calling the dog. "Buster! Buster, here, boy!"

He went to her, grabbed her arm and hauled her back a few feet. She tried to shake him off, but he held on. "Don't," he warned. "It could be dangerous."

"But Buster…" Frantic tears clogged her voice.

He shone the light on the ground at the edge he'd dragged her back from. Hard to tell, but it looked pretty solid. "Careful, okay?" Reluctantly, he let her go. "Just take it easy… slow."

Together they moved toward the cliff again. He shone the flashlight down into the darkness, spotted the small ledge created by two joined sets of tree roots maybe thirty feet down. Buster was young and agile. All he would have needed was something to break his fall and chances were he would have been okay.

No sign of him on that ledge, though.

"Buster!" Willa called again, more frantic than before. "Buster!"

Not knowing what else to do, Collin put his fingers between his teeth and let out with the whistle that always brought the dogs running. He glanced over at Willa, at the tears already streaming down her soft cheeks.

He was just about to start blaming himself, when he heard the scrabbling sounds over the side, up the road a little, near where he'd stopped the truck.

Willa whipped around toward the noise. "Buster!" Collin turned the light on her, so she wouldn't trip on the uneven road surface as she took off again in the direction of the sounds.

About then, the white dog scrambled up over the bank, apparently unhurt. He got to the road and shook himself.

"Buster!" Willa dropped to a crouch and threw her arms around him. The dog whined and swiped his sloppy tongue all over her face and wagged his tail as though he'd just done something pretty spectacular.

And maybe he had.

Collin went to them. With another happy cry, Willa jumped up and threw her arms around *him*. "He's fine. He's okay. Oh, thank God." She buried her face against his neck.

He held her close and tried not to let himself think about how right she always felt in his arms.

Buster rode the last short stretch inside the cab, sandwiched between Willa's feet.

Collin didn't much care for dogs in the front. But he wasn't complaining. A couple of minutes after they'd piled in the truck again, Collin parked in the flat space not far from the front door to his house.

"We made it," Willa said softly. "I can hardly believe it."

He reached over and grabbed his bag out from under Buster's big feet. "I'm starving. Let's scare up something to eat."

Inside, he got Libby's bowl down from a cupboard and filled it with kibble leftover from last winter. Buster went right to work on the food.

Willa stood holding her black plastic bag, her pack slung on one shoulder, staring out the wall of windows that faced the valley. With the lamps on and the antler chandelier overhead casting its warm glow, there was nothing to see but her reflection in the glass. "This is so beautiful, Collin."

He left the open kitchen area and went to stand beside her. "Pretty dark down there tonight. Usually, even with the great room all lit up, you can see the lights of town."

She turned to him, her eyes so soft and bright. "You'll be seeing them again before you know it."

He took her arm and tried not to feel too happy to have her there, in his house, alone. "Come on. I'll show you the guest room and the spare bath."

Her face lit up. "A shower? You mean it?"

"Right this way."

Willa pushed her empty plate away. "Steak. A baked potato. Even a salad." She sent him a mock glare. "And to think, if I hadn't made you bring me along, it would have been macaroni and canned ham all over again."

He gave her one of those grins that always made her pulse speed up. "Is that what the church ladies are serving tonight?"

"I believe so, yes." She sat back and looked around her. The living area was all one room, with a comfy-looking sofa and chairs grouped around a rustic fireplace. He'd built a small fire that crackled cheerfully. Up on the mountain, even summer nights had a bite to them.

The galley-type kitchen had butcher-block counters, the cabinets painted a woodsy green.

She asked, "This place was your uncle's?"

"That's right." He polished off his beer. "Uncle Casper was an independent old coot—and he was always good to me."

She remembered Casper Traub. He had a handlebar mustache and he always wore a white Resistol hat. "A confirmed bachelor."

"Damn straight. Uncle Casper and I got along. We just seemed to understand each other—but I've made a lot of changes to the house since he passed. This area had a wall down the middle before, the kitchen separate from the living room. I like it open. And I had bigger windows put in to take advantage of the view."

"You did a great job." She stared up at all the lights strung on the antler chandelier. "It's comfortable and homey. Inviting, but not cluttered."

"That's good." He gestured with his empty beer bottle. "It's pretty much what I was going for."

"You got it right."

He was watching her. "But not what you expected." It wasn't a question.

She confessed, "Not really. I was thinking you would have more of a woodsy man-cave, to tell the truth."

Twin creases formed between his brows. "It's not a woodsy man-cave?"

"Collin. You can't have a man-cave with all those windows. With a man-cave, there would be stacks of girlie magazines. And the decor would focus on empty liquor bottles lining the walls."

He pretended to look wounded. "You're serious. You see me saving empty liquor bottles to use for decoration, surrounded by girlie magazines...."

"Oh, come on. You know I'm just kidding."

He shrugged and pointed the beer bottle at the big-screen TV. "Well, I've got the right TV anyway. And I get cable up here now, believe it or not—or I do when the cable service isn't down. Even my cell phone works most of the time." He grinned that wicked grin of his. "Admit it. You're impressed."

"Bowled over." She took a small sip of the beer he'd given her. "You miss your uncle?"

He gave her a slow nod. "Every day. He taught me all I know about the business and he left it to me with the house when we lost him. My shop's in the basement."

"*You* make the saddles now?"

He sent her a wounded glance. "Who would if I didn't? You think I keep a bunch of elves down there?"

"Of course not." But she *was* surprised. She'd known that Casper Traub had left everything to his favorite nephew, but somehow she hadn't really thought about what exactly that would mean—and that made her feel a little ashamed. The past few years, she'd been so busy judging him, she'd never stopped to think about who he was as a person, how he might have changed and grown from the wild, rude boy who used to spy on her out in the back pasture.

He got up, got a second beer from the fridge and twisted the top off. "You want one?"

She still had half of hers. "I'm good."

He came back to her and dropped into his chair again. "What? You're having trouble believing that I work for a living?" He took a drink, his Adam's apple sliding up and down in his strong brown throat. "You have one of my saddles in the tack room of your dad's barn."

Yet another surprise. "My dad's precious CT Saddle? *You* made it?"

"I did."

"But he got that saddle three years ago."

"I've been making saddles since before high school. Uncle Casper had me working with him as soon as I was tall enough to stand at a workbench."

"Oh. I…didn't know."

He grunted and shook his head. And she felt really bad. He seemed to sense her distress, and leaned across the table toward her. "What'd I do? Willa, come on. You look like you're about to cry."

She waved a hand. And then she sighed. "You didn't do anything. Honestly. It's only that I'm disappointed in myself, I guess."

"Why?" He asked it so quietly. Like he didn't want to push her, but he really did want an answer.

She gave him the truth. "We live in a very small town, where everyone knows everything about everyone else. Yet, I didn't know you made the most beautiful saddles in Montana. I didn't know much at all about you. In high school, I never wanted anyone to know that I was…" Her throat clutched. She gulped to loosen it. "Um, attracted to you. So I made real sure that I acted like I couldn't care less whenever anyone mentioned your name. That meant I never learned anything about you—about who you really are. Except that everyone said half the girls had been with you and the other half wished they might."

"Willa…" His voice was husky and his eyes were so soft.

She suddenly felt all warm and quivery inside and she had to force herself to say the rest. "And then, well, after that night at the Ace in the Hole, I was just so…bitter. So angry at you. And that meant I kept on not letting myself know anything about you, kept on judging you without even knowing you. It was all just so narrow-minded and, well, *small* of me, you know? And I like to think of myself as an open-minded and fair person. But maybe I'm not. Maybe I'm already just an old busybody, listening to rumors, believing the worst about people. Never stopping to find out what's really going on."

"You're too young to be an old busybody."

She wanted to smile—but he was letting her off too easy. "Don't be nice to me about this. I don't deserve it."

He set down his beer, got up and came around the table to her, dropping to a crouch beside her chair. "Hey." He took her hand. Heat flowed up her arm, into her heart. And lower down, too. "And I have to tell you, I kind of got a kick out of you avoiding me for four years."

She groaned. "You didn't."

"Oh, yeah. You were so determined. I'd walk in a room—and out you went through the other door."

"But still. Be honest. It did hurt your feelings a little, didn't it?"

"I survived."

She looked down at their joined hands and then back up into those beautiful deep-set eyes of his. "So you forgive me?"

"There's nothing to forgive." He seemed so earnest right then, his face tipped up to her, that lock of hair falling over his forehead the way it always seemed to do.

She couldn't stop herself—she didn't *want* to stop herself. She dared to smooth it back. It was just as she'd always imagined it might be—thick and warm and so very silky, a little bit damp from his recent shower. "I don't know what I would have done in these past few days without you."

"You would have been fine."

She grew bolder. She pressed her palm to his cheek. It was smooth, freshly shaved. "I would have drowned that first day. You know it as well as I do."

"Uh-uh. You're too ornery to drown."

"You think so?"

"Oh, yeah. You would have gotten that door open and made it to safety." His voice was rough and tender, both at once.

Her breath caught in her throat. *A kiss,* she thought.

What could a kiss hurt?

Just one. No harm in that.

His gaze seemed to burn her and his sensual mouth was slightly parted. He smelled so good, clean and fresh and manly.

"Oh, Collin…" She dared to bend closer—and then blinked in surprise when he caught her wrist and gently guided her hand away from his face.

He swept to his feet, grabbed up his empty plate and the salad bowl and carried them to the sink. Without turning back to look at her, he said, "You want to watch a movie or something? I've got a bookcase full of DVDs."

Her face was flaming. Talk about making a fool of herself.

What was her problem anyway? The poor guy couldn't be nice to her without her trying to jump his bones.

She reminded herself, as she'd reminded herself about a hundred times in the past few days, that he liked her and he was her friend. But he was not interested in her in *that* way and she needed get that in her head and keep it there.

His friendship mattered to her. She was not going to lose him because she couldn't stop throwing herself at him.

He still had his back to her as he rinsed out the salad bowl and then scraped off his plate in the garbage and stuck it in the dishwasher.

She picked up her plate and carried it over there.

He took it from her. "So. Movie?"

"As long as I get to choose which one."

He did let her choose. His taste ranged from horror to Western and action/adventure to raunchy guy comedies. Not a tender romance to be found.

She chose a Jason Statham shoot-'em-up. It was fast-paced and entertaining. When it was over, she let Buster out and waited on the step for him to take care of business. Back inside, she told Collin good-night and headed for the guest room, Buster at her heels.

The bed was big and comfortable and she'd worked hard all afternoon. She should have gone right to sleep.

But, no. She kept thinking about what an idiot she'd been at the dinner table, kept wondering if she should have done something other than pretend for the rest of the evening that nothing had happened.

Then again, if not that, what? Certainly they didn't have to discuss the fact that she regretted throwing herself at him and would try really, really hard not to do it again.

Sheesh. How pathetic. That was a conversation she just didn't need to have.

Willa plumped her pillow and turned over. Then she turned over again. Then she sat up and pushed back all the covers but the sheet.

Then she pulled the covers back over herself again.

It was hopeless. Sleep was not in the offing. She turned on the lamp and got her book from the bag and tried to read.

But she couldn't concentrate. The clock by the bed said ten after one.

Maybe she could find some cocoa in the kitchen. Or just some milk to heat up. Or *something*.

She threw back the covers. On the rug by the bed, Buster lifted his head—and then settled back to sleep with a soft doggy sigh. She yanked on a worn plaid shirt over the camisole and knit shorts she'd worn to sleep in and decided to just go barefoot. Flip-flops made too much noise anyway. She didn't want to take the chance of disturbing Collin. At least one of them should be allowed to get a decent night's sleep.

His bedroom was down at the far end of the hall. The door was open, but there was no light on in there.

Not that it mattered. She had no intention of bothering him. Willa went the other way, out to the great room and into the kitchen.

She flicked on the light and was heading for the fridge when Collin said, "Go back to bed, Willa. How many times do I have to tell you? I'm not having sex with you."

With a cry of surprise, she whirled toward the sound of his voice. He stood over in the living area, wearing his jeans and nothing else, his strong legs planted wide apart, hands linked behind him, staring out the wall of windows on the dark town below.

She didn't know whether to laugh or throw something at him…but wait.

On second thought, she did know. The latter. Definitely.

Okay, she'd tried to kiss him and she shouldn't have. But he didn't have to be mean about it. In fact, the more she thought about it, the more she realized how sick and tired she was of hearing him say he wouldn't have sex with her. It had been funny, for a while—but tonight, well, it was downright hurtful.

She zipped around the island counter that separated the living area from the kitchen and marched right for him. "Oh, please. Will you give that up? I couldn't sleep, that's all." She halted a few feet from him and glared at his broad back. "Nobody here is thinking about sex."

"Speak for yourself." Slowly, he turned and faced her. She gasped at the yearning she saw in his eyes.

Chapter Ten

Collin couldn't take it anymore.

The sight of her, in those little purple velour shorts and that skimpy, lacy top…well, it was too much. Even if she did have on an old plaid shirt over the top. That old shirt wasn't hiding anything. She hadn't even bothered to button it up.

He could see her nipples very clearly, poking at him through the thin fabric, could make out the tempting, ripe curves of her breasts. She was driving him crazy, that was what she was doing. He'd held out for years, done the right thing by her, even though she'd ended up hating him for it.

But tonight, well, it was too much.

And hadn't he known that it would be? She shouldn't have kept after him until he brought her up here with him. She shouldn't have tried to kiss him. Shouldn't have come out of her room dressed in those soft purple shorts and that skimpy silky top that didn't hide a damn thing.

He burned. He was on fire—to take her breasts in his two hands. To touch the skin of her thighs, to rub his rough palms along all that smooth softness, to inch his fingers upward, under the hem of those shorts, to touch her at last where he knew she would be hot and wet and waiting for him.

He wanted her, wanted sweet Willa Christensen, probably always had, from way back. From before he even realized what he was wanting. Oh, yeah. He wanted her.

And to hell with what was best for her. She wanted him, too. She'd made that more than clear on more than one occasion.

Tonight, he was going to give her exactly what she wanted.

Reaching out, he took her by the arms and hauled her up close to him, reveling in the feel of her body brushing along the front him, making him ache all the harder for her.

He brought his face good and close to hers, so close he could taste the heat of her breath. "You should have stayed in town tonight like I told you to, you know that, don't you?"

She licked her lips and gulped. "Um. I…" Her eyes were so wide. Wide and soft and wanting.

Those eyes of hers called to him. They always had. Those eyes said she knew him, was waiting for him to finally reach out and take her. Those eyes said she would do anything he wanted.

Truth to tell, those eyes had always scared the crap out of him. They seemed to hint of things a guy like him didn't deserve to know.

Things like forever. Things like a lifetime.

Things he wasn't planning for. He lived his life alone.

Which led back around to the basic issue: he shouldn't be doing this.

But too bad. He *was* doing this.

He was through making jokes about it, through trying to discourage her from wanting a little hot fun with the town troublemaker. If she wanted him so much, who was he to tell her no?

"Oh, Collin..." She said it so softly. So willingly. And then her eyes changed. All at once, they weren't so open and sweet anymore. They'd gone determined. They were sparking fire. "No. Uh-uh. I should *not* have stayed down in town. I'm here with you and I'm *glad* I'm here."

Some final scrap of that protectiveness he'd always felt for her prompted him to give her one last out. He met those eyes of hers. He didn't look away. "What I'm saying is, just tell me no, Willa. Just do it. Do it now."

She let out a strangled sound. It might have been a laugh. Or a sob. "Are you kidding? Don't try and pretend that you don't get it. All I've ever wanted was the chance to tell you yes."

It was the last straw.

"Tell me yes, then. You go ahead. You say it right out loud to me."

She didn't even hesitate. "Yes, oh, yes. Please, please make love to me."

So much for her last out. She'd refused to take it. So be it.

He closed that small distance between her mouth and his. He kissed her.

For the very first time.

He touched her mouth with his and it was...everything. A forbidden dream realized.

A promise so long denied, finally kept.

She kissed him back, sighing so sweetly. She melted into him, all that pride and orneriness and softness. Everything that was Willa.

Right there. In his arms.

Her breasts flattened against his bare chest, the way they'd only done in his dreams up till then. Through the flimsy material of that lacy top, he could feel her nipples, hot. Hard. She opened her mouth to him. He swept his hungry tongue inside and the kiss became something more than a dream. Deeper than a promise.

She moaned as he kissed her, and she ran her slim hands up over his shoulders, into his hair.

He needed...more of her. *All* of her. He had his arms good and tight around her, his aching hardness pressed into her belly. He let his hands roam freely, over the slim, smooth shape of her back, up under that cotton shirt, and then down to the cove at the base of her spine.

Her hair was loose. It brushed his forearms and the backs of his hands. Like feathers. Like a cloud of silk. He speared his fingers up into it, fisted them, pulling her head back so he could scrape his teeth along the slim, pure curve of her white throat.

She cried his name. He covered her mouth again and drank the sound.

He needed...more. More of her.

He had to have the feel of her bare skin under his hands. The plaid shirt was in the way. He fisted it by the sides and peeled it back over her slim shoulders. She moaned a little, as though in protest at having to let go of him, but she let him guide her arms down so he could push the shirt off. He whipped it away and tossed it in the general direction of a chair.

Then he clasped her bare shoulders. So smooth and tender, her skin. White, but with a pink flush on it. Beautiful.

He cupped her shoulders, pressed his palms against her upper chest—and lower, until he had her sweet breasts in his two hands with only the thin fabric of that clingy silky thing to protect her from his hungry touch.

She lifted up to him, sighing, offering him whatever he wanted from her.

And he knew what he wanted. To taste her.

He kissed his way down her slim throat again, scattered more kisses along the ridge of her collarbone, down the sweet-smelling skin of her upper chest and lower, over the tender swell of her breast.

He reached the goal at last and latched onto her nipple, sucking it through the silky fabric, flicking it with his tongue.

She clutched at him, holding him to her, whispering, "Yes. Oh, Collin, yes…"

He couldn't have agreed with her more. She smelled like flowers and lemons and a little bit musky, too. All woman, his Willa.

His? Well, fine, maybe not. Not forever. But at least for tonight.

The lacy thing—what did women call those things?— a cami. Yeah. The cami had to go. He grabbed the hem of it…and then got lost in the feel of her skin again. He eased his fingers up under it, stroking the tender flesh of her back, and then bringing both hands around to the front of her, caressing her flat, smooth belly.

She was breathing so frantically. He lifted his head and kissed her again. She moaned into his mouth.

And he moved his hands higher. He cupped her bare breasts under the cami. They were so perfect, so firm and round—not too big, not small, either. They fit just right in his hands.

He thought about seeing her naked.

He wanted to do that. Right away.

Now.

She made no objections, only moaned eagerly and whispered "yes," and "yes" again, as he pulled off the cami and took down the little shorts.

There.

At last.

He had everything off her. She was silk and fire and magic, all he'd ever wanted. Right there in his arms.

He bent enough to wrap his hands around the twin globes of her bottom. She moaned again and he went on kissing her as he lifted her up, dragging all that softness against him. He moaned, too.

It felt so good. *She* felt so good.

She wrapped those soft, smooth thighs around him and hooked her ankles behind his back.

Now he could feel her, feel the womanly heart of her, right there, pressed tight to his fly. He was so hard it hurt. Hurt in the best, most extreme, most perfect kind of way.

And then, still kissing her, her hair a froth of silk and shadows sliding across his skin, her mouth to his mouth, his breath to hers, he started walking.

Well, reeling was more like it.

He reeled across the great room and down the hall to his room at the end. She held on. She went on kissing him. She wrapped those soft, long arms and slim, strong legs around him like she would never, ever let him go.

In the doorway, he paused. Or more like staggered. He braced his back against the door frame and indulged in just kissing her. She didn't seem to mind that he'd stopped moving toward the bed. She just went on kissing him, went on rocking her hips against him, went on making him want to get out of his jeans and into her softness, pronto.

But then again...

No.

He didn't want to rush it. How many times in his life did

a man hold a dream in his arms? Once, if he was lucky. A man would be a fool to rush something like that.

Yeah, okay, he had a whole boatload of faults. And maybe he was a fool in some ways. But not when it came to holding Willa in his arms. He was taking his time about this.

He was making it last if it killed him.

And he was kind of afraid it just might.

She framed his face in her two slim hands. "Collin…"

He opened his eyes, stared into hers, which were shining so bright, even in the dim light from all the way back in the kitchen. "Willa."

She wrapped her legs tighter around him. He groaned at the perfect friction as all that willowy softness slid along the front of him. "You do have protection?"

He nodded on another groan.

"Oh, good." And she sighed and kissed him again.

Paradise. They went on kissing, there in the darkened doorway. Endlessly.

Until a terrible thought occurred to him. He broke the kiss so suddenly that his head bounced against the door frame.

She cried out, "Oh! I'll bet that hurt." And she clucked her tongue and fussed over him, rubbing the bumped spot in a gentle, soothing way. "Be careful…."

Gruffly, he reassured her. "I'll live—Willa, look at me."

She blinked at him owlishly, adorably. In the faint glow of light from up the hallway, her dark hair was a wild tangle all around her sweet, flushed face. A dream. No doubt. This had to be a dream. "What?" she demanded. "What's the matter now?"

"I need you to tell me. Is this your first time?" He did not have sex with virgins.

She pressed those amazing lips together, nervous. Unsure. And then she buried her face against his neck. "No." She said it softly.

"Good." Relief was coursing through him. That fat-headed idiot from high school, Derek Andrews, no doubt. And probably Mr. Wonderful, who wanted to marry her.

Mr. Wonderful, who was another reason Collin shouldn't be seducing Willa. She deserved a bright future with the right kind of guy.

But somehow, at that moment, he wasn't feeling all that guilty about Mr. Wonderful. What guy in his right mind proposed marriage and then went to Australia? Mr. Wonderful deserved a little competition for leaving her on her own at the mercy of a guy like him.

She pressed her plump lips to the side of his throat and he felt her tongue slide along his skin. He groaned and wrapped his arms tighter around her and was very, very glad that she wasn't a virgin.

He supposed he should have known she wasn't. She didn't act like a virgin. She acted like a woman who knew what she wanted.

"Willa," he whispered, and then again, "Willa…" He'd always loved the feel of her name in his mouth.

"I'm right here." She lifted her head from his shoulder and nuzzled his ear as he kissed his way across her cheek to take her mouth once more.

Then he gathered her tighter, closer, and launched them from the doorway, making it to the bed in four long strides. He laid her gently down and turned on the lamp, and then he just stood there above her, looking down at her, so slim and pretty, naked to his sight.

At last.

"So beautiful…" The words came out of him on a bare husk of sound.

She met his eyes—or at least she did at first. But then

she grew shy. She did that thing that women do—an arm across her pink-tipped breasts, a hand to cover the shining brown curls in the cove of her silky thighs.

"Don't…" His voice sounded desperate, ragged to his own ears.

And she reached out. She put a hand against his belly, palm flat. A groan escaped him when she did that. Her touch felt so good, so exactly right. Like the scent of her that seemed to call to him, to beckon him to her.

She said, gently, politely, "Take off your jeans, please."

He couldn't do what she wanted fast enough. Two of the buttons were undone anyway. He undid the rest and shucked them off and away.

"Oh, Collin, you're so…you're beautiful, you are."

"Men aren't beautiful," he argued gruffly.

"Oh, yes. They are." She held out her arms to him. "I'm so happy. After all this time, I never thought…never imagined…" She seemed to run out of words. It was all right. He understood, he knew exactly what she meant. "Come down here. With me…."

He pulled open the bedside drawer and got a condom from the box in there. And then he went down to her. He stretched out beside her, covered her mouth with his and let his hands wander.

Her body moved beneath his touch, so tempting, so soft. He kissed her as he stroked her hair, her throat, the smooth roundness of her shoulder.

So much to explore, all of her. Beautiful and willing and pliant and tender. The slim curve of her waist called to him. He stroked his hand from her rib cage to the swell of her hip and lower, down the long sweep of her thigh.

He palmed her knee and gently guided it open. Then he did what he'd dreamed of doing, sliding his palm up the inside of her thigh as she rolled her hips and tossed her head and moaned his name in hungry encouragement.

The dark curls were already wet with her excitement. He parted them. She cried his name out good and loud then.

He kissed her slow and deep. He whispered against her lips, "Like this, Willa?"

She gasped. "Yes, oh! Yes…"

He slipped a finger in. Two. Wet silk inside, warm and slick, welcoming him. Her hips moved rhythmically now, her thighs open, offering him everything. So much. All she had to give.

"Collin…" She said his name against his mouth. And then she gave him her tongue to suck. He kissed her endlessly as he stroked her.

And by then, touching her in that most intimate place wasn't enough. He had to taste her there.

He kissed his way down the center of her. She clutched his shoulders, murmured his name over and over, like she couldn't get enough of saying it. He just kept kissing her, all of her, as he lifted up and slid over and settled between her open thighs. She shifted, adjusting herself with a long, slow sigh, bracing her heels on his shoulders.

The scent of her was so sweet, lemons and musk. And the taste? Exactly as he'd dreamed it. Only better. Endlessly better…

He used his fingers and his mouth and she moved against him, sighing, her hands in his hair, her head tossing on the pillow. She was rising, reaching for the peak, and he stayed with her, all the way. Until at last she went over, crying his name as the soft explosion of her climax pulsed against his tongue.

The condom had been lost somewhere in the tangle of bedclothes. He felt around for it—and got lucky. His fingers closed around it as she sighed once more and went all loose and lazy.

He didn't stop kissing her. She tasted so good.

She moaned his name. And finally, she pleaded, "Oh, please. Oh, my. I can't…it's too much…"

With a low chuckle, he relented, backing off a little, resting his head on her thigh. She stroked his hair, traced the shape of his ear. He was aching to continue. He'd been hard and getting harder forever, it felt like right then.

But at the same time, he was satisfied just to lie with her that way, naked. Together. Unashamed.

A few minutes later, he sat back on his knees. She followed him, sitting up, brushing her wild hair out of her eyes, laughing. "Here. Let me…"

So he gave her the pouch. She tore the end off with her teeth. Hottest thing he ever saw. A guy didn't need those girlie magazines she'd teased him about having in his mancave. Not with Willa Christensen naked in his bed.

She peeled away the wrapper and set it neatly on the bedside table. Then she bent close to him. She rolled it down over him.

He shut his eyes and tipped his head back and tried not to lose it just from the feel of her sliding it down over him.

"Collin?"

He let a low groan be his answer.

And then the bed shifted as she rose up on her knees and bent close to him, all tart and sweet and womanly. Her hair brushed his shoulder and her mouth touched his, lightly, teasing him.

It was too much. He rose up and took her shoulders and rolled her under him.

She let out a little cry and a soft laugh. And then he was on top of her, his elbows braced on either side of her, framing her sweet face in his hands, her hair all around them. He stared down at her and she looked up at him.

"Willa…"

"Collin."

"Willa, I…" There were no words. And it didn't matter. He was right where he'd never dared dream he would be.

"I'm so glad," she whispered.

He had her arms trapped at her sides. But she could move her legs.

And she did, lifting them, hooking them around the backs of his thighs. He was positioned just right, nudging her where she was so soft and wet and open.

She felt like heaven. Like some lost paradise, found at last, after he'd given up believing he would ever get there.

He entered her slowly, by aching degrees. And he held her gaze the whole time. He needed the sight of her face as he claimed her, so beautifully flushed. Lips softly parted.

Completely willing, with nothing held back from him.

She moaned as he went deeper. He made an answering sound and kept pressing, filling her.

Finally, he couldn't go slowly anymore. With a forceful thrust, he was all the way in.

She gasped. Her eyes widened. Her sweet lips invited.

He lowered his mouth to her and kissed her as he began to move.

After that, time folded in on itself. He lost control and rocked wildly against her. She held him closer, tighter than before.

She made soft, willing sounds that only drove him higher. Deeper. Harder.

His mind was gone, shattered. There was only her body and his body inside her, the feel of her soft, willing mouth pressed to his.

He hit the peak and sailed over, knowing a faint echo

of regret that he couldn't hold out for her—and then, all at once, learning he hadn't left her behind, after all. Her body pulsed around him, drawing him deeper. Pushing him higher.

Hurling him outward through a midnight-blue universe of fast-spinning stars.

Chapter Eleven

Faintly, far away, Willa heard music playing. It was that Joe Nichols song, "Tequila Makes Her Clothes Fall Off."

She smiled. She'd always thought that song was kind of cute.

The song stopped. And the bed shifted. She remembered.

It was Collin's bed....

"My cell," said a groggy, very masculine voice not far from her ear. He nuzzled her hair. "I left it charging in the kitchen...."

"Um." She cuddled closer to his big, hard, naked body. He wrapped a muscular arm around her and drew her closer, tucking her into him, spoon style, settling the covers more snugly around them.

She smiled some more and opened her eyes to morning light.

Amazing. It really had happened with Collin. Just like

in all her forbidden fantasies. It had been incredible and it had lasted all night long.

He smoothed her hair away from her neck and kissed her there. "You smell good...." Down the hallway, the phone beeped.

"Voice mail," she said on a lazy yawn.

His lips brushed her neck again. "It's after eight. I'd better go see if it's anything important."

She grabbed the arm he had wrapped around her and pretended to sulk. "Oh, no..."

But he only kissed her hair and pushed back the covers, pausing to tuck them around her again. "I'll be right back."

She rolled over and watched him get up. He looked so good without his clothes on. He had a cute little happy trail and a real, true six-pack.

And a beautiful tattoo on the hard bulge of his right shoulder, one of those tribal designs. She'd spent a while the night before studying it, tracing its curves and angles with her fingers. It looked a little like a mask, with horns and a pair of eyes that also seemed to resemble sharks, somehow. She'd asked him what it was supposed to represent and in typical Collin fashion, he'd answered, "Whatever you want it to represent."

He put on his jeans and buttoned them partway, which somehow only made him look manlier and more naked. "Keep the bed warm."

"Will do. Let the dog out?" Buster, who'd ended up on the rug by the bed, was already up and wagging his tail.

He nodded. "C'mon, Buster."

She watched him go, Buster close behind. The view of him walking away was every bit as inspiring as the one from the front.

She heard the outside door open and shut as he let Buster out. And then he came back.

He held out the phone to her. "Your brother."

She sat up, pulling the sheet with her to cover her breasts, and took the phone from him. "Um. Thanks." She hit the icon for voice mail.

Gage's voice said, "Collin, this is Gage. I'm in town. And looking for my sister. Could you have her call me?" He didn't sound especially cordial.

Collin was watching her. "Good old Gage. Finally made it into town and he's wondering where the hell his baby sister's gotten off to."

Willa hitched up her chin and put on a smile. "Oh, I doubt he's wondering. I'm sure someone in town has already told him exactly where I am."

His dark gaze ran over her. She thought of the night before and a hot shiver went through her. "Not feelin' quite so *unimpeachable* now, are you, Willa?"

She pursed up her mouth at him and narrowed her eyes. "Don't start. I do not regret a thing. Last night was beautiful. I mean that. Do you understand?"

He gave her a slow, insolent once-over. "Yes, ma'am."

She puffed out her cheeks with a frustrated breath. And then she whispered, "Come here. Please?"

His fine mouth curled. "You should call your brother back."

She reached out her hand.

He looked at it for a count of five. Her heart sank. She was certain he would turn and walk away.

But then he reached out, too. Their hands met, fingers lacing together. Relief, sweet and good as a long drink of cool water, washed through her.

He dropped down onto the bed at her side. "I feel bad, okay? I don't want to cause you problems with your family."

She dropped the phone onto the sheet and wrapped

her other hand around their joined ones. "You're not. You couldn't."

He leaned closer. She tipped her mouth up to him and their lips met. "Call him," he said against her lips. "I'll let Buster back inside and put the coffee on." He lifted their hands and kissed the back of hers.

Reluctantly, she let him go, picked up the phone again and called her brother back. He answered on the first ring.

"Gage, it's me."

"Willa. Where are you?"

She could tell by his tone that he already knew. "I'm up at Collin's. We drove up yesterday. The road's a mess. I helped him clear the way."

A silence on Gage's end, then, "I don't get it. You never even liked Collin Traub, and all of a sudden, you two are— what? What's going on, Willa? What about you and Dane?"

Dane. Oh, Lord. She'd really messed up with Dane. She never should have let him talk her into taking time to think things over. She'd put off the inevitable and now she felt like a two-timer.

"Willa, are you still there?"

"Yes. Right here." And no way was she getting into all this on the phone. "Listen. I'll call you as soon as we get back down into town. We can talk then—or, whenever you can get a minute."

"*When* will you be back in town?"

"I don't know for sure yet. Collin may have things he has to do up here. And we cleared the road as best we could, but there are some rough spots and some places where the cliff side collapsed. It could take a while to get down."

"Buster okay?"

"He's fine. Yes."

"And you?" He sounded worried. "You...okay?"

Love washed through her. Her brother was such a great guy. "I am just fine. I promise you. And I'm glad you're here. So glad." Rust Creek Falls really needed him now. But she didn't say that. She knew him, knew he had to be beating himself up that he hadn't been there when the levee broke. Telling him how much he was needed would only make him feel worse about everything.

"Call me," he said. "As soon as you're back in town."

When she entered the kitchen, Buster was in the corner, his nose buried in Libby's old food bowl. The coffee was brewing. And Collin stood at the stove, laying strips of bacon in a pan.

She leaned a hip against the counter and stuck her hands in the pockets of the flannel robe she'd found on the back of his bathroom door. "I hope you don't mind. I stole your robe." Her purple shorts, cami and plaid shirt were strewn around the living room.

He glanced over. "Looks better on you than on me anyway."

She wanted to go to him, brush his hair back off his forehead, tell him…

What?

She wasn't quite sure. "That bacon smells so good."

He tipped his head toward the open shelves with the dishes on them. "Put the plates on the table?"

She nodded and then got busy setting the table. He cooked the bacon and scrambled some eggs. She made the toast and poured the coffee.

They sat down to eat, the silence between them both sharp-edged and a little too deep.

She made herself break it. "Gage is fine. I said I would call him when we got back down into town."

"You need to get going right away, then?"

She sipped her coffee. "No. There's no hurry."

"You sure about that, Willa?"

The question seemed to hang heavy in the air between them.

Willa pushed back her chair. He watched her, dark eyes wary, as she went around the table to his side and did what she'd wanted to do since she entered the kitchen. She smoothed his hair back off his forehead. "I'm sure. No hurry."

He caught her hand. But he didn't push it away. Instead, he brought her fingers to his lips and kissed the tips of them. "Your food will get cold...."

"Um. Can't have that." She bent and he tipped his head up. They shared a quick kiss and she returned to her chair.

After that, the silence didn't seem so oppressive. But the romantic and sensual mood of the night before, of that morning before the phone rang, was definitely absent.

She wanted to talk—about everything. About how she was never going to marry Dane Everhart and she'd been wrong not to simply say no when Dane proposed, about how her brother would be fine with her and Collin being together, once she had a chance to talk with him. About how beautiful last night had been and how she was looking forward to more nights just like it.

But somehow, she didn't know where to begin. And that had her looking back wistfully at their recent nights on the front steps of the town hall, when talking with Collin had been as simple and easy as breathing.

And now, here they were. Lovers, at last. And it was suddenly neither easy nor simple. She had so much to say—and yet she feared she might mess things up if she started talking. She might end up blurting out something that would turn him off.

Was it true then, what they said about sex ruining a perfectly good friendship? She did hope not.

Collin knew he had to get her back to town as soon as possible. Her brother's call had been like a bucket of icy water in the face. It had snapped him back to reality hard and fast.

He shouldn't have taken her to bed. He knew that. Really, where was it going to go with them?

Nowhere. Things were crazy now, after the flood. Their whole world had been turned pretty much upside down. He knew that was all it was with the two of them: one of those things that happen when a man and a woman were thrown together by necessity in a crisis, with emotions running high.

It could never be anything permanent. She was a nice girl with a certain kind of life ahead of her. And his life suited him fine as it was. He liked his independence, always had. And she was going to marry a big shot from Colorado. She would remember that soon enough.

Probably already had. She'd been pretty damn quiet ever since she'd talked to Gage. Collin figured that just the sound of her brother's voice had gotten her to thinking twice. She'd realized it was a bad idea, what they'd done last night, that it never should have happened and it needed to stop now.

They loaded the contents of his freezer into coolers, strapped them into the pickup bed, and left for town.

The trip down went smoothly, all things considered. Collin knew the places to be extra careful—and they'd cleared away the worst of the storm debris on the way up.

He handed her his cell when they reached the base of the mountain. "Call Gage."

She made the call.

It was, "Hi, it's me...Yes...All right, I will...A few minutes...Okay." She handed him back his phone and asked him to let her off at the sheriff's office.

He pulled up to the curb.

She hooked Buster's leash to his collar and turned a dewy smile his way. "I...well, I can't tell you to call me, since I don't have a phone." She really did sound like she *wanted* him to call her.

But that had to be wishful thinking on his part. His chest was tight and his throat felt like it had a log stuck in it. "I'll see you." It came out way too gruff and low.

She searched his face. Whatever she was looking for, he didn't think she found it. He reminded himself how that was for the best. "Um. Okay, then. Have a good one."

"Yeah. Say hi to Gage."

"Will do." Another blinding, too-wide smile. And then she shouldered her pack, grabbed her big plastic bag of stuff and got out. Buster jumped down after her.

He didn't allow himself to watch her walk away. As soon as she shut the door, he put it in gear and got the hell out of there.

Gage was waiting for Willa in his office. He was on a cell phone arguing with someone about roadblocks or something, but he cut it short when he looked up and saw her in the doorway.

"Willa." He gave her a tired smile and ended the call. Then he got up and came around the desk to her. She ran to him and he hugged her close. He said in a voice rough with emotion, "I'm so glad you're all right." She let her bag and pack drop to the floor and hugged him back, hard. He'd always made her feel safe and protected. And right then, after the way Collin had seemed so eager to get rid of her, well, it felt good to have her big brother's arms around her.

When he let her go, she asked, "Have you been out to the ranch?"

His mouth formed a grim line. "Yeah. What a mess. I'll be staying down the street, in a FEMA trailer for a while."

"Why not stay at Mom and Dad's?"

"It's better if I'm right here in town, where I need to be." There was a tap on the door. He went over and opened it and said to the dispatcher, "I need a few minutes here. Won't be long." Then he shut the door again and turned to her. "Buster?"

"He's good. I tied him out in front."

He came back to her, clasped her shoulder and glanced down at the pile of belongings she'd dropped at her feet. "I heard you've been staying over at the town hall on a cot—until last night anyway."

She nodded, her gaze on his handsome face. He looked so weary, the faint lines around his eyes etched deeper than before. "It worked out."

He took charge, the way he always did. "So, then. You need a car, a phone and a place to stay."

She *had* a place to stay—with Collin. Or at least, she'd thought she did until a couple of hours ago. "A car and a phone would really help." She was going to have a long talk with Collin that evening, whether he liked it or not. And then, if that didn't go well, she'd find somewhere else to stay. "I need to get hold of the insurance people—for the house and for the Subaru."

"Have a seat." Gage gestured at one of the guest chairs and then went back to sit behind his desk, where he pulled open a drawer and took out another cell phone, a charger and the key to his pickup. "I've got cells I can use and the county provides me with a vehicle. For now, you take my cell and the pickup."

"Oh, Gage. I can't take your truck."

"Oh, yes, you can. And you will." He shoved it all across at her. "I programmed the number of the cell I'll be using into this phone. So you know where to reach me whenever you need me. Get a hold of your insurance agent. And call Mom. She's been asking about you."

"I will. Thanks."

"And with the truck, you can get around. Got money?"

She admitted, "I lost my wallet in the Forester."

He passed her some cash and a credit card. "You should get over to Kalispell and replace your license. And you need to call about your credit cards...."

She granted him a patient glance. "Yes, big brother."

He went right on. "There's gas available, too. The garage just got its tanks refilled. With the truck, you'll be able to stay at the ranch."

She wasn't committing to that. At least not until she'd had it out with Collin. "I'll be okay. Please don't worry."

He was looking way too bleak. She knew what was coming next. And she was right. "So...you spent the night at Collin Traub's." He practically winced when he said Collin's name.

She sat up straighter. "Yes, I did—and you can just stop giving me that pained look. Collin's not what I always thought, Gage. I'm ashamed of how completely I misjudged him. He's a great guy."

He had a one-word response to that. "Dane?"

"Dane is not the issue here."

"Willa." He used her name as a rebuke. "The man asked you to marry him. I thought you were considering it."

"I blew it, all right? I never should have told Dane I would think it over when he proposed. There's nothing to think over. Dane is not the man for me."

"You say that now...."

"Yes. And I should have said it from the first. As soon

as Dane's back in the country, I will apologize to him for keeping him hanging."

"Dane's a good man. Are you sure you want to just cut him loose?"

"I am absolutely certain."

"Well, even if that's so, it doesn't make the Traub wild man right for you. Willa, come on. You know about Collin Traub. He's not a man to hang your hopes on. The guy never met a heart he didn't break. And he's spent more than one night cooling his heels in the jail cell out there for being drunk and disorderly and picking a fight."

She refused to waver. "People mature. They change. Collin grew up without a lot of supervision. Yes, he went a little wild."

"A *little?*"

"He's just not like that anymore. I…I care for him and I respect him." Gage started to speak, but she didn't let him get a word in. "Listen. I know you only want to protect me and I love you for it. But I don't want or need protecting. I'm an adult and I know what I'm doing." *I hope.*

"Well, I don't like it."

"Gage…"

He surprised her and admitted, "All right. I know that he's made a go of his uncle's saddle-making business. I give him credit for that." Willa started to relax a little. At least Gage realized that Collin had created a productive life for himself. But then he went on, "However, when it comes to women, Collin Traub is bad news. I want you to stay away from him. Can you just do that, just stay away from him for my sake? Please."

"I'm sorry. No. You're the best brother any girl could have. But being the best doesn't give you the right to tell me how to run my life."

He started to rise. "Now, you listen here—"

"Sit down, Gage," she instructed in her best school-teacher tone. Surprisingly, he sank back to his chair. And she pressed her advantage. "I'm a grown woman. And I am fully capable of making my own decisions about my life—and the men in it. I want you to give Collin a chance."

"A chance to what?" he demanded. "To hurt you and mess you over?"

"No. A chance to make you see that there's more to him than your old ideas about him. All you have to do is ask around town and you'll learn a thing or two about everything he's done for Rust Creek Falls since the flood. He saved my life, Gage. He's been at the front line of the rescue efforts and the cleanup. He's a natural leader and he's right there when he's needed—and no, I can't say if what's happening with Collin and me is going to last forever. But I do know that, however it ends up with us, I will never regret being with him."

Gage gave her a long, dark look. And then he grabbed a pencil, pulled open his pencil drawer and tossed it in. He shut the drawer good and hard. "I'm not happy about this."

"That's your prerogative."

"But what can I say?"

She gazed at him coaxingly. "That you'll give Collin a chance."

He blew out a breath. "Fine. I'll stay out of it. For now. I'll just knock myself out being open-minded about Collin Traub."

She beamed him her fondest smile. "Thank you."

"But if that wild man breaks your heart, you can be damn sure I'll be first in line to break *his* face."

Willa spent the day taking care of personal business.

She used the cell Gage had loaned her to call her insurance agent and the FEMA flood insurance number.

The clerks she talked to took her number and promised she'd get calls back from adjusters within twenty-four hours—for the car and for the house and for her separate government-run flood insurance policy. Next, she made calls about her credit cards. That took a while, since she no longer had the cards, she was calling from someone else's phone and her records had been turned to mush in the flood. But in the end, she gave the ranch as a temporary address and was promised that new cards would arrive there within the week. After that, she decided to go ahead and drive to Kalispell to visit her bank and her cell phone provider, and to get a new driver's license.

As soon as she got her new phone in her hand, she called everyone back and told them she had her own phone now. Then she called her mom in Livingston.

"You got your phone back," her mother said when she answered. "Oh, honey. We miss you...."

"I miss you, too, Mom."

"I talked to Gage just today..."

"Yeah. He finally made it back. He loaned me his truck."

"Good. There are still a lot of problems with the roads, so we thought we'd just stay here in Livingston a little longer."

"That sounds wise, Mom."

"Gage says they're giving him a trailer so he can stay in town."

"Yes. You know him. He needs to be where the action is."

"Honey, I've been meaning to ask. You *are* staying at the ranch, aren't you?"

"Uh, no."

"But why not?"

Willa didn't want to go into her relationship with Collin. Not now. Not on the phone—and not after last night and the awkwardness of that morning. It was all too new and exciting and scary. Not to mention, up in the air. And evidently, Gage had stayed out of it and said nothing to their parents about where she'd slept last night.

Thank you, big brother.

"Willa? Are you there?"

"Right here. And I've been staying in the town hall." It was true. She had been. Until last night. "They have cots set up for people whose homes were flooded."

"But surely you should be out at the ranch. Even with the power out, it seems to me that you would be so much more comfortable there than sleeping on a hard, narrow cot in a public building...."

"Mom. I'm managing. It's working out fine."

"Just think about it, won't you? Consider it."

"I'll manage, Mom."

Her mother muttered something under her breath. "Always so independent."

"I love you, Mom. Give my love to Daddy. I have to go...."

"And we love you. You're eating right, aren't you? Taking care of yourself...?"

"I'm perfectly healthy and I'm getting plenty to eat. And I do have to go."

With a sigh, her mother said goodbye.

Willa and Buster got back to Rust Creek Falls at a little past three in the afternoon. She stopped in at Gage's office and returned his cell phone. Then she visited the town hall and the Community Church in hopes that Collin might be at one or the other.

He wasn't. She tried not to feel too disappointed. The

man could be back up on the mountain working in his shop, or out on flood cleanup—or just about anywhere.

She considered calling him, but decided to wait. Tonight, one way or another, she would track him down.

Summer school was out by then, so she went to Paige's house. Shelby was there with her little girl, Caitlin, who would be in Willa's class next year. Willa got a full report on the day's activities at the park. Shelby said the day had gone well and volunteered to fill in again for Willa whenever she needed a hand.

Willa thanked her. She really liked Shelby, who was a wonderful mother and a talented teacher. Shelby wasn't having an easy time of it raising her little girl alone. A blonde, blue-eyed beauty who had once been the most popular girl at Rust Creek Falls High, now Shelby made ends meet tending bar at the Ace in the Hole. Willa had been encouraging her to apply for a full-time teaching position with the district.

When Shelby and Caitlin left, Willa stayed to brainstorm with Paige on new projects for their summer school kids—projects that would lend themselves to an outdoor classroom setting.

At five-thirty, Willa put Buster on his leash and Paige walked with them to the church for dinner. The gas had never stopped working on the north side of town, but the power was still out. Paige had no generator, which meant she couldn't keep food refrigerated. The church, with the help of donations from a number of sources, would continue to provide meals for the community as long as people needed them. Refrigerated trucks brought in food daily.

Halfway there, Paige asked gingerly, "Are things okay with you and Collin?"

Willa sent her a sideways glance. "Ask me in a day or two."

"I'm here and ready to listen anytime you need me."

Willa hooked an arm around her friend's slim shoulders. "I know. It's just another reason why I'm so glad you're my friend."

At the church, Willa spotted Jerry Dobbs sitting at a table with three other members of Collin's cleanup team. Collin wasn't with them.

Willa told Paige she'd join her in a moment. She got a bowl of dog food from one of the church ladies and took it outside to Buster. As the dog wolfed down his dinner, she gave Collin a call.

He didn't answer.

She left a message. "Hey. It's Willa. Note this number. It's mine. I went to Kalispell and replaced my cell phone today, along with my driver's license. I also dealt with replacing my credit cards, insurance adjusters and with my bank…" And really, did he need a blow-by-blow? She realized she was nervous because he hadn't picked up when she called. She tried again. "Right now, I'm down at the church for dinner. No sign of you. Give me a call…." She couldn't think of anything else to say, so she left it at that.

Back inside, she went through the serving line and sat down with Paige. Throughout the meal, she kept waiting for the phone to ring.

Didn't happen.

She couldn't help but feel a little bit dumped. Which was ridiculous, and she knew it. How could she be dumped? To be dumped implied that you'd shared some sort of at least semi-committed relationship with a guy. She and Collin? They were friends who'd slept together. One time.

So then, did that make her just another of Collin Traub's one-night stands?

Oh, dear Lord. She did hope not. Collin couldn't be that disappointing and hurtful. Could he?

She wished she could stop remembering her argument with Gage that morning.

Was Collin going to go and prove her big brother right? *No.*

She needed to stop this. She was not going to think like this. If she kept on in this vein, she'd be right back where she started before the flood: racing out of rooms just because Collin Traub entered them.

That morning, she'd argued fervently with Gage on Collin's behalf. She'd said how Collin had grown and changed from the no-strings wild boy he used to be. And she had absolutely believed what she'd said.

Collin *had* changed. And if he could do it, so could she.

The friendship they'd found since the flood meant a lot to her. And last night had been beautiful—no matter what happened next. One way or another, she was working this out with him. If he didn't want to be with her in a man-woman way, well, that would hurt.

A lot.

But she would get over it.

Right now, what she needed to do was talk this out with him. And to do that, she had to *find* him.

Jerry Dobbs had finished his meal. He was busy putting his tray away, tossing his trash and separating his dishes from his flatware.

Willa told Paige she'd see her tomorrow, picked up her tray and went to ask Jerry if he might know where Collin had gone.

Collin tried to concentrate on the intricate pattern of leaves and vines, on the good, clean smell of veg tan top-grain leather, on the slow, exacting process of stamping the custom design with his stylus and mallet.

But his mind was not cooperating. His mind was on a

certain brown-eyed woman. On the scent of lemons, on the way it had felt to have her tucked up against him naked all night long.

She had called over an hour ago. He hadn't answered and he hadn't called her back, though he *had* played her message. Three times. So far.

Yeah, he was being a real jerk and he knew it.

Still, he kept thinking it was better this way. Let her be completely disappointed in him, start avoiding him again.

Better for everyone.

Being her friend was one thing. But taking it further...

Bad idea. He'd blown it and he knew it. He shouldn't have given in to that thing he'd always had for her. He'd seriously stepped over the line and he wasn't going to let it happen again.

The sound from upstairs stopped his thoughts in midramble and his mallet in midair.

Someone was knocking on his front door.

He dropped the mallet and stylus and headed for the stairs as fast as his boots would carry him.

"Why do I get the feeling you're avoiding me?" she asked when he pulled open the door. She stood there in old jeans and a frayed T-shirt, her hair loose on her shoulders, Buster at her feet. He'd never in his life seen a sight quite so beautiful. She tapped her booted foot. "Do I get to come in or not?"

Chapter Twelve

Collin glanced past her shoulder, saw her brother's pickup parked next to his. Of course, Gage would have seen to it that she had transportation.

He accused, "The road up here is still dangerous."

"You'll be happy to know that Buster and I made it just fine." She stuck out her chin at him. "Ahem. May I come in?"

It was a bad idea. And he was way too crazy happy to see her.

"Collin. *Hello?*"

He stepped back automatically. She moved forward, the dog right behind her. He edged around her, shut the door and turned to her. "What?"

She squared her shoulders, kind of bracing herself. "Look. If you regret last night, that's fine. I can deal with that. I would rather you *didn't* regret it. I would rather be, um…" She paused, swallowed. He watched the warm color flood upward over her sweet, soft cheeks. "I would rather be your lover. But if you don't want that, well, okay. If you think it was a big mistake, what we did last night, okay. I won't like it and it...hurts me. But I *will* get over it. Because what I really want, most of all, Collin Traub, is to still be your friend."

He drank in the sight of her. It occurred to him that he would never get tired of seeing her pretty, clean-scrubbed, earnest face. "My friend." It came out low and kind of threatening, though he didn't really mean it that way. "You want to be my friend."

She hitched her chin higher. "Yes. I do. I want to *remain* your friend, above all."

"What about that guy you're going to marry?"

"Collin. I'm not marrying Dane. And I will tell him that as soon as I get a chance to talk to him."

He wasn't sure he believed her. "Why keep the guy hanging if you're only going to say no?"

"I'm not keeping him hanging. He asked me to think it over. I said I would. I *have* thought it over and I'm not going to marry him."

Collin still wasn't really buying it, still had that feeling that this thing between them was only temporary, something born out of the chaos caused by the flood. Not the kind of thing that lasted.

Which should have been fine with him. He'd never been a guy who worried about whether or not what he had with a woman was going to last.

Because for him, it never did.

Three steps separated them. He took the first one. Couldn't help himself. Looking at her was like drowning in a whirlpool, the spinning current dizzying, sucking him down.

And then, when he was only two steps away, well, he had to get even closer. He took the second step.

And the scent of her came to him: sweet and tart and way too womanly.

That did it.

To hell with trying to do the right thing here. She wanted him and he wanted her and why shouldn't they both have what they wanted?

He snaked out a hand and caught her wrist.

She gasped. "Collin! What...?"

He pulled her to him, wrapped an arm around her. How could she be so perfect, so slim and soft and way too exciting, bringing the scent of lemons and Ivory soap to drive him wild? She stared up at him, her eyes so wide. Heat flared in his groin. "Right now, Willa, I'm not really thinking about being your friend."

That full mouth formed a round O. "Well." Breathless. Hopeful. "It's all...workable. Don't you think?"

"Thinking," he said roughly. "Who's thinking?"

And then she lifted a hand and cradled the side of his face. "Don't be afraid...."

Another wave of heat blasted through him. He put on a scowl. "I'm not afraid."

"Right." Soft. Indulgent. Way too knowing. Her eyes had that gleam in them now.

He still couldn't really believe she was here, in his house. In his arms. "You shouldn't have come up here."

"Yes. Yes, I should have."

"Your brother warned you about me, right?"

"Gage is willing to be open-minded."

"You mean he warned you and you argued with him."

"And now he's willing to be open-minded."

"I know how you are, Willa. So damn determined."

She smiled then, dimples flashing. "I am, yes. It's one of my most sterling qualities."

He bent his head closer, nuzzled her hair, breathed her in. Nothing. No one. Ever. Not like her. "Willa…" It came out harsh, low. Hungry.

She clung to him. She felt like heaven. She closed her eyes and pressed her lips to his throat. "Yes." She kissed the word into his skin, once. And then again. "Yes."

He put a finger under that stubborn chin of hers. With a sigh, she opened her eyes. He advised, "I should send you back down the mountain right now."

"Oh, but you won't." She clucked her tongue. Softly. "It's much too dangerous, remember?"

He pulled her even closer. "*This* is what's dangerous." There were a thousand reasons they should stop right now. He tried to remember at least a few of them, but it wasn't happening. "I'm not the right guy for you."

"That's for me to decide. All you have to figure out is whether *I'm* the right girl for *you*."

"I don't—"

"Shh." She put two fingers against his mouth. It took all his will not to close his teeth around them and suck them inside. "We don't have to decide anything now," she whispered. "We can just…be together, you and me. Just enjoy every minute we have, for now. Just kind of wing it and see where it takes us."

"It's not a good idea, Willa." He formed the words against the soft pads of her fingers.

"Your mouth says one thing, but the rest of you is sending another message altogether." She pressed herself against him, snugger. Tighter.

He caught her fingers, touched his lips to them. Somehow, he couldn't help it—couldn't help holding her, touching her. Wanting her. "You're getting pretty bold lately…."

She lifted her mouth higher, offering it to him. "Must be the company I'm keeping."

That did it. He dipped his head and settled his lips on hers.

She sighed in welcome.

He wrapped his arms tighter around her and kissed her slowly. With care and attention and longing and heat.

She responded by sliding her hands up his chest to his shoulders, by sifting those soft fingers up into his hair. By sighing her willingness against his parted lips.

And by then, he'd pretty much forgotten all the reasons they shouldn't be doing this.

If she wanted to be with him, he could only put up so much resistance. After all, *he* wanted to be with her.

He burned to be with her.

And now, tonight, again, at last, he *would* be with her.

He started undressing her, right there in the entryway.

She didn't object—on the contrary, she started undressing *him*. He got rid of her T-shirt and she returned the favor. He unhooked her bra. She undid his jeans.

And then he lifted her high and carried her down the hall to his bedroom. He set her on the bed and knelt to unlace her boots. He got one off, and the sock beneath it, and he was starting on the other one when she reached out and laid her palm on his hair.

He looked up.

She gazed down at him, her eyes and her mouth so soft. So tender. "Collin...."

He kind of lost it then. He got her other boot off, ripped away the sock. And then she was clasping his shoulder, pulling him up to her.

It all happened so fast. He got the condom from the drawer as she pulled down her jeans and panties and kicked them away.

Her hands were on him again, pushing his jeans down. He still had his boots on. Neither of them cared.

He rolled the condom on and then went down to her. He tried to take it slow, to make sure she was ready.

But she tugged at him. She was so insistent, making tender sounds of need and encouragement, wrapping her arms and her long legs around him and pressing herself up to him, inviting him.

What could he do, given an invitation like that?

Accept. With enthusiasm.

And he did. He kissed her deeply as she slid her arm down between their bodies. She closed her soft fingers around him and guided him home.

After that, he was lost. Lost in the best, sweetest, hottest way.

She was all around him, all woman and softness and heat.

He surrendered. She moved against him, calling him down.

He was lost in her. As his climax rolled through him, he couldn't help hoping he might never be found.

When he could move again, he took off the rest of his clothes and pulled the covers up over them.

They made love again, more slowly that time.

And then, for a while, they just lay there, arms around each other, watching the shadows lengthen out the window across from his bed. He started talking about his Thunder Canyon relatives, about the wedding of his long-lost cousin that had taken place over the Fourth of July.

She asked, "Why didn't you go to the wedding with the rest of your family?"

He stroked her hair. "I had work that needed doing. And anyway, weddings have never been my kind of good time. They're like family reunions—there was one of those going on down in Thunder Canyon, too, over the Fourth— both are just excuses for the old folks to ask me when I'm getting married and how come I'm such a troublemaker."

She laughed. "Well, when *are* you getting married? And why are you such a troublemaker?"

"I'm not getting married. And troublemaking's fun."

She wrapped her leg across him, ran a soft finger down his arm in a slow, teasing caress and whispered, "I think you've put a big dent in your troublemaker reputation lately."

"Naw."

"Yeah. Jerry Dobbs told me you talked old Mrs. Lathrop into putting her shotgun away and relocating to a FEMA trailer today."

He traced the wings of her eyebrows, one and then the other. "You know Mrs. Lathrop. She's so, so proud. She moved back into her house, even though it's not safe in there since the flood. We had to talk her into leaving."

"Jerry said *you* talked her into leaving—and that she had her shotgun on you while you did it."

"Jerry exaggerates. And is he the one who told you I'd gone on up the mountain?"

"Mmm-hmm."

"Jerry's also got a big mouth."

"Oh, now. You like Jerry. You and Jerry get along."

He pressed his nose against her throat. He loved the texture of her skin almost as much as the way she smelled. He also cupped her breast. Because he could. Because it felt so good. Because it fit his hand just right. "Stop trying to make a hero out of me."

She laughed again, husky and low. "Oh, I'm not trying anything. You're being a hero all by yourself."

* * *

Willa had decided to take the advice she'd given Collin that Tuesday evening.

She was going to take it day by day. Enjoy being with him.

And she wasn't expecting anything. She was letting this beautiful, exciting thing between them unfold in its own way.

She taught summer school both Wednesday and Thursday. In the afternoons, she met with insurance adjusters.

She and Gage, as it turned out, were two of the "lucky" ones. Their houses would have to be taken down to the studs and rebuilt—but at least they had flood insurance. Too many didn't.

In the evenings, Willa and Buster went up the mountain, where Collin was waiting. Those two nights were glorious, perfect. Just Willa and Collin all wrapped up tight in each other's arms.

Friday, Willa got a call from her insurance company. They would provide her a rental car until the replacement check came through. After summer school was done for the day, she gave Gage back his truck and Collin drove her to Kalispell, where she got the keys to a green Forester.

By then it was after six, so they stopped in at a little Italian place Collin liked. It was wonderful, to sit in a restaurant lit by actual electricity and be served crisp salads, fragrant garlic bread and piping-hot lasagna. She was feeling so festive she even had a glass of red wine while Collin enjoyed a cold beer.

"I could sit here forever," she confided when her plate was empty and the waitress had whisked it away. "It's funny how easy it is to take simple things like restaurants and electricity for granted. I keep telling myself that I'll never consider basic services as a given again."

He was looking at her so…intimately. A look that curled her toes and made her think of the night to come. "How 'bout dessert?"

They ordered gelato with yummy waffle biscuits. Willa took her time savoring the cool, creamy treat.

It was almost nine when they started back to Rust Creek Falls. The plan was to skip stopping in town and caravan up the mountain, but when Willa saw that the Sawmill Street Bridge lights were on, she honked at Collin, who was in the lead.

He pulled over and she swung in behind him, jumping out to run to his side window. He rolled it down. "Looks like the power's back on."

She felt like a little kid at Christmas. "I can't believe it. I sat in that restaurant fantasizing about all the lights coming on. And what do you know?"

"Let's go into town. See what's going on." His eyes had a gleam to them, one she completely understood. He had that troublemaker image he sometimes hid behind, but she wasn't fooled, not anymore, not since the flood. He loved Rust Creek Falls as much as she did. Every step toward recovery from the disaster that had wiped out half the town mattered. To both of them.

She glanced across the bridge. It wasn't fully dark yet, but the streetlights were on. "Yes!" She ran back to her rental car and followed him across the bridge.

Main was blocked off between Sawmill and Cedar. They parked in the Masonic Hall parking lot. Willa left the windows down partway for Buster and they went to investigate.

It was a street dance.

They ran into Thelma on the corner. She told them that not only was the power back on, the landline phones were operational again, too. People had decided to celebrate by throwing a party.

At least half the town was there. Several local musicians had grabbed their instruments and formed an impromptu band. They were set up on the sidewalk midway between the two roadblocks. Folks stood around, clapping and laughing. And the street was full of dancers, everyone spinning and whirling under the streetlights. Willa spotted Paige dancing with her dad and Shelby and little Caitlin dancing together. Gage stood over by Nathan Crawford across the street from the musicians. He spotted Willa and gave her a wave.

Collin grabbed her hand. "Come on." He led her out into the crowd and they danced a couple of fast ones. And then came a slow one. He pulled her against him. She went into his arms and closed her eyes and swayed with him beneath the streetlights, thinking how the moment was about the most perfect that ever could be: dancing with Collin in the middle of Main Street on the night the lights came back on.

The next day, Saturday, Collin's parents and brothers returned at last from Thunder Canyon. They all rolled in to the Triple T in the early afternoon.

Collin was in his workshop up on the mountain when his mother called.

Ellie had a lot to tell him. She and his dad and his brothers and Dallas's three kids hadn't come home alone. They'd brought friends from Thunder Canyon, people who wanted to help and who had the kinds of skills that would be needed to begin to rebuild the south side of town. There were several members of the Pritchett family, who owned a carpentry business. And there were also Matt Cates and his dad, Frank, of Cates Construction, among others. Lots of others.

"You come on down to the ranch for dinner tonight," his mom commanded.

He thought of Willa. He'd been indulging himself in a big way with her, spending every spare moment at her side. She'd gone down the mountain to help with a food drive at the church that morning, but she would be back around five. He'd been looking forward to that—to a quiet dinner, just the two of them.

To another whole night with her in his bed.

On the floor by his feet, Buster raised his head from his paws and twitched an ear at him. Collin bent and gave the dog a pat. It had just seemed a natural thing that Buster would stay on the mountain with him while Willa went to help out down in town.

They were getting real…settled in together, him and Willa. He probably needed to dial it back a notch with her.

But somehow, every time he thought about that, about putting a little space between the two of them, he got this ache in the center of his chest. It was the kind of ache a man gets when he's making himself do something he doesn't want to do.

Because he didn't want to dial it back with Willa. He only thought it would be better for her if he did.

But not for him. Uh-uh. He liked it with her.

He liked everything about being with her.

He liked it too much.

"Collin?" His mother's voice sent his dark thoughts scattering. "You're too quiet. What's going on?"

"Not a thing. I'm right here."

"You come home for dinner."

"Tomorrow, okay? Tonight, I have plans."

"I said, tonight. Your family's home and we want to see you. Bring that sweet Willa Christensen. I'm so glad you're seeing her. I always did like that girl."

Swear words scrolled through his mind. His mom already knew about Willa.

Was he surprised?

Not particularly. His mom knew everyone and he had no illusions that he was the only one in town she'd been talking to while she was away.

"Who told you about me and Willa?" He knew he shouldn't ask. But he was kind of curious.

"Are you kidding me? Who didn't? She's a prize, that girl. I never dared to hope. My own Last Straw and the dear little Christensen girl." *The Last Straw.* It was his mom's pet name for him. She always claimed it was only because he was the last of her children. He knew better and so did everyone else. She called him the Last Straw because he'd given her so much grief with his bad behavior and untamed ways. "I'm very pleased," she added. "Very. Don't you blow it with her, now. Hear me?"

"S'cuse me, Mom. But what's going on between Willa and me has got nothing to do with you."

Ellie sighed. Deeply. "Dear Lord in heaven, you are a trial to me. I only asked you to come to dinner tonight and bring Willa. Please. Six o'clock. Don't be late."

"Mom, I…" He let the objection die unfinished. He was talking to dead air anyway.

Willa's cell rang as she carried a case of baked beans into the church's multiuse room.

She passed the beans to Mindy Krebs and took the phone from her pocket. The display read "Collin." Her heart did a happy dance and she was grinning like a love-struck fool as she answered. "What?"

"My mom, my brothers and about half of Thunder Canyon just arrived in town. Mom knows about you and me. And she wants us both to come to the ranch for dinner."

Willa couldn't help laughing. "Collin. You should hear yourself. You sound like a covert operative passing state secrets."

"She drives me nuts."

Willa had a hard time believing that. "But your mom's so thoughtful and generous and smart and perceptive. I just love her."

He made a low, growling sound. "So does everyone else in town. And she's a good mom, don't get me wrong. She's just way too damn pushy sometimes, that's all. At least when she's dealing with me."

"Because you never did do what she told you to do."

"That's right. It's kind of a point of pride with me never to do what my mother says."

"You know that's childish, right?"

A silence on his end, then, in a surly tone, "Will you come to dinner at the Triple T with me tonight?"

She smiled widely. "Of course. Dinner at the Triple T would be lovely."

Ellie and Bob Traub knew how to throw a barbecue.

Their house was packed with people. Neighbors, friends, ranch hands, Thunder Canyon visitors and a whole lot of family spilled out onto the wide front porch and into the yard, where Bob had two smokers going along with a grill.

Gage was there. Willa spotted him on the front porch when she and Collin arrived. She worked her way through the groups of people to give him a hug.

He offered his hand to Collin. The two men shook.

And Gage said, "Been hearing good things about you lately."

Willa felt a wash of love and appreciation for her brother. He'd done what he'd promised, kept an open mind about Collin and been willing to listen when people told him all Collin had done for their town since the flood.

Collin grunted. "But you know not to believe everything you hear, right?"

Gage chuckled. "Word is you have good ideas, you don't lose your head and you're willing to pitch in." He grew serious. "So I'm asking you for what Rust Creek Falls needs from you. I'm asking for your help with the big job ahead of us."

Willa hid her smile at Collin's wary expression. "Sure," he said at last. "What can I do?"

"Come to the town hall Monday morning at ten? We're putting a group together. We'll start figuring out ways to get funding and volunteers to rebuild south-side homes for folks who had no flood insurance. Also, there's the clinic. We want to get it operational again. And most important, the elementary school. The high school isn't big enough to hold the younger kids, too. We have to do something so the K through eighth graders have a place to go in the fall."

Willa was nodding. "Good. September is just around the corner."

Gage asked, "So what do you say, Collin?"

He didn't hesitate. "I'll be there."

"Willa, dear." Ellie Traub descended on them, all smiles. "I'm so glad to see you!" She grabbed Willa in a bear hug.

Willa laughed in surprise at being clutched so close by Collin's mom. "Good to see you, too, Ellie."

Ellie took her by the shoulders. "I heard you were flooded out—and Gage, too." She sent Willa's brother a sympathetic frown. "It's horrible. Awful…."

"We'll survive," Willa said. "And we'll rebuild."

"Lavinia and Wayne…?" Ellie asked about Willa and Gage's parents.

"They're fine," Gage assured her. "I talked to them just

an hour or so ago. They should be back at the ranch some-time tomorrow."

Collin said, "They were in Livingston, at the big rodeo, when the storm hit."

"So was I," Gage told Ellie, regret in his voice. "Mom wouldn't leave me alone until I agreed to go with them. She had some idea I was working too hard and needed to take a break and forget everything for the holiday."

"She knows what you need better than you do, huh?" Collin sent his mother a meaningful glance.

"Yes, she does," Gage confirmed, sounding weary. "Just ask her."

Ellie grabbed Collin. "We only do it because we love you. Now, give me a hug," she demanded fondly.

"Aw, Mom…" Collin embraced her with obvious af-fection.

Then Ellie hooked one arm with Collin's and the other with Willa's. "Gage, there's beer in the cooler out on the lawn."

"Thanks, Ellie."

Eyes shining, Ellie commanded, "You two come with me. I want everyone to know how pleased and happy I am that you're both here—together."

"It was embarrassing," Collin grumbled much later that night, when they were alone in his bed. "Dragging us all over the yard, announcing over and over again that you were with *me*."

Willa lay with her head on his broad chest. She could hear his heartbeat, so strong and steady. There was no place in the world she would rather be than right there, held close in Collin's strong arms. "She loves you. She's proud of you."

He made one of those low, growly sounds. "She can't

believe that someone as amazing as you would be hanging around with me."

"That's not so."

"Yeah, it is." He pressed his lips to her hair.

"No."

"Yeah—and what do you want to bet that Nathan Crawford will be at that meeting your brother talked me into
going to Monday morning?"

She tipped her head back and kissed his beard-scratchy
chin. "Probably. But you can handle him."

He looked down into her eyes and said gruffly, "You
realize my mom is right, don't you? You're much too fine
a woman to be wasting your time with me."

"I am not wasting my time. And I really get annoyed
with you when you put yourself down."

"It's only the truth."

"No, it isn't." She tried to look stern. "Will you stop
it? Please?"

He smoothed her hair and answered grudgingly, "Yes,
ma'am."

She gave him a slow smile. "Actually, I'm a lot like
your mother."

He widened his eyes in a comical way and faked a gasp
of shock. "Don't say that. Anything but that."

"Oh, but I *am* like Ellie. I'm pushy. And determined.
And very sure of what's good for the people I love…."

Love. She'd said the word so casually.

But then, as soon as it was out, she didn't feel casual
at all.

Love. Once the word had escaped her lips, it seemed to
hang by a thread inside her mind, slowly swinging. Tempting her to grab it and run with it.

Love.

The big word, the one that mattered. The word that changed everything.

She dared for the first time to admit to herself what was happening to her, how her life had become something new and fresh and beautiful. The world had a glow to it now.

Because of him.

I love you, Collin Traub.

Buoyant light seemed to fill her. All at once, she was weightless, defying gravity through pure joy.

I love you, Collin Traub.

She opened her mouth to say it—and then she shut it without making a sound.

Saying it out loud would be dangerous. Risky.

He was frowning down at her. "Hey."

She kissed his chin again. "Umm?"

"You okay?" Cautious. A little worried. "You seemed a thousand miles away just now."

"I'm right here." She took his arm, wrapped it snugly around her and settled herself more comfortably against his warm, broad chest. "And I'm fine. Better than fine."

He chuckled then. "You certainly are—and never admit you're like my mother, unless you're purposely trying to creep me out."

She laughed and promised, "Never again," as her heart cried, *I love you, Collin. I love you, I do.* The simple phrases seemed to tickle the back of her throat, working themselves closer to being said.

But she didn't say them.

Not yet. It had only been nine days since the flood, and only five since that first night she'd spent in his arms.

Yes, to her, what they had together now wasn't all that surprising. It felt like a simple progression, a natural unfolding of something that had been there all along. She'd known him all her life, wanted him for so long, been waiting, even when she thought that she hated him, for a chance with him.

She was more than ready to talk about that. About their lives, about their future.

About love.

But she was no fool. She knew that *he* wasn't ready.

So, then, she could wait.

She had a feeling it wouldn't be long.

The time wasn't right yet.

But it would be.

Soon....

Chapter Thirteen

Collin had an ever-growing backlog of work he needed to get going on down in his shop. The next morning, as they were finishing breakfast, he told Willa he would have to spend the whole day at it.

She pushed her empty plate away and rose slowly from her chair.

He stared at her, feeling suddenly wary. "I'm not sure I trust that look in your eye."

She gave him one of those sweet, innocent school-teacher smiles of hers as she came around to his side of the table. He gazed up at her, narrow eyed. He knew she was up to something. She sat on his lap.

He growled her name in warning.

She only brushed his hair back from his forehead with her soft, cool fingers and then kissed his cheek. "Come to church with me."

"Willa…"

"Please. It'll only take a couple of hours, total, including the drive up and down the mountain. After church, I promise I'll leave you alone to work in peace for the rest of the day."

The problem with her sitting on him was that the feel of her only made him want to touch her. To kiss her. And then to kiss her some more.

He caught her earlobe between his teeth and worried it lightly, because he couldn't quite stop himself. She trembled and let out one of those reluctant little moans that always drove him crazy.

"Shame on you, Willa Christensen," he scolded. "Talking about church while you're sitting on my lap. You know very well what happens when you sit on my lap...."

She wiggled her bottom against him and then he was the one trying not to moan. "Church," she whispered way too damn seductively. "It'll be over before you know it and then you can come right back up here and work all day and half the night if you want to...."

"Wiggle like that again and I won't be getting any work done. We won't be going to church, either. We won't be going anywhere but back down the hall to bed."

"Church. You take your truck and I'll take the Forester. That way, as soon as the service is over, you can head right back up the mountain." She kissed him. And then she slid to the floor and stood above him.

He grabbed her hand. "Get back down here...."

She bent close and kissed him again. "I'll be ready in twenty minutes."

They went to church.

It was kind of nice, really, Collin thought. His family was there, his mom all smiles at the sight of him and Willa together. Pastor Alderson gave a sermon about finding joy in simple things.

Collin could relate to that, especially lately. Just being around Willa all the time, that was a pretty damn joyful thing for him.

Yeah, it was partly the sex, which was amazing...and which he probably shouldn't be thinking about in church.

But the thing was, the sex wasn't everything.

It wasn't even the most important thing.

Willa herself. *She* was the important thing. The way she would laugh, kind of husky and happy both at once. The way she cuddled up close to him, her ear against his chest like she only wanted to listen to the sound of his heart beating. The way she listened so close when he talked, but then had no problem speaking up if she didn't like something he'd said.

The way she could be so kind and gentle—and then turn right around and be tough as nails when something mattered to her. The way she could pull on a pair of work gloves and keep up with him clearing storm debris all the way up the mountain. The way she wasn't ashamed to be with him in front of everyone. Even if she *was* a school-teacher with a certain reputation she really ought to be looking out for.

He'd thought he was happy before Willa.

But the past few days, he'd started thinking that before Willa, he hadn't even known what happiness was.

He was living in a dream, and he knew it. This thing with her, well, it couldn't last. He was who he was and he'd always seen himself in an honest light. He'd grown up wild and he hadn't been to college. He could change some, but not completely.

Not enough to be with a woman like Willa in a forever kind of way.

The pastor told them all to rise. They sang an old hymn that Collin had known since childhood.

Out of the corner of his eye, in the pew across the center aisle, he caught sight of Nathan Crawford, standing so tall and proud, singing good and loud. Nathan saw him looking and shot back a narrow-eyed glare. Nathan would probably be ticked off that Gage had asked him to the meeting about flood relief tomorrow.

Well, too bad. Collin was going. He had a few ideas for raising money and getting folks together to rebuild what they'd lost. And he wanted to help in any way he could.

There were other Crawfords in church that day. He got a few scowls from more than one of them. They'd always looked down on him. Not only was he a Traub, he was the no-good, skirt-chasing, *troublemaking* Traub.

Since he and Willa started in together, he'd worried that the Crawfords might come after her for being with him, might smear her good name. So far, that hadn't happened. But it still nagged at him. In a little town like Rust Creek Falls, people had certain standards. They didn't like to think of their schoolteachers living in sin. Especially not with the local bad boy.

Willa nudged him with her elbow. He sent her a glance. She sang even louder, brown eyes full of teasing laughter.

He forgot his worries and let himself enjoy just being with her. It couldn't last forever, but as long as it did, he intended to enjoy himself.

After church, Willa longed to ask Collin to take her to the doughnut shop for a Sunday snack. The shop had reopened the day before and it was a Sunday tradition in town. Folks went to church and then to the Wings to Go or Daisy's Donuts over on North Broomtail Road.

But he did need to work and she'd already made her

deal with him. So she kept her word and sent him back up the mountain.

When he got in his pickup, Buster whined to go with him. Collin shot her a questioning look.

"Go ahead," she said indulgently. "Take him." So Collin got out and let the dog in—ever since the day Buster fell from the pickup bed on the way up the mountain, they'd been letting him ride in front. "I'll be back by five or six," she promised. Thelma was expecting her to help sort donated clothing for flooded-out families.

Collin kissed her, a warm brush of his lips against her cheek—and then he climbed back up behind the wheel and headed for Sawmill Street.

Willa's mother called her from the ranch at a little past two. "We're home," she announced, then, "Where are you? We've missed you."

"I'm at Thelma McGee's, helping out."

"Honey, we would love to see you. Can you come on over?"

"I'll check with Thelma…"

The older woman made a shooing gesture. "Go on, now. Go see your mother. Give her my best."

When Willa arrived, her dad was out in the northeast pasture somewhere, repairing a fence.

Her mom had the coffee ready and a box of bakery sweet rolls she'd picked up in Kalispell. After hugs and greetings, they sat at the table together, each with a steaming mug and a treat from the bakery box.

Willa knew her mother. She could tell by the way her mom sipped her coffee thoughtfully and then said nothing for a moment, her head tipped to the side, that she was working up to broaching an uncomfortable subject.

"Ellie Traub came by," Lavinia said at last.

Willa got the message then. Ellie must have mentioned her and Collin. Willa picked up her fork and ate a bite of cheese Danish. "I'm sure she's happy to have you home safe and sound."

Lavinia took a big sip of coffee and set the mug down a little too firmly. "Ellie's *happy* because she's always liked you so much. She's always hoped that you might end up with one of her boys."

"I like Ellie, too, Mom. But then, you know that."

Her mom gave up on subtlety. She leaned across the table. "Oh, honey. *Collin?*"

Willa drew in a slow, calming breath and reminded herself that she'd gotten through to Gage about Collin and she could get through to her mom, too. "I care for Collin. I care for him a lot. Since the flood, I've gotten to know him—really know him. He's strong and good and brave. And he doesn't give himself enough credit, but I'm working on getting him to see that he's a much better man than he's willing to admit. And I've been staying with him, up at his house, since last Monday night."

Her mother winced and sipped more coffee. "Staying."

"Yes."

"But is that wise?"

"I'm proud to be with him, Mom. He's a wonderful man. He's done a lot to help people, to keep people's spirits up, since the flood. Ask around town. Please. Ask Gage. *He'll* tell you."

Her mother frowned. "Gage hasn't said a word to me about you and Collin Traub."

"I'm sure Gage was waiting for me to talk to you first. I appreciate his staying out of it."

"But you never even seemed to *like* Collin. And what about Dane Everhart?"

"I *always* liked Collin. A lot more than I ever wanted to admit."

"But—"

"And as for Dane, it was never going to work with him and me." Lord, she was tired of explaining about Dane. It was her own fault, though, and she had to remember that. She should have had the courage to say no when she meant no. "Dane's a great guy. He's just not the guy for me."

"But Collin is?"

Willa sat back in her chair and folded her arms across her chest. "I love you, Mom. A lot. I will always be there if you need me. But I'm twenty-five years old and perfectly capable of managing my own life. I can't say what the future will bring, but I am with Collin now and I am proud to be with him."

Her mother tipped her head to the side again. Willa braced herself for another onslaught. But her mom surprised her and slowly smiled. "I always did kind of wonder about you and Collin. I had a feeling there might be a spark or two between you…"

A burst of relieved laughter escaped Willa. Her mom was going to be all right with Collin, after all. She teased, "No way."

Lavinia nodded, looking smug. "Yes." And then she scolded, "But you really must clear things up with Dane as soon as possible."

"You're right. And I plan to. I'll be going to see him as soon as he gets back from Australia."

Her mom got up, brought the coffeepot over and refilled their mugs. "Collin has done well with the saddle-making business. He made your dad's CT Saddle, did you know?"

"I didn't know. Until Collin told me."

"And I hear that he's turned that old cabin of Casper's into something quite beautiful."

"Yes, he has. You and Daddy will have to come up for dinner. Maybe next weekend."

"We would enjoy that, honey. Very much."

* * *

Willa got back to Collin's at five. The main floor was deserted.

She called down the stairs. "I'm here!"

Buster came bounding up. As she scratched his ears in greeting, Collin called from below, "Half an hour?"

"Take your time!"

She fed Buster. There was leftover meat loaf and several servings of browned potatoes in the fridge. She put them in the oven to reheat and cut up a salad. Then she set the table.

By then, fifteen minutes had passed. The oven was on a timer, so she felt safe grabbing a quick shower.

She was rinsing off when the shower door opened and Collin stepped in.

"S'cuse me," he said with that slow smile that seemed to fire all her circuits at once. "Just need to freshen up a little...."

She laughed as he grabbed her close. "Don't get my hair wet!"

Of course, he took that as a challenge, turning her beneath the spray so the water poured down directly over her head. "Oops."

"Collin!" she sputtered, trying to wiggle free.

But she didn't try too hard.

And then he kissed her again. She realized it didn't matter that her hair was soaking wet.

All that mattered was that his mouth was pressed to hers and his arms were nice and tight around her.

The meat loaf was a little dry when they finally sat down to eat.

"Delicious," he said, and poured on the ketchup.

She asked him how the work was going. He said he'd

made progress, but there was still a lot to catch up on. To-morrow he had that morning meeting in the town hall, but after that, he would come right back up the mountain and work for the rest of the day.

"I've been thinking I'm going to need to hire someone to work with me," he said. "Not right now. But it's coming. I know a couple talented saddle makers in Kalispell. I'm going to contact them, see if they have any interest in joining forces with CT Saddles. They could work in their own shops, but put in some of their time on projects I bring them."

"Growing the business. Excellent. And you can't do everything yourself—especially when you also want to help out with the rebuilding effort."

"There should be more hours in a day."

"No argument there." She ate a bite of potato. "Thelma told me today that she thinks you should run for mayor. She thinks you're the one to carry on, to build on what Hunter started."

He sent her a look from under his thick eyelashes. "Don't."

"Don't what?" She widened her eyes at him.

"Don't start in about me running for mayor. It's not going to happen."

She cut off a bite of meat loaf neatly. "I think it is."

"You don't know what you're talking about."

She set down her fork and put up a hand. "All right. Subject closed." She pressed her lips together to keep from smiling. "For now."

He made a low, grumbling sound, but let it go at that.

She ate the bite of meat loaf. And then she said, "My parents got back today. I went out to the ranch and had a nice visit with my mom."

He studied her for a moment, his grumpy expression

softening. "Sometimes I don't believe you're actually here, in my place, heating up the meat loaf, naked in my shower, harassing me over dinner...."

Tenderness filled her. "I like it, being here with you. I like it a lot." For a moment or two, they simply gazed at each other. They were both smiling by then. She remembered what she'd been about to tell him. "*Your* mother got to *my* mom before I did."

He forked up more meat loaf. "That doesn't sound good."

"Well, it was kind of scary when Mom started in on me, I'll admit."

"Started in on you about being with me?"

"She was surprised, that's all."

"Your mother knows you're too good for me," he said in that voice that seemed to be joking—but really wasn't.

She set down her fork. "No. She doesn't think that. She doesn't think that at all."

"Yeah, right."

"And neither do I, which you really ought to know by now."

He grabbed the big glass of milk he'd poured himself and guzzled about half of it. "This is a dumb thing to argue about."

"I agree. As soon as you admit what a great guy you are, we can *stop* arguing about this."

He actually rolled his eyes. "Okay, okay. I'm great. I'm terrific."

She raised her own glass of milk in a toast. "Yes, you are." She drank. When she set the glass down, she asked, "Would you mind if we had my parents up here for dinner? Maybe Friday or Saturday night? I was thinking we could have your folks, too. And maybe Gage and any of your brothers who wanted to come."

He was silent. A definite hesitation. "I have a lot of work I need to be doing, Willa."

"I understand. But I would do the dinner. You only have to come upstairs when everyone gets here."

"The road is still iffy."

"I go up and down it every day. As long as you know the spots to watch for, it's fine. I'll just tell them all where to be extra careful." She waited. He said nothing. Finally, she said, "If you don't want to have the family here, I think you ought to just say so."

He looked away. "It's not that."

"Then what is it?"

He pushed his plate away. "Come on, Willa. People get...expectations. Especially in this town. You saw how my mom was last night, dragging us all over the yard, making sure everyone got that you and me are together."

She had a sad, sinking feeling—at the same time as she told herself not to be in such a hurry about everything. She needed to let him adjust to what they shared in his own way, in his own time. She reminded herself that it had only been six days since they became more than friends, and that only a few minutes ago, he'd told her how happy he was just to be with her.

"So." She made an effort to keep her voice calm and reasonable. "You don't want to have the family up here for dinner this weekend. Am I right?"

He gave it to her straight, at least. "That's right."

Something shifted within her. Something died just a little. For the first time since they became lovers, she found herself thinking that it was simply not going to work out with them.

And then she told herself to stop. Just stop.

Maybe it was pushing it a little, to have the whole family over for dinner so soon. He did have a lot of work to do. And he was also unaccustomed to being half of a couple.

In fact, from things he'd said in the past, she had a sense that he'd never planned to be part of a couple. She needed to let him deal, give him the time and the space to start to see himself in a new light.

"You're mad," he said softly. Sadly.

She swallowed and shook her head. "No. It's okay. Really. It's fine."

The rest of the evening was lovely, Willa thought.

Collin was tender and attentive. He was passionate in bed. They talked for over an hour before they fell asleep. There was laughter. He held her close.

He honestly did seem happy just to be with her. More than happy.

Still, Willa couldn't shake the feeling that he'd drawn a line between them when he told her he didn't want the family over. An invisible but uncrossable line, a line that cut them off from a future together.

For him, they were lovers. The best of friends.

But no more than that.

Never more than that.

On Monday, Willa told her mother that she would have to put the family dinner on hold for a bit. Her mom didn't push. She said she understood. Everyone was scrambling since the flood, trying to catch up with their lives, to get things back to normal. Of course, Collin needed to focus on his work. They would all get together for an evening soon enough.

Willa smiled and nodded. But she was thinking, *I love him. I love him so much.*

And she was starting to get the feeling that loving him

wasn't enough, that he would never want to hear her say what was in her heart for him.

That she would never wear his ring.

Collin knew that he'd hurt Willa when he'd dug in his heels about having the family over.

He was trying not to think about that, about how he'd hurt her. He was trying to keep her with him, even though he knew that in the end, what she wanted and what he wanted were two different things.

Tuesday afternoon he sat through a second endless meeting with Gage, Nathan, Thelma and the rest of the group of community leaders they'd put together to come up with ways to speed flood recovery. When he finally left the town hall, he spotted Dallas, his oldest brother, coming toward him on the sidewalk, looking bleak.

But then, who wouldn't be bleak in Dallas's position? His wife, Laurel, had left him and their children last year. He was a single dad raising three boys on his own.

The brothers shook hands and clapped each other on the back. Dallas said he'd driven into town to pick the boys up from summer school.

"You got a little time to kill?" Collin asked him. "We could grab a beer at the Ace...." It was one of those invitations made only for form's sake. Collin had work waiting on the mountain and didn't really expect Dallas to say yes.

But his glum-faced brother surprised him. "Sure. I got about a half an hour until they turn the boys loose. Let's go."

They sat at the bar and ordered a couple of longnecks.

Collin asked how things were going and his brother said, "I'm proud of my boys and I'm getting by—and what's going on with you and Willa Christensen?"

Great. Getting grilled about Willa by his gloomy big

brother. That hadn't really been in the plan. Collin sipped his beer and tried to decide how to answer.

Dallas kept after him. "You've made Mom happy for once. I'll say that. But come on. Everyone knows Willa's living up at your place. Yeah, you're the hero of the day and all. You definitely manned up when the flood hit. But do you really think moving Willa in with you was such a great idea?"

By then, Collin just wanted to cut through the crap. "Dallas. What are you getting at?"

"Willa's a great person. And you're not so bad yourself. But she's the marrying kind and we both know it. The big question is, are you?"

Collin wanted to tell his brother to mind his own business. Unfortunately, Dallas had a point. "I'm nuts over her," he said low, so only his brother would hear him. "I've got it bad."

"I kind of noticed that. But let me point out the obvious. You don't move a nice girl like Willa into your place unless you're putting a ring on her finger real soon. Especially not when she's the kindergarten teacher. That's not a thing a man should do—well, maybe in New York City. But not in Rust Creek Falls."

Collin thought about what his brother had said. He thought about it a lot—constantly, as a matter of fact.

He felt bad. Rotten. Low.

He never should have let Willa move in with him. It wasn't good for her. He should have thought of her first, instead of how much he wanted to be with her, instead of indulging himself just because he couldn't shake the hold of needing her so bad.

Wednesday night, she asked him if something was bothering him.

He didn't know how to answer. If he told her that he was feeling like a low-down loser for living with her when he never intended to marry her, well, where would that lead?

To her moving out.

He knew her. There was no way she was going to hang around if he told her to her face that it was going nowhere between them.

And he couldn't let her move out. Everyone would say that he'd dumped her. She would be shamed in front of the whole town. He couldn't ever let that happen to her.

Plus, he didn't *want* her to move out. He just wanted to be with her. And not to have to think about what was going to happen next.

But then, he *did* think. He thought way too much. His mind was like a hamster on a wheel. A hamster on speed, thoughts going nowhere fast, endlessly chasing themselves in a circle.

He thought about that other guy, that guy from Colorado, the one who'd asked her to marry him. The other guy was a stand-up guy, she'd said.

She'd also said she was telling him no.

But *should* she be telling him no?

It made Collin feel sick in the pit of his stomach to think of her with that other guy. But what if the other guy was the *better* guy?

Collin wanted her. A lot. But he also wanted the best for her. And if the best for her was that other guy, well, Collin ought to step aside and give her some space to make the right decision.

He could do that much for her, at least.

But he did nothing.

Every day, every hour, his thoughts got more and more tangled up and confused. He didn't know how to talk to her about all of it. So he didn't talk to her.

He lied and acted oblivious and said there was nothing wrong—and that only made him more disgusted with himself. He started thinking how he really had a problem with seeing ahead to the consequences of his own actions. He had a part missing, emotionwise. He'd always been that way, chasing the thrill, hungry for excitement. Not thinking who would be hurt or damaged by his doing exactly what he wanted to do when he wanted to do it.

All day Thursday and half of Friday, as he worked in his shop to catch up on his orders, he tried to figure out what he was going to do to make things right with Willa. By three in the afternoon on Friday, he finally came to an actual decision. He realized there was only one choice for him now, only one thing to do.

He took a quick shower, put Buster in the pickup and headed for Kalispell.

It was no good lately with Collin, and Willa knew it.

Things had only gotten worse with every day that passed since Sunday, the day he'd told her he didn't want the family over. Every day since then, he'd become more distant, more uncommunicative. And she wasn't sleeping well at night now. She kept waking up and staring at the ceiling and trying to lie very still so that Collin wouldn't notice she wasn't asleep.

Wednesday, she'd asked him about it, about what might be on his mind. He'd looked right in her face and told her there was nothing.

She'd wanted to believe him. But she didn't believe him.

There was a falseness now between them. And it was growing. She needed to break through it.

But how?

It was starting to seem to her that there was only one

way to get through to him. She needed to put herself out there, tell him the hardest thing.

She'd wanted to wait a while, to simply be with him and let the closeness between them grow. But the only way they were growing since Sunday was further apart.

Yes, opening her heart to him was a big risk. She could end up without him. From the way he'd been behaving lately, she probably *would* end up without him as soon as she uttered those three oh-so-dangerous words.

But who was she kidding? In the deep ways, the ways that mattered, she was already without him.

So why keep lying to herself? She might as well go for it, might as well pull out the stops, put her heart on the line and accept the consequences. At least then she would know she'd given it her best shot.

On the way up the mountain Friday afternoon, she decided she would tell him as soon as he came upstairs from his workshop.

But when she got there, the house was empty. He'd left a note on the table: *Quick trip to Kalispell. Took Buster. Back by six.*

All right, she thought. She would tell him when he got back.

She could start dinner....

But no. Dinner could wait. She was much too on edge to think about food right then. She had lesson planning she could do, so she went to the spare room, where she'd set up a desk and computer, and she got to work firming up her choices for activities for the following week, making lists of materials she hadn't pulled together yet.

An hour dragged by. She finished at the computer and went back out to the kitchen to face the prospect of cooking something.

Anything to keep busy until he returned.

She was standing at the refrigerator with the door wide-open, staring blankly inside, when she heard the crunch of tries on gravel outside.

Her heart gave a sick lurch inside her chest and then started beating so fast she felt dizzy. She shut the refrigerator door and turned toward the hall and the short entry area.

The door opened. She heard his boots on the wide planks of the hardwood floor, heard the door close, knew he would be pausing at the coatrack to hang up his hat.

Buster came bounding in ahead of him. She knelt and pressed her face to the warm, sweet scruff of his neck. He wiggled and made happy whining sounds—and then left her to lap water from his bowl.

Slowly, her knees feeling absurdly shaky, she rose.

And there he was. "Willa." He wore clean jeans and a blue chambray shirt rolled to the elbows and her heart just ached at the sight of him. "Come here…." He held out his hands.

She hesitated. She couldn't…read him, had no idea what was going on with him. He seemed to be looking at her so seriously, with such determined intention. "I…" Words simply failed her.

And then he was right there, so close. In front of her. He smelled of mountain air, of pine trees. He took her hand. "Come on…" And he pulled her with him, around the jut of the counter, into the main living area, over to a fat brown chair by the window. "Sit down."

She did what he told her to do.

And then he was kneeling at her feet, looking up at her, his jaw set, his full mouth a determined line. He had something in his hand.

And then he was sliding it on her finger.

A ring. A beautiful diamond solitaire on a platinum

band. Exactly the kind of ring she would have chosen for herself. She stared at it, gaping. "Collin, what…?"

And then he said, "Marry me, Willa. Be my wife."

It was just what she'd hoped to hear him say someday. And for a moment, she knew the purest, most wonderful spiking of absolute joy.

It was all going to work out, after all. She would have her life with him. They would be married, have children. Be happy forever, just as she'd almost stopped dreaming they might be….

She opened her mouth to tell him how glad she was, to say how much she loved him and how scared she had been that it was all unraveling, all going wrong.

But then, before a single sound got out, she saw that it wasn't right, after all. She realized what he *hadn't* said. It was the part about how he loved her. He'd left that out.

And instead of saying *Yes,* or *Oh, Collin, I do love you,* what came out of her mouth was, "Why?"

He blinked.

He actually blinked.

And that was when she knew that it wasn't going to work.

To his credit, he managed to pull it together. Sort of. "It's the right thing. And I'm nuts for you. That's not going away anytime soon. It's the right thing and…"

She stopped him by reaching out and pressing a finger to his lips. "The right thing, why?"

He swallowed. "Well, we *are* living together. And I want to keep on living with you and I…" He paused, tried again. "Okay. I love you, all right? I love you and I want to marry you and all you have to do is say yes."

She laughed. It wasn't a happy sound. The laugh caught in her throat and ended on something very much like a sob. "Oh, Collin. You're not telling me the truth. I know it. *You* know it. Can't you just say it? Just tell me what's going on with you, whatever it is."

He gazed up at her. He looked absolutely miserable. "You're not going to say yes to me, are you?"

She took off the beautiful ring. "I can't say yes to you. Not like this. I just can't." She reached for his hand. Reluctantly, he gave it to her. She put the ring in his palm and folded his warm, strong fingers over it. "You don't really want to get married, do you?"

He rose then. He gazed down at her, dark eyes so deep, full of turmoil and frustration.

She stared up at him and asked him again, "Do you?"

His mouth curved downward; his big body stiffened. And then he turned from her to the wide windows that overlooked their town. He stared out, showing her his broad, proud back. "What I want is you. What I want is for you to be happy, for you to have what *you* want. I don't want folks in town saying crappy things about you. I want you to have the best of everything. I don't really think I'm it, but you've told me over and over you won't marry that other guy, so it kind of seems to me that you'd better marry me."

"You *want* me to marry Dane?"

"No." On that, he didn't hesitate. "But you deserve the best. Is he the best? The way you talked about him the night of the flood, I guess so."

"I was stupid and small and petty the night of the flood. I wanted to get to you, to hurt you. I'm sorry I did that. It was wrong. Now, how many times do I have to tell you, Dane is not the guy for me?"

He didn't say anything. He only shook his head.

She tried again. "Who said crappy things about me?"

He still wouldn't look at her. "No one. I don't know. I just… I don't want them to, okay? And as long as you're living up here with me without my ring on your finger, well, they could, all right? In a small town like ours, they might. Especially the damn Crawfords. They'd do it just because I'm a Traub—the troublemaking, skirt-chasing Traub—and you're with me."

She got up then. And she went to him. When she stood at his shoulder, she said, "But they haven't."

He faced her at last. "Not that I know of." It was a grudging admission.

She wanted to touch him, to clasp his muscled shoulder, to lay her palm against his cheek. To lift up and press her lips to his, to kiss him until he pulled her close and kissed her back, until she forgot everything but the taste of him, the heat and wonder of him in her arms.

But no. Better not.

She said, "You keep evading the basic question. So I'll tell you what I think. I think you are a wonderful man—a much *better* man than you're willing to give yourself credit for. But I don't think that you want to get married. And you know what? I want *you* to have what *you* want. What you need."

He scowled down at her. "I don't like the sound of this, Willa."

Her throat clutched. The hot tears were pushing at the back of it. She refused to let them fall. "I love you," she got out on a bare husk of sound. "With all of my heart. And that's why I'm going to pack up my things and go."

Chapter Fourteen

It was five minutes to eight when Willa arrived at the ranch that night. Buster leading the way, she came in the door carrying two big boxes full of her things. Her parents, settled into their recliners for a quiet evening at home, glanced over at her with matching expressions of surprise.

Her mom jumped up. "Willa. What in the world...?"

The tears broke free then. They streamed down her cheeks. "Collin asked me to marry him. He bought me the most beautiful ring. The perfect ring. And I said no."

Her dad got up, too, then. He came and put his big, rough, rancher's hand on her hair, pressed a kiss to her forehead. And then he took the boxes from her and carried them down the hall to her old room.

"Oh, honey..." Her mom held out her arms.

Willa went into them, into the kind of a comfort only a mom can give. "Oh, Mom. I love him."

"I know, I know...."

"But it's not… Oh, Mom. It's just…not…"

"Shh. Shh, now. It's okay. It's all right."

She was openly sobbing by then. She couldn't seem to stop herself. "It's not. No, it's just not…"

And her mom held her and stroked her hair and patted her back and kept saying how everything was going to work out. Her dad came back up the hall. Buster followed him out as he went to get the rest of her things.

After Willa left him, Collin went down to his shop and he went to work. He worked straight through Friday night. When the sun came up Saturday morning, he climbed the stairs, plodded down the hall and fell into bed.

He slept for a couple of hours, his dreams full of Willa. It was still morning when he woke up, by himself, in the bed that he'd gotten way too damn used to sharing with her.

In those first few seconds when consciousness found him, he forgot she wasn't there. He reached for her, but there was only emptiness on the other side of the bed.

That was when it all came flooding back. She was gone.

He got up and went back down to work.

Willa woke up early that Saturday. There was no summer school, but she went to town anyway. She wanted to talk to her brother before somebody else told him that she and Collin were through.

Gage was in his office.

She went in, closed the door and said, "I broke up with Collin. It's not what you think, so please don't try any big-brother heroics."

He was already looking thunderous. "What do you mean, it's not what I think?"

"He asked me to marry him. I turned him down. I made the decision to move out, not him. He wanted me to stay—

and do not ask me why I left, because I'm not explaining myself. All I'm saying is that he only wanted to do the right thing."

Gage got up from behind his desk then. He came around and he took her by the shoulders. For several seconds, he simply held her gaze. And then he pulled her close and gave her a hug. When he stepped back, he said, "So what you're saying is, you want me to stay out of it. You don't want me to bust his face in. And you want me to keep him on the Recovery Committee, to treat him like nothing has changed."

"Yes," she answered softly. "That is exactly what I'm saying."

Around five in the afternoon that day, Collin trudged back upstairs. He drank a quart of milk and ate a tuna sandwich standing up at the counter. Then he went down the hall and fell across the bed. When he woke up a few hours later, he returned to the lower floor and worked some more.

That was kind of the tone for the whole weekend. He didn't bother to shower or shave or even use a toothbrush. He worked. When he started to feel like he might fall over or hurt himself with his own tools, he went upstairs, grabbed something to eat, fell across his bed for an hour or two—and then woke up, remembered all over again that Willa was gone and staggered back down to his shop.

On Sunday, his mother called twice. He let the calls go to voice mail.

He might have stayed on the mountain indefinitely, but on Monday morning as he stood at the counter, staring blankly into space, downing a mug of coffee, he heard a scratching noise. And then a whine.

He went to the front door and opened it.

Buster.

The dog whined again and wagged his tail. When Collin only stared down at him, he plunked his butt on the porch boards and whined some more.

"You're not supposed to be here."

Tongue lolling, the dog stared up at him hopefully.

"Fine." Collin stepped back and Buster came in. He went right to his water bowl and lapped up what was left in it. Then he sniffed the food bowl. "Oh, pardon me. I had no clue you were coming." Collin laid on the sarcasm. Unfortunately, it was wasted on Buster. "Okay, okay." He went and got the bag of kibble. Buster sat and waited as he filled the bowl. "Go for it." And Buster did exactly that.

Willa was probably worried about the mutt. He would have to call her....

His heart lurched into overdrive and his throat felt tight, his tongue thick and heavy in his mouth as he autodialed her cell.

She answered on the second ring. "Collin." A small voice, so soft. And then she must have realized why he'd called. "You have Buster?"

"Yeah. He just now showed up at the door."

"Oh. I'm glad. We were worried...."

"I'll bring him down today."

"You don't have to. I can drive up after—"

"I said I'll bring him. I have a meeting anyway." A meeting he hadn't planned to go to, but hey. He couldn't hide in his shop forever. Life went on. Such as it was.

"I have summer school."

"Yeah, I know." He was aching for the smell of lemons, for that soft place in the curve of her throat. He loved to kiss her there.

"I'll call Thelma. She never minds watching him."

"But she's going to the meeting."

"It's okay. I'll ask her to wait for you. He's fine in the house without her. I'll pick him up there after school."

So, then. He wouldn't see her. That was good. Or so he tried to make himself believe. "All right, then."

"Thank you for bringing him...."

He tried to think of what to say next.

But then it didn't matter. She was gone.

Off the phone. Not in his house. Out of his life.

I love you, she'd told him. *With all of my heart.*

The bleak numbness of the weekend was fading. He'd started getting the feeling that he'd messed up bad, that he'd gotten stuck somewhere in his mind, stuck being some guy he really wasn't anymore. He'd thrown away what he wanted most because he didn't have the sense to say the things Willa needed to hear. It was all doubly discouraging because the things she needed to hear really were there, inside him, even though he'd gone and pretended they weren't.

He'd pretty much told her to go marry that other guy. The more he thought about that, the more disgusted he got with himself. It would serve him right if she took his advice.

Thinking about it all made his head spin. A spinning head and a broken heart were a real unpleasant combination.

He told himself that now, to be fair, he had to wait. He had to let her work it out with Dane Everhart one way or another. If she turned down the guy from Colorado, then maybe...

Maybe what? Seriously, what was the matter with him? What he needed to do was leave her alone. If there'd ever been any hope for him with her, he'd pretty much blown that by the way he'd treated her.

He scrambled some eggs and ate them, took a shower,

loaded Buster into his pickup and drove down the mountain. He dropped off the dog and went to the meeting.

Gage was there. Once or twice, Collin caught the other man watching him. But Gage didn't say a word about Willa. They discussed the donations that were coming in—and how to get more. They talked about the volunteers who'd come in from Thunder Canyon and elsewhere and how best to put them all to work rebuilding Rust Creek Falls. The meeting lasted three hours and they were still only two-thirds down the agenda. They agreed to meet Wednesday, same time, and finish up.

Collin drove to Kalispell and stocked up on groceries. He went home and went back to work—and deleted, unheard, all the messages his mom had left him over the weekend and that day.

The next morning, there was Buster, big as life, waiting at his front door. That time he texted Willa instead of calling. It just seemed wiser not to talk to her. Not to put his overworked heart under that kind of pressure, not to give himself any opportunity to make an idiot of himself all over again by begging for another chance. He took the dog to Thelma's and went back up the mountain.

On Wednesday morning, he couldn't help expecting Buster to show up again. But he didn't. They must be keeping a closer eye on him.

Which was good. For the best.

He was standing at the counter drinking his coffee, staring into the middle distance, wondering what Willa might be doing at that moment, when someone knocked at the door.

Willa?

He choked in midsip and his pulse started racing. Hot coffee sloshed across his knuckles as he set the mug down too hard. He wiped the coffee off on his Wranglers and made for the door.

It couldn't be her....

And it wasn't.

It was his mom, wearing tan pants, riding boots and an old plaid shirt, her straw Resistol in her gloved hands. She'd come on horseback, ridden her favorite mare, Sweetie, who was hobbled at the foot of the steps, nipping at the sparse grass.

"You deleted my phone messages, didn't you?" She asked the question softly. Kind of sadly. And that, somehow, was a thousand times worse than if she'd just started lecturing him as usual, if she'd called him her Last Straw and threatened to hit him upside the head to knock some sense into him.

He shrugged. "Yeah. I deleted them."

"Are you all right?"

"No."

"Sometimes you can be your own worst enemy."

"That's a fact."

"Not so much now as when you were younger, though." She almost smiled, but not quite. "I'll call that progress."

"You want to come in?"

She shook her head. "I'm just checkin' on you. I didn't check on you enough when you were little. Too late to make up for all that now, I guess."

"You're doing all right."

She put her hat back on. "You keeping fed?"

"Mostly."

"There's no law says you can't try again, and do a better job than you did before. Messing up is just practice for the next time, when you get it right." She turned and started down the steps.

"I love you, Mom," he said softly to her retreating back.

The words felt strange in his mouth. He knew he hadn't said them to her enough. And this time she probably hadn't even heard him.

Gathering the reins, she mounted. "Love you, too." She clicked her tongue and the horse turned and started back down the road. He stayed in front of the open door, watching her, until she disappeared from sight.

About then, he heard a whine. He glanced over and saw Buster sitting in the scrub grass beside the porch.

For the first time in days, Collin smiled. He slapped his thigh.

The dog barked, jumped to his feet and came running.

That morning, Willa got the call she'd been dreading.

The one from Dane. "Willa. My God. I just came from the airport, just heard how bad the flooding was in Rust Creek Falls. Are you all right?"

"I'm fine. Really." *Except for the little matter of my shattered heart.* "I lost my house and my car, though."

"Oh, sweetheart. I'm so sorry."

"Dane. Listen. I need to see you. I'm coming to Boulder, right away." Shelby could fill in for her. And Buster had taken off again, but it was no mystery where he'd gone. Maybe she would just call Collin and ask him if he could look after the dog until she got back.

"Coming to Boulder?" Dane boomed. "Not on your life."

"But, Dane, I—"

"I'm coming to you."

"No. Really, I'll find a flight and—"

He interrupted her. Again. "Sit tight, honey. I've got a plan."

Lord. She blew out a long breath. "Don't you always?"

He laughed, a bold, booming sound. "I'll be there before noon, you watch me."

"We'll have to arrange to meet somewhere. As I said, my house is a total loss." And she didn't want to meet him at the ranch. Too awkward, with her parents there....

"How about the middle of Main Street? You'll see me coming. I'll be the one in the CU helicopter."

"A helicopter?" How very, very Dane.

"Yeah. I'm getting the use of it courtesy of a generous alumnus. I'm coming, honey. I am as good as on my way...."

Collin, Gage and the rest of the committee were finishing up their endless meeting in one of the town hall conference rooms when they heard a helicopter overhead.

Nathan frowned. "We're not expecting a visit from the governor."

But then the helo loomed outside the window, coming in. Apparently, it was going to land in the street out in front. It was black and silver, with a giant gold CU painted on the belly.

Gage leveled that steady gaze of his on Collin. "Looks like Coach Everhart is dropping in to see how Willa's doing."

Collin reminded himself that he had to stay out of it. He needed to let Willa figure out what she wanted for herself.

But then, he couldn't do it. He could not just sit there.

He shot to his feet and headed for the door. Behind him, he thought he heard a low chuckle from Gage.

Willa was waiting on the sidewalk as the helicopter touched down. There were people all around her, folks she'd known all her life. They'd come running out of the library, the church and the town hall. Others had halted on the street. Everyone stared upward. It wasn't every day that a helicopter flew down and landed in the middle of town.

Leave it to Dane to make his arrival an event.

The chopper touched down. Dane jumped out before the blades stopped whirling, bending low to keep his handsome blond head out of danger. "Willa!" He ran toward her, rising to his full six feet six inches as he cleared the slowing blades.

Dread and misery and a healthy dose of embarrassment formed a leadlike ball in the pit of her stomach. She wrapped her arms around herself and waited grimly for him to reach her. Paige had given her the use of her house so she and Dane could be alone when she said the things she had to say.

"Willa!" The wonderful, rough deep voice came from behind her.

She stiffened, gasped, certain she couldn't have heard right. And then she whirled toward that voice, her heart in her throat.

Collin.

He was real. He was there. He reached out and put his warm, strong hands on her shoulders and she trembled with happiness just at his touch.

"Willa…" He stared at her with such frank longing in those beautiful dark eyes. She blinked at him, hardly daring to believe, and a ragged, hopeful sound escaped her. And he said, "Willa, damn it. I want you and I love you. Maybe I've always loved you, since way back when we were kids and I used spy on you playing with your Barbie dolls out in your dad's back pasture. Yeah, I know…" He tipped his head in the direction of the tall man behind her. "That other guy may be a better man. But there's no way he loves you like I do. And there's also no way I'm not trying again, no way I'm letting you go without pulling out all the stops." And then he dropped to his knees in front of her, the way he had last Friday. Only, somehow, nothing at all like last Friday. Because that had been all wrong.

And this, now, this moment? It was so very right.

He grabbed her hand and said fervently, "Stay, Willa. I'm asking. I'm begging. Stay here in Rust Creek Falls and be my wife."

People started clapping. Some shouted encouragements.

"You tell her, Collin!"

"Say it like you feel it!"

"Don't let her get away!"

There were whistles and catcalls.

Willa hardly heard them. For her, at that moment, there was only Collin, though he was looking kind of hazy through her happy tears. She confessed, "You really had me worried there."

"I know. I messed up. But I swear to you, right here on Main Street, in front of God, the library, that other guy—and way too many of our friends and neighbors—that when it comes to you and me, I won't mess up again."

She tugged on his hand. "Come here. Up here to me." And he swept to his feet once more. "I love you, Collin Traub," she told him. "I will always love you. And yes. Absolutely. You and me. From this day forward."

"Willa…" He grabbed her close and kissed her, a real kiss, deep and long and sweet. Everybody clapped all the harder.

When he lifted his head, she blinked up at him, dazed with joy. "Buster?"

"At Thelma's." He bent to kiss her again.

"Ahem," said the man behind her.

Willa pressed her hands to Collin's warm, hard chest. They shared a long, steady look, one of perfect understanding. And then, together, they turned to face Dane.

As it happened, Dane Everhart was not only a great guy, he was also a good sport. He said wryly, "Looks to me like I don't have a chance here."

Willa answered gently, "You're a good man, Dane. And I was wrong not to be straight with you from the first."

Dane gave a low chuckle. "Sometimes I'm a little pushy when it comes to going after what I want." He nodded at Collin. "You're a lucky man."

Collin pulled Willa closer to his side. "You're right. And I know it. I'm the luckiest man alive."

Dane held out his hand to Willa. She took it and they shook. "Be happy," he said.

"I will."

And then he turned and ran to the helicopter. The blades started whirling again.

Willa threw herself into Collin's waiting arms. They didn't see Dane go. They were too busy sharing another long, hot, perfect kiss, one that sealed their mutual commitment to their town, to each other and to the future they would build together with their own loving hands.

They were married three days later, on Saturday, July 27 with Pastor Alderson presiding.

It was a simple afternoon ceremony in the Community Church. The whole town attended and there was a big potluck afterward. Willa wore her mother's wedding dress. Paige stood up as her maid of honor and Collin asked his brother Sutter to come out from Seattle to be his best man.

If people whispered about how the maid of honor and the best man used to be together, they didn't whisper for long. Paige and Sutter conducted themselves with quiet dignity and the talk quickly died down.

It was one of those weddings where all the guests were smiling, a feel-good kind of day. Rust Creek Falls may have suffered through the flood of the century. But now the sun was shining and love ruled the day. Everyone could see that the bride and groom were meant for each other. Willa glowed with pure happiness.

And the former Traub bad boy had eyes only for his bride.

* * * * *

AN INCONVENIENT AFFAIR

CATHERINE MANN

To my stellar editor, Stacy Boyd! Thank you for the wonderful brainstorming session that gave birth to The Alpha Brotherhood. It's a joy working with you.

Prologue

North Carolina Military Prep
17 years ago

They'd shaved his head and sent him to a reform school.

Could life suck any worse? Probably. Since he was only fifteen, he had years under the system's thumb to find out.

Hanging around in the doorway to the barracks, Troy Donavan scanned the room for his rack. The dozen bunk beds were half-full of guys with heads shaved as buzz-short as his—another victory for dear old dad, getting rid of his son's long hair. God forbid anyone embarrass the almighty Dr. Donavan. Although, catching the illustrious doc's son breaking into the Department of Defense's computer system did take public embarrassment to a whole new level.

Now he'd been shuttled off to this "jail," politely disguised as a military boarding preparatory program in the hills of North Carolina, as per his plea agreement with the judge back home in Virginia. A judge his father had bought off. Troy clenched his hand around his duffel as he resisted the urge to put his fist through a window just to get some air.

Damn it, he was proud of what he'd done. He didn't want it swept under the rug, and he didn't want to be hidden like some bad secret. If the decision had been left up to him, he would have gone to juvie, or prison even. But for his mom, he'd taken the deal. He would finish high school in this uptight place, but if he kept his grades up and his nose clean until he turned twenty-one, he could have his life back.

He just had to survive living here without his head exploding.

Bunk by bunk, he walked to the last row where he found *Donavan, T. E.* printed on a label attached to the foot of the bed. He slung his duffel bag of boring crap onto the empty bottom bed.

A foot in a spit-shined shoe swung off the top bunk, lazing. "So you're the Robin Hood Hacker." A sarcastic voice drifted down. "Welcome to hell."

Great. "Thanks, and don't call me that."

He hated the whole Robin Hood Hacker headline that had blazed through the news when the story first broke. It made what he did sound like a kid's fairy tale. Which was probably more of his dad's influence, downplaying how his teenage son had exposed corrupt crap that the government had been covering up.

"Don't call you that…or what?" asked the smart-ass on the top bunk with a tag that read: *Hughes, C. T.* "You'll steal my identity and wreck my credit, computer boy?"

Troy rocked back on his heels to check the top bunk and make sure he didn't have the spawn of Satan sleeping above him. If so, the devil wore glasses and read the *Wall Street Journal.*

"Apparently you don't know who I am." With a snap of the page, Hughes ducked back behind his paper. "Loser."

Loser?

Screw that. Troy was a freakin' genius, straight As, already aced the ACT and SAT. Not that his parents seemed to notice or give a damn. His older brother was the real loser—smoking weed, failing out of his second college, knocking up cheerleaders. But their old man considered those forgivable offenses. Problems one's money could easily sweep under the rug.

Getting caught using illegal means to expose corrupt DOD contractors and a couple of congressmen was a little tougher to hide. Therefore, *Troy* had committed the unforgivable crime—making mommy and daddy look bad in front of their friends. Which had been his intent at the start, a lame attempt to get his parents' attention. But once he'd realized what he'd stumbled into—the graft, the bribes, the corruption—the puzzle solver inside him hadn't been able to stop until he'd uncovered it all.

No matter how you looked at it, he hadn't been some Robin Hood do-gooder, damn it.

He yanked open his duffel bag full of uniforms and underwear, trying to keep his eyes off the small mirror on his locker. His shaved head might reflect the light and blind him. And since rumor had it half the guys here had also struck deals, he needed to watch his back and recon until he figured out what each of them had done to land here.

If only he had his computer. He wasn't so good at face-to-face reads. The court-appointed shrink that evaluated him for trial said he had trouble connecting with people and lost himself in the cyberworld as a replacement. The Freud wannabe had been right.

And now he was stuck in a freaking barracks full of people. Definitely his idea of hell.

He hadn't even been able to access a computer to research the criminal losers stuck here with him. Thanks to the judge, he was limited to supervised use of the internet for schoolwork only—in spite of the fact he could handle the academics with his eyes closed.

Boring.

He dropped down to sit beside his bag. There had to be a way out of this place. The swinging foot slowed and a hand slid down.

Mr. Wall Street Journal held a portable video game.

It wasn't a computer, but thank God it was electronic. Something to calm the part of him that was totally freaking over being unplugged. Troy didn't even have to think twice. He palmed the game and kicked back in his bunk. Mr. Wall Street Hughes stayed quiet, no gloating. The guy might actually be legit. No agenda.

For now, Troy had found a way through the monotony. Not just because of the video game. But because there was someone else not all wrapped up tight in the rules.

Maybe his fellow juvie refugees might turn out to be not so bad after all. And if he was wrong—his thumbs flew across the keyboard, blasting through to the next level—at least he had a distraction from his first day in hell.

One

Present Day

Hillary Wright seriously needed a distraction during her flight from D.C. to Chicago. But not if it meant sitting behind a newlywed couple intent on joining the Mile High Club.

Her cheeks puffed with a big blast of recycled air as she dropped into her window seat and made fast work of hooking up the headset. She would have preferred to watch a movie or even sitcom reruns, but that would mean keeping her eyes open with the risk of seeing the duo in front of her making out under a blanket. She just wanted to get to Chicago, where she could finally put the worst mistake of her life behind her.

Hillary switched from the best of Kenny G before it put her to sleep, clicking through the stations until she settled on a Broadway channel piping in "The Sound of

Music." Passengers pushed down the aisle, a family with a baby and a toddler, then a handful of businessmen and women, all moving past her to the cheap seats where she usually sat. But not today. Today, her first-class seat had been purchased for her by the CIA. And how crazy was that? Until this month, her knowledge of the CIA only came from television shows. Now she had to help them in order to clear her name and stay out of jail.

A moan drifted from the brand-new Mrs. Somebody in front of her.

Oh God, Hillary sagged back into her seat, covering her eyes with her arm. She was so nervous she couldn't even enjoy her first visit to Chicago. She'd dreamed about getting out of her small Vermont hometown. Her job as an event planner in D.C. had seemed like a godsend at first. She met the exciting people she would have only read about in the news otherwise—politicians, movie stars, even royalty.

She'd been starstruck by her wealthy boyfriend's lifestyle. Stupidly so. Until she allowed herself to be blinded to Barry's real intentions in managing philanthropic donations, his lack of a moral compass.

Now she had to dig herself out from under the mess she'd made of her life by trusting the wrong guy, by believing his do-gooder act of tricking rich associates into donating large sums of money to bogus charities, then funneling the money overseas into a Swiss bank account. She'd proven herself to be every bit the gullible, small-town girl she'd wanted to leave behind.

As of today, her blinders were off.

A flash of skin and pink bra showed between the seats.

She squeezed her eyes shut and lost herself in the do-re-mi refrain even as people bumped past. *Focus. Will away the nerves. Get through the weekend.*

She would identify her scumbag ex-boyfriend's crooked banking acquaintance at the Chicago shindig. Give her official statement to Interpol so they could stop the international money-laundering scheme. Then she could have her life back and save her job.

Once she was back in her boss's good graces, she would again be throwing the kinds of parties she'd wanted to oversee when she'd first become an event planner. Her career would skyrocket with her parties featured in the social section of all major newspapers. Her loser ex would read about her in tabloid magazines in prison and realize how she'd moved on, baby. Maybe she would even appear in some of those photos looking so damn hot Barry would suffer in his celibate cell.

The jackass.

She pinched the bridge of her nose against the welling of tears.

A tap on her shoulder forced her out of her silly self-pity. She tugged off an earbud and looked over at a...suit. A dark blue suit, with a Hugo Boss tie and a vintage tie clip.

"Excuse me, ma'am. You're in my seat."

A low voice, nice, and not cranky-sounding like some travelers could be. His face was shadowed, the sunlight streaking through the small window behind him. She could just make out his dark brown hair, which was long enough to brush his ears and the top of his collar. From the Patek Philippe watch to his edgy Caraceni suit—all name brands she wouldn't have heard of, much less recognized, before her work with high-end D.C. clients.

And she *was* in his seat.

Wincing, she pretended to look at her ticket even though she already knew what it read. God, she hated the aisle and she'd prayed she would luck out and have an empty next to her. "I'm sorry. You're right."

"You know what?" He rested a hand on the back of the empty seat. "If you prefer the window, that's cool by me. I'll sit here instead."

"I don't want to take advantage." Take advantage? The cheesy double entendre made her wince. A moan from the lovebirds a row ahead only made it worse.

"No worries." He stowed his briefcase in the overhead before sidling in to sit down.

Then he turned to her, the light above bringing him fully into focus— And holy cows on her hometown Vermont farm, he was *hot*. Angular. But with long lashes that kept drawing her gaze back to his green eyes. He was probably in his early thirties, gauging from the creases when he smiled with the open kind of grin that made him more approachable.

She tilted her head to the side, studying him more closely. He looked familiar, but she couldn't quite place him.... She shook off the feeling. She'd met so many people at the parties she'd planned in D.C. They could have crossed paths at any number of places. Although, she must have seen him from a distance, because if they'd met up close, she definitely wouldn't have forgotten him.

His seat belt clicked as the plane began taxiing. "You don't like flying."

"Why do you say that?"

"You want the window seat, but have the shade closed. You've already plugged into the radio. And you've got the armrest in a death grip."

Handsome and observant. Hmm…

Better to claim fear of flying than to go into the whole embarrassing mess she'd made of her life. "Busted. You caught me." She nodded toward the row in front of her just as one of the seats reclined providing too clear a view of a man's hand sliding into the woman's waistband. "And the lovebirds up there aren't making things any more comfortable."

His smile faded into a scowl. "I'll call for the flight attendant."

He reached for the button overhead. She touched his wrist. Static snapped. At least she hoped it was just static and not a spark of attraction.

Clearing her throat, she folded her arms over her chest, tucking her hands away. "No need. The flight attendant's in the middle of her in-flight brief—" she lowered her voice "—and giving us the death glare for talking."

He leaned toward her conspiratorially. "Or I can kick the back of their seat until they realize they're not invisible—and that they're being damned inconsiderate."

Except now that he was so close, she didn't notice them. Her gaze locked on the glinting green eyes staring at her with undisguised, unrepentant interest.

A salve to her ego. And an excellent distraction. "I guess we can live and let live."

"We can."

"Although, honestly, it doesn't seem fair the flight attendant isn't giving the evil eye to the handsy twosome."

"Maybe they're celebrating their anniversary."

She snorted.

"Cynic?"

"And you're trying to tell me you're a true believer in flowery romance?" She took in his expensive suit, his dimpled smile and his easy charm. "No offense, truly, but you seem more like a player to me."

A second after the words left her mouth, she worried she might have been rude.

He just laughed softly and flattened a hand to his chest.

"You think the worst of me. I'm hurt to the core," he said with overplayed drama.

Her snort turned into a laugh. Shaking her head, she kept on laughing, tension uncurling inside. Her laughter faded as she felt the weight of his gaze on her.

He pointed to the window. "We're airborne now. You can open the shade and relax."

Relax? His words confused her for a second and then she remembered her excuse for nerves. And then remembered the real reason for her nerves. Her ex-boyfriend. Barry the Bastard Bum. Who she was hoping to help put in prison once she identified his accomplice in Chicago—if she didn't get offed by the bad guy first.

She thumbed her silver seat belt buckle. "Thank you for the help…"

"Troy." He extended his hand. "My name is Troy, from Virginia."

"I'm Hillary, from D.C." Prepping herself for the static this time, she wrapped her fingers around his, shaking once. And, yep. *Snap. Snap.* Heat tingled up her arm in spite of all those good intentions to keep all guys at bay. But then what was wrong with simply being attracted to another person?

Her ex had taken so much from her, and yes, turned a farm-fresh girl like her into a cynic, making her doubt everyone around her. Until she now questioned the motives of a guy who just wanted to indulge in a little harmless flirtation on a plane.

Damn it, there was nothing bad about chatting with this guy during the flight. He had helped her through her nerves about identifying Barry's accomplice at the fundraiser this weekend. A very slippery accomplice who had a way of avoiding cameras. Very few people had ever seen him. She'd only seen him twice, once by showing up at

Barry's condo unannounced and another time at Barry's office. Would the man remember her? Her nerves doubled.

She desperately needed to take full advantage of the distraction this man beside her offered. Talking to Troy beat the hell out of getting sloshed off the drink cart, especially since she didn't even drink.

"So, Troy, what's taking you to Chicago?"

Troy had recognized Hillary Wright the minute he'd stepped on the plane. She looked just like her Interpol file photo, right down to the freckles on her nose and the natural sun streaks through her red hair.

The photo hadn't, however, shown anything below the neck—a regrettable oversight because she was…hot. Leggy with curves and an unadorned innocence that normally wasn't his type. But then when had he ever given a crap about walking the expected path?

That's why he'd shown up here, on her flight, rather than following the plan laid out by the CIA operatives, who were working in conjunction with the American branch of Interpol. To see what she was like in an unguarded moment.

Lucky for him that window seat was empty so he'd been able to wrangle his way in beside her. It had been too easy, and she was totally unsuspecting. She might as well have "fresh off the farm" tattooed across her freckled nose.

A sexy uptipped nose he wouldn't mind kissing as he worked his way around to her ear. He'd expected pretty from her picture, but he hadn't been prepared for the undefinable energy that radiated off her. It was as damn near tangible as her innocence.

This plane on the way to Chicago was the last place she should be. More so, that viper's nest gala this weekend was *absolutely* the last place she should be.

Damn, damn, damn the "powers that be" for making her a part of some crazy power play. He could have accomplished the identification in Chicago without her, but they'd insisted on having her backup confirmation. It was obvious to him now that she was too naive to brush elbows with the sharks at that gala—a bunch of crooks using a fundraiser to cover up their international money laundering.

"Troy? Hello?" Hillary waved her hand in front of his face, her nails chewed to the quick. "What takes you to Chicago?"

"Business trip." Truth. "I'm in computers." More truth. Enough for now. She would see him again soon enough after they landed and when she learned who he really was... Well, she would likely change, close up or suck up. People judged him based on either his past or his money. "What takes *you* to Chicago?" he asked, even though he already knew.

"A fundraiser gala. I'm an event planner and, uhm, my boss is sending me to check out a chef at this weekend retreat."

She was a really crummy liar. Even if he didn't already know her real reason for going to Chicago, he would have sensed something was off in her story.

"A chef... In Chicago... And you work in D.C. You work for lobbyists?"

"I specialize in fundraisers for charities, not campaigns. I didn't plan the one in Chicago. I'm just, uh, scoping out competition. It's a pretty big deal, kicking off Friday night, running all the way to Sunday afternoon with parties and—" She paused self-consciously. "I'm babbling. You don't need the agenda."

"You specialize in polishing the halos of the rich and famous." He smiled on the outside.

Her lips pursed tightly. "Think what you want. I don't need your approval."

A sentiment he applauded. So why was he yanking her chain? Because she looked so damn pretty with righteous indignation sparking from her eyes.

That kind of "in your face" mentality was rare. But it also could land a person in trouble.

He knew too well. It had taken all his self-control to buckle down and meet the judge's requirements when he'd been sentenced at fifteen. Although, he'd found more than he expected at the military school. He'd found friends and a new code to live by. He'd learned how to play by the rules. He'd slowly gotten back computer access and started a video games company that had him rolling in more money than his pedigreed, doctor old man had ever brought home—three times over.

But the access had come with a price. His every move had been monitored by the FBI. They seemed to sense that the taste of megapower he'd felt delving into the DOD would be addictive. Irresistibly so. At twenty-one, he'd been approached with an enticing offer. If he ever wanted a chance at that high again, he would need to loan his "skills" to the American branch of Interpol on occasion.

He'd chafed at the idea at twenty-one. By thirty-two, he'd come to begrudgingly accept that he had to play by a few of their rules, and he'd even found a rush in being a sort of "on call" guy to assist in major international sting operations. He was committed to the job, as he'd proven every time they'd tapped him for a new assignment.

Over time, they also began utilizing him for more than computer help. His wealth gave him access to high-power circles. When Interpol needed a contact on the inside quickly, they used him—and other freelance agents like him. For the most part, he still provided behind-the-scenes computer advice. He was only called upon for something out in the open like this about once a year, so as not to overuse his cover.

Some of that caution would have been nice now, rather than recklessly including Hillary Wright in this joint operation being run by the CIA and Interpol. She wouldn't be able to carry off the charade this weekend. She couldn't blend in.

He'd known it the second he read her profile, even if they'd missed it. God only knew why they called him a genius and then refused to listen to him. So he'd arranged to meet her on this flight to confirm his suspicions. He was never wrong. He would stick by her side all weekend and make sure she didn't blow the whole operation.

Granted, that wouldn't be a hardship, sticking near her for the weekend.

For the first time in years he wasn't bored. Something about this woman intrigued him, and there weren't many puzzles in life for him. So he would stay right here for the rest of the flight and play this through. When she found out his full name—his public, infamous identity—she would pull away. She would likely never know his real reason for being part of this sting, and someone like Hillary Wright wouldn't go for a guy with the reputation of Troy Donavan, especially so soon after getting her fingers burned in the relationship department.

Not that he would let that affect his decision to stick by her. She needed him to get through this weekend, whether she knew it or not.

A flight attendant ducked to ask, "Could I get either of you a complimentary beverage? Wine? A mixed drink?"

Hillary's smile froze, the lightheartedness fading from

her face with the one simple request. The mention of alcohol stirred painful memories. "No, thank you.

Troy shook his head. "I'm good. Thanks." He turned back to Hillary. "Are you sure you don't want a glass of wine or something? A lot of folks drink to get over the fear."

She inched away from the wall and sat upright self-consciously. "I don't drink."

"Ever?"

She refused to risk ending up like her mother, in and out of alcohol rehabs every other year while her father continued to hold out hope that this time, the program would stick. It never did.

There was nothing for her at home. D.C. was her chance at a real life. She couldn't let anything risk ruining this opportunity. Not a drink. Not some charming guy, either.

"Never," she answered. "I never drink."

"There's a story there." He toyed with his platinum cuff links.

"There is." And honest to God, the bay rum scent of him was intoxicating enough.

"But you're not sharing."

"Not with a total stranger." She was an expert at keeping family secrets, of sweeping up the mess so they would look normal to the outside world. Planning high-profile galas for the D.C. elite was a piece of cake after keeping up appearances as a teenager.

She might look like a naive farm girl, but life had already done its fair share to leave her jaded. Which might be why she found herself questioning the ease of her past hour with Troy.

Nothing about him was what she'd expected once he'd first flashed that bad-boy grin in her direction. They'd spent the entire flight just...talking. They'd discussed favorite artists and foods. Found they both liked jazz music and hokey horror movies. He was surprisingly well-read, could quote Shakespeare and had a sharp sense of humor. There was interest in his eyes, but his words stayed light all the way to the start of the plane's descent.

His eyes narrowed at her silence. "Is something wrong?"

"You're not hitting on me," she blurted out.

He blinked in surprise just once before that wicked slow smile spread across his face. "Do you want me to?"

"Actually, I'm having fun just like this."

She sat back and waited for him to stop grinning when he realized she wasn't coming on to him. Was she? She never went for this kind of guy, hair too long and a couple of tiny scars on his face like he was always getting into some kind of trouble. A line through one eyebrow. Another on his chin. And yet another on his forehead that played peekaboo when his hair shifted.

But then Barry had been Mr. Buttoned-Up, clean-cut and respectful. Except it had all been a cover for a deceitful nature.

Troy stared deeper into her eyes. "You don't get to have fun often, do you?"

Who had time for fun? She'd worked hard these past three years building a new life for herself, far away from a gossipy small town that knew her as the daughter of a drunk mother. Barry had tarnished her reputation with his shady dealings—stealing scholarship money for God's sake. And unless she proved otherwise, people would always think she was involved, as well. They wouldn't trust her.

Her boss wouldn't trust her.

She picked at the hem of her skirt. "Why would you say I'm a wet blanket?"

"Not a wet blanket. Just a workaholic. The portfolio under your seat is stuffed with official-looking papers, rather than a book or magazine. The chewed-down nails on your otherwise beautiful hands—sure shout stress."

She'd tried balancing her career and a relationship. That hadn't gone very well for her. Thank you very much, Barry, for being a white-collar crook—and not even all that good of an embezzler, given how easily he'd been caught. She'd been so busy with her job that she'd completely missed the signs that he'd been using her to get close to her clients—and sucker them in.

"Troy, I'm simply devoted to my career." Which would be wrecked if she didn't make sure everyone knew she was a hundred percent against what Barry had done. Her boss would fire her and no one else would hire her since the clients would never trust her. "Aren't you?"

What exactly did he do in computers? She was just beginning to realize that they'd talked all about her and not so much about him and the flight was already almost over.

"Work rocks—as do vacations. So if you were taking this plane trip for pleasure, no work worries and you could pick up any connecting flight when we touch down—where would you go?"

"Overseas." She answered fast before realizing that again, he'd turned the conversation away from himself.

"That's a broad choice," he said as the ground grew larger and larger, downtown Chicago coming into focus.

"I would close my eyes and pick, some place far away." Far, far away from the Windy City gala.

"Ah, the old escape idea. I get that, totally. When I was in boarding school, I made plans for places to live and visit, places without fences."

Boarding school? Interesting and so far removed from her childhood riding the ancient bus with cracked leather seats each morning with all the friends from her neighborhood.

She settled deeper into her seat. "Isn't that the whole point of a vacation? To do something that is totally the opposite of your daily routine. Like open spaces being different from the walls of your old boarding school."

"You have a point." His smile went tight for a flash before his face cleared. "Where are you from originally—so I can get a sense of your daily routine when I'm choosing our great escape?"

Our? "Theoretically of course."

"Theoretically? Nu-uh. You're wrecking the fantasy."

"Right, sorry about that." His magnetism had a way of drawing her into this fantasy. No harm in that. "I'm from Vermont, a tiny town nobody's heard of. Coming to D.C. was a big enough change for me—and now I'm going to Chicago."

"But you don't look happy about it."

She forced herself not to flinch. He was too perceptive. Time to put some distance between them, let him show himself to be a jerk so she could move on. "I'm scared of flying, remember? And this is where you're supposed to ask me for my phone number."

"Would you give it to me if I did?"

"No," she said, almost believing what she was saying. "I'm not in a good place to date anyone right now. So you can stop trying to charm me."

"Can't a guy be nice without wanting something other than engaging conversation?"

She couldn't help but smile. "Did you really just say that?"

He slumped back in his seat, respect glinting in his eyes. "Okay, you're right. I would like to ask for your phone number—because I am single, in case you were wondering—but since you've made it clear you're not open to my advances, I'll satisfy my broken heart and soothe my wounded ego with the pleasure of your company for a little while longer."

God, he was good. Funny and charming, so confident he didn't think twice about making a joke at his own expense. "Do you practice lines like that or are you just really good at improvisation?"

"You're a smart woman. I'm confident you'll figure it out."

She liked him. Damn it. "You're funny."

"And you are enchanting. It was my pleasure to sit next to you on the flight."

They'd landed? She looked around as if waking up from a nap to find more time had passed than she realized. Passengers were sliding from their seats. The aircraft had stopped.

Troy stood, hauling her simple black roll bag from the overhead. "Yours?"

"How did you know?"

He tapped the little dairy cow name tag attached to the handle. "Vermont. Highest cows to people ratio in the country."

"Right you are." She stood, stopping beside him. Close beside him. All the other passengers crowded the aisle until her breasts brushed his chest.

His rock-hard chest. That suit covered one hundred percent honed man, whipcord lean. The bay rum scent of him wrapping around her completely now, rather than just teasing—tempting—her senses.

But still, he didn't touch her or hit on her or act in the least bit skeezy. "Have a great visit in the Windy City."

She chewed her bottom lip, resisting the overwhelming urge to tug his silk tie.

The flight attendant spoke over the loudspeaker. "If you could please return to your seats. We have a slight delay before we can disembark at the gate."

Hillary pulled away quickly, ducking into her seat so fast she almost hit her head. Troy reclaimed his seat slowly while the flight attendant opened the hatch. The yawning opening revealed the long metal stairs that had been rolled up outside. Confused, Hillary yanked up her window shade. They'd stopped just shy of the terminal. A large black SUV with some kind of official insignia on the door waited a few feet away. Two men wearing black suits and sunglasses jogged up the stairs and entered the plane.

The first one nodded to the flight attendant. "Thank you, ma'am. We'll be quick with our business."

The identical duo angled sideways.

Her stomach tumbled over itself. Was there a problem? In spite of what she'd told Troy, she hadn't been freaked out about flying, but now she felt that lie come back to bite her as fears fluttered inside her. How long before she knew what was wr—

Not long at all, apparently.

The dark-suited men stopped beside her row. "Troy Donavan?"

Troy Donavan?

Her stomach lurched faster than a major turbulence plunge. Oh God, she recognized that name. She waited for him to deny it...even though she already knew he wouldn't.

"Yes, that's me. Is there a problem, gentlemen?"

Troy Donavan.

He'd confirmed it. He was far from a nice guy, far from some computer geek just passing time on a commuter flight. His reputation for partying hard and living on the edge made it into the social pages on a regular basis.

"Mr. Donavan, would you step out of your seat, please?"

Troy shot an apologetic look her way before he angled out to stand in front of the two men. "We could have met up at the gate like regular folks."

The older man, the guy who seemed in charge, shook his head. "It's better this way. We don't want to keep Colonel Salvatore waiting."

"Of course. Can't inconvenience the colonel." Muscles bunched in Troy's arms, his hands fisting at his sides.

What the hell was going on?

The "men in black" retrieved Troy's Italian leather briefcase and placed a streamlined linen fedora on his head, the same look that had been featured in countless articles. If she'd seen him in his signature hat, she would have recognized him in a heartbeat.

He was infamous in D.C. for having hacked the Department of Defense's computer system seventeen years ago. She'd been all of ten at the time but he'd become an icon. From then on, any computer hacking was called "pulling a Donavan." He'd made it into pop culture lexicons. He'd become a folk legend for the way he'd leaked information that exposed graft and weaknesses within the system. Some argued he'd merely stepped in where authorities and politicians should have. But there was no denying he'd broken major laws. If he'd been an adult, he would have spent his life in jail.

After a slap-on-the-wrist sentence in some military school, he'd been free to make billions and live out his life in a totally decadent swirl of travel and conspicuous consumption. And she'd fallen for his lying charm. She'd even liked him. She hadn't learned a damn thing from Barry.

She bit her lip against the disappointment in herself. She was here to put the past behind her—not complicate her future. She pressed her back against the body of the plane, unable to get far enough away from the man who'd charmed the good sense right out of her.

Troy reached for his briefcase, but the younger man took a step back.

The older of the two men held out...*handcuffs*.

Cocking an eyebrow, Troy said, "Are these really needed?"

"I'm afraid they are." *Click. Click.* "Troy Donavan, you're under arrest."

Two

"Were the handcuffs necessary?" Holding up his shackled hands, Troy sprawled in the backseat of the armored SUV as they powered away from the airport. The duo that had arrested him sat in the front. His mentor and former military school headmaster—Colonel John Salvatore—sat beside him with a smirk on his face.

As always, he wore a gray suit and red tie, no variation, same thing every day as if wearing a uniform even though he'd long ago left the army.

"Yes, Troy, actually they are required, as per the demands of the grand dame throwing this gala. She's determined to have a bachelor auction like one she read about in a romance novel and she thought, given your checkered past, the handcuffs would generate buzz. And honest to God, the photos in the paper will only help your image, and therefore our purposes, as well."

It was always about their purposes. Their agreement.

He'd struck a deal with Colonel Salvatore at twenty-one years old, once his official sentence was complete. Salvatore had been the headmaster of that military reform school—and more. Apparently he helped recruit freelancers for Interpol who could assist with difficult assignments—such as using Troy's computer skills and later utilizing his access to high-power circles. Other graduates of the military school had been recruited, as well, people who could use their overprivileged existence to quickly move in high-profile circles. For these freelancers, no setup was needed for a cover story, a huge time and money saver for the government.

A person might be called on once. Or once a year. Maybe more. Salvatore offered things no one else in Troy's life had ever given him. A real chance to atone.

He may not have felt guilty at fifteen, but over time he'd come to realize the repercussions of what he'd done were far-reaching. His big DOD computer exposé as a teen had inadvertently exposed two undercover operatives. And even though they hadn't died, their careers had been cut short, their usefulness in the field ruined.

He should have taken his information to the authorities rather than giving it to the press. He'd been full of ego and the need to piss off his father. He knew better now, and had the opportunity to make up for what he'd cost the government and those two agents.

And yeah, he still enjoyed the rush of flying close to the flame while doing it.

Troy worked his hands inside the cuffs. "You could have waited. There was no need to freak out Hillary Wright. I would think you'd want her calm."

Her horrified, disillusioned blue eyes were burned in his memory as deeply as the sound of her laugh and the genuine warmth of her smile.

Sighing, Salvatore swiped a hand over his closely shorn head. "If you'd been on the private jet like you were supposed to be none of this would have happened. Stop caring what Hillary Wright thinks of you. She'll be out of your life by Monday. Your time will be your own soon enough and, with luck, I won't need to call on you again for a long while."

The years stretched ahead in monotony. His company all but ran itself now. The past eleven months since he'd been called upon had been boring as hell.

His mind zipped back to Hillary and how he would see her for the rest of the weekend—how she would see him. "A bachelor auction, huh? That grand dame can't expect me to strut down some catwalk."

"When did *you* start worrying about appearances?"

"When did *you* start using innocents like Hillary?" he snapped back, unsettled by the protective surge pumping through him. At least he would have a chance to explain to her some of what had happened on the plane. He could claim the event swore him to secrecy about the handcuffing gig, even if he wasn't authorized to tell her about his role with Interpol. "I thought your gig was to, uh, collaborate with the fallen."

"My 'gig' is to mentor people with potential. Always has been."

"Mentor. Jailer."

Salvatore smirked. "Someone's grouchy."

Troy rattled his cuffs as they drove deeper into the skyscraper-filled city. "Could you just take the cuffs off?"

He hated being confined and Salvatore knew that, damn it. Although looking at the cuffs now, other uses scrolled through his head, sexy fantasies of using them with Hillary. Maybe he would lock his wrist to hers, and take it from there.

"The mistress of ceremonies has the key."

"You're joking." He had to be. "That's hours away."

"When have I ever had a sense of humor?"

"Valid point." Troy's hands fell in his lap. He might as well settle in for the scenic ride through downtown Chicago. He would be free, eventually, and then he would check on Hillary. For now, he was stuck with Salvatore.

The colonel was one eccentric dude.

Sure, Salvatore was the Interpol handler for the group of freelancers whose lifestyles gave them a speedy entrée into a high-profile circle when fast action was needed. But it must blow to be an overgrown babysitter for Troy at some shindig hosted by a local grand dame at a downtown hotel. Tonight's gala kicked off a whole weekend of partying for the rich and famous, under the pretense of charity work.

And apparently Salvatore wasn't just here for Troy, but helping the CIA by being here for Hillary, too.

"Colonel, I am curious, though, why do we need Hillary for this? How much does she know?"

The more Troy learned about her, the more of an edge he would have over her the next time he saw her.

"She's here to identify contacts of her former boyfriend. And because we and the CIA need to be sure she's truly as innocent as she seems."

Was his protectiveness misplaced? Could he have so misread her? Either way, it didn't dim how damn badly he wanted to peel her power suit off with his teeth. "This is really just to test her?"

The colonel waved aside Troy's indignation. "Speaking of Hillary Wright. Your little stunt—switching from the private jet to her flight? Not cool. I had to cancel lunch with an ambassador to get here in time."

"You're breaking my heart."

Sighing, Salvatore shook his head. "How the hell did you even get on that plane?"

"Really?" Troy cocked an eyebrow. "Do you even have to ask *me*, the guy who broke through the school's supposedly impenetrable computer firewalls in order to hack your bank account and send flowers to the Latin teacher on your behalf?"

A laugh rumbled in the old guy's chest. "As I recall, that trick didn't go so well for you since she and I were quietly seeing each other and I'd already sent her flowers. She figured out fast who pulled that off."

"But the flowers I chose were better—Casablanca lilies, if I recall."

"And I learned from that. Same way you should accept you can learn from others once in a while." Salvatore and the teacher had eventually married—and divorced. The man's laughter faded into a scowl. "The internet is not your personal plaything."

Troy held up his cuffed wrists. "These give me hives *and* flashbacks."

Salvatore's eyes narrowed. "I don't know why I put up with you."

"Because I'll get the job done. I always do. I'll find our mystery guy either in person or through the hotel's security system. I will make sure this time that he doesn't get away with hiding from the cameras. We will track his accounts and nail the bastard." He'd only caught a glimpse of the guy once, a month ago shortly before they'd taken down Barry Curtis. If only they'd caught both men then... "But now, as far as I'm concerned, my job also includes making sure Hillary Wright stays safe in that pool of piranhas posing as scions of society."

"As long as you don't make a spectacle of yourself or her, I can live with that. Keep it low-key for once."

"Okay, deal," he agreed, perhaps a bit too quickly because Salvatore's eyes narrowed suspiciously. Time for a diversion. "One last thing, though."

"You're pushy today."

"Look in my briefcase. I brought John Junior—" Salvatore's only kid "—a copy of Alpha Realms IV. He'll have a month's head start mastering it before it hits the market."

"Bribery's a crime." But Salvatore still reached for the Italian leather case. "What's the favor?"

"It's just a gift for your son from my software company. No strings attached."

"What's the favor?" he repeated.

"I don't agree with your pulling Hillary Wright into this. She's too naive and uninformed. After the party tonight, I want her sent home to D.C. Scrap keeping her around for the weekend."

Troy would figure out a way to contact her in D.C., without all the hidden agenda crap. But make no mistake, he would see her again.

"She's not so innocent if she was involved with Barry Curtis." The colonel slid the video game into his black briefcase. "She'll prove herself this weekend—or not."

"Guilty of bad judgment, that's all." Troy was sure of that. What he didn't know—something that bothered him even more—was if Hillary still had feelings for the creep.

God, why did he feel such a connection to a woman he'd only just met? Maybe because she possessed an innocence he'd never had.

"Are you so sure about her?" The leather seats creaked as Salvatore shifted back into place.

Troy was certain he couldn't let her go into a ballroom full of crooks alone. "I'm sticking with her tonight and putting her on a plane in the morning."

Salvatore patted his briefcase. "You should really keep

me happy if you want me to put in a good word with your brother's parole officer."

Troy looked up sharply. Pulling in his brother was dirty pool, even for Salvatore.

"I'm not an enabler." His brother, Devon, had more than a drug problem. He'd blown through his trust fund and had been sent to jail for dealing to feed his cocaine addiction. Troy forced himself to say blandly, "Do whatever you want with him."

"Tough love or sibling rivalry?"

Anger pulsed—at Salvatore for jabbing at old wounds. "You'd better tell the driver to move this along so I can get out of these handcuffs before I have to take a leak. Otherwise you'll have to help."

"Bathroom humor is beneath you, Donavan."

"I wasn't joking." He pinned Salvatore with an impassive look as the SUV stopped in front of the towering hotel.

Salvatore reached for the door handle as the driver opened Troy's side. "Time to rock and roll."

Standing in the elevator in the Chicago hotel, Hillary smoothed her sweaty palms down the length of her simple black dress. Strapless and floor length, it was her favorite. She'd brought it, along with her good luck charm clipped to her clutch purse, to bolster her and steady her nerves. It wasn't working. Her hands went nervously to her hair, which was straight with a simple crystal clasp sweeping back one side.

She'd been nervous enough about this weekend from the moment she'd been asked to come to Chicago, but at least she'd had a plan. She'd thought she had her head on straight—and then she'd fallen right into flirting with a notorious guy seconds away from handcuffs. The experience had thrown her. Right now, she wasn't sure of much of anything.

There'd been a time, as a little girl, when she'd dreamed of staying in a five-star hotel like this one, in a big city, with all the glitz included. As a kid, after she'd finished her chores on the dairy farm, she'd hidden in her room, away from her drunken mother. For hours and hours, Hillary had played on the internet, escaping into another world. Researching other places and other ways to live. Clean places. Pretty, even.

With tables full of food.

She'd spent a lot of time thinking about the cuisine, learning recipes, planning meals and parties to fill her solitary world. Even if only in her imagination.

Once she'd turned eighteen, she scrounged together enough college loans to get a degree in hospitality and economics. Three years ago, she'd landed with a major D.C. corporation that contracted out events planners. Someday, she hoped to start her own company. Be in charge of her own business. She refused to live her life as the scared little country girl she'd once been, hiding in her room, too afraid to slip out and grab a mushy apple from behind mom's beer.

The elevator doors slid open and she smiled her thanks to the attendant before stepping out into the wide hall, sconces lighting the way into the glittering ballroom. Nerves ate at her stomach like battery acid. She just had to get through this weekend. She'd make the proper identifications, which would help confirm her innocence. Or at least get her off the hook, even if they still didn't believe she'd known nothing about what Barry had in mind for those supposed college scholarships.

Forging ahead, she passed her invitation to the tuxedoed man protecting the elite fundraising bash from party crashers. Media cameras flashed. Even with spots in front of her eyes, she already recognized at least two movie stars, an opera singer and three politicians. This party rivaled anything she'd seen or planned—and her standards were top-notch. The ballroom glittered with refracted lights from the crystal chandeliers. Columns and crown molding were gilded; plush carpets held red-and-brass swirls.

A harpist and a violinist played—for now—but from the looks of the instruments set up throughout the room, the music would obviously be staggered. The stage was set for a string quartet. A grand piano filled a corner, with a 1940s-era mic in place alongside.

The dance—at two thousand dollars a head—was slated to fund scholarships. But then that was the root of Barry's scam—collecting money for scholarships, most of which were never awarded, then funneling the cash out of the country into a Swiss bank account.

Bile rose in her throat. She thumbed the charm clipped to her bag, rubbing the tiny silver cow pin like a talisman, a reminder of where she'd come from and all she intended to accomplish.

Men wore tuxedos or military uniforms, the women were in long dresses and dripping jewels that would have funded endless numbers of scholarships. Well, everyone wore formal attire except for the gentleman in a gray suit with a red tie. Her contact.

Colonel Salvatore.

She'd been introduced to him by her lawyer. Apparently, the colonel worked for international authorities. The CIA had promised he would ensure her safety and oversee her cooperation while she was in Chicago. Only one more weekend and she could put this all behind her.

The colonel stepped up beside her and offered his arm.

"Miss Wright, you're here early. I would have escorted you down if I'd known you were ready."

"I couldn't wait any longer to get this evening under way." She tucked her hand into the crook of his arm. "I hope you understand."

"Of course." He started into the ballroom, moving toward the seating section with a runway thrust into the middle.

She recalled there being some mention of an auction of items donated by the elite from around the globe.

More money laundering? Couldn't anyone or anything be genuine anymore? Was everything tainted with greed and agendas?

Salvatore gestured her toward a seat reserved with his name and "guest". They took their places five rows back, not conspicuously in the front. She was also in the perfect spot to see both of the screens panning shots of the guests while a matriarch of Chicago high society took the stage to emcee the auction. Of course Colonel Salvatore had planned everything.

Hillary forced herself to focus on studying each face on the screen, on searching for the two familiar individuals who Barry had claimed were his "silent partners"—not that Barry was talking to authorities now that he'd lawyered up.

But then when had she ever been able to count on a man? Her father certainly hadn't done anything to stop her mother from drinking or to protect Hillary and her sister. He'd buried himself in working in the fields, and as long as she worked alongside him, she was safe.

The hard work of her childhood had taught her to work hard as an adult. Life was just hard. Plain and simple. She was still trying to keep herself safe so her efforts could finally pay off.

As bid after bid went by for posh vacations, jewelry and even private concerts, her thoughts raced back to Troy Donavan and that hour of lighthearted banter on the plane. For a short snap, life had felt fun and uncomplicated.

Yet, it had all been a lie. She couldn't have bantered with a more complicated person. Troy was a perfect example of the cold, hard truth. Everyone wanted something from someone else. People didn't do things exclusively out of the goodness of their hearts. There was always a pay-off of some sort expected. The sooner she accepted that and quit believing otherwise, the happier she would be.

Madame Emcee moved closer to the microphone, her gold taffeta dress smooshed against the podium. "And now, before we move on to dancing the night away, we have one final auction left for the evening, one not on your programs." She swept a bejeweled hand toward the large flat screens. "If you'll turn your attention to our video feed, you'll see media footage you may have caught earlier."

Troy Donavan's face filled the screen.

Oh. God.

Hillary clenched her hands around her handbag, the silver charm cutting into her palm. She glanced quickly at the colonel to see if he'd noticed her panic. But her escort simply sat with his arms folded, watching along with everyone else.

In full color, high-definition, the whole runway scenario played out again in front of her. Troy, walking off the plane in handcuffs, wearing that quirky, undeniably sexy hat. Troy, escorted into some official-looking SUV. Hillary had been so rushed getting checked in and ready for the kickoff gala, she hadn't even turned on the television in her room.

Madame Emcee continued, "But what does that have to do with us tonight? Prepare yourself."

The lights shut off. The ballroom went pitch-black. Gasps rippled. A woman squeaked.

After a squeal of microphone feedback, the emcee continued, "For our final bid of the night, we have for you..."

A spotlight illuminated a circle on stage.

Troy Donavan stood in the middle, wearing a tuxedo now instead of his suit, but still cuffed with his hands in front of him. A white silk scarf gave him the same quirky air he'd had on the plane. Her eyes took in the whole man. How could she not? He'd been hot in a suit—in a tuxedo, he stole the air from the room.

"Yes," Madame continued, her fat diamond earrings sparkling disco ball refractions all around her face. "Troy Donavan has offered himself as a date for the weekend. But first, someone must 'bid' him out of our custody in an auction. He's been a bad, bad boy, ladies. You'll want to handle with caution and by no means, let this computer whiz get his hands on your software."

Laughter echoed up into the rafters from everyone—except Hillary. She sat stunned; her hands gripped the sides of her seat so tightly her fingers went numb. The whole arrest had been a gag, a publicity stunt for this party. She'd spent the entire afternoon thinking of him in a jail cell—and yes, sad over that in spite of her anger.

Now she was just mad. He had to have known what she thought in those last minutes on the airplane and he'd said nothing to reassure her. He didn't even bother to lean down and whisper "Sorry" in her ear.

She should be relieved he wasn't in trouble, and she was. But she couldn't forget. He was still the Robin Hood Hacker.

Still playing games.

The bidding began—and of course it soared. Half the women and a couple of men were falling all over themselves to win a weekend with him. The war continued, shouts growing louder and escalating to over seventy thousand dollars. The ruckus continued until just three bidders remained.

Winning at the moment was a woman wearing skin-tight silver and chunky sapphires, with a sheen of plastic surgery to her stretched skin.

Not far behind, a college-aged student who'd begged Daddy for more money twice already.

And coolly chiming in occasionally, a sedate woman in a simple black sheath.

College girl dropped out after her daddy shook his head at the auctioneer and drew his hand across his throat in the universal "cut off" signal. Still the bidding rose another ten thousand dollars, money that would go to underprivileged schoolkids who needed scholarships. This was all in fun, right?

Yet, the way these people tossed around money in games left her…unsettled. Why not just write a check, plus cancel the event and donate that amount, too? Of course if they did that, she would be out of a job.

Who was she to stand in judgment of others? Of Troy?

As much as she wanted to look away from his cocky smile, which had so charmed her earlier, she couldn't. The way she stayed glued to the bidding upset her. A lot.

She found herself rooting for the one less likely to entice him. Not that she really knew anything about him. But a part of her sensed—or hoped—Ms. Plastic Surgery with her wedding ring wouldn't be at all alluring to Troy. And if she was, then how much easier it would be to wipe him from her mind.

But the sedate woman in the black dress? She could have been Hillary's cousin. And that gave her pause. If that woman won and if she was his type, then that meant he could have been genuine on the airplane when he flirted....

As fast as "going, going, gone" echoed through the room, Ms. Sedate had a date with Troy Donavan for the weekend, won by an eighty-nine-thousand-dollar bid. And gauging from his huge "cat ate the canary smile" he was happy with the results.

The depth of Hillary's disappointment was ridiculous, damn it. She'd spoken to the guy for all of an hour on a flight. Yes, she'd been inordinately attracted to him—felt a zap of chemistry she hadn't felt before—but she could chalk that up to her vulnerable state right now. She was raw, with her emotions tender and close to the surface. After this ordeal with Barry was over, she would get stronger.

The emcee moved closer to Troy in a loud crackle of gold taffeta, which carried through the microphone. She keyed open the cuffs and he tucked them into his tuxedo pocket. He kissed her hand before taking the mic from her.

"Ladies and gentlemen," he said in that same carefree voice that had so enticed Hillary earlier as he'd calmed her nerves on the plane, "I'm pleased to be a part of such a generous outpouring tonight—all in the Robin Hood spirit and not a single computer hacked."

There was no denying it. The crowd loved him. They all but ate up his irreverence and charm. All except Colonel Salvatore. He seemed—skeptical.

"As you're all aware, I'm not known for playing by the rules. And tonight's no different." He motioned to the reserved woman who'd won the bidding battle. "My assistant here has been placing bids for me so I'll have the opportunity to pick the lady of my choice for the weekend."

Gasps, whispers and a couple of disgruntled murmurs chased through the partiers.

"I know—" Troy shrugged "—not completely fair, but I can't be accused of driving someone else to pay more since I took the burden of the highest bid upon myself."

Madame Emcee leaned in to the mic. "And it is a quite generous donation, may I add." She nodded to Troy. "But please, continue."

"Since we're all here in support of a worthy cause, I hope my request will be honored by the woman I choose. After all, it would be a double standard if this bachelor auction didn't work both ways."

His cocky logic took root and cheers bounced from person to person like beach balls at a raucous Jimmy Buffett concert. Troy started down the steps with a lazy long-legged lope, microphone in hand. The men and women around Hillary whooped and shouted louder while Troy continued to speak into the mic. He paused at the first row, then moved on to the second and the third, playing the crowd like a fiddle as each woman wondered if she would be chosen. The spotlight followed him farther still, showcasing every angle of a face too handsome to belong to someone who couldn't be trusted to use that charm wisely.

Abruptly, he stopped.

Troy stood at the end of row five. Her row. He stood beside Colonel Salvatore. The older gentleman—her contact—scowled at Troy.

And why not? He was making it difficult for her to stay low profile this weekend, which was what she'd been instructed to do. But then he couldn't possibly know how much trouble he could cause just by bringing the spotlight to this row.

Troy extended his hand and looked Hillary straight in the eyes. "I choose you."

Three

Her stomach fell as quickly as her anger rose, which was mighty darn hard and fast. What game was he playing now? She had no clue.

She did know that every single pair of eyes in this room was glued to her. She looked farther—and crap—her horrified face was plastered right there in full color on the wide screens.

Undaunted, Troy dropped to one knee.

Damn his theatrical soul.

"Hillary—" his voice boomed through the speakers "—think of the children and their scholarships. Be my date for the weekend."

She wanted to shove him on his arrogant ass.

Troy shifted his attention to the colonel. "I assume you won't mind me stealing your date?"

The colonel cleared his throat and said, "She's my niece. I trust you'll treat her well."

Niece? Whatever. Sheesh. This was nuts.

A steadying hand palmed her back. Salvatore. Her skin turned fiery with embarrassment. She turned to him for help.

Salvatore smiled one of those grins that didn't come close to reaching his pale blue eyes. "You should dance, Hillary."

Right. She should get her feet moving and then people would stop staring at her. Determined to feel nothing, she put her hand in Troy's—and still her stomach did a flip. She was not sixteen, for crying out loud. Although his grip felt so warm—callused and tender at the same time. Her body freakin' tingled to life. She'd always prided herself on being in control of her emotions. The second she'd found out what an immoral creep Barry was, she'd felt nothing but repulsion at his touch.

She knew Troy was a liar, a crook and a playboy. Still her body sang at the notion of stepping into his arms and gliding across the dance floor.

Plus, he'd just bid nearly ninety thousand dollars to spend the weekend with her. Gulp.

The pianist began playing. A singer in a red dress cupped the microphone and launched into a sultry rendition of a 1940s love song.

Troy tucked her to his side and led her to the center of the empty dance floor. The spotlight warmed her already-heating cheeks. His silk scarf teased her hand as he held it against his chest and swept her into the glide of the music. She should have known he would be a smooth dancer.

She blurted out, "Is there anything you don't do well?"

"I take it that's not a compliment."

"I don't mean to be rude, but I'm here to work this weekend, not play games."

"Believe me, this is no game." He pulled her close.

She inhaled sharply at the press of his muscled body against hers. He wasn't some soft desk jockey. He was a toned, honed *man.* Her mouth dried and her pulse sped up.

"Just relax and dance." His warm breath caressed her ear. "And I promise not to sing along. Because, in answer to your question, I'm tone-deaf."

"Thanks for sharing. But it's not helping. You can't truly expect me to relax," she hissed, even as her feet synced perfectly with his. His strong legs brushed ever so subtly against hers with each dance step. "You just told a roomful of people and a pack of reporters that you paid nearly ninety-thousand dollars to spend the weekend with me. Me. A woman you've known for less than a day. We've only spoken for an hour."

He guided her around the floor as other couples joined in. The shifting mass of other bodies created a sense of privacy now that all eyes weren't so fiercely focused on them.

"Well, Troy?" she pressed. "What are you hoping to accomplish?"

"Don't you believe in love at first sight?" He nuzzled her hair, inhaling deeply.

She stumbled, bumped into another couple, then righted her steps, if not her racing pulse. "No, I do not. I believe in lust at first sight, but not love. Don't confuse the two."

All the same, she couldn't help but draw in another whiff of his bay rum scent now that she was as close to him as she'd ever been. Swaying, she resisted the urge to press her cheek to his and savor the bristle of late-day stubble. The kind of slightly unshaven look that wasn't scruffy, but shouted *testosterone* to a woman's basic instincts.

But the music slowed and she rested her cheek against his chest, just over the silken scarf for a moment.

"Hmm." His chest rumbled with approval. "So you admit you're attracted to me."

Of course she was. That didn't mean she intended to tell him. "Correction—I was stating that you are simply attracted to me."

He laughed softly, spanning her waist with a bold, broad palm. "Your confidence is compelling."

"Not confidence, exactly." She leaned back to study his eyes. "Why else would you have gone to all this outrageous trouble to spend time with me? Although I guess you're so wealthy that perhaps the obscene amount of money doesn't mean anything to you."

He sketched his knuckles along her jawline. "I wanted the chance to spend time with you."

"Why not go about that the normal way?"

"Tough to do if I'd ended up as someone else's date for the weekend."

"How did you even know I was here?"

"I saw you when I was backstage. My assistant was here. Giving her instructions on what to do was as simple as a text."

"But the ballroom was full of people."

"You could have been in a football stadium, and I would have seen you," he said intensely. His fingers skimmed along the sensitive curve of her neck. "Now let's stop arguing and just enjoy ourselves—unless you plan to renege on the agreement you made in front of all these people. But I have to warn you, everyone will be very disappointed in you if you cost the charity eighty-nine-thousand dollars."

His touch almost distracted her from his manipulative words.

She clasped his wrist and placed his hand back on her shoulder. Her bare shoulder. Maybe not such a good idea after all. "People won't like *you* very much either if you don't follow through on your assistant's bid."

"Everyone knows I've never cared what other people

think of me." His fingers caressed her subtly, enticingly. "But you do care about people's opinions. Rejecting the bid, refusing to play along, causing a scene could all damage your credibility as an event planner—"

"Oh stop it." Stop teasing her. Touching her. Tempting her. "We both know I'm not going to cause a scene, and you're going to pay the charity. How about we shut up and dance in peace?" While she thought about what to do next. At least dancing with Troy gave her an easy excuse to check every face on the dance floor.

He tut-tutted. "My mother always said it isn't nice to tell people to shut up."

"You are really infuriating."

"At least you aren't indifferent."

"That's safe to say." She huffed a hefty exhale. "I want to get this date out of the way so I can go back to my real reason for being here this weekend."

"To check out the chef."

"Right, the food."

Something shifted in his eyes, then his expression cleared again. "Our date is for the whole weekend."

An entire weekend of his touch? His humor and charm? Even with her real reasons for being here, it seemed she didn't have a choice on that. So she could either fight him or use this situation to her advantage.

She could be his "bought for the weekend date," and she could use that role to mingle with everyone, see if she could catch a glimpse of the mystery man Barry had claimed was his business partner. No one would question why she was here and if Colonel Salvatore hadn't liked the idea he would have objected when Troy asked her to dance. Now, people would be too focused on who she was with to worry about why she was here. He would actually make the perfect cover.

All she had to do was resist the overwhelming urge to pull him into a dark corner and kiss him senseless.

Troy had been trying to figure out how to get Hillary away from the crowd for the past two hours.

And yes, he wouldn't mind having her alone after one hundred and twenty-two minutes with her pressed against him, either dancing or tucked by his side as they sampled the array of tiny desserts. The soft feminine feel and minty scent of her was damn near driving him bonkers.

Except he had a plan. He'd already executed the first part through the bidding war. Salvatore's scowl had shot daggers his way all evening, a price worth paying. Hillary could still make her identification, and she would have him as a bodyguard, even if she didn't know it.

He guided her along the pastry line, then over to the drinks table—seltzer water with lime for them both—then out on the balcony where tables were set up. Lights were strung and twinkling, the sounds and smells of the lake carrying on the wind. He picked the table against the wall, overlooking the rest of the small outdoor area and out of clear view of the security cameras.

They could sit beside each other, shielded by the shadows. No one would approach without him seeing them first, and she could watch the party, even though she didn't know they were on the same side. His instincts told him she was honest, but he couldn't risk telling her of his affiliation with Salvatore until both he and Salvatore were certain of her innocence.

Bluesy jazz music drifted through the open French doors. A saxophone player had joined the pianist and singer. All of the musicians tonight were big names who'd donated their talent to the event. One of them was even a buddy from reform school and a Salvatore recruit, as well. This place was crawling with money and agendas.

Including his own.

He took his seat beside her, the handcuffs in his pocket jingling a reminder of his earlier fantasies about cuffing them together—all night long. He tipped back his glass and allowed himself the luxury of studying her out of the corner of his eye. There was no way to hide a woman like her. Sure she wore a simple strapless black gown, her hair clasped back on one side. Yet in a place full of women in designer gowns and priceless heirloom jewels, she stood out from the simplicity of her presence alone. Her unassuming grace, the way she didn't seek the spotlight—and yet, it followed her. She drew the light.

She drew him.

Troy watched her over the top of his glass. "Are you still angry about the auction?"

Slowly, she placed her seltzer water back on the shiny steel table and stirred the lime around deliberately. "I'm upset that you didn't tell me the truth on the airplane. I don't appreciate being lied to."

"I didn't lie." He'd been careful with his words.

She looked up sharply. "You left out parts. You quibbled about your identity." Her freckled nose crinkled ever so slightly in disgust. "Quibbling is the same as lying."

She sounded like Colonel Salvatore. He cursed softly.

"What was that?" She arched a brow, again just like his mentor.

"If I'd told you my full name on the plane, would you have spoken with me during the flight?" He leaned forward, taking her cool hand in his, the minty scent of her carrying on the late-night breeze. "Or if you did speak, would it have been the fun, easy exchange we shared?"

She stayed silent, but she didn't pull away.

"Exactly." He thumbed the inside of her wrist, enjoying the satiny softness of her skin, the speeding throb of her pulse. "I wanted to talk to you, so I didn't pull out a calling card that says hey, I'm the Robin Hood Hacker."

"Okay, okay—" she chewed her bottom lip, which glistened with a simple gloss, all of her makeup minimal "—but can you at least acknowledge that you deliberately misled me?"

"I did." He clasped her hand with both of his and squeezed once. He was making progress. Getting closer. Anticipation thrummed through his veins in time with the bluesy music. "And I'm sorry that has upset you, because honest to God, from the moment I saw you on the plane, I've just wanted to spend time with you. I want you to see *me,* not my Wikipedia page."

She released her bottom lip from between her teeth. "You make a compelling argument."

"Good. Then consider this. We're both here for the weekend. So let's make the most of it. Don't think past Sunday. I'll be patient through all your visits with the chef."

"You don't have to."

"I'm in Chicago because I'm obligated to be here. You've made a dull weekend much more interesting." His eyes lingered on the way the stars and lights brought out streaks of gold in her sleek red hair. His fingers ached to thread through each strand. "If we hang out together for the rest of this gala, we don't have to make awkward conversation with others."

"Better the devil I know than the devil I don't?"

"I can live with that if it means I get to spend more time with you."

Her midnight-blue eyes narrowing, she traced a finger

over the top of their clasped hands. "Are you seriously hitting on me?"

"Yes." And for once he wasn't holding anything back.

"You must be really hard up."

"Or just h—"

"Don't even say it."

"Hungry for your company."

"You're not funny." Her mouth twitched anyway.

"Yes, I am. But it's not something I take pride in. I'm a smart guy, and intelligence is a genetic lottery. What really matters is how I use those winnings."

She swayed forward just a hint. "There's sense in some of that egotistical ranting of yours."

He canted closer until only a sliver of air separated them. He waited. Her breath puffed faster and faster with the quickening rise and fall of her chest. Her pupils widened as she met and held his gaze.

Then her lashes fluttered closed. All the invitation he needed.

Taking advantage of their shadowy corner, Troy slanted his mouth over hers, testing the soft give of her full lips. Tasting the lingering lime flavor of her drink. He squeezed her hand more firmly and claimed her. Completely.

He slid his arm around her shoulder and deepened the kiss, teasing along the seam of her mouth until she opened for him. Her sigh filled him with a surge of triumph. He'd been imagining this since the second he'd clapped eyes on her on the airplane. She didn't just melt, she participated, stroke for stroke.

His fingers tangled in the silky glide of her hair along her shoulders. The strands clung to his fingers with a snap of static and something more snapping through his veins.

There was chemistry here, a connection and crackle he burned to explore along with the curve of her hips, her breasts. He wanted to kiss the crook of her arm, behind her knee and find the places that made her go weak with pleasure. This weekend presented the perfect opportunity to indulge in the countless fantasies exploding to life in his brain.

Her hand flattened to his chest, her fingers gripping his silk scarf and bringing him even closer.

His heart ramped up at the strength of her passion. And the thought of her tugging that scarf off, of peeling the rest of their clothes away and touching him without the barrier of fabric… A possessive growl rumbled deep inside him, almost pushing him over the edge.

He pulled himself from her before he took this too far in such a public setting. She gasped, then looked around quickly.

Her eyes wide, she pressed the back of her trembling wrist to her mouth. "That was…"

"Damned amazing."

"Not a good idea."

"I thought you might say that." But given her reaction to him, he wasn't daunted in the least.

She flattened her palms to the table and drew in a shaky breath. "You've got to understand, I have exceptionally crummy taste in men. It's like I have a radar for finding the most dishonest, untrustworthy guy in the room. So the fact that I like you makes you very dangerous for me."

"You like me." He nudged her loose hairpin back into place. "But, wow, you sure know how to throw a guy hope and smack him back down again at the same time."

"I'm sorry, but it's true, and honestly—" she looked around nervously "—now's also a really horrible time for me to even think about dating."

She seemed to be searching for an escape route, but then he knew that she also needed to stay here, at the party.

Watching. Just as he did. So, pressing her to stay at the table shouldn't be too tough.

He wanted to kiss her again. But he would settle for hearing the sound of her voice, which was more amazing than even the professional singer and musicians back in the ballroom.

"Tell me more about these horrible men you chose."

She started to stand, to leave. "I don't appreciate being made fun of."

He stroked her arm, the heat of their kiss still firing through him. "Stay, please. I'm serious. I want to learn more about you. Unless you have somewhere else to be?"

Pressing two fingers against her temple as if combatting a headache, she looked through the doors at the crowded ballroom, then shook her head. "I should stay until…the chef is free."

"Then pass your time with me. Tell me about the losers."

She turned slowly back to him. "Fine, if you insist." She held up three fingers. "In high school, I dated three guys. One cheated on me." She tucked down a finger. "The other was just using me to get to my best friend." She tucked down another. "Number three liked to mix vodka in his sports drink and dumped me in the middle of the homecoming dance. And the pattern continued on through college and the few times I've risked the whole relationship gig as an adult. I'm some sort of a scumbag magnet."

She said it all dispassionately, as if she'd built a defense against the hurt, but somehow, he knew it was an act. Guilt pinched inside him over the things he wasn't telling her, that he wasn't authorized to tell her. His intermittent work for Interpol depended on him keeping up a carefree, jet-setting lifestyle. But if she ever found out his real reason for being here, she would have to know that for once, someone was actually putting her welfare first.

"Hillary, it's not nice to call me scum."

"I'm sorry, really, but you must be if you're drawn to me. Or maybe it's because I'm drawn to you." Her pupils widened again in response, just as they had right before he'd kissed her.

"Or maybe you're just going through lots of frogs until you find your prince."

Her laughter reached out to him on the night air. "You're mixing up your fairy tales. You're not a prince. You're Robin Hood."

He winced. "God, I hate being called that."

"Robin Hood's been a beloved fella throughout history." She toyed with a lock of her hair. "He took care of the less fortunate. Exposed corruption."

"He wasn't in it for the glory."

Her praise was making him itchy.

"So it's the adoration you object to." She tapped his wrist, already showing a bruise from where he'd first fought the handcuffs earlier. "That's actually rather honorable."

"Watch it. You're falling under my scummy spell."

"Right." She inched her hand away. "Thanks for the reminder."

"I just want to keep you safe from me." He winked.

She rolled her eyes. "I'm twenty-seven. It's time I looked out for myself."

"Does that mean you're going to stop fighting the notion of being my date for the weekend?" This whole weekend would be so much easier if she went with the flow. Easier, yes, but he also couldn't deny he found bantering with her exciting.

Intoxicating.

"I thought the auction was for tonight?"

"No, you didn't." He took her hand again. "But nice try." He kissed the inside of her wrist, lingering.

Her throat moved with a long swallow. She shot to her feet. "About the weekend, I do have to work. I can't spend every waking moment with you."

"I'll just hang out while you work. I can even sample some pâté, give you my opinion on petits fours. My friends say I'm quite enlightened." He slid his arm around her shoulders, pulling her against him so quickly she forgot to protest. "I'm amazingly footloose, too much money and not enough to do. So I'm all yours."

"That's not a good idea." As they moved away from the table and entered the hallway, she glanced over her shoulder, back at the ballroom.

"Why not?" Because if the way they'd danced together was any indication, they could be very, very good together.

She weaved past two women whispering on their way to the restroom, jewel-encrusted clutch purses in hand. "You'll be bored."

He stopped in front of the gilded elevator and jabbed the up button. "Let me make that call. I really can help you, you know." He chose his words carefully, so she would think he meant the chefs, but so she would also realize he could get her more access overall. "If you're with me, you will meet more people, make more connections for your entertaining business."

She looked up at him through narrowed eyes. "Do you think everyone's Machiavellian?"

"I *know* they are," he answered without so much as blinking. "And knowing that makes life easier."

"Troy?" She touched his silk scarf lightly, her blue eyes darkening with…sadness? "That's no way to live your life."

She swayed into him, and he wondered how the hell he'd gotten closer to her at the moment he'd been trying the least. Something about Hillary Wright had him off balance, as it had from the start.

Right now, he wanted nothing more than to head up to his penthouse suite and make love to her all night long. To tell her again and again how damn perfect she was. To show her she could trust he was one hundred percent into her. That he was a man who didn't want to take anything from her. He just wanted to give.

The elevator slid open.

Colonel Salvatore stood alone inside, mirrors capturing his scowling reflection. He held Hillary's little black clutch bag in one big fist. "I've been looking for the two of you."

Four

Hillary's high heels darn near grew roots into the plush carpet as she stared at Colonel Salvatore glowering at her from the elevator.

She couldn't seem to make herself move forward and end this evening with Troy. An amazing evening. Unconventional, sure, but fun. He'd surprised her with an engaging mix of arrogance, humor, intelligence and perception.

Plus, he kissed like molten sin.

She forced her feet to drag forward without pitching on her face. Inside the elevator, she held out her hand for her thrift-store purse. "I must have left it at the auction. Thank you for keeping it safe."

Silently, Troy stepped in after her, and she realized he must be curious about Salvatore even though he'd written off the man as her "uncle" just before he'd whisked her away to dance. She searched for the words to explain without saying things she shouldn't.

"Troy, this is my friend, Colonel—"

"No need, Ms. Wright," Salvatore interrupted. "Troy and I know each other well."

Something dark in his voice, an undercurrent she didn't comprehend, sent shivers down her spine. She looked from one man to the other. Troy slid in the key card to access the penthouse floor and the colonel kept his hands behind his back. She reached to press the button for her floor.

Salvatore shook his head as the doors slid closed. "We're all going together. It's time the three of us had a talk."

Together?

Ding. Ding. Ding. The floors went past.

These two men more than just knew each other. Suddenly she realized that Troy was somehow tied into her reason for being here. Given his sketchy background could he be part of Barry's mess, too? Her stomach plummeted even as the elevator rose.

Although she could swear she'd never seen him with her ex-boyfriend. So many questions and fears churned through her head, stirring up anger and a horrible out-of-control feeling. All her life, she'd tried to play by the rules. She'd worked hard to get ahead and somehow she kept screwing up.

The elevator dinged a final time, opening to a domed hallway with brass sconces and fresh flowers. A door loomed on either side, leading to two penthouses. Troy angled left, guiding them inside the three-room suite that sported a 1920s Great Gatsby opulence.

Any other time she would have enjoyed examining the tapestry upholsteries and dark polished woods—not to mention the breathtaking view from a wall of windows overlooking the Windy City. Skyscrapers and the lake blended together in a mix of modern prosperity with a layer of history. She loved cities, craved the bustle and excitement—the ultimate contrast to how she'd grown up. She rubbed the silver cow charm on her purse and turned to face the two men.

Colonel Salvatore paced with his hands behind his back, his heavy steps making fast tracks over the Persian carpets in the living area. Troy leaned lazily on the bar, flipping a crystal drink stirrer between his fingers.

The silence stretched until Hillary was ready to pull her hair out. "Will someone please tell me what's going on?"

"Fine." Salvatore stopped abruptly. "I expected better from both of you. While you two were playing footsie on the balcony, our guy was slipping away. My sources say he left sometime this evening and is probably already on a private jet out of the country."

Her legs folded and she sank onto the edge of a camel-backed sofa. "*Our* guy?"

Pivoting sharply, Salvatore pinned Troy with a laser glare. "You really didn't tell her *anything* about your role here? Damn it, Donavan, why is it you chose now to follow the rules when you've rarely concerned yourself with keeping me happy in the past?" His sigh hissed between his teeth as he shifted his attention back to Hillary. "Troy Donavan's in Chicago for the same reason you are. To help ID Barry Curtis's associate."

Of course he was.

She'd known the truth on some level, from the moment those elevator doors slid open and Colonel Salvatore said he was looking for both of them. Except, up to the last second, she'd been holding out hope—foolish hope—that she was wrong. Apparently her bad-boy radar was in full working order.

Troy knew about her reason for being here and hadn't said a word to her. He'd made her believe he really wanted to spend time with her. She must have looked so ridiculous to him, talking about needing to see the chef. It had all been a game to him, playing along with her. Likely he'd been keeping this from her even on the airplane.

She forced her attention back to Salvatore's words. For better or worse, she still had to get through this weekend in order to reclaim her life.

"The guy we're after is insanely good at staying away from security cameras. It's as if he has an inside scoop. But I would still like the two of you to review the recordings of tonight's events, make use of Troy's exceptional tech skills and see if you can find even a glimpse."

She struggled to sort through so much information coming at her so fast. "Why do you need both of us to identify him?"

Troy snapped the crystal drink stirrer. "Yes, Colonel, please do enlighten us, because I've been wondering the same thing."

"Some things in life are on a need-to-know basis and neither of you need to know why I chose to play it this way. Troy, my tech guy has forwarded you all the security footage from tonight. I hope to hear good news from you both by morning." He nodded to Hillary. "Your luggage has already been brought here so you can change out of your formal wear."

Share a suite with Troy? She eyed the two doors leading to bedrooms. Where was the colonel staying? "And if we find who we're looking for in the video feed right away, we can all go home? This is over?"

"Troy will contact me in my suite across the hall. Once we've reviewed what you found, you'll be free to leave. If anyone sees you leaving the hotel, let the partiers here think you're spending your weekend together somewhere else."

"You're just sending Hillary back to D.C. unprotected after making her a target?" Troy snorted. "Think again."

A target? Surely, he was exaggerating.

"And don't you think she was every bit as much a target before? Helping us is her best shot at getting back a normal life. Good luck convincing her to do anything your way after the masterfully foolish way you've pissed her off," Colonel Salvatore shot over his shoulder before walking out the door.

The door clicked. Then clicked twice more as Troy secured all of the locks, sealing her inside with him.

Hillary shot to her feet and charged over to the panoramic window, suddenly claustrophobic and needing to embrace the open space of the outside. "I can't believe I was such an idiot."

Troy walked up beside her, hands stuffed in his tuxedo pockets. He didn't look surprised. And why not? He'd been playing her from the start.

"Damn you, Troy Donavon." She smacked her palm on the glass. "I was kicking myself for falling for your act on the plane. I knew better than to trust you, and still I bought into your line of bull only a few hours later. You must have been laughing the whole time at how gullible I was."

"Hey, I'm the good guy. There's nothing wrong with your instincts." Broken stirrer in hand, he tapped the glass right by her hand. "And I can promise I was never laughing at you. I just wanted to keep you safe."

She folded her arms over her chest. "How are you a good guy? I'm working with the colonel to get myself out of trouble because of a stupid choice I made in who I trusted. If the colonel's coercing you to be here as well, that isn't exactly a vote of confidence for the man to keep me safe."

"Let's just say he's a friend and he needed my help—

all of which I'm sure he will confirm." Troy leaned closer, the heat of him reaching out to her in the air-conditioned suite. "When I saw you and realized what you were walking into, I thought you could use some… reinforcements."

"But you lied to me. Again, after the auction." And that hurt, too much for someone she'd just met. "On the dance floor, and every second on the balcony when you didn't tell me you knew why I'm here. When you kissed me. You lied by not explaining you're here for the same reason. You played me for a fool."

His deep green gaze glinted with so much sincerity it hurt. "I wasn't playing you, and I never, never thought you were foolish. My only concern from the second I saw you on the plane has been protecting you from any fallout."

"And seducing me? Is that part of protecting me?" The memory of his kiss steamed through her so tangibly she could swear it might fog the window.

He stepped closer. "Protecting you and being attracted to you don't have to be mutually exclusive."

She pressed a hand to his chest to stop him, that damn silk scarf of his teasing her fingers, making her burn to tug him even nearer. "Doesn't that break some kind of code of ethics?"

"I'm not a cop or detective or military guy or even a James Bond spy." He tossed aside the broken drink stick he'd been holding and pressed his hand over hers. "So, no. Seducing you doesn't interfere with my ethics."

"You're just…what? Please do explain." She stared into his eyes, hoping to find some window into his soul, some way to understand what was real about this whole crazy evening with him.

"I'm a concerned citizen with the power to help out, as you are." His voice rang true, but there was a cadence to his answer that sounded too practiced. There had to be something more to his story, to why he was here. But from the set of his jaw, clearly he didn't intend to tell her.

"Then *why* did you kiss me?" To have that toe-curling moment tainted was just the final slap.

"Because I wanted to. I still do." He didn't lean in, but his fingers curved around hers until their hands were linked. The connection between them crackled all over again, even without the kiss.

God, what was wrong with her?

She snatched her hand away. "Well, that's damn well never going to happen again." She backed away from him and his too-tempting smile. "Would you please set up your computer while I change? We have work to do. I would like to finish as fast as possible so we can say goodbye to each other and to this whole horrible mess."

Hillary locked herself in the spare bedroom and sagged back against the six-paneled door. Crystal knob in hand, she propped herself up. But just barely.

As if the day hadn't promised to be stressful enough, she'd been blindsided by Troy again and again.

She scanned the room, her temporary sanctuary with flock fleur-de-lis wallpaper and a dark mahogany bed. Whereas the sitting area had been wide-open with a wall of windows, this room was heavily curtained, perfect for sleeping or curling up in a French, art deco chaise by the fireplace.

For now, she needed to focus on her suitcase, which rested on an antique luggage rack at the end of the carved four-poster bed. She pitched her clutch bag on the duvet and sifted through what she'd packed for something appropriate to wear. What did a person choose for an evening with a guy she wanted, but needed to hold at arm's length? Confidently casual, with a hint of sparkle for her bruised pride—

Her phone vibrated inside her clutch, sending the purse bouncing along the mattress. She raced to grab the cell— and saw her sister Claudia's phone number.

Claudia had stayed in Vermont with her husband and her three kids, where she taught school and watched out for their mother. Her older sister was the "perfect" person, the strong one who met life on her own terms. She never hid from anything or anyone. She admired her sister and her ability to let go of the past enough to move smoothly into her own future.

Claudia would have never been fooled by someone like Barry.

Hillary thumbed the on button. "Hello, Claudia."

"Is that all you have to say? *Hello, Claudia?*" her sister said with more humor than worry. "Hillary Elizabeth Wright, why haven't you returned all seven of my calls?"

She tucked the phone under her chin and unzipped the side of her evening gown. "I've only been gone a day. There's no need to freak out."

"And what a day you've had, sister," Claudia said, pausing for what sounded like a sip of her ever-present Diet Coke. "You should have told me."

"Told you what?" She shimmied down her dress and kicked it to the side in a pool of black satin.

"That you know Troy Donavan—*the* Troy Donavan, Robin Hood Hacker, billionaire bad boy."

Hillary stopped halfway stepping into her jeans. "What are you talking about? I don't *know* him."

Now who was quibbling with the truth? But she needed to stall and gather her thoughts.

"Then you have a doppelganger, because there are

photos of you with him all over the media. Your Google numbers are through the roof."

Oh great.

Of course they were. She should have known. She yanked her pants on the rest of the way. "I just met him earlier today."

Was it only one day?

"Nuh-uh, sister dear. That story's not flying. He bid a *hundred thousand dollars* for a weekend with you?"

"Eighty-nine-thousand dollars, if you want to be technical." She tugged on a flowy pink poet's shirt. "The reporters must have rounded up."

"*Eighty. Nine. Thousand. Dollars.* Ho-lee crap. I can't get my husband to foot the bill for a waffle cone at the ice-cream shop."

"Billy's a great guy and you've been head over heels for him since you sat beside him in sophomore geometry class."

"I know, and I adore every penny-pinching part of him since he's so generous in other ways." Claudia purred over the phone not too subtly. "I'm just living vicariously through you for a minute. It's nice to fantasize about no mortgage and no diapers. So, spill it. I want deets. Now."

"It's crazy." Hillary fingered her silver chain belt link by link. "I'm sure he's just bored and I said no, which he took as a challenge."

"Then keep right on challenging him until you get some jewelry."

"That's an awful thing to say." She hooked the belt around her waist loosely.

"Ahh," her sister said knowingly. "You like this guy."

"No. I don't. I *can't.*" She flopped back on the four-poster bed, staring up at the intricately carved molding around the tray ceiling. "I haven't known him long enough to draw that kind of conclusion."

"That hot, is he?"

"Hotter."

"You lucky, lucky lady." Claudia paused for a long gulp of her drink. "Did you have a crazy one-night stand with him?"

"God, no." Hillary sat upright. "Since he bought this weekend with me, sleeping with him would feel…cheap."

Still, her mind filled with images of lying back with him on this broad bed until her fingers twisted in the lacy spread.

"I hate to be the one to break it to you, but eighty-nine-thousand dollars isn't cheap, sister."

"You know what I mean."

"I do. I'm just teasing." The phone crackled with the sound of her shuffling the phone from one ear to the other. "Would you have slept with him if there hadn't been the infamous auction?"

"No. Definitely not." She hesitated. "I don't think so."

"Wow." Her sister's teasing tone faded. "He really has gotten to you."

"He's—" a knock sounded on her door "—here. I need to go."

"Call me. Just check in to let me know you're okay." Claudia's voice dripped with big-sister concern. "It's been a tough year for you."

"For all of us." Their father had died of a heart attack in his sleep. Their mother was in rehab—again. And then in her grief, Hillary had lost herself in a relationship with Barry. It was time for luck to swing over to the positive side. "Love you tons, but I gotta run."

She disconnected and reached for the door. Now, she

just had to make it through the whole night without thinking about how Troy's kiss brought her body to life in a way Barry's never had.

Love you tons.

Hillary's voice whispered in Troy's head as he watched her walk deeper into the suite's living room. Who had she been talking to on the phone while she changed clothes?

She'd been buttoned-up sexy in her power suit on the plane. She'd been gorgeously hot in her strapless black gown.

And now she was totally, approachably hot in tight jeans and a long pink poet's shirt with a slim silver chain belt resting low on her hips. She made comfy look damn good.

He pivoted away hard and fast, shoving up the sleeves on his button-down—he'd changed into jeans, too. On the coffee table, he'd fired up his laptop. Now he just needed to log on to the secure network to retrieve the colonel's video feed.

How like the old guy to make sure Hillary was royally pissed off before leaving her here for the rest of the night. Colonel Salvatore had definitely gotten his revenge over the auction stunt.

They'd played back-and-forth games like this since school. Troy would reprogram the class period alarms. The colonel extended evening study period by an hour, which pissed off Troy's classmates, who rained hell down on him in other ways.

Usually the mind games and power plays with Salvatore were fun. But not tonight. At least having Hillary here in his suite made it easier to keep an eye on her.

Troy called to Hillary without looking up from the keyboard, "I ordered coffee and some food in case it turns into a long night."

"I'll take the coffee but pass on the food. Let's not waste time." Her bare feet sounded softly along the Persian rugs. "We have a job to do."

"I've wired my laptop into the wide-screen TV so we don't have to hunch over a computer. The images will be larger, nuances easier to catch." He'd also run the pixilation through a new converter he'd been developing for use with military satellites.

"That looks high-tech, but it makes sense you would have the best toys."

Toys? He wasn't dealing in Little Tikes, but then he wasn't into bragging, either. He didn't need to.

His "toys" spoke for themselves. "You might want to reconsider the food. This will take a while. It's not like watching footage of the night once and we're done. There are different camera angles, inside and outside. We'll be reliving the night five or six times from different bird's-eye views."

"Are *we* on there?" She gripped the back of the chaise.

"We will be. Yes." Would she see how damn much she affected him? Good thing he was in control of what played across that screen.

"What about out on the balcony? The kiss? Is that one on camera for anyone to see?"

"I'm also fairly good at dodging security cameras when I choose." He glanced at her, took in every sleek line of her long legs as she walked to the room-service cart. "I can assure you. That moment was private."

Her footsteps faltered for a heartbeat. "Thank you for that much, at least."

"You're welcome." He grinned and couldn't resist adding, "Although, there's still the film of us dancing so close it's almost like we're—"

"I get the picture. Turn on the TV." She poured a cup

of coffee from the silver carafe, cradled the china in her hands and curled up on a vintage chaise.

He sat on the sofa, in front of his laptop. He split the TV screen into four views. "We can save time using the multiple views on some of the sparser scenes, then go back to single screen for the more populated cuts."

"Why is it that so few people have seen this guy?" She blew into her coffee.

"It's not that so few have seen him. It's that they're all afraid to talk." He fast-forwarded through four squares of empty halls, empty rooms. "You should be afraid, as well."

"Why aren't you?"

"I'm afraid for you. Does that count?"

He slowed the feed of cleaning and waitstaff setting up. Caterers. Florists. Just because their informant said the guy would be at the party didn't mean he couldn't be using a cover of his own. Troy clicked to zoom in on a face with the enhanced pixilation software that could even read the bar code still stuck to the bottom of a box of candles.

Glancing left, he checked for a reaction from Hillary, but nothing showed in her expression except pleasure over the sip of coffee. He took in the bliss in her eyes over a simple taste of java. What he wouldn't give to bring that look to her face. He turned back to the TV mounted over the fireplace.

Even keeping his attention on the screen and computer, he was still hyperaware of Hillary sitting an arm's reach away. Every shift on the chaise, every time she lifted the mug of coffee to her lips, he was in tune to it all.

The air conditioners kicked on silently, swirling the air around, mixing the smell of java with her fresh mint scent. Was it her shampoo or some kind of perfume? He could picture her in a bubbling bath with mint leaves floating around her....

"Troy?"

Her husky voice broke into his thoughts.

He froze the image on the screen. "Do you see something?"

"No, nothing. Keep running the feed." She set aside her china cup and saucer with a clink. "I'm just wondering... How did you meet up with Colonel Salvatore? And please, for once, be honest the first time I ask a question."

She wanted to talk while they watched and worked? He was cool with that. He could share things that were public knowledge. "The colonel was the headmaster at the military boarding school I was sent to as a teenager. He's since retired to...other work."

"You still stay in touch with him?"

"I do." As did a few other select alumni. "Let's just say I'm obligated to him for the life I lead now, and he's calling in a favor."

She slid from the chaise and walked to the room-service cart. She rolled it closer to him and poured *two* cups.

A peace offering?

She set down a cup and saucer beside his computer. "What was your high school like?"

"Imprisoning." He didn't bother telling her about his no-liquids-around-computers rule, especially when the computer was equipped with experimental software worth a disgustingly large amount of money. Instead, he lifted the cup and drained half in one too-hot gulp.

"I meant, what was school like, what was your life like before you were sent to reform school?"

"Boring." He drank the rest of the coffee and set aside the empty china.

"Is that why you broke into the DOD's computer system?" She sat beside him, her drink on her knee. "Because you were bored?"

"That would make me a rather shallow person."

"Are you?"

"What do you think?"

On the screen, the auction area began to fill. He manipulated the focus to capture images of people with their backs to the cameras, reflections in mirrors, glass and even a crystal punch bowl.

She leaned forward, her slim leg alongside his. "I believe you're probably a genius and a regular academic environment may not have been the right place for you."

"My parents sent me to the best private schools—" again and again, to get kicked out over and over "—before I went to the military academy."

"You were bored there, too."

Did she know she'd inclined closer to him?

"Teachers did try," he said, working the keyboard with one hand, draping his other arm over the back of the sofa. "But they had a class full of students to teach. So I was given lots of independent studies."

"Computer work." She set her cup on the far end of the coffee table. "Alone?"

Hell, yes, alone. All damn day long. "The choice was that or be a social outcast in a class with people five or more years older."

She tapped the pause key on his laptop and turned toward him. "Sounds very lonely for a child."

"My social skills weren't the best. I was happier alone."

"How could the teachers and your parents expect your social skills to improve if they isolated you?" Her eyes went deep blue with compassion.

He didn't want her pity. Frustration roiled over how she'd managed to slip past his defenses, to pry things out of him that he usually didn't share. He snapped, "Would you like to tutor me?"

She flinched. "You seemed to have mastered the art of communication just fine."

Anger was his fatal flaw. Always had been. He leveled his breathing. "I have the brotherhood to thank for the social skills."

And the anger management.

"The brotherhood?"

He reached for the keyboard again, setting the screen back into motion, losing himself in the technology of manipulating the image. "Military reform school was a sentence, sure, but I found my first friends there. They were people like me in a lot of ways. I learned how to be part of a pack."

"Military reform school—so they had issues, too?"

"You mean criminal records."

"I'm not judging." She leaned back until her hair slithered along his arm. "Just asking."

Was she flirting? What was her angle? Why was she asking more about him? Regardless, he wouldn't miss out on the chance to reel her in, and perhaps win back her trust.

"A lot of the guys in the school were there because they wanted a military education prior to going into the service." He wrapped a lock around his finger, unseen behind her back. "Some of us were *sent* there to learn to be more self-disciplined."

Touching her hair, just her hair and nothing more, required all the self-control he'd ever gained. But nothing could will away the blood surging south, the hot pounding urge to undress her.

"And you formed a brotherhood with those people, rebels like yourself?"

"I did." That much he could say honestly, and without

mentioning the whole Salvatore/Interpol connection. "To-gether, we learned how to play within the rules."

She nodded toward the image of him on the runway at the bachelor auction, taking the mic and crowing to the audience about how he'd played them. "You don't look particularly conformist to me."

"You should have seen me back in the day." Hair always too long for regs and an attitude he'd worn like his own personal uniform.

"Do you have pictures of yourself from that time stored somewhere on this computer?" She leaned forward and he let go of her hair quickly.

"Sealed under lock and key. Trust me, you'll never find any old yearbook photos of me."

"Hmm…"

She went silent again, and he wondered what she was thinking. He clicked the computer keys to freeze on the frame of the ballroom filling the screen. She leaned her head on his shoulder.

His body went harder, if that was even possible. He almost reached to pull her over, kiss her again, tuck her underneath him and—

"Troy, there's a photo of me sitting on the Easter Bunny's lap."

What? She was giving him conversational whiplash. "What's so bad about that?"

"I was thirteen."

"Aww…" Now he understood. She'd been trying to make him feel better by sharing her own secret embar-rassment. So sweet, he didn't have the heart to tell her he'd left those concerns behind him a long time ago. "Your mom made you."

"Hell, no." She froze the image again and angled side-ways to face him full-on. "I was there because I wanted to believe. In the Easter Bunny. In Santa. In the Tooth Fairy. I was teased in school until I learned it was best to keep some things to myself. There wasn't a Sisterhood of the Tooth Fairy at my junior high."

God, she was freaking amazing. After all the ways he'd lied to her, quibbled, maneuvered, whatever, she was still worried about him being hurt by some slights back when he was a kid.

He gathered up a fistful of her hair. "You really are too awesome for your own good."

"Compliments will not get me into your bed," she said, her lips moving so close to his they were almost touching.

His fingers tangled in her hair, he stared into her blue eyes, which were deepening with awareness. "What if I came to *yours?*"

Five

The feel of his hand in her hair, his fingers rubbing firm circles against her scalp, offered a sensual mixture of setting her nerves on fire and melting her all at once. Right now, she wanted to be the type of person who could just lean into him for more than a kiss and damn the consequences. She wanted to do something she'd never done before—have a one-night stand with a virtual stranger. He was so close their breath mingled until she couldn't tell if the coffee scent came from him or from her.

"I told you we were never going to kiss again."

"I heard you. I was there, remember? While I enjoy the hell out of kissing you, it's not mandatory for going to bed together. Admit it," he growled softly, "you're tempted."

"I'm tempted to eat all the marshmallows out of a box of Lucky Charms, but that doesn't mean I intend to do it."

"Never?" he challenged.

"Okay," she conceded. "Maybe I did it once. Doesn't mean that was a smart thing to do."

"Then how about a kiss just for a kiss's sake, so you can prove to me whatever we felt downstairs was a fluke."

A fluke? Oh, she already knew what she'd felt, and it was real. That didn't mean she intended to jump into bed with a guy just because the kiss rocked her socks. Perhaps that was the lesson Mr. Have It All needed to learn. She could turn the tables, knock him off balance with a mind-numbing kiss and show him she could—and would—still walk away. Excitement pooled low in her belly at the thought. She trailed her fingers along his forehead, over the eyebrow with a slash of a scar through it, then cupped his jaw in her hands.

With slow deliberation, she took his bottom lip between her teeth, tugging before teasing her tongue along his mouth. His eyes glinted emerald sparks of desire, and then she didn't see anything. Her eyes closed, she sealed herself to him, her mouth, her chest, her hungry hands and hungrier body.

This kiss was different than the reserved connection on the balcony where there'd been the threat of interruption. Here, they were alone. She was free to explore the breadth of his shoulders, the flexing muscles in his arms as he hauled her close.

Her breasts pressed against the hard wall of his chest. Her nipples tightened to needy buds against him, hot and achy, yearning for the soothing stroke of his tongue. A tingling spread inside her, so intense it almost hurt. She wriggled to get even closer, shifting to sit on his lap, straddling him. And...

Oh. My. She arched into him, against the rigid length of his arousal pressing so perfectly against her.

A purr of pleasure clawed up her throat, echoed by his

growl of approval. Apparently this was a language optional make-out session.

His hands slid from her hair, roved down her back and slid under her bottom. In a fluid move, he flipped her onto her back and stretched over her on the sofa. The weight of him felt good, so very good, intensifying every pulsing sensation. The fabric of the sofa rubbed a sweet abrasion against her tingling nerves.

She hooked a leg over his, throwing back her head as he kissed along her jaw and over to her ear. His hot breath caressed her skin with the promise of how good that mouth would feel all over her body. She tipped her face, shaking her hair back and giving him fuller access as he tugged on her earlobe with his teeth. In an out-of-control moment, she flung out an arm to steady herself. Her fingers clenched the coffee table—

Sending her full china cup clattering to the ground.

Troy froze, then looked to the side sharply before sweeping his computer away from the spilled coffee. The rush of air along her overheated body brought a splash of much-needed reason. What the hell was she doing? She'd only just met the guy and already she'd kissed him twice. She'd wanted to show him how she could kiss and walk away, and she'd ended up beneath him.

Gasping, she swung her feet back to the ground, her toes digging into the plush Persian cotton. The rush back to earth was slower than she expected; her senses were still on tingling alert. Giving in to the temptation to kiss him hadn't been her best idea. She should be focused on the video feed, on finding Mr. Mystery Cohort as soon as—

Squinting, she studied a far corner of the screen, just a hint of a flashy gold ring that looked familiar, with some kind of coin embedded on the top. The fog of passion parted enough for her to process what was right in front of her eyes.

"Troy, hold on a second." She grabbed his shoulder. Her fingers curled instinctively around him for a second before she pulled back.

"What's wrong?" He looked over his shoulder.

"On the TV, can you play with the image for me? There…" She pointed to the top left corner as he righted his computer and sat again. "Can you find a reflection of the face of that guy wearing the ugly gold ring?"

"Of course I can." He dropped back onto the sofa with his laptop, his hair still askew from her frenzied fingers. She seriously needed to rein in her out-of-control emotions.

She clenched her fists against the temptation to finger comb his hair back into place and focused her attention forward. In a flash, the picture zoomed in, with a clarity that boggled her mind. Whatever software he had beat the hell out of anything she'd seen on *Law & Order* reruns. The picture moved and inverted as he shuffled the views, pulling up reflections off a number of sources until…

Bingo.

"That's him," Hillary said, standing and walking closer even though she didn't need any further confirmation. "That's Barry's business partner."

Two hours later, Troy leaned in the open doorway to Hillary's room as she packed her small suitcase.

After she had ID'd the face in the video feed, they'd contacted Salvatore. Troy had only caught one glimpse of Barry Curtis's cohort at a regatta race in Miami, but he agreed the face fit what he remembered. Now Salvatore was off making his calls to contacts. Since they had a face to run through international visual recognition systems, hopefully soon they would have a name. An honest to God lead, a trail to follow. They would have the guy in custody soon.

But in the interim, Troy needed to make sure no backlash came Hillary's way for bringing down a multibillion-dollar international money laundering operation. He needed to keep her in his sights. And lucky for him, thanks to the bachelor auction, going their separate ways wasn't going to be that easy to accomplish. Aside from the fact that everyone in that ballroom had seen them together, the tabloids had snapped photos that were already circulating around the blogosphere. Follow-ups would come their way, questions on how they'd spent their weekend together. She couldn't just duck out of sight, and he couldn't let her stand alone and vulnerable in the spotlight.

He had to admit, time with Hillary would not be a hardship in the least.

Thanks to a pair of killer high heels, her already-amazing legs looked even more train-stopping. Her black tank top and wide belt drew his eyes to every curve he'd felt pressed against him earlier. Curves he was determined to explore at length someday in the not-too-distant future.

He might be completely the wrong man for a rose-colored glasses chick, but that last kiss from Hillary made it impossible for him to turn away. She would be his. The only question was when.

Now that their first goal of the weekend had been accomplished, he would have time with her to figure that out. She might think she was going home to D.C., but he had other plans. He just needed to persuade her.

Hillary flicked her damp ponytail over her shoulder. "What's wrong, Troy? Aren't you happy? We helped them identify the guy." She zipped her roll bag closed. "He won't be able to rip people off anymore. You delivered justice today."

"He's not in custody, and he's smart." Troy shoved away from the door, taking her question as an invitation to enter her bedroom in the shared suite. "If he realizes you're the one who identified him… No, I'm not ready to celebrate yet."

"I'll be fine." Her confidence was hot.

Too bad it was also misguided.

"You're too damn naive about this. You're going to take time off from work and come with me. I know a great, low-profile place where you can put your feet up and relax until this all blows over."

"That he-man act may work with some women, but not with me. I'm going home. The whole reason I came to Chicago was to ID this guy so I could go back to the job I love." She hefted up her suitcase.

He thought about taking the bag from her, but a tug-of-war would likely make her pull back all the more. He sat on the end of the chaise by the window. "You can't return to D.C. Not yet. You need to lie low until the authorities bring him in."

"That's a rather open-ended timeline." She dropped the bag to the ground and sat on it. "I can't just duck out of my life indefinitely."

Good. At least she wasn't walking out the door. "The colonel assures me it will be a week, two weeks tops. Take emergency leave—say you've got a sick mother."

"Sick mom? Really?" She crossed her feet at the ankles. "You think up lies easily."

"Say whatever the hell you want." He tapped the toe of her high heels with his Ferragamo-clad foot. "But let me help."

"No, thanks." She tapped him right back. "I can take my own vacation without you."

His foot worked up to her ankle. "Can you just walk away from this?"

Her lashes fluttered for an instant before she said, "It's just physical reaction."

"Is that such a bad thing?"

"It can be." She pulled her foot back and crossed her legs.

Gorgeous legs. Miles long. The sort made for wrapping around a man's waist.

"Then come away with me for a week, err on the side of caution." He winked. "I promise to come through for you."

"Argh!" She stomped both heels on the carpet. "Can't you just talk to me? Drop the charming, polished act and just speak."

His grin spread. "You think I'm charming?"

She shot to her feet and grabbed her bag by the handle. "Forget it—"

He stepped in front of her. "I'm sorry. I just… I don't want you to leave. What the hell do you want from me?"

"Honesty. Why are you pushing so hard when this is already settled? Our work here is done, and I'm not a defenseless kid."

"Hillary, damn it…" He struggled for the words to convince her when she'd hamstrung him by telling him not to use any charm. Kissing her again wouldn't gain him any traction right now, either. "You confuse the hell out of me. I'm worried about you, and hell, yes, I want to make love to you on the beach in every continent. But I also want time with you."

"Honestly?"

"As truthful as I know how to be. Spend a week with

me. Be safe. Get me out of your system so you can return to your regular life without regrets."

"What makes you think you're in my system?"

"Really? Are you going to look me in the eye and tell me you don't feel the attraction, too? And before you answer, remember I was there when we kissed."

"Okay, I'll admit there's…chemistry."

"Explosive chemistry, but it's clear neither one of us is ready for something long-term. So let's let whatever this is between us play out before we return to our regular lives."

She studied his face, and he could have sworn she swayed toward him. But it was just her head moving back and forth.

"I can't, Troy. I'm sorry." She backed away, pulling her roller bag with her. "I'm going home to Washington, to my normal, wonderfully *boring* life."

Ouch.

There wasn't a comeback for that.

Stunned, he watched her walk away. She was actually leaving, opting for her everyday job in D.C. rather than signing on for the adventure of following their attraction wherever it led. Some might call it ego for him to be so stunned, but honest to God, he was floored by the power of their attraction. He knew it wasn't one-sided. That she would turn her back on the promise of something so unique, so fantastic—so very much *not* boring— blew him away.

He wasn't sure exactly why it was so important to him that he follow her. The attraction. Keeping her safe. The challenge of her saying no. Maybe all three reasons.

Regardless, she'd vastly underestimated him if she thought they were through. If she wouldn't come with him then he would simply have to make do with helping her hide out in the nation's capital.

* * *

She'd actually done it. She'd walked away from Troy Donavan.

That made her either the strongest woman in the world—or the most afraid. Because the thought of spending the next week or two with Troy was the scariest and most tempting offer she'd ever received. Walking away hadn't been easy, and she still didn't know if that made her decision to do so right or wrong.

Her roller bag jammed in the revolving door.

Figured.

She yanked and yanked until finally the door bounced back and released her suitcase. Freed, she stepped outside the hotel, scanning for a cab. She would worry about the expense of changing her ticket return date later.

Of course it was raining, turning an already-muggy early morning all the more humid and dank and overcast. Four more aggressive commuters snagged cabs before her. Exhausted, frustrated and close to tears, she sat on her suitcase again.

"Need a ride?"

Hillary almost fell off the bag.

"Colonel Salvatore?" She steadied herself—darn heels she'd vainly chosen because of Troy. "I'm just trying to catch a cab to the airport."

Her eccentric contact again wore a gray suit and red tie, his buzz-cut hair exposed to the elements. She couldn't help but think about Troy's linen fedora and all the thin-brimmed hats he wore in the photos of him that filled the press.

"Then let me take you. I owe you that, as well as arranging for your change in flight plans."

Resisting would be foolish, and she really did need to leave before she raced back up to Troy's suite—which she couldn't even do since she didn't have a penthouse key card. "Thank you. I gratefully accept."

A driver was already opening the doors to a dark SUV with tinted windows. She slid inside for what had to be the most awkward car ride of her life. Colonel Salvatore didn't speak for their whole drive through the city to Chicago's O'Hare International. He simply typed away on his tablet computer. After five minutes of silence, she focused her attention on final views of the city slicked with rain. Who knew when or if she would return?

Her eyes drifted over to study the colonel, the former headmaster of Troy's military high school. Troy had said he "helped out" but how deeply did that connection go? She'd been working with local authorities when she met the colonel.... None of it mattered. Time to put the past— Barry— behind her and start fresh.

Right?

But once they reached the airport, the SUV didn't stop at the terminal. "Colonel?"

Holding up a hand, he focused on whatever he was working on at the moment.

"Sir," she pressed as the muffled sound of jet engines grew louder, closer, "where are we going?"

He clapped the cover closed on his tablet. "To the private planes. I'm taking a personal jet."

"But I'm going to D.C. Regular coach status is okay with me."

"You have options."

"I've done what you asked me. It's time for me to go home."

"Troy will follow you because he's convinced you need watching until we have everything neatly tied up."

A thrill shot through her before she could steel herself,

an unstoppable excitement over the thought of seeing him again after all. "He's free to go where he chooses."

"Or you could go with him to someplace...different."

Confusion cleared, like the mist rolling away to reveal the line of private jets beyond the colonel's. "He's in one of those planes, isn't he? Is it his personal aircraft or is he waiting inside yours?"

"You're a quick one. Good. Troy needs someone sharp to keep up with him." He nodded toward the row of silver planes nestled in the morning mist. "Mine's next in line, and yes, the one closest is Troy's private aircraft."

"You expect me to just hitch a ride with him? Don't I need to check in or something?"

"I've okayed everything with the pilot. You have your luggage with you." He smiled for the first time. "Admit it. You're tempted to spend time with him. So why not go away with him for a week?"

She bristled at his confidence. "You're awfully sure of yourself."

"Just hedging my bets," he said so matter-of-factly that they could have been discussing breakfast—not the idea of her hopping on a near stranger's plane to go God only knew where.

"You have an answer for everything."

"I study people and make calculated decisions based on how I believe they will react." He straightened his already-impeccable red tie.

"And you're calling me predictable." How could he when she didn't even have a clue what to do next?

"I just bargained on you doing the right thing for Troy."

"The right thing for *Troy?*" That brought her up short. "What are you talking about?"

"I gave you credit for being smarter than this."

She leveled a steady gaze at him and wished she could

wield something a little harsher. She was at the end of her patience here, exhaustion and emotional turmoil having worn her out. "You're not a very nice man."

"But I'm effective."

"Please, get to your point," she snapped. "Or I am leaving."

"I have to agree with Troy that life would be easier and less complicated for all of us if the two of you took a remote vacation. Running around D.C. is too obvious a place for you to be when there is a rich and powerful individual still at large who has reason to be quite unhappy with you and Troy. And if Troy follows you straight to your home, anyone who might be upset over this sting will be able to find Troy, too.... Do I need to keep spelling out all the extremely uncomfortable scenarios for you?"

Her skin went cold. She'd been worried about her future—as in her freedom—but she'd never considered that white-collar criminals might resort to force. "You're not playing fair. And what did you plan to do with me once I ID'd the guy? Did you have a plan to keep me safe?"

"I had hoped we would have the man in custody, and when he got away, I assumed you would be leaving with Troy, based on seeing the two of you together."

The attraction was that obvious to others? "Well, you guessed wrong, and now you're telling me *I'm* responsible for Troy's safety? That's your job, isn't it?"

"I'm doing my job right now. I'm saying what has to be said, for both of your sakes. Get on his plane. By letting him think he's protecting you, you'll be protecting him."

She hesitated.

His eyes flickered with the first signs of something other than calculation or cool disdain. He looked like he actually...cared. "Ms. Wright, please, be the first person in Troy's life to put his interests ahead of your own."

His words sucker punched the air right out of her.

Whether or not his words were genuine or calculated, he'd found a means of coercion so much stronger than force. For whatever reason, she had a connection to Troy, a man she'd only known for a day. He had an influence over her emotions that she couldn't explain.

Maybe it was because she understood what it was like not to have anyone put her first in their lives. Or maybe it was the memory of all he'd told her about his time in school. Or maybe it was that she wanted more kisses.

Whatever the reason, she was climbing on board that airplane.

Dropping his hat on his head, Troy slid from the limo outside his aircraft just as the colonel boarded his Learjet. Ironic. Apparently everyone was getting the hell out of Dodge.

He tugged out his briefcase and jogged through the light rain to the stairs. Once he made it inside, he would need to confer with the pilot about changing their flight plan, rerouting for D.C.

Even with the delay, at least he could work since his plane was a fully outfitted office and completely familiar. He'd built a pod he could move from the hold of any aircraft to another, with an office, a small kitchenette and sleeping quarters. Some seemed surprised at the lack of luxury, but he didn't need the trappings. He had what was important to him: his own portable technological nirvana.

He ducked through the hatch inside and stopped short.

Hillary. Here. On his private jet.

She lounged at his desk, her iPad open in front of her. Early-morning sunrise streamed through a window and outlined her in an amber glow.

Amber glow?

Good God, this woman was turning him into some kind of a poet.

She spun the chair to face him. "I assume that was an open invitation to go with you, but don't gloat. It's not an attractive trait."

He placed his briefcase on the white leather sofa and pulled his hat off. "Well, I certainly wouldn't want to do anything that would make me unappealing to you."

"Good. We're on the same page then." She returned to her iPad and started typing.

"Everything okay?" He resisted the urge to offer her one of the tablets he had on board, prototypes beyond anything the public had seen yet.

"I'm sending a couple of emails to rearrange things at work so I can take an emergency vacation for personal reasons." She looked up. "I'm not comfortable with a convenient 'my mom is sick' lie."

"Fair enough." He placed his hat on his desk in front of her.

She closed her iPad. "Just so we're clear, I'm here for safety's sake. Not for sex."

God, the spark in her eyes made him hot. Although now might not be the best time to point that out.

"Can't be much clearer than that."

"Good. Now where are we going?"

"Monte Carlo."

"Monte Carlo?" she squeaked, her composure slipping. "What about passports?"

"Taken care of. If you recall, when the CIA first questioned you, they required you to turn over your passport to ensure you wouldn't flee the country. Now that you're in the clear, you can have it back. We'll make a brief refueling stop in D.C.—your passport is already there waiting to be picked up." While Hillary talked, he pulled out his phone and typed instructions to his assistant and Salvatore to make sure her passport *would* be there.

"And what about clothes for me to be gone that long? Appropriate for that locale and weather?"

"Got it covered." He dashed off another text to his assistant before tucking his phone back inside his suit.

"You were that confident I would join you? I'm not sure I like being that predictable."

"Hillary, you are anything but predictable." He scooped up his hat and dropped it on her head, sliding his fingers along the brim.

"Why Monte Carlo?"

"Why not?" He tugged her by the hand to sit on the sofa beside him. He flicked the seat belt toward her and they both buckled in for takeoff.

"Do you live your life that way?" She touched his hat self-consciously. "With a perpetual why not?"

"Works for me." Right now, he was living for the day he saw her wearing that hat and nothing else.

"Why Monte Carlo?" she repeated.

Because he had backup there, and he needed help from someone he could trust. Sometimes, the brotherhood reached out to each other, without Salvatore in the mix. This would be one of those times.

Of all his military school friends, Conrad Hughes, the very first person he'd met on the first day of school, would understand how a woman messed with a man's head. Conrad wouldn't judge. "I'm touching base with a friend who can help cover our tracks. Ever been to Monte Carlo?"

She took off his hat and dropped it on his lap. "I went to Atlantic City once."

"Did you like it?"

"Yes, I did."

"Then you're in for a treat beyond anything the Tooth Fairy would shove under your pillow." He put his hat on, tugged it over his eyes and stretched out to nap.

Six

Monte Carlo was everything she'd imagined—and more.

They'd landed at an oceanside private airstrip near the Ports de Monaco, where a limo awaited them. A thrilling ride later, along the Mediterranean coastline, they'd arrived at a casino that overlooked a rocky cove and packed marina. The beige stucco resort, while clearly pristinely new, had a historical design with Roman columns and arches, statues and sculptures spotlighted in the moonless dark.

Deep inside, there were no windows, but plenty of lights so bright it was impossible to tell day from night. Troy walked through without stopping at the check-in desk. She didn't bother asking questions. She'd already seen how regular rules didn't seem to apply to him.

The air was filled with the cacophony of machines, bells, whistles and gambling calls, but more than that, she heard music, laughter and the splash of a mammoth fountain. Her high heels clicked along the marble mosaic tiles as she and Troy weaved through the crush of vacationers. A mix of languages came at her from all directions, a little like mingling in some of the D.C. parties she'd planned.

Except eyes followed them here. People whispered and pointed, recognizing Troy Donavan.

He pulled off his signature hat. "Let's try our luck once before we head up. Your choice. Cards? Roulette? Slots?"

Exhaustion took a backseat to excitement. Monte Carlo had been in her top ten fantasy places to visit as a kid. She'd researched it, dreaming of James Bond and Grace Kelly. But photos and movies and tabloids just didn't capture the vivid colors, clashing sounds, exotic scents. She'd even fantasized about a fascinating man on her arm, and the reality on that count far surpassed any dreams.

"I'm a little underdressed for cards or roulette." She swept her hands down her jeans.

"You're welcome anywhere I say you are."

Ooooh-kay. "I'm good with a slot machine."

"Fair enough." He guided her to a line of looming machines with high leather bar stools in front.

He offered his hand as she settled in place. Tokens? She'd totally forgotten about getting—

A woman in uniform stopped beside them, smiling at Troy. "*Bonjour,* Mr. Donavan," she said in heavily accented English. She passed him a leather pouch. "Compliments of the house. Mr. Hughes sends his regards."

"*Merci, mademoiselle.*" He opened the pouch and Hillary caught a glimpse of tokens, chips, key cards and cash. He pulled out a fistful of tokens and extended his open palm to Hillary.

"Only one token, thanks. For luck before we go to our rooms to freshen up."

Hillary plucked a single coin from his hand and hitched

up into the chair. *Ching,* she set the lights flashing and waited for the results.... Troy stood behind her, leaning in ever so slightly until his bay rum scent mixed with the perfume of live flowers.

She'd given up trying to understand how she could still be so drawn to, so aware of, a man she knew led a secret life and wouldn't hesitate to stretch the truth if he thought it was "for her own good." Here she was in Monte Carlo and all she could think about was how glad she was to be here with Troy. For the moment, at least, she would embrace the adventure. She would revel in the sensations and refuse to let herself get too attached.

The slot machine ended on a losing note, and she didn't even care. She was here, and her nerves all tingled as if she'd hit a jackpot.

Chemistry. What a crazy thing.

She smiled over her shoulder at him, which brought their mouths so close. She could see the widening of his pupils, see every detail of the scar through his eyebrow. Her breathing grew heavier but she couldn't seem to control the betraying reaction that gave away just how much she wanted his mouth on hers again. She froze, waiting for him to make a move....

He simply smiled and stepped back, offering his hand for her to slide from the high bar stool.

"Whenever you're ready," he said.

Her breath gushed out in a rush. Disappointment over that lost chance for a quick kiss taunted her. She put her hand in his. "Thanks. Or should I say *merci?*"

His hand warmed her the whole way to the elevator, which was made mostly of glass, for riders to watch the whole casino on the way up. Her stomach dropped as the lift rose. She'd always prided herself on being so practical in her plans for her life, but the way she wanted to be with Troy was completely illogical. And now they were as far away from Salvatore, chaperones and intrusions as possible.

What did she want from this time with him while they waited for the all clear from Salvatore?

The answer came to her, as clear as the elevator glass— so smudge-free she almost felt like she could walk right through and into the open air. She wanted to learn more about Troy—and yes, she wanted to sleep with him. She needed to sort through his charm to find out what was real about him, then figure out how to walk away without regrets and restless dreams once she returned home.

The elevator doors slid open as she once again headed to a hotel suite. With Troy.

He palmed her back and guided her into the luxurious, apartment-sized space with a balcony view of the marina. High ceilings and white furniture with powder-blue accents gave the Parisian-style room an airy feel after the heavier Gatsby tapestries of their Chicago penthouse. She stared out at the glistening waters as the bellhop unloaded their bags and slipped away quietly.

Troy walked through her peripheral vision. "Something to drink before we head down for dinner?"

"I didn't sleep at all last night and while you may have had an amazing nap on the plane—" damn his nonchalant soul "—I did not. I just want room service and a good night's rest. Can we 'do' Monte Carlo tomorrow when I'll be awake enough to enjoy it?"

"Absolutely." He tossed his hat on the sleek sofa before walking to the wet bar. "What would you like to drink?"

"Club soda, please," she answered automatically. "Thank you."

He poured the carbonated water into a cut crystal tumbler, clinking two cubes of ice inside. "That's not the first time you've turned down alcohol."

"I told you before." She took the glass from him, fingers brushing with an increasing familiarity. "I don't drink. Ever."

"Have I been around long enough to hear the story yet?" He rattled the ice in his own soda water.

Why not? It wasn't a secret. "My mother was an alcoholic who hit rock bottom so many times she should have had a quarry named after her."

"I'm very sorry."

"It's not your fault."

He brushed her shoulder, skimming back her ponytail. "I'm still sorry you had to go through that."

"I learned a lot about keeping up appearances." She sipped her drink and watched boats come in for the day and others head out with lights already blazing for night travel. "It's served me well in my current profession."

"That's an interesting way of making lemonade out of lemons."

Enough about her and her old wounds. The point of this time in Monte Carlo, for her, was to learn more about him.

She pivoted to face him, leaning against the warm windowpane. "What about you?"

"What do you mean?" he answered evasively.

"Your childhood? Tell me more about it."

"I had two parents supremely interested in appearances—which meant I never had to learn how to play nice. They were always ready to cover up any mistakes we made." His eyes glinted wickedly as he stared at her over his glass.

"Us?"

"My older brother and I."

"You have a brother? I don't recall—"

"Ahh…" He tapped her nose. "So you did read my Wikipedia page."

"Of course I did." She'd been trying to find some leverage, since this man tipped her world about seventeen times a minute. "It doesn't mention your brother."

"Those pages can be tweaked you know. The internet is fluid, rewritable."

She shivered from more than the air conditioner. "You erased your brother from your history?"

"It's for his own safety." He stared into his drink moodily before downing it.

"How so? What does your brother do now?"

"He's in jail." He returned to the bar and reached for a bottle of scotch—Chivas Regal Royal Salute, which she happened to know from event planning sold at about ten thousand dollars a bottle. "If the other inmates know the kind of connections he has, the access to money…"

She watched him pour the amber whiskey into a glass—damn near liquid gold. "What's he in prison for?"

"Drug dealing." He swirled his drink along the insides of the glass, just shy of the top, without spilling a drop.

"Did your parents cover up for him?"

"Periodically, they checked him into rehabs, before they took off for Europe or China or Australia. He checked himself out as soon as they left the continental U.S." He knocked back half an inch.

"You blame them."

"I blame him." He set down his glass beside the open bottle. "He made his own choices the same way I have made mine."

"But drug dealing… Drug addiction." She'd seen the fallout of addiction for the family members, and as much as she wanted to pour that ten-thousand-dollar bottle of booze down the sink, she also wanted to wrap her arms around Troy's waist, rest her head on his shoulder and let him know she understood how confusing and painful his home life must have been.

"Yes, he was an addict. He detoxed in prison." He looked up with conflicted, wounded eyes. "Is it wrong of me to hope he stays there? I'm afraid that if he gets out…"

Her unshed tears burned. She reached for his arm.

He grinned down at her wryly. "You and I probably shouldn't have children together. Our genes could prove problematic. Sure the kids would be brilliant and gorgeous." He stepped back, clearly using humor to put distance between them as a defense against a conversation that was getting too deep, too fast. "But with so much substance abuse—"

"Troy," she interrupted, putting her club soda down slowly. This guy was good at steering conversations, but she was onto his tactics now. "It's not going to work."

"What do you mean?"

"Trying to scare me off by saying startling things."

His eyes narrowed, and he stepped closer predatorily. "Does that mean you want to try and make a baby?"

She cradled his face in her hands, calling his bluff and standing him down, toe to toe. "You're totally outrageous."

"And you're outrageously hot." He rocked his hips against hers. "So let's have lots of very well-protected sex together."

She brushed her thumb over his mouth even though the gesture cost her. Big-time. Her body was on fire. "Abstinence is the best protection of all."

"Killjoy." He nipped the sensitive pad of her thumb before stepping back. "I'll go downstairs and leave you to your rest then. Order anything you want from room service. Everything you'll need is in your room. Enjoy a bubble bath. God knows, I'll be enjoying thinking of you in one."

He scooped up the bottle of Chivas on his way out of the suite.

Great. She'd won. And never had she felt more completely awake in her life.

He sure as hell wasn't going to get any sleep tonight, not with Hillary sleeping nearby.

Without question, he intended to make love to her. But not tonight. He had business to take care of, ensuring he covered their trail and that she was safely tucked away. Then, he would be free to seduce every beautiful inch of her taste by taste, touch by touch, without worry that some criminal would come looking for her.

First, he needed to find Conrad Hughes.

Luckily, the leather pouch included a key card to Conrad's private quarters. At last count, Conrad owned seven, but the one in his casino was his favorite and his primary residence since he'd split with his wife.

The second the elevator doors parted, Conrad was there, waiting. Of course he'd seen Troy coming. Nothing happened in this place without the owner knowing.

"Hello, brother." Conrad waved him inside, brandy snifter in hand. "Welcome to my little slice of heaven."

Conrad Hughes, Mr. Wall Street, and Troy's first friend at the military reform school, led him into the ultimate man cave, full of massive leather furniture and a gigantic television screen hidden behind an oil painting. There was a sense of high-end style like the rest of the place, but without the feminine frills.

Apparently, Conrad had stripped those away when he and his wife separated.

Troy held up the Chivas. "I brought refreshments."

"But you didn't bring your lady friend. I'm disappointed not to meet her."

"She's changing after our trip." Images of her in the spa tub were a helluva lot more intoxicating than anything in the top-shelf bottle he carried. "I figured this would be a good chance to speak with you on my own. Check in, catch up and whatnot."

They had a long history together—two of the three founding members of The Alpha Brotherhood.

Conrad had been a step away from juvie when they'd met in reform school. His crime? Manipulating the stock market, crashing businesses with strategic infusions of cash in competing companies, manipulating the rise and fall of share prices. He would have been hung out to dry by the court and the press, except someone stumbled on the fact that every targeted company had been guilty of using child laborers in sweatshops overseas.

Once the press got hold of that part of his case, he'd been lauded as a white knight. The judge had offered a deal similar to Troy's. Through the colonel's mentorship, they'd learned to channel their passionate beliefs about right and wrong. Now they had the chance to right wrongs within the parameters of the law.

Their friendship had lasted seventeen years. Troy trusted this man without question. And now was one of those times he would have to call upon his help.

His wiry, lanky buddy had turned into someone who looked more like a pro athlete these days than a pencil-pushing businessman. The women had always gone wild over Conrad's broody act—but he'd only ever fallen for one woman.

Conrad had gone darker these days, edging closer to the sarcastic bastard he'd been in the old days. A sarcastic bastard with dark circles under his eyes and a dining tray full of half-eaten food. His friend looked like he'd been to hell and back very recently.

Troy sprawled in a massive leather wingback chair across from Conrad. "I need to tuck Hillary away for a week or so, but I don't want anyone looking for us."

"Is this Salvatore-related or just a need for personal time with a lady friend?"

Conrad was one of the few people on the earth he could be completely honest with. "Started as the first, became both."

"Fine, I can handle things from this end."

Troy trusted Conrad to do what was asked, but he wasn't quite as clear on Conrad's methods, and these days, Troy was more careful about life. Right now more than ever, he couldn't afford to let his impulsive nature take over. Control was paramount.

"Want to share how you intend to do that?"

"Because you're worried I can't handle it? I'm hurt, brother, truly wounded." Conrad drained his drink and poured another.

"Because I want to learn from the master."

"Nice salve to my ego." He smirked. "But I get it. A woman's involved. You can't just leave it all to trust. I can cover for you."

He thumbed on the wide-screen TV and a video of Hillary with Troy at the slot machine played. "I assume this little snippet here was a public display for gossipmongers and the press or you would have used my secure, private entrance."

"Of course it was." He and Conrad had secret access to each other's homes around the world at any time. Yes, he had wanted people to see him with Hillary here, and he should have realized Conrad would have already intuited his plan. "Kudos to your security people for capturing my good side."

"My casino staff aims to please." Conrad cleared the screen. "I'll loop some reels on the security tapes of you, play with the technology so it looks like you're wearing different clothes on different days. My secretary will submit some photos to society pages. The world will think you're here kicking up your heels like a carefree playboy with his next conquest."

"Thanks." He stifled a wince at the word *conquest*. Somehow Hillary had become...more. "I appreciate your help."

"Your plane trip here will cement the story. It would help if you forwarded me some photos from the different airports."

"Consider it done." And that quickly, business was taken care of, which only left the personal stuff. "How are you, brother?"

"I'm good."

"You look like crap. Have you slept recently? Eaten a meal?"

"Who turned you into the veggie police?"

"Fair enough." Troy lifted his drink in a toast. "Just worried about how you're doing since you and Jayne split."

Even the woman's name made Conrad curse.

The breakup had been a surprise to everyone who knew them and so far neither of them was spilling details. Even the social pages had been strangely quiet on the issue and God knows, if either had been cheating, some telephoto lens would have caught something.

Not that his friend would have ever cheated on Jayne. The two had been crazy in love, but a restless traveler didn't work well with a white-picket-fence woman. And those middle of the night calls to assist Colonel Salvatore probably hadn't helped, either.

Conrad rolled his glass between his palms. "Jayne took a job in the States."

"She's a nurse, right?" he asked, more for keeping his friend talking than a need to know.

"Home health care. My altruistic, estranged wife is taking care of a dying old guy, even though she has millions in her checking account. Money she won't touch." His hands pressed tighter on the cut crystal until something had to give. Soon. "She hates me that much. But hey, by all means, don't let my catastrophe of a marriage turn you off of relationships. Not all of them end up slicing and dicing your heart."

He flung his glass into the fireplace, crystal shattering. He reached for the bottle.

"Dude, you really need to lay off the booze. It's making you maudlin."

"And mean. Yeah, I know." He set the bottle down again. "Let's play cards."

"Believe I'll pass tonight. I prefer not to have my ass handed to me." And truthfully, he was itching to get back to Hillary now that he'd taken care of business. But he couldn't leave until he was sure his buddy would be okay.

"You're no fun. And after I did you this great favor."

"Hey, we could play Alpha Realms IV."

"So you can hand me my ass? No, thanks." He thumbed the television back on. "What do you say we catch—"

A sound at the door cut him off short and they both shot to their feet. Hillary stood on the threshold with the leather pouch in her hands and a master access key card in her other hand. "Alpha Realms IV? Really? How old are you two? Ten?"

Conrad set aside the bottle slowly, a calculating gleam in his eyes that had Troy's instincts blaring. *Mine.*

"Ah, so this is Hillary Wright in the flesh. Or should I call you Troy's Achilles's heel?"

Seven

Hillary stood self-consciously in the open archway leading into what could only be described as the man cave to end all man caves.

She'd finished her bath and her meal only to find she'd discovered her second wind. She'd put on a chic yellow silk dress and gone in search of Troy. The guard outside her door had informed her that the leather pouch was her golden ticket to whatever she needed at the casino. Then her own personal body guard had escorted her here to find Troy and his buddy, the casino owner.

Good God, there was a lot of testosterone in this room. Whereas Troy was unconventionally handsome, edgy even, his buddy was traditional: tall, dark, buffed and broody.

Personally, she preferred edgy.

"I'm Conrad Hughes," the dark-haired Adonis extended a not-so-steady hand. "Mr. Alpha Realms's best friend."

Troy hooked an arm around his shoulders. "And he's a perpetual liar, so disregard anything he says."

Like the part about her being his Achilles's heel?

Conrad simply laughed. "As for being ten, yeah. We're men. We're perpetually ten in some aspects."

In which case, she should probably just go. "I'll just leave you to it. I'm sorry I bothered you."

Troy grasped her elbow. "Hold on. I'm done here." He glanced over his shoulder. "Right, bud?"

Nodding once, Conrad said, "We're good. Now go, have fun. What's mine is yours. Nice to meet you, Hillary."

She was back in the elevator with her guard excused before she could register being ushered out. "I think you and your buddy Conrad both need to sleep it off rather than play video games."

"I'm not drunk. Not even drinking anymore beyond the one I had in the room and one when I came down here." He brushed his lips across her forehead. "You're welcome to check my breath."

She tipped her head to his, their mouths so close. And as she looked deeply in his eyes, she could see he was completely sober. He hadn't lied. He'd controlled himself. There hadn't been some "out with the boys" bender. He was here for her, and that was definitely more intoxicating than alcohol.

"I'm not sure I understand you."

"Hillary, the last thing I would do is show up drunk in our room. You have understandable issues on the subject. If I stumbled in sloshed I would be less likely to score."

And that fast he eased the tension that had been growing too heavy and fast for her.

Laughing, she strode ahead of him out of the elevator, back at their suite. "Oh my God, did you really just say that?"

She glanced over her shoulder and caught him watching her with unmistakable appreciation.

"I did. And you're a little turned on." Walking behind her, he stroked a finger up her spine. "Admit it."

Hell, yes. She was burning up inside from a simple touch along her back.

"I'm a little exasperated." She bantered right back without brushing his hand away. Funny, how she was becoming more and more comfortable with his hands on her. Maybe too much so.

"Let's see what I can do about that."

She spun around, hand on her hips. "Seriously, are you suffering from some kind of Peter Pan syndrome? You crack jokes at inappropriate times and you still play video games."

"I develop software, yes."

Her thoughts screeched to a halt. She was learning fast to pick apart his words since he had a deft way of dodging questions with wordplay. "Not just video games?"

"Did I say that?"

There was something here. "Why do I get the sense you're toying with me?"

"Maybe because I would like to toy with you, all night long." His hands fell to rest on her shoulders. "But we need to leave Monte Carlo first thing in the morning so you really should get some sleep."

"We just got here. I thought we were going to play." Is that what she wanted? To play? All she knew was that she didn't want to say goodbye to him, not yet.

"We didn't come here to play. We came here to get you out of the public eye." All lightheartedness left his gaze and she saw the cool calculation at the foundation of everything he'd done. "First thing in the morning, we're going to leave through Conrad's private entrance. The world will think we're here in Monte Carlo somewhere, in case anyone's looking."

"Where are we really going?"

"To my house."

His house? She struggled to thread through his rapidly changing plans. "Didn't you say you live in Virginia? Doesn't that defeat the whole purpose of lying low?"

"I said I'm from Virginia. I do have my business based there, the corporate offices. But I have a second home where I get away to do the creative part of my job—or just to get the hell away, period."

With each word he confirmed there was so much more to him than she'd realized. She hadn't looked below the surface, not really. Maybe because the steady logical man in front of her made the charming playboy all the more appealing. "Where would that be? Who knows where we're going? I'm all for hiding out, but there needs to be someone to look for us if we fall off the planet."

"Smart woman. I respect that about you." He cradled her face in his hands, thumbs grazing her jaw, the calluses rasping over her tingling skin. "I assume you trust Colonel Salvatore."

"As much as I trust anyone these days. The whole trust thing is…scary."

"Good. Those concerns are there to keep you safe in life." With a nod, he stepped away. "We'll make a pit stop at Interpol headquarters in Lyon, France, and update him personally on our way."

"On our way to where?" Her eyes followed him as he walked toward his room without pressing her to accompany him. Which of course only made her want to go with him all the more.

"Costa Rica. But before we get there, I have a surprise."

* * *

Dinner in France?

Hillary was blown away by Troy's incredibly thoughtful surprise. He'd remembered her wish to talk to the chefs in Chicago, and he'd taken that dream up a notch.

Some of the finest chefs in the world worked in Lyon. She'd expected to zip into Interpol and be whisked right out of the country. But Troy had given her a hat of her own and sunglasses, changed his signature fedora for a ball cap and they'd become typical tourists in a heartbeat. After an early dinner, he'd suggested a sunset walk at the municipal gardens—*Jardin botanique de Lyon*—in the Golden Head Park. *Garden* didn't come close to describing the magnificence of everything from tropical flowers to peonies and lilies, to a massive greenhouse with camellias over a hundred years old.

The scent alone was positively orgasmic.

His hand wrapped around hers felt mighty damn special, too.

Holding hands while walking in the park was something so fundamental, so basic anywhere in the world, yet she strolled with a world-renowned guy in France, no less. Still, he made it seem like an everyday sort of date.

And there was no question but that this was an honest-to-goodness date.

Of course, this was the guy who'd cut his teeth on breaking into the Department of Defense's network. Who was he, this man who ran in such high-profile circles but appreciated simple things? A man who worried so deeply about his brother, even as he pretended to cut himself off from deeper feelings with a carefree attitude?

Troy was getting to her, in spite of all her wary instincts shouting out for self-preservation. She wanted for once to find out the yearnings of her heart could be trusted.

She leaned in to smell a camellia. "Why did you do it?"

"Do what?" His thumb caressed the inside of her wrist.

"Really?" She glanced sideways at him through her lashes. "Doesn't everyone ask you about it?"

He brushed an intimate kiss along her ear. "Why did I break into the Department of Defense's computer system?"

"Yeah."

"I told you already." His mouth flirted closer to the corner of her lips. "I was bored."

"I'm not buying it." She spoke against his mouth.

"Then you tell me. Why do you think I did it?" Pulling back, he held her eyes as firmly as he held her hand.

She studied him for a second before answering honestly. "I think you want me to say something awful so you can get pissed off."

"Why the hell would I do that?" He scowled.

"And yet, you're getting pissed anyway, which gives you a convenient wall between us." She tapped the furrows in his forehead.

He backed her against a roped-off area. "You want more? Walls down, total openness and everything that comes with that?"

"You'll only find out if you answer." She smoothed aside the long hair on his forehead, his normally cool-guy 'do pushed down by his ball cap. "If you don't want to tell me the real reason, just say so, but it's unrealistic to think people—especially people close to you—wouldn't want to know."

"You're close to me?" He linked both arms around her, bringing her closer.

"Aren't I?" Butterflies filled her stomach as she thought about how close she wanted to get, how deeply she wanted to trust Troy.

His arms fell away and he backed away a step. "Okay,

fine…" He whipped off the cap and thrust his hands through his hair before jamming the hat on his head again. "Everyone says I had this altruistic reason for what I did, but honest to God, I was unsupervised, spoiled and pissed off at my parents for not—hell, I don't know."

"You did it to get their attention." An image of him as a boy started to take shape, one that tugged at her heart. She suspected there was more to the story but that he was only going to tell her at his own pace.

"I wasn't five." He steered her out of the way of an older couple snapping photos of flowers, touching her with such ease, as if they were lovers. "I was fifteen."

"But you weren't an adult."

"Lucky for me or I'd have been in prison." He stuffed his hands in his suit pockets. "Hell, if I'd done the same thing today, even as a teen, I wouldn't have gotten off so easy."

"So the brotherhood, the guys like you at the military high school, they were really more of the family you never had."

Defensiveness eased from his shoulders. "They were."

"The casino owner? He's a brother?"

"What do you think?"

Her mind skipped to the obvious question. "What did he do?"

He hesitated for an instant before shrugging those broad shoulders that endlessly drew her eyes. "It's public knowledge anyway. Remember the big fluctuation in the stock market a little over seventeen years ago?"

"No kidding?" She gasped. She'd only been about ten at the time, but her teachers had used it in a lesson plan on government and economics. Newscasters and economists still referred to it on occasion. "That was him?"

She sank down on a park bench as other tourists milled past.

"He accessed his father's account, invested money, made a crapton. So his dad let him keep right on investing." He sat beside her, his warm thigh pressing against hers. "But when he caught a couple of his dad's friends assaulting his sister…"

"He crashed the friend's business?"

Troy stretched his arm along the bench, touching her, taking part in more universal dating rituals. "He did. And once he was in the system, he uncovered a cesspool of companies using child laborers overseas. The press lauded him as a hero, but he never considered himself one since his initial intent was revenge."

"So even though what he did was wrong, he had an emotionally intense reason for it, as did you."

"Don't try to glorify what we did. Any of us. We all broke the law. We were all criminals heading down a dark path that would have only gotten darker if we hadn't gotten caught." He tugged a lock of her hair, bringing it close to his face and inhaling. "There was this one guy—a musical prodigy—whose parents sent him to reform school instead of to drug rehab."

She turned on the bench, sliding her hand under his suit jacket to press against his heart. "That had to be painful for you to see, because of your brother."

He didn't answer, just stared back at her with those jewel-tone green eyes, and she wondered if he would kiss her just to end the conversation. She wouldn't stop him.

Then something niggled in the back of her brain. "I think what you did had something to do with your brother."

He looked down and away.

"Troy?" She cupped his face and urged him to look at her again. "Troy?"

"My brother failed out of college, enlisted in the army, then got busted and sent to jail." He held up a hand. "I'm not defending Devon. What he did was wrong. But there were others in his unit dealing, and two of them got off because their dads were generals."

Her heart broke over the image of a younger brother dispensing justice for his older brother.

"Once I got into the system, I stumbled on other… problems…and I decided I might as well do a thorough job while I was in there."

"Wow…" She sagged back. "You sure set the world on its ear."

"The irony of it all? My dad used his influence to keep me from serving time." He bolted to his feet. "Time's up. We need to head back to the airport."

He didn't take her hand this time. Just clasped her elbow and guided her back out of the gardens. His expression said it all.

Date over. There would be no kiss at the door. And honestly, as vulnerable as she felt right now, she could use a little emotional distance herself.

On a plane leaving Lyon, France, Troy knew he should be pleased with how his meeting had gone today with Salvatore at Interpol Headquarters. His plans were falling into place. Hillary was safe. The world believed they were sharing a romantic week in Monte Carlo. No one except the colonel and Conrad knew about their true destination as they flew through the night sky.

Costa Rica.

They would be there by sunrise. He should be pleased, but still he felt restless. Unsettled.

Hillary was snoozing in the sleeping compartment. The transferable pod made his location less traceable as he came and left in different crafts, while still having all of his personal comforts available.

He preferred his life simple, although he couldn't miss the excitement in Hillary's eyes over dining in France. She'd told him from the start that she'd chosen her job to get away from her rural roots, that she was looking for glamour and big-city excitement. He could give her that, and he wanted to. Although he could do without more soul-searching, like what they'd done in the gardens. But he also wondered how she would feel about his more scaled back lifestyle in Costa Rica. He knew his life was not what anyone would call simple, but amidst the travel and business, he preferred things to be…less pretentious, less complicated.

Maybe those days in the military school had left an imprint on him in ways he hadn't thought about before. At the academy, all he'd had was a bunk, a locker trunk and his friends. He'd lived that way even after leaving school and growing his hair again, even with clothes as far from a military school uniform as he could make them. He'd kept his world Spartan, when it came to letting new people into his life. Until now.

Right now, he felt like that fifteen-year-old kid whose life had been turned upside down, leaving him on shaky ground as he figured out who to trust.

Troy tossed his uniform hat on the bottom bunk along with his day planner, pissed off, as usual, and he was only six months into his sentence. "What the hell are you doing here?" he asked Conrad, who was pretending to be asleep.

Conrad called from the top bed. "You're blowing my cover."

"What cover?"

"That I missed formation because I fell asleep," he said,

his voice echoing in the barracks, which were empty other than one other guy who actually was snoozing. "What's your excuse for blowing off a mandatory formation?"

"I got my ass handed to me in trig class today. Just didn't have the stomach to get ripped again by Salvatore because of imaginary spots on my brass buckle."

Conrad extended an arm with his spiral notebook, marked Trigonometry. "Be my guest. Can't help you with the buckle, though."

"Thanks."

Conrad dropped the book and Troy caught it in midair, accepting it without hesitation. He'd helped Conrad out last week with hacking into a news site for stock returns. The limited computer access hadn't been quite as tight as they'd claimed. Except in one realm. "How is it that I can get into any system except where they keep their tests?"

"Uh, hello, they know you're here." His arm arced down and he swatted Troy with a pillow. "They must be paying Bill Gates a fortune to keep that out of reach."

"Funny." Not. It was frustrating being confined to this place. He flopped back and started thumbing through Conrad's notes. Notes that were damn near Greek. "Must be nice being a friggin' math genius."

"If I was a genius I wouldn't have gotten caught. I would be at some after-homecoming dance getting blown by a debutante who gets off on the fact that my old man is rich enough to buy me a Porsche for my sixteenth birthday."

"I think you wanted to get found out."

Conrad ducked his head to the side, looking down. "You think I wanted this? You're nuts. Why did you do it?"

"I'm not sure. 'Mommy' and 'Daddy's' attention instead of a new toy? Fame and recognition? Who knows? The court-appointed shrink just says I'm antisocial." And

how damn weird was it that now, here, he finally had a real friend. "How did you get caught?"

"I let a female knock me off my game. I got sloppy. It's my own fault. Women have always been my weakness. Take it from me, man. Never let a woman be your Achilles's heel." He ducked back to rest on his own bed again. "But you, you never do anything you don't mean to."

In his six months here, he'd never seen Conrad's confidence shaken.

"Sure, I do, Hughes. I blurt out crap all the time that I don't mean to say. Teachers really hate that, by the way."

His buddy laughed, shaking off some of the darkness. "So I see every day. You do take the attention off the rest of us, and for that, we thank you, man."

From the far corner, the guy he'd thought was asleep jackknifed up and threw two fistfuls of brass buckles across the room. "Do you think you two could hold it down? Take the belt buckles, just go and let me sleep in peace. I've got some sort of stomach bug. Leave or you might catch it."

Stomach bug? The loser was probably coming down off something. He was some piano prodigy who'd been busted for drugs and shipped here.

Troy tossed a belt buckle. "No, thanks, Mozart. I'll pass on Marching 101."

"Really, dude—" Mozart swung his legs over the side of his bed, holding his stomach and wincing "—if you would stop worrying about being a moody whiner all the time, you could learn something. To infiltrate the system, learn to work it from the inside. Use those brains of yours to play the game. Polish your damn brass."

Conrad did that uppity sneer thing he had down to an art form. "You're actually telling us to kiss ass, Beethoven? Because you sure as hell don't."

"Exactly." Mozart/Beethoven *grabbed the Pepto-Bismol from his bedside table. "There are other ways...."*

Troy scooped up a remaining buckle and tossed it from hand to hand. *"You make people laugh. Good for you. That's your gig. You're a people person."*

After guzzling a quarter of the bottle of stomach meds, he swiped his wrist over his mouth, smearing away the pink stain. *"Studies say that a sense of humor is the true measure of intelligence."*

"Just because you took that psychology class, Bach, don't think you can trick me into doing things your way by playing mind games."

"Whatever. I'm offering you a new tool for your arsenal." Mozart/Beethoven/Bach—aka Malcolm Douglas—shrugged, stretching back out again. *"It's up to you if you want to take it."*

"Knock-knock jokes, Douglas?" Troy tossed the final buckle back. *"Are you for real?"*

Douglas applauded. *"See, that was well-played sarcasm. You've got potential."*

The door exploded open across the room.

Colonel John Salvatore stood framed in the opening. *"Gentlemen, you'd damn well better be hurling right this second or you will be by the time I'm done running you."*

Troy shoved up from his computer workstation and pushed open the door to where Hillary slept. Curled up on her side, she hugged the wool blanket he'd picked up on an African safari. Her red hair splashed an auburn swath over the white Egyptian cotton. His hand itched to cup the curve of her hip. He ached to slip into bed and lie behind her, tucking her body into his. He would wrap his arm around her waist, the undersides of her breasts resting against his skin. He would breathe in the scent of her shampoo, stay right there until she woke up and rolled into his embrace, inviting him to indulge in more.

Indulge in everything.

He wanted Hillary in his bed for real, not just to sleep, and he had wanted that since he'd first seen her. But he needed to have his thoughts in order, be in control of himself. He wasn't the impulsive teen anymore who blasted through security firewalls without thinking of the consequences.

And as he thought this through, he was beginning to realize his preference for keeping things simple wasn't going to work with her. She was the type of woman that asked for, demanded, more from a man. She had a way of getting him to talk that no one had managed before. Maybe because she wasn't some groupie who glamorized what he'd done. Even when she didn't agree with his choices, she listened. She wanted the real story.

That was mighty damn rare and enticing.

As he watched the even rise and fall of her chest as they powered across the ocean toward the Costa Rica coastline, he couldn't deny it any longer. He would do anything to sleep with her. Anything.

And he would need everything he'd learned from Salvatore, from Hughes and from Douglas to win her over.

Eight

His Costa Rican getaway wasn't at all what she'd expected.

She slid out of the Land Rover, sounds of the tropical wilds wrapping around her. The chorus of isolation, of escape, echoed. Birds and monkeys called from the dense walls of trees. His home rested on a bluff, with a waterfall off to the side that fed into a lagoon. Wherever he looked out from his home, he would have an incredible view.

Sure, it was a pricey pad, without question. But not in a flashy way. She'd expected a sleek beach place with gothic columns and swaths of gauzy cabanas on a crystal-white beach.

Instead, she found more of a tree house. The rustic wooden structure was built on stilts—which made sense for surviving fierce storms. Built in an octagonal shape, its windows provided a panoramic view of not only the water but also the lush jungle. Splashes of blooming colors and ripening fruits dotted the landscape like tropical Christmas lights.

This wasn't a beach vacation place for parties. This was a retreat, a haven for solitude. There wasn't even a crew of servants waiting. She carried a travel bag while Troy unloaded their luggage. He'd been strangely pensive since their flight, studying her like a puzzle to figure out.

Although she was probably looking at him in exactly the same way.

He glanced over. "Elevator or stairs?"

"Stairs," she said without pause, "I wouldn't miss a second of seeing this from all angles."

Climbing the winding wooden stairs, she drew in the exotic perfume of lush fertility seasoned with salty sea air. The spray of the waterfall misted the already-humid morning air. She cleared the final step to the wraparound balcony.

The man who would choose this type of home intrigued her, and she suspected the house would only get better. She wanted to believe that, as if the house was an indicator of the real Troy. It was ironic that after she'd fought so hard to leave the isolation of the farm, that somehow this secluded place felt amazingly right.

He ran his fingers along a wood shingle, and it opened to reveal an elaborate panel of buttons and lights. He'd keyed codes into elaborate security gates along the drive to the house. Apparently there was a final barrier to breach. He pressed his palm to a panel and the front door opened.

She stepped into a wide space full of rattan sofas and chaise lounges with upholstered cushions of deep rusts and greens. With the windows, it seemed as if the inside and outside melded seamlessly. No period pieces or antiques.

Just well-constructed comfort.

Troy tapped another small panel on the inside wall and

the lights came on. "There are multiple bedrooms. You can choose which suits you best. We're on our own here, so no worries about where the staff might sleep."

Music hummed softly; ceiling fans swirled. "Is the whole place wired like a clap on/clap off commercial?"

"A bit more high-tech than that, but yes. I may dress better these days—" he sailed his hat toward a coat tree with perfect aim "—but I'm still the same computer geek inside. The whole place is wired for internet, satellite, solar panels."

"Everything here is fresh. I thought there wasn't a staff?" The place had clearly been serviced, from the fresh basket of fruit on the kitchen island to the thriving plants climbing toward the vaulted ceiling.

"There isn't an official crew here. Not full-time, anyway." He set their luggage by a sofa. "A service comes in once a month to air the place out, dust the knickknacks. Fill the pantry before I arrive. Then they leave. I come here for solitude."

"But you brought me."

"Yes, I did," he said from beside the fireplace, one foot braced on the stone hearth. "That should tell you how important you are to me."

The seriousness of his statement caught her off guard. "Does that line usually work with women?"

"Your choice. Trust me or don't."

And that's what it all boiled down to for her. Trust. The toughest of all things for her to give. "Could I just give you my right arm instead?"

He shoved away from the wall. "What do you say we take this a step at a time?"

With each step that brought him closer, her temperature rose, her desire for him flamed even as wariness lingered. "What do you mean?"

"Rather than jumping all-in, you can test the waters, so to speak." He lifted a strand of her hair, sliding it between his fingers with slow deliberation.

"Test the waters how?" Like make out on the sofa? Play strip poker? Progress to third base? Nerves were stirring her into a near hysteria, because if her body ignited when he was just touching her hair, there wasn't a chance in hell she would be able to hold out against a full-out touch. And there was nothing and no one here to stop them.

He let her hair go shimmering free. "Go swimming, of course. So which will it be? The pool or the waterfall?"

Hillary stripped out of her travel clothes, a dress she'd slept in on the plane. She needed a shower, but since they were heading to the waterfall… She would just take shampoo with her.

Her suitcases waited at the foot of the bed, but the open doors on the teak wardrobe showed rows and shelves full of clothes, all her size.

He truly had prepared for her visit. What would he have instructed buyers to choose for her? She thumbed through sundresses, jeans, shorts, gauzy shirts—and a half-dozen swimsuits with sarongs. Two-pieces and one-pieces, giving her choices.

One-piece, for sure. She tugged out a basic black suit and stepped into it before reaching for the phone to check in with her sister. Her hand half in and half out of her bag, she paused. What did a call from Costa Rica cost? And would it be traceable, thus risking their safety? She should probably check with Troy on that.

She yanked on a matching cover-up, then stuck her head out the door. "Troy?" she called out. "What're the rules on phoning home? I meant to call my sister while we were in France, and I, uh, forgot."

Their date had so filled her mind, she'd lost sight of everything else.

"Use the phone by the bed," he answered from somewhere around the kitchen. "It's a secure line."

"Thanks, I'll only be a minute."

"Take as long as you need." The sound of cabinets opening and closing echoed. "The only rules here are that there are no rules, no schedules."

She slid back into the room, the easy exchange so enticingly normal, so couple-ish. Plus a ka-billion-dollar vacation home and a world-renowned computer mogul she'd met while they both helped international law enforcement solve a case.

Yeah, totally normal.

And how would she even know "normal" if it bit her on the nose? She certainly hadn't seen a lot of healthy relationships in her life.

Sagging onto the edge of the bamboo-frame bed, she dialed her sister's number from memory. Since there was only an hour's time difference, her sister should be awake. The ringing connection was so clear, she could have been calling from next door. Of course Troy had crazy good technology.

"Uh, hello?" her sister said hesitantly, probably because the caller ID wouldn't have been familiar.

"It's me, Claudia, not a telemarketer."

"God, Hillary, it's great to hear your voice. How's Monte Carlo? Are you winning a fortune? The photos of you are gorgeous, by the way." The sound of Claudia sipping her signature soda filled the airwaves for a second. "I've been saving everything I can get my hands on and downloading the computer articles so you can see it all when you get home. We could have a scrapbooking weekend to organize everything."

Monte Carlo. Their cover story. Telling her sister every-thing would only worry her so she simply said, "Thank you. You can show me when I visit next."

"We could both be in our retirement rockers by then. Try to make it sooner."

"Fair enough. I promise." She always promised, but when push came to shove, somehow something always interfered.... And why? Her sister was wonderful; her brother-in-law was a great guy. She loved the kids. Their family was actually an example of how a healthy family *could* work. Had she avoided them because it was painful to see everything she didn't have? "I just wanted to check in and tell you I love you. I'll send the kids cool T-shirts."

"How about just have fun with that überhot guy. He beats the hell out of Barry the Bastard Cutthroat."

"He does. He really does. I'm actually getting some of that R & R you're always telling me I need. We're going swimming in a few minutes."

"Please tell me you're wearing a sexy two-piece so I can continue to live vicariously through you."

She looked down at the conservative black swimsuit with the simple black cover-up. "Um, sure."

"Atta girl. You deserve to play, date, flirt. Everything doesn't have to be intense. Enjoy the chase. Love you, but I have to run to clean the guest room."

"You're having company?"

"Uh…yeah. Listen, I really need to go. The kids are killing each other over who gets the last packet of gum-mies. Bye—" The phone connection cut off.

Phone still pressed to her ear, Hillary eyed the open wardrobe and that stack of bathing suits…. She tossed the receiver down and bolted across the room. Before she could change her mind, she tore off the black suit and snatched up an aqua-colored bikini, crocheted with flesh colored lining. It was suggestive and sexy and something she never would have dared pick out for herself.

If it had been the only suit on the shelf, she might have been angry. But there was such a wide range to choose from, this wasn't forced on her. The store tags on everything made it clear the items had been bought for her.

And she felt good wearing it.

She pulled on the frothy cover-up that matched, the nearly sheer silk sliding seductively over her skin like a lover's kiss. She arched up on her toes to snag a beach towel from the next shelf up. The white-and-black patterned cotton slid down in a tumble all around her, a huge towel made for sunbathing. She whipped it forward to refold…

What in the world?

Blinking, she looked again and sure enough, Troy had somehow, someway ordered a towel with a big Holstein cow pattern. No way could this be coincidental. The man was too smart and too observant. He had to have noticed her cow-patterned luggage tag and the silver pin on her evening bag.

Her sister was right. Things didn't have to be intense. She could play. Flirt. This wasn't an all-or-nothing proposition. A guy who gave cow towels definitely understood the lighter side of life. Her bruised heart could use some soothing after all she'd been through the past month.

Cow towel cradled to her stomach, she charged through the door, ready to meet her adventure head-on.

Troy needed to give his assistant a big fat bonus.

Palm flat against the kitchen counter, he took his time staring at Hillary from head to toe. There were no words other than *wow*—just wow—for how mouthwateringly hot she looked. The sea-green, almost-sheer cover-up rippled over her skin like waves of water, touching her in all the places he ached to caress.

He'd told his assistant to order a variety of clothes for any occasion. His only specific instruction had been to include a few cow-patterned accessories for fun. His assistant had been smart enough not to question or laugh.

That's why he paid her well.

He cleared his throat. "Did you find everything you need?"

"And more." She held up the cow-patterned towel. "This is amazing. Thank you."

"Thank my assistant. She did all the work."

"I'm guessing that she didn't decide on her own to pick out a beach towel with a bovine theme."

"I may have given her some direction. I'm glad you like it." He couldn't wait to see what she thought of the other surprises he'd ordered for her.

His own personal mermaid walked toward him, stealing a little bit of his sanity and will with every long-legged stride. Her eyes slid over him, lingering on his black board shorts and plain white T-shirt with the sleeves cut off.

She held up a small beach tote. "Do you mind if I wash my hair at the waterfall?"

He slid an arm around her and pulled her flush against him. "You can do any damn thing you want to."

"I do believe that's a compliment." She shook her hair back to glide down her spine.

"All that and more." He placed a floppy sun hat on her head before reaching for his straw fedora.

Hooking an arm around her shoulders, he grabbed his own bag of supplies for their morning—food and more towels. He guided her through his house and out onto the balcony. Her jaw dropped in awe, her feet slowing as she looked around her. For a moment, he saw his house through fresh eyes. Somewhere along the line, he'd lost sight of the details, just seeing the place as home.

The space widened into a veranda with a hot tub and a sunken pool built up to the edge. In spite of his carefully cultivated playboy reputation, he didn't take much time off. Even when he came here, he worked. Enjoying a morning at a waterfall with Hillary was an indulgence for him.

"Troy, this is incredible." Kneeling, she played her fingers through the crystal water. "I've seen infinity pools before but nothing like this one. With the way it's sunk into the balcony, it's like the pool is suspended in midair. What an architectural wonder. Did you come up with the design?"

"I had an idea in my mind for something like this, but I had to leave it up to the experts to make it happen. I have an architectural contact. He's more of an artist, actually."

Standing, she shook her hand dry. "One of your school pals?"

"Not this time." He slid his arm around her waist and started down the winding stairs that led from the house, down the bluff and toward the lagoon. "The architect is the stepbrother of my business partner. He had the place built from all regional materials. Most of the wood comes from Guanacaste trees...the fabrics are local weaves—"

"Whoa, hold on." She touched his stomach lightly. "You have a business partner?"

"In my software company, yes." Their flip-flops slapped each wooden plank on the way. "He provided the start-up funds."

"But I thought you came from old money? The press all said your father—" She stopped short.

"That my father bought a big company for me." He pushed past the sting of her assumption. He'd long ago accepted there were people who would always see him as a trust-fund kid. He could live with that, especially since it helped him when Salvatore needed him.

"What's the real story?"

He glanced over at her, surprised she asked. "A school friend provided an infusion of start-up cash to get things rolling. So I can't claim I did it all myself."

"I'm guessing your friend earned his money back many times over."

"Our company has done…well." Troy plucked a blue bloom from a sprawling Gallinazo tree and tucked it behind her ear.

Smiling, she touched the flower as a toucan flapped on a branch above. "You said his stepbrother designed the place. Who is this architect?"

"Jonah Landis."

"Of *the* Landis family?" Her eyebrows shot upward. "The stepbrother…is a Renshaw? Wow, you do have connections."

The Landis-Renshaw family were financial and political powerhouses. They understood his intense need to protect his privacy.

This place offered the ultimate in seclusion, with nature's soundproofing of a roaring waterfall and chattering monkeys.

His feet slowed as they reached the secluded lagoon. He set his bag on a mossy outcropping and tossed his hat on top, kicking off his sandals. He peeled his T-shirt over his head and—

Hillary stood on the edge of the shore in a bikini that glued his tongue to the roof of his mouth. Her smile was pure seduction as she backed into the water, bottle of shampoo in hand.

His erection was so damn obvious in his swim trunks, immediate, total immersion in the waterfall would be the best course of action. He climbed up the nearest rock ledge and dived in.

He parted the water with his hands, swimming closer and closer to Hillary. Her aqua-colored suit blended with the shades in the water until she appeared naked. Just what his libido needed. Yes, he wanted to seduce her. But he wanted to be in control when he did it.

Right now, he felt anything but in control.

He surfaced next to her and plucked the shampoo bottle from her hand. "Mind if I help?"

"Knock yourself out." She gave him the shampoo and disappeared underwater. The flower in her hair floated free. She shot back up again, her hair drenched and slicked back.

He squeezed shampoo in his palm then pitched the bottle back to shore. Facing her, he smoothed the shampoo along her soaked auburn locks. "How was your sister?"

The feel of her hair in his hands struck a primal chord deep inside him.

"Busy. As usual. She has the husband and kids and the big farmhouse. Our parents' old house, actually." Her head lolled back into his hands. "Where are your parents now?"

"I honestly don't know or care." His fingers clenched the rope of sudsy hair in his hands.

Her head tipped to the side as she studied him through narrowed eyes. "I didn't mean to upset you."

"Nothing upsetting about it. Just facts. You left home. So did I." Stepping behind her so she couldn't read his expression, he worked up the lather, massaging along her scalp. "Go ahead and say what you're thinking."

"I still keep in contact with my mother."

"I'm glad for you."

"I'm sorry for you. And I'm sorry I even brought this up."

"Don't be sorry." He slid his soapy hands along her shoulders, down her arms. Her silky skin sent lust throbbing through his veins, made him ache to peel away Hillary's suit and explore every soft inch of her rather than talk about his damn family. "My folks are living happily ever after, soaking in the sympathy of their friends over the huge disappointments their children have been."

"You're a billionaire, a successful software entrepreneur. You've turned your life around." She started to shift around to face him, but he stopped her, bringing her back flush against him instead. "They should be proud."

Her voice hitched, and she relaxed against him, her bottom nestled against his erection.

"I'm a self-centered playboy," he said against the top of her head, breathing in the scent of her minty shampoo. "But of course I do outscore my jailbird brother."

"What made him start using in the first place?" She reached back to cradle his cheek. "Where were your parents then? Or when he was in rehab?"

"We're adults. We take responsibility for our own actions." His heart pumped faster the harder she pushed the subject.

"But you weren't adults then."

Enough.

Enough of her trying to rationalize his past so he fit her mold of morality. He gripped her shoulders and turned her around to face him, needing her to see him, him as he really was. "We were old enough to know right from wrong and we both chose to do the wrong thing. There are consequences for that."

"Were the two of you close?" She clasped his wrists and just held on, her touch gentle but firm.

"We alternated between hating each other and being best buds. He sent me care packages at school—almost got me expelled with some of the crap he included." The memory made him smile…for a second, anyway. "I visited him in rehab to return the favor. A lot of the families there had reasons for what happened—abuse or depression leading to drug use. My brother had the same excuse I did. He was bored."

She squeezed his wrists. "I'm sorry, but I'm not letting your parents off that easily. At the very least, they were neglectful."

This conversation wasn't going the way he'd intended and this outing sure as hell wasn't going the way he'd planned.

"Troy—" she stepped closer, leaning into him "—tell me something…happy. Surely you've got some positive memories with your brother. You're a good person. I know the colonel and your brotherhood were there when you needed them, but there had to be some kind of foundation for that goodness inside you."

He wasn't sure he bought into her line of reasoning, but if it would get her smiling again, he would dig deep for something. "When we were kids, we had a nanny. When our parents weren't around we would even call her Mom."

"She sounds sweet." Hillary gifted him with a smile.

"She was tough as nails, just what two out-of-control boys needed. She was one step ahead of our pranks—and the first to reward us when we behaved."

"Reward you how?"

"Take us to baseball games, swimming at the lake, building tree houses and forts." And until now he hadn't thought about how his home here echoed those early tree houses—on a grander scale. "She even got us a couple of puppies and taught us how to take care of them."

"What kind of puppies?"

Hillary's breasts brushed his chest as they stood toe to

toe. He would keep right on happy talking for this kind of result.

"Pound puppies, of course. She told us a person's worth isn't measured by pedigree or looks. It's not about what something costs." She'd been a smart woman. He'd learned a lot from her, life lessons that stuck. "I picked a lab-bulldog mutt and my brother chose a shepherd mix."

Her smile faded. "You said you went to boarding schools, before the military school. What happened to the dogs? Did your nanny watch them?"

The water chilled around him. "When I was eight and my brother was ten, our parents fired the nanny."

"Because you were going to boarding school?"

His eyes closed. "Because they overheard us call her Mom." Her gasp pushed him to add wryly. "At least we knew she would take care of our dogs."

"Your parents gave away your dogs, too?" There was no escaping the heartbreak in her voice with just the two of them, out here alone.

He plastered on his best smile. "Damn, you asked for a happy memory. Sorry about the detour."

Sympathy shone in her eyes, along with a glint of something else. Determination. Her cool hands splayed on his chest as she stepped between his legs in a message of unmistakable seduction. "What do you say we make a great memory now?"

What the hell?

Now she wanted to make love? After he'd damn near opened a vein? Or *because* he'd opened that vein?

Realization dawned. She was feeling sorry for the kid he'd been, and was probably acting out of stirred-up emotions. He should tell her no. Wait until she was thinking clearly.

But then he'd never been particularly big on playing by the rules.

Nine

Hillary's heart was in her throat. The revelations about Troy's childhood had touched something deep inside her. She'd planned on being with him when they walked out here to the waterfall, but she'd underestimated how much he could move her. She'd deluded herself into thinking she could have a simple fling with him.

Somehow, Troy had gotten under her skin in only a few days. A few days that felt like a lifetime. She splayed her hands across his hard muscled chest sheened with water.

Troy cupped the back of her neck, his pupils dilating with arousal. "Are you seducing me?"

"Are you seducible?" She trailed her fingers down his chest.

"Totally."

He cupped her face and kissed her, openmouthed and without hesitation. She met him just as fully, wanting everything from him, determined to rock his foundation as surely as he did hers.

The taste of morning coffee lingered on his tongue. She wrapped her arms around his neck and kissed him right back, her mouth, her hands, her whole body in the moment. Finally, allowing herself to feel everything, no holding anything in reserve for later. There was no later. Everything inside her screamed *now*.

The water swirled around her, around them both, each bold caress of his hand sending the fresh currents over her. Her feet slipped on the slick stone floor and he steadied her with his hands under her bottom. The strength of his hands thrilled her. The rasp of his callused fingertips along her skin doubled the pleasure of his touch. She sketched her foot up his calf, then hooked both her legs around his waist.

The sun shone down on her head and her shoulders, but the sparks behind her eyelids had more to do with the man than the rays. And then they sank slowly underwater. Bubbles swirled around them as the rest of the shampoo left her hair. His mouth still over hers, he pumped his feet again and again, swimming backward until the suds stopped. For once, she surrendered control and let his strength carry them through the clear waters of the lagoon.

He broke the surface and she gasped for air against his shoulder. Their bodies fit, their legs brushing underwater in tantalizing swipes. She leaned into him, sealing them skin to skin.

His erection pressed against her, a solid welcome pressure against the ache building inside her. His hand braced between her shoulder blades, and she let her head fall back as he lavished attention along the exposed curves of her breasts. His mouth worked over her, teasing her through the swimsuit fabric until she reached a fever pitch.

Her hands fell away from his shoulders, and she reached behind herself. She untied the bikini strings at her neck. He smiled against her skin and made fast work of untying the rest. The scraps of aqua fabric floated away. The rippling surface brought her nipples to even tauter peaks.

He tucked an arm behind her back, tugging her hair gently until she arched farther for him, easing her breasts from the water. His mouth skimmed over one then the other, kissing and plucking as he bared her to the morning sun. He dipped his chin in the water and took her nipple lightly between his teeth, rolling and suckling, tugging just enough to send her writhing against him. Everything was brighter here, pristine when seen through the glistening droplets of water spraying from the falls. She felt like she was part of a fantasy or story or film.

From the start, she'd been drawn to Troy. They'd been leading up to this moment. Regardless of what happened afterward, she would regret it if she didn't experience today to the fullest. She wanted him inside her. Now.

She grabbed his shoulders and raised herself up again, sliding her legs to the rocky floor, pressing her body flush against his. "Do you have birth control? A condom? Because if I'm not mistaken, we're both one instant away from losing it."

"Back at the house," he murmured against her mouth. "Condoms are back at the house, damn it."

"Then we need to get there. Come on…"

He brushed his bristly, unshaven face against her cheek, whispering in her ear, "Or, we can take our time here, carefully, safely, still very pleasurably."

Possibilities swirled through her mind like the spiraling whirlpools rippling around the jutting rocks. "What exactly did you have in mind?"

He swiped his hand through the water, stirring the current between her legs until finally he cupped her. "I could touch you here." He clasped her wrist. "And if you're so inclined, you could—"

She palmed the length of his erection, stroking down, down, down and then up again, learning the thick, impressive length of him. "Is that what you mean?"

"Uh…" His head fell back and his throat moved with a slow gulp. "Yep, you're right on target."

With a deft hand, he untied the strings along her hips and the rest of her swimsuit floated away. She reached to grab it and he clasped her hand.

"I'll get you another suit just like it if you want, but right now I have more ideas for us."

His fingers slid between her legs, searching, teasing, finding the right places and pressure against the nub of nerves. Pleasure coiled tighter inside her, building. The buoyancy of the water held her up, and good thing it did, as her knees were quickly turning to jelly.

She tugged at the waistband of his trunks, her hands clumsier than she would have liked, but he was wreaking havoc with her equilibrium right now. He slid two fingers inside, crooking them just enough to send sparks exploding behind her eyelids.…

To hell with taking off his shorts, she reached inside and found him, thick and long, all for her. She explored him with her hands, stroking his throbbing erection until he growled primitively in her ear. She gripped him a bit more firmly, the water slicking her hand as she worked him every bit as intensely as he tormented her. He took her to the edge, so close to fulfillment, then shifted his hands away deliberately, sipping along her neck, whispering against her skin how much he wanted her. How desperately he wanted to make her come apart, until she cried out and sank her teeth into his shoulder from the burning ache to finish.

He scooped an arm under her bottom and lifted her, walking with her toward the shore and she thought, yes, finally they would go inside and make love on his bed. Or the sofa.

Or hell, a sturdy table would suffice right now.

He kissed her, his tongue thrusting and sweeping until her eyes closed and she lost herself in the bliss of him. Step by step, he moved closer to the shoreline, until they were waist-deep in the water. His hands spanned her waist and he lifted her. She opened her eyes, disoriented, confused.

The water dripped from her skin as he set her on a moss-covered stone outcropping. He pressed her backward until she lay along the smooth, earthy rock with her legs draped over his shoulders while he still stood in the water. His intent became very clear a second before he closed his mouth over the core of her.

Her arms flung wide and dug into the mossy carpet. His tongue stroked and soothed, circling and pressing. His hands glided up her hips then over her breasts, doubling the sensation as he toyed with her. Still, she squirmed to get closer, closer still as she burned for him to finish even as she wanted the liquid fire to continue forever. Each thrum of her heart accented the pulsing pleasure growing stronger and stronger until she couldn't hold it back any longer.

She cried out her release, no holds barred. Their complete isolation gave her the freedom to ride the orgasm through each blissful aftershock. Her fingers scraped deeper into the moss, her back bowing upward as Troy laved every last sensation from her body until she collapsed, her bones all but melting into the stony outcropping.

A light breeze whispered over her bared flesh, bringing her back gust by gust. Troy lifted her off the rock and into the water again, body to body.

"Hmm…" She hummed her pleasure at this most perfect moment, but had to ask. "What about you?"

"We'll get there." Sliding an arm under her legs, he cradled her against his chest and started toward the shore. "I'm not worried."

"Where are we going?" She leaned into him, resting in his arms. Her body was all but a muscleless mass after the explosive orgasm he'd just given her.

"Back to the house before you're too sunburned to enjoy the rest of what I have planned for you."

"Smart man." She threaded her fingers through his hair, loving the length, enjoying everything about this unbelievably unique and special man.

Something insanely out of control was happening to her, and as much as she'd told herself she had crummy judgment in men, right now she felt like she'd merely been passing time until this man came into her life.

Troy carried Hillary up the winding stairs, back to the sprawling pool area. Every step he prayed for the self-control to wait until they made it back to the house. The press of her naked curves against him was damn near driving him insane with the urge to drop to the ground right here, right now and thrust inside her, out here in the open air, on the lush earth, with the scent of crushed foliage and flowers all around them.

Except he needed protection. He couldn't forget about keeping her safe in all realms. He'd stocked condoms everywhere in the house and on the patio, but he hadn't thought to pack them in their picnic lunch.

But honest to God, she'd caught him unaware down there. He'd planned to swim with her, wow her with his home. Except she'd been the one to wow him with how she'd melted over a lame story about his brother and puppies.

But then Hillary had been surprising him from the start. The only predictable thing about Hillary was her unpredictability, and for a smart guy used to figuring things out at least twenty-five steps ahead of the rest of the world, he was enjoying the hell out of the unending surprises she doled out.

And if she kept that up with her mouth on his chest, he was in danger of losing his footing, sending them both crashing down. If he rolled on the ground with her for even a second, he would lose control. Totally. Damned, though, if he could bring himself to tell her to stop what she was doing with her tongue.

Finally—thank heaven—he reached the pool area built into the balcony. He set Hillary down on a lounger, double-sized and covered by a gauzy cabana.

She reached up to cup his face. "Please say you have condoms here."

"I do." In the table by the lounger. He stretched out over her.

She skimmed her foot up and down his calf, which brought the heat of her more fully against his erection straining like hell to get out of his boxers.

"You sure were confident in your plan, Troy."

"Confident in how damned hot we both get the second you walk into the room, or into my thoughts."

"That's actually pretty romantic."

"I'm trying." Now probably wasn't the time to tell her he'd taken the edge off in the shower the night before. But he was grateful he'd done so, because no way in hell was he going to waste this chance with her on some quick trigger finish. He would be in control, damn it. Holding himself in check at the waterfall had been worth it. "And as for being confident about today? Not exactly. I'm never certain of anything around you. You surprise me on a regular basis. So while you were changing, I stored condoms in about a dozen different places."

"Why not by the waterfall—or in a beach bag for when we went to the lagoon?"

"You surprised me." And they'd improvised well.

He had no complaints about the appeal of carrying this fiery-haired beauty—*his* fiery-haired beauty—up to his lair. He was damn glad for the privacy and security that allowed him to roam the grounds freely with her. The couple who serviced the home lived five miles away, and they never came unless he called. No one would get past the wired gates without his say-so.

He and Hillary had free run to do whatever, whenever they wanted here.

"*I* surprised *you?*" She tugged the hair along his neck gently. "Very cool. Because you've been surprising the hell out of me since the second you talked your way into the seat beside me on the plane."

"Any objections?" He slipped his hand between them, gently rolling her nipple between his thumb and forefinger.

"Only that you're talking a lot, and I have better plans for your mouth right now, like using those teeth to tear into a condom wrapper."

He pressed his thigh between her legs until she moaned. "I do like a woman who knows what she wants."

"In that case, this time, I want control."

Power plays were cool by him since they were both going to be winners here. "I'm all yours."

"Well, we can start by getting rid of your board shorts." She tugged at his waistband and together they sent his swim trunks flying into the pool.

Her eyes and hands went to his hips, then curved around his arousal. He passed her one of the condoms, and she sheathed him with torturously slow precision that threatened to send him over the edge, here and now, with the monkeys laughing at his lack of restraint. But then she'd vowed this was about her turn to be in control.

Rolling with her, he shifted to his back, bringing her on top of him. She straddled his hips and lowered herself onto him inch by inch, stretching, accepting him into her body. He guided her with his hands on her hips, thrusting into her over and over as they found their rhythm. Her husky purrs of pleasure spurred him on, made him want to bring her over the edge again. He cradled her breasts, and she rewarded him with a breathy gasp. He couldn't take his eyes off the beauty of her. The way her hair slithered over her shoulders as she rode him. How her breasts moved in his hands.

The pleasure on her face.

With each stroke, he claimed her as his, again and again. Or maybe she was claiming him. Right now, all he cared about was that he had her. And he would have her over and over this week. The thought of losing this, of losing her, ripped through him, and his fingers dug into her hips, guiding her harder and faster, watching for the signals that she was close to completion, as well.

A flush rose up her chest.

The pulse in her neck throbbed faster.

Her head flung back, auburn hair streaming as she—

Yes. He thrust into her a final time, the silken vise of her body pulsing around him as he came, powerfully and completely. He pumped into her one last time and wrung yet another cry of pleasure from her. His arms went around her, gathering her as she melted onto his chest. He kissed her forehead, tasting the salty dots of perspiration along her brow. Their sweat-slicked bodies sealed and holy hell, he was in trouble.

For the past seventeen years he'd told himself he was done with family. Only claiming a group of brothers equally as cynical and world-weary as he was.

Today, with Hillary, he wanted more.

Three days later, Hillary reclined against Troy in the bubbling hot tub, mint leaves floating around them and scenting the night air. She'd had more sex since arriving here than she'd had in her entire life.

Okay, perhaps a slight exaggeration, but she certainly had never been this satisfied. Troy's meticulous attention to detail, his determination to study every possible way to make her come was mighty enticing. She'd never had a man this devoted to giving at least as much pleasure as he received. Sagging back against his chest, she let the pulsing jets work their magic on her well-loved muscles.

She tipped her head back to look at him, taking in his now-familiar face. "Thank you for my cow towel."

"You already thanked me," his voice rumbled against her.

"And for the big fuzzy cow slippers."

"Wouldn't want your feet to get cold at night." His hands slid just under her breasts, massaging her ribs, her stomach, soothing and arousing even though her body was too exhausted to comply.

"Coffee definitely tastes better in a cow mug." She twisted to kiss his shoulder, right over the spot where she'd nipped a little too hard earlier. He had a way of driving her crazy like that. "Although the hula cow by my toothbrush was a little strange, but it made me laugh."

"Then I've done my job well."

She'd laughed herself sore when she'd realized all the

computers—and there were many in his house—had Holstein cow screen savers.

"You've been very generous and thoughtful—and fascinatingly original."

"God forbid I ever be boring." His strong fingers worked along her thighs. "Would you like a black-and-white diamond pendant to go with your collection?"

"You're being outrageous." Outrageous—and so charming she didn't know how she would go back to the real world again, where this fantasy would fade. Because she knew without question, the fantasy always faded.

"Damn, does that mean I have to take it back to the store?"

What was he saying? Something about a diamond cow necklace? "You didn't actually…"

"You'll have to wait and see, won't you?" His massaging hands slid between her legs, arousing her again after all.

As her knees eased apart, she realized the fantasy was going to live a while longer.

Troy propped his feet on his desk using an upgraded video phone that could put the competitors under if he released it. He still hadn't decided.

Sometimes it was better not to upset the order of things. Leave the market alone for now and save the technology for a time it might make a significant difference rather than just adding yet another upgrade for folks to buy while tossing out products still in perfectly good working order.

All the same, he enjoyed his toys and kept the best of the best here in his own personal, techie version of a man cave. More than just a wall of computers, he had shelves of parts and storage, old and new. For now, he focused on his video call. His brother—the military school kind—

was on the other end of the conversation, still wearing his rumpled tux from the concert he'd given the night before.

"Mozart, I appreciate the help. You're the man, as always."

"It's all good, my friend." Malcolm Douglas popped an antacid in his mouth then set aside the plastic jar—already half-empty. Troy's musical protégé buddy had come a long way from his days at the military reform school—but he still had a finicky stomach. "Consider the favor done within the hour."

The casino cover story was starting to grow stale. Some might begin to suspect the truth, since Troy wasn't renowned for staying in one place for any length of time. Salvatore assured him they had leads; they were on the guy's trail, just a little longer.

But Troy wasn't willing to sit back and bet on it. Backup plans were always in order. So he'd sent photos to online magazines and gossip blogs of him with Hillary having a candlelit dinner. Spliced in with some older photos of him with Malcolm taken last month, the press and the public—and anyone else watching—would think they were in New York City, that they'd had dinner followed by attending a concert.

"Congrats on the latest gig, by the way. Not too shabby playing Carnegie Hall."

"Minor compared to what's going on in your world right now." Malcolm brushed off praise as he always had. "The new woman in your life is smokin' hot. A California dime, no doubt."

"Thanks, and careful. That's my 'ten.'"

"Hey, just sayin'." His buddy continued to push Troy's buttons for fun. It's what they did.

"Note to self, no more candlelight photos for Mozart."

Malcolm pointed. "I'm not talking about your romantic dinner pics, buddy. She's rocking the fluffy robe."

Troy spun his chair around fast, feet back on the ground. Sure enough, Hillary stood behind him in her robe, her eyes wide. "Are you talking to *the* Malcolm Douglas?"

Jealousy spiked, fast and furious and irrational. He forced himself not to go all caveman just because the woman he cared about happened to be a groupie for this generation's cross between Harry Connick Jr. and Michael Buble.

Tearing his eyes off Hillary, Troy pivoted back to the screen. "Gotta run, pal. Thanks again for the help. I owe you."

"And I will collect. Count on it."

The screen went blank.

Strolling deeper in the room, she angled her head to the side, auburn hair still tousled from sex and sleep, then more sex and sleep. "Your brothers run in high circles. The friend who helped you at the casino and now him." She gestured to the empty screen. "There sure are a lot of you."

"I wouldn't say 'a lot' of us exactly." He rocked back in his office chair. "That would make us so…cookie cutter."

"Trust me, no one would ever call you cookie cutter." She held up her hand, a platinum necklace with a white-and-black diamond cow charm dangling from her fingers. "You are one hundred percent original."

He grabbed her wrist and tugged her into his lap. "Now that is the hottest thing you've ever said to me."

"I must not be holding up my end of the seduction then." She wriggled in his lap until she settled.

"You're killing me here. I need an energy drink."

"Which I'll be happy to get for you if you'll make me one promise."

"What's that?"

"I adore the necklace and gladly accept it. But from here on out, dial back on the extravagant gifts. Okay?"

"Fair enough."

He slid the necklace from her hand. He swept aside her hair and hooked the chain around her neck. He might not be the most romantic guy in the world, but he prided himself on his originality, and he would do everything in his power to obliterate the memory of Barry Curtis.

He pressed a kiss to the latched chain.

She glanced back at him, their mouths and eyes so close they almost touched. "What are you thinking?"

"Something a smart man wouldn't say." A wry smile tugged at him.

"What do you mean?"

"Why would you want to know if I've already warned you it might upset you?" Standing, he set her on her feet, cow slippers poking out from the hem of her robe.

"Because..." She tugged his T-shirt holding him closer. "If you really didn't want me to know, you would have said something like...'nothing' or 'I'm thinking about breakfast or what goofy hat I'm going to buy next.'"

"You think my hats are goofy?"

"I'll answer you if you answer me."

Ah, what the hell? Might as well. "I was thinking about you and your jackass of an ex-boyfriend. I was wondering if you're still in love with him."

Whoa? Wait. That wasn't exactly what he'd been thinking. He'd just wanted to be sure she was over him. The *love* word hadn't entered his mind. But now that he'd gone there with the conversation, there was no going back.

She sank down into his empty chair, confusion on her face as she studied him. "Looking back, I can see I was never in love with him. I was definitely infatuated—very infatuated." She grimaced, fingering the diamond necklace. "Dazzled a little. But I like to think I would have seen through the glitz to the real guy underneath at some point."

He leaned back against a table of surveillance proto-types, listening. Hoping for what, he wasn't sure.

"What can I say?" She shrugged. "I told you right from the start that I have a history for picking bad guys. Eventually, I figure it out. In this case, Barry's arrest just sped up the realization process."

Usually he rocked at being analytical underneath all the jokes, but right now it was tougher than usual. Still, he forced himself to sift through the words. She didn't love Barry Curtis.

"Okay, then. I can live with that."

Too bad one realization led to another. She doubted her ability to choose the right guy to love, period.

Leaning her elbows on her knees, she pinned him with her eyes. "How can you be jealous when you've only known me a few days?"

"Who says I'm jealous?" Lame answer for a smart dude.

"Really? You want to try and bluff?" She laughed... then realized her robe was gaping. She straightened fast and held the part closed. She was shutting down and if he didn't do or say something fast, he could lose headway in his goal of... What?

He knew damn well what. It didn't matter how long he'd known her. He was certain. He wanted her in his life. Permanently. But he wasn't sure she was ready to hear that yet. She might not have loved Barry, but she'd been burned badly by the relationship.

The timing needed to be right. He couldn't afford to screw this up.

So he shoved away from the table and stalked toward her, at least letting all the possessive feelings show. "I'm not jealous so much as pissed off that the bastard hurt you."

He pressed his hands on either side of the chair, bringing their faces nose to nose. "I want to beat the crap out of him then hack his identity and wreck his credit. Got a problem with that?"

A slow smile spread over her face. "No problem at all." She tugged his bottom lip between her teeth. "And just so we're totally clear, I think your hats are sexy as hell."

Ten

Her time here was surely coming to a close.

Hillary floated on a raft, warm waters of the infinity pool lapping over her. She watched Troy swim the length of the pool. Lights underwater illuminated him powering through the depths, while the stars twinkled above on a cloudless night.

She and Troy had all but lived outside and at the lagoon since they'd arrived five days ago. They'd taken walks—made love in the forest—shared exotic delicacies—made love in the cabana. Learned personal details from political views to a shared preference for scary movies. Eventually they'd made their way inside to dodge the rain, enjoying a horror film in the theater-style screening room.

Like a real date.

But real life intruded often enough to keep her from getting too comfortable, too complacent, too eager to believe in something beyond the fantasy. Daily calls from

Salvatore let them know he was getting closer. Barry Curtis's accomplice had been tracked slipping over the channel into Belgium. They were on his tail and expected to catch him at any time.

What amazed her most was how easily Troy and Salvatore had maneuvered this whole situation while keeping things anonymous. Calls from her sister indicated the public was eating up tabloid stories of Hillary and Troy gallivanting around the globe, wining and dining in a different country every night.

While she'd enjoyed their dinner in France, she had to admit, the time alone with him was more precious.

Troy surged to the surface beside her. "Hey, beautiful." He lifted her hand and kissed each fingertip. "We're going to be waterlogged by the time we leave this place."

"Is that a bad thing?" Especially given the attention he was lavishing on her hand at the moment.

"Not at all." He rested his elbows on the edge of her raft. "Just checking to make sure you're cool with how little time we've spent in an actual bed."

He'd been attentive, romantic, and she was so tempted to think there was more going on here. But she needed to remember this would end soon. Life back in D.C.—in the real world—would be different. It always was. Still, she would miss the peacefulness of this place.

She toyed with his hair, longer now that it was wet. "Sleeping in the cabana was romantic. And watching the sunrise on the balcony—amazing. The past five days have been better than any vacation I could imagine. You've got the perks of this place down to an art."

"An art? What do you mean?" He trailed the backs of his fingers along her breast, down her side and over her bare hip. They'd never gotten around to putting on clothes today.

She was totally naked other than wearing her diamond cow necklace.

"If you've never brought anyone here, where did you romance all those women you were linked with in the tabloids?" She hated the hint of jealousy leaking into her tone regardless of how hard she tried to tamp it down.

"Are you jealous?"

Hell, yes. "Curious."

"Everything in the tabloids? All false." His face was stamped with deep sincerity. "I was a virgin until I met you."

Snorting on a laugh, she rolled her eyes. "Right."

"Serious," he continued, with overplayed drama. "I've lived like a monk. My staff put saltpeter in all my drinking water so I could save myself until the day I met you."

She splashed him in the face. "You're outrageous."

"So you've told me." He snagged her hand before she could splash him again, his face truly earnest now. "Would you rather I detailed past affairs? Because that's all they were. Affairs. Not relationships. Not serious. And never permanent."

Her stomach fluttered at the turn in the conversation. "Is that what we're doing here? Having an affair?"

"Damned inconvenient time for an affair, if you ask me."

"Okay then, are we having an inconvenient affair?" Those butterflies worked overtime, so much so she couldn't even pretend she didn't care about his answer.

"What if I said this isn't an affair?" He pinned her with his eyes as they floated together in the center of the pool. "I saw you, and I had to have you."

The possessive ring in his voice carried on the wind. Exciting in some ways, and perhaps a hint Cro-Magnon in others.

"That sounds more like I was a piece of cheesecake on a tray at a restaurant."

He winked. "I do like cheesecake."

"Could you be serious?" She flicked a light spray into his face.

He tugged her in with him, and they pushed away from the float. Sliding deeper into the pool, she treaded water, face-to-face with Troy. She looped her arms around his neck and their feet worked below the surface keeping them both afloat.

"Do you want me to be serious?" His hands cupped her bottom, their bodies a seamless fit against each other. "Because I can be, very much so. Except I get the sense that the timing is off, and if I tell you exactly what I'm thinking, you'll run."

His perceptiveness surprised her. She'd spent so much time enjoying his lighthearted ways and trying to remind herself this was a fantasy that would end, she hadn't considered he might be thinking of more after this week.

And he was one hundred percent right that the thought of life after Costa Rica scared her. "You're a very wise man."

Disappointment flickered through his eyes for an instant before his easygoing smile returned. "Then let's get back to having an inconvenient affair."

He sidestroked them to the edge of the pool. Her back met the tiled wall where his feet just touched the ground. He kissed her neck in the sensitive crook, paying extra attention to the place just below her ear that made her...*sigh*.

The hard muscles of his chest pressed to her breasts. Heat tingled through her veins, surging and gathering low. She explored the planes of his shoulder blades, his broad shoulders and his arms that held her so securely. He hitched her legs around his waist and started walking toward the semicircle of concrete stairs, kissing her every step of the way.

Climbing the stairs, still he held her. The air washed over their damp bodies. Goose bumps rose along her skin, every bit as much from Troy as from the night air. She tangled her fingers in his hair, loving the unconventional, uncut look of him.

With her legs looped around his waist, he carried her into the spacious house. Through the living area where they'd made love on a chaise lounge with the windows open. Past the kitchen counter where they'd had breakfast and each other. And down the hall to his bedroom where they'd yet to spend a night under the covers together.

He lowered her onto the towering carved bed draped with mosquito netting, like another tree house inside the ultimate tree house. The rest of the room was sparse, with only a wardrobe and a mammoth leather chair by the window. He presented such a fascinating mix of wealth and Spartan living.

But right now, she didn't want to think about his decor. Only feel. "This whole week has been a fantasy."

"You like fantasies?"

"What exactly do you have in mind?"

He eased back to his feet and went to the wardrobe. He tugged out his tuxedo jacket and shook it. Something rattled in the pocket. He pitched the jacket to her and she fished inside to find…

"Handcuffs?" She spun them on a finger. "Do you carry these around as a regular accessory?" Her mind filled with sensual possibilities, games she would only play with someone she trusted, and yes, at some point she'd learned to trust him. A scary thought, if she let herself ponder it for too long. So she again focused on the moment, on Troy and on the pleasure they were going to give each other very, very soon.

"They're from when I was auctioned off. I tucked them in my pocket and forgot about them until you mentioned fantasies." He closed the wardrobe, the dim lamplight casting a warm glow over his lean naked body. "The cuffs would have ended up at the cleaners when my tuxedo went in to be dry-cleaned, but we rushed out of the hotel so fast I never got around to it."

"The bachelor auction and the way you turned it around was quite a stunt." She'd been drawn to him then, in spite of her frustration over how little he'd told her on the plane.

He knelt on the edge of the bed, moving up the mattress until he covered her. "The auction was uncomfortable as hell, but it worked out well."

"I have to confess…" She stroked back his still-damp hair, the scent of mint and furniture polish riding the humid air. "I was jealous of your assistant, before I knew who she was, when I thought she'd won a weekend with you."

"Jealous, huh?" He hooked two fingers in the other side of the cuff, tugging lightly. "Feel free to elaborate."

"I was hoping plastic surgery chick would win."

"She wouldn't have," he said confidently. A drop of water from his wet hair spilled on her overheated flesh, trickling between her breasts.

Her nipples tightened from just that one droplet. She shivered in anticipation of how much more there was in store for them.

"The bidding could have gone much higher."

"I still would have won." His eyes blazed with flinty determination. "My assistant was authorized to do whatever it took."

"Just so you could choose me?" How far would he have gone?

"I didn't believe Salvatore was doing enough to protect you." He linked fingers with her, the handcuffs clasped in their joined hands. "I had to come up with a way to keep watch over you and that seemed the easiest way."

His words about safety chilled her, reminding her of their reason for being here in the first place. While she didn't doubt he was attracted to her, would they have ended up here on their own? Would he have pursued her had he just met her on the street? Old insecurities niggled.

"Spending eighty-nine-thousand dollars was easy?" She attempted to hide her unease with a joke like he did so often. "Why not hire a bodyguard? It would have been cheaper."

"You know how you said you were jealous of my assistant?" He held both her hands, pressing them into the mattress, his erection thick against her stomach. "I felt the same at the thought of turning you over to some security guy."

She arched up into him, enjoying the heat flaming hotter in his eyes. The scent of native flowers drifted on the breeze through the open windows, providing an intoxicating moment when she realized just how aware she was around this man.

A sense of power pulsed through her, and she embraced it, needing to feel in control of something here. "The attraction between us was pretty instantaneous."

"Once the auction rolled around, I was so damn happy to see you out there in the audience." He grinned down at her. "And then I was so turned on I had to keep my hands in front of me."

Now that would have made headlines. "I thought that was just because of the handcuffs."

"Oh, it was the handcuffs all right." He squeezed her hand in his, still holding the handcuffs. "Thinking about ways that you and I could use them had me sweating bullets. Which brings us back to fantasies."

"You've had fantasies, about me and handcuffs?" The simmering heat inside her flamed to life. "What exactly would you like to do with those handcuffs?"

"I wouldn't want to shock a Vermont farm girl."

"Please…" She tugged the handcuffs from him and dangled them in front of his face. "Shock me."

Troy had never been one to turn down a challenge.

And the challenge in Hillary's eyes was one he very much looked forward to fulfilling. He snapped one cuff around her right wrist and the other around his left, so they were shackled while facing each other. The past five days with Hillary had been beyond incredible, and with time running out, he hoped he could cement their bond before they left.

She blinked up at him in surprise. "I thought you were going to cuff me to the bed, Viking style."

"Then I did surprise you." He sketched his hand along her breast, which brought her hand to herself, as well.

She slid her free hand between them to stroke him but he manacled her wrist and pinned it against the bed.

"Troy," she said, writhing against him, the ache inside her building, "I want to touch you, too."

"We'll get around to that. We have all night." And if he had his way, they would have even longer.

"Who says you get to be in control?" She pressed back, knowing there was no way she could actually win in a contest of pure muscle, but maybe she had a chance in the battle of wills. "My. Turn."

He laughed softly against her, the puff of air along her

breasts sending fresh shivers down her spine. Then he rolled to his back, taking her with him. "Consider me at your command."

Her smile of pure feminine power launched a fresh flood of testosterone pounding through him in answer. Her hands still linked with his, she kissed her way over his chest, lingering and laving her way down until…holy crap, her lips closed around him. His head dug back into the pillow as he lost himself in the moist and warm temptation of her mouth, the tempting sweep of her tongue. She shouldn't be able to take him to the edge so fast, but then nothing was as he expected with Hillary.

The only thing he knew for sure was that he didn't want this to end.

He tugged their cuffed wrists and hauled her upward, unyielding, and flipped her to her back again, the length of him pressed between her legs. The silky dampness of her let him know she was every bit as ready as he was. With his free hand, he tugged on a condom in record time and slid into her welcoming heat. He knew her body after all they'd done together, yet still he couldn't get enough of her. Of the soaring sensation of being inside her with the scent of their mutual arousal perfuming the air.

The link between them was real, damn it. Every bit as real as the handcuffs binding them together. She had to see that, to believe it. He just needed to be patient and work past her insistence that her judgment in men was off. He needed to win her trust.

She hooked her ankles behind his back and took him deeper inside her, rolling her hips and bringing them both closer to completion. He wanted to wait—he had to wait—for her. Gritting his teeth, he held back his release, until finally, thank heaven, her breath hitched with the special sound that preceded her…cries of completion.

His own control snapped and he thrust again deeper, shouting with his own release jetting through him. Again. And again. Until he sagged on top of her, just barely managing to hold the bulk of his weight off her by levering on his elbows. He rolled to his side, their hands still locked together. He flung his other arm over his eyes, his defenses stripped back until he was unable to hide from the secret he'd been holding all day.

Salvatore had called after supper. Barry Curtis's accomplice had been picked up trying to slip into Switzerland. Extradition was already underway.

Hillary was cleared to return to D.C.

While the morning sun climbed, Hillary rested her chin on her hands on Troy's chest. The handcuffs rested on the pillow beside her. She would have to remember to tuck them away to play with again on another day. The whole Viking scenario held a certain appeal.

She kissed his chin. "You most definitely are not a monk."

"Nice to know you noticed," he said, his fingers tracing lazy circles on her back. "Have you checked under your pillow?"

Her hand went to her diamond necklace then over to her pillow. She tumbled underneath and her fingers closed around... Metal? She closed her fist around something square and pulled out...

"A cowbell?" Laughing, she rolled to her back, clanging the copper bell.

"Everything's better with a little cowbell."

"I can't believe you got this."

He rolled to his side, eyes on her face intensely, like he was looking for something. "You said I couldn't buy you extravagant gifts, so I've been working within your system."

"It's sweet. Really." She kissed him quickly. "I can honestly say I have never gotten one before."

"What till you hear my cow jokes. What do you call a sleeping cow?"

"A bull dozer."

"Okay, too easy." He threw a leg over hers, the ceiling fan stirring the mosquito netting. "Mooo-ving on."

She groaned.

"Why do milking stools only have three legs? Because the cow has the udder."

She swatted him with a pillow, the cuffs clattering to the floor. "That's awful."

"I know. I went through a lot of corny jokes at school until I learned the nuances of humor."

Something shifted inside her at those words, at the image of him "learning" to be funny, trying to fit in as he was tossed from school to school, his parents abdicating their roles in his life.

He flung his arms wide. "What? You don't have any ammo to toss back? Roll out the computer geek jokes. Take your best shot. I'm bulletproof. More than that, I'm a bullet catcher."

"You're a cocky bastard." But she sensed he hadn't always been that way. But saying as much would take them to a serious level she wasn't ready for, not yet. So she scrounged for a joke.… "Ethernet—something to catch the Ether Bunny."

"Oh," he groaned. "Talk about bad. You're a rookie."

She pushed for more, determined to keep it light and make the most of their time here before he told her they had to leave. "The truth is out there…if only I had the URL."

"Better."

"There are ten types of people. The ones who understand binary code and the ones who don't."

"Ahh," he said as he sighed, pulling her close. "Now you're making me hot."

She splayed her fingers over his chest, traced four scratch marks she'd left earlier. "You're crazy."

"That's very possible."

A darkness in his eyes unsettled her. "I was joking."

"I wasn't. This genetic lottery thing…" He tapped his temple. "It's enabled me to do some incredible things with my life. But sometimes it fails me on the basic things in life, things that everyone else has and takes for granted."

So much for staying away from deeper subjects. She should have known there was no hiding, especially not with Troy. And she found she actually wanted to know. She needed to understand him. "Such as?"

"A family. One that functions and talks to each other and eats Sunday dinners together."

"Troy," she gasped, gripping his shoulders insistently. "You can't blame yourself for your family friction."

"I played my part. You know, I could have just sucked it up and gone to medical school like my father wanted. It wouldn't have been that difficult for me academically," he said with confidence but not arrogance. He hooked his finger in her necklace, sliding it back and forth. "I could have done some kind of research gig where I wouldn't be around people."

God, he was breaking her heart here. "I don't know where in hell you got this idea that you're not good with people. You're charming and funny." She covered his hand on her necklace. "A total original."

"Like I said, it's a game I learned and I'm cool with that."

"Not a game." She shook her head. "I think maybe you learned to share parts of yourself, in a way others can understand."

She pressed her mouth to his before he could argue with her, her heart tumbling over itself with love for this man and sadness that she would soon have to leave him behind.

Eleven

Troy stood on the balcony, cell phone to his ear, trying to outtalk the monkeys and birds yammering in the trees. "Thanks for the update, Colonel. Glad to know Curtis is finally spilling his guts."

"It's a race between the two to make a deal. International money laundering doesn't sit well with the authorities. And stealing from disadvantaged kids' college scholarship funds plays even worse in the press." Salvatore's heavy sigh carried through the airwaves. "When are you and Hillary Wright coming in this morning?"

"Not this morning. But soon." When he got around to telling her.

"Donavan," the colonel said in the suspicious headmaster tone he'd honed over the years. "You've informed Hillary that all's clear. Right?"

"Of course I will, tonight." He leaned back against the rail, splinters snagging on his board shorts.

"Ah, Donavan." Salvatore all but tut-tutted at him. "How can a man so smart be so damn stupid?"

"Thanks for the vote of confidence, sir." Troy gripped the balcony harder, splinters digging straight into his palms. "If that's all, how about you roll me to the bottom of your on-call list?"

Salvatore's mocking laugh faded as Troy hit the end call button and set the cell on the rail.

Time was running out. Even the cackling monkeys in the trees seemed to be mocking him for being an idiot. Salvatore was right; he couldn't keep Hillary here indefinitely. He would take her home and just ask her out like a regular guy once they returned to the States.

Except he'd never done the "regular guy" gig all that well.

He heard Hillary's near-silent footsteps approaching a few seconds before she placed her hand in the middle of his back, her fingers curving in with familiarity.

"Was that good news on the phone?"

"Yeah…" He looked down at the lagoon where he'd made love to Hillary for the first time. Would she come back here or was this some fantasy escape for her, one that would be over and done when she was back home? He would tell her after lunch. She would still be back before the end of her hastily scheduled vacation. He needed to use this last pocket of time to seal the deal. "Work stuff. Mergers. Money. Boring office crap."

Hillary slid in front of him, wearing a floral sarong knotted over her breasts, a flower tucked behind her ear. She had sun-kissed cheeks and an ease to her that hadn't been there before they'd come here. When they returned, would she wear those buttoned-up suits like armor to keep him out?

"I would think you'd be happy." She sketched her fingers over his forehead. "You look worried."

"I am happy." He nodded, trying to shake the whole gloom-and-doom air weighing down his mojo. What the hell was up with that? He was the guy of the fedora hats and cool scarves.

She toyed with the string on his board shorts. "Let's take brunch up to the roof today. I think it's the only place where we haven't made love yet."

The vision of her with the waterfall in the background, mist in the air, wild outdoors all around them, took his breath away. He couldn't lose her. He needed to bind her to him before they left, ensure they had a future.

"Do you ever think about having kids?"

Hillary leaned back, her eyes wide. "Are you trying to tell me the condom broke?"

"No! God, no." Although the thought of a kid with Hillary didn't scare him as much as it should.

A sigh moved visibly through her. "Then that seems to be a rather premature question." She slid her arms around his waist. "Shouldn't we figure out if we're going to see each other after we leave here?"

"Lady, that's a given." At least he hoped it was. And if not, he intended to make it one. "And as for the kid question, I didn't say *our* kids, I said kids. Period. When people date—like we're talking about doing when we get back to the States—then they discuss their views on life stuff. Like having children."

"Okay," she said slowly, her voice wary, "then yes, sometimes I think about it."

"And your verdict?"

Why the hell had that jumped out of his mouth now? Her answer mattered to him, more than he was comfortable with. He was supposed to be romancing her to seal the deal, not freaking her out with a full-court press.

"Honestly, Troy, the thought scares the hell out of me. What do I know about being a mom?" She spread her arms wide before tapping his chest. "And you mentioned genetics once. What about that? What if between our genes and the patterns we've seen, our kids... I mean... Ah, hell." She shoved against his chest. "Why are you bringing this up now? We should be talking about whether to go out for pizza or steak."

He shifted away from her, leaning back against the balcony. "I always thought I would adopt."

His answer stopped her. She turned to face him again. "Really?"

"Sure, once I found the right woman to spend my life with, because I don't know that I'm up to the task of parenting alone."

"And you would adopt because of the genetics fears you talked about?"

"In part, maybe. But I also figure I have all of this money and flexibility and there are kids out there without homes. Maybe I could just say to hell with worrying about someone getting into trouble and go ahead and adopt a troubled kid. Help them turn it around, give a kid the same break I got."

"You would do that?" She came back to him, leaning a hip against the rail. "Take in a child you already knew had problems?"

"If I had a biological kid who got into trouble like me and my brother did, I wouldn't just write him or her off." Memories of fights with his dad reverberated in his head. "And by problems, maybe I would take in a kid with medical problems, someone overlooked. I could pay for anything that kid needed. And hats. Lots of little hats for the kid."

Her eyes welled with tears as she touched his cheek. "Are you for real? Or is this an act to make women love you?"

"Would you believe me even if I said every word is true?"

He pushed back a wince at how he'd delayed for a day in telling her they could leave Costa Rica. He hadn't lied, he'd just...

Quibbled.

That's what Hillary would call it, and she wouldn't be forgiving of what she considered a lie. But how could he let her go not knowing if she'd agree to see him again?

"The thought of believing everything you're saying scares me. The fantasy is so much easier." She pulled a wobbly smile. "Even with the handcuffs."

"You're worried I'll hurt you." Even the thought of anyone hurting her made him want to haul her in and hold her tight.

"Remember when we talked about your happy childhood memory?" She folded her arms over her chest. "When my sisters and I were little, we would ride around on the tractor with Dad. He told us we were princesses and that was our chariot. It was fun to pretend."

"If you loved the farm so much, why were you so hungry to leave?"

"Because I realized all those times on the 'chariot'— that was just to protect the queen while she was toasted." She wrapped her arms around herself tighter, all but putting a wall between them.

"He was protecting his kids, you mean," he said, trying to put a positive spin on things, to give her something happier to hold on to.

"If he'd been protecting us, he wouldn't have enabled her. He loved her, but he was scared of her. He was scared if he pressed her to change, she would leave him." She stopped and held up her hand. "Whoa. Wait. I screwed up that happy memory exchange, too. Anyhow, I left the farm, but I don't hate it. I still go back to visit—my sister lives there with her family now that our dad's gone. Mom lives in an apartment—when she's not in rehab."

To hell with distance. He hauled her against his chest again. "I'm sorry for all you've been through. I can see how that would make you wary. But you can trust me, Hillary—"

His cell rang on the porch railing.

She looked quickly at the phone. "You should get that."

"Ignore it."

"It could be important."

Sighing, he snatched up the damn phone, knowing she was right. His assistant's name scrolled across the caller ID. If this had anything to do with Hillary's safety, he couldn't afford to ignore it.

"What?" he barked into the phone, resenting the intrusion of the outside world. "This better be important."

"It is. Hillary Wright's sister is going crazy trying to get in touch with her. Says it's something to do with their mother."

In the privacy of her room, Hillary cradled the phone and dialed her sister. After the intense conversation with Troy, she needed her space to face a call about her mother.

Why in the world did he have to bring up kids now? So early in their relationship? She was still adjusting to being in love with him. And then he had to roll out those incredibly enticing images of him as a dad, of him opening his life and heart to a kid who desperately needed a family. He was making her think he might want a future with her. Had she willingly signed on for another heartbreak by coming here with him?

The ringing in the phone receiver stopped and her youngest niece started chattering into the phone, "Aunt Hillary, Aunt Hillary, Grandma's moving in with us!"

Shock froze her. Her sister had always been softer where their mother was concerned, but she couldn't have actually caved on this. What about the children? "Could you please put your mommy on the phone?"

"Okeydokey. Love you, Aunt Hillary."

She clutched the phone tighter. "Love you, too, sweetie. See you when you come to Washington for your family vacation."

The sound of her niece shouting, "Mommm, telephone, Aunt Hillary," sounded in the background. Footsteps grew louder, then the rustling of the phone being passed over.

"Hillary?" her sister gasped into the phone.

"Claudia, what is going on there? I got an emergency SOS to call and now I hear Mom's moving in with you. Are you nuts?" All her fears and frustrations poured out in nervous babbling. "This is taking the codependent thing a little far, don't you think? You can't really expect to have her there with your children, can you? Maybe you don't remember what it was like, but I do."

"Hillary," Claudia interrupted. "Slow down, okay? I need to tell you something and it's a tough one."

"I'm already sitting." But she scooted farther back on the bed, nerves frothing in her stomach. "What's wrong?"

"While Mom was in the rehab clinic, the doctors found out she has a mass on her liver…." Claudia paused, her voice catching. "It's cancer, Hillary, and it's bad. End stage. The doctors say she has a couple of months left, tops. Her apartment isn't an assisted living type of setup. She has nowhere else to go."

Shock numbed Hillary as she absorbed the last thing she'd expected to hear. She'd spent her whole life figuring out how to cope with having an alcoholic mother. She'd never thought about how to cope with not having her mother at all. "I'm coming to Vermont."

"You don't have to rush right away—"

"Yes, I believe I do." She leaped from the bed, trying to deny the voice whispering in her mind that she wasn't running to her mother.

She was running away from Troy and the fear of him rejecting her love.

Troy stood in the open doorway of Hillary's room watching her pace frantically around, throwing clothes into her suitcase. From her tense shoulders to the sheen of tears in her eyes, he knew.

"I assume it was bad news on the phone."

She nodded tightly, folding her cow towel quickly and pressing it on top of everything else in her roller bag. "It is." She sat on the case and zipped. "My mother is ill, very ill. She has liver cancer. She doesn't have long left. I need to go home now and help my sister get Mom's affairs in order. We have to set up hospice, so many details."

She ticked through the to-do list efficiently. Even in a sarong, she could still harness the buttoned-up suit-type organization. She all but wrapped herself in competence.

"Oh God, Hillary." He pushed away from the door, reaching for her. "I'm sorry. Is there something I can do to help? Doctors? Specialists?"

She stopped in her tracks. "Actually, I do need something. I need for you to be sure my family won't be in any kind of danger if I'm there."

Ah, hell. She thought they still had to hide out here, away from Barry Curtis's accomplice. He could almost hear Salvatore's mocking laughter in his ears, followed by an *I told you so* for not letting Hillary in on the news sooner.

He took her hands in his. "No worries on that front. Actually, we're cleared to leave anytime."

"Really? Did they catch the mystery guy we identified in the surveillance footage?" Confusion chased across her face. "Are we sure there won't be retaliation against us for making the identification?"

"They have him in custody. Barry Curtis is talking now. They are in a rush to outconfess each other, so Interpol doesn't need our testimony." And he was damn grateful he didn't need to worry about her safety, although he knew now he would never stop being concerned for her. "We're just icing on the cake for them."

"That's awesome, and crazy convenient in the timing." She pressed a hand to her forehead, then, slowly, realization dawned in her eyes. "That call this morning, the good news, it wasn't about work was it? It was Salvatore."

"Yes, it was." He couldn't deny it.

"Why didn't you tell me? When did he find out?"

He hesitated a second too long.

Disillusionment flooded her face, followed by anger. "You knew before this morning, didn't you?"

Resolution settled deep in his gut, along with the urge to kick himself for being worse than an idiot. "I heard late yesterday afternoon."

"Why? Why wouldn't you tell me?" Pain laced her every word. "Why would you let me worry and wonder? It's almost like you kidnapped me, handcuffing me here with a lie."

"I intended to tell you today. I just wanted to enjoy a final night with you."

"That wasn't your decision to make." Her eyes went cynical as she backed away. "But then maybe you already knew that. Consciously or subconsciously, you sabotaged this relationship because you don't want the reality, just this tree house fantasy."

"Damn it, Hillary, that's not true. Give me a chance to explain." He gripped her by the shoulders.

But her body was like ice under his hands.

"I only have one question for you, Troy." She met his gaze unflinchingly, beautiful and so vulnerable. "Why couldn't you have just been honest with me? Why did you have to go to such lengths to break my heart?"

Her words stabbed him clean through. He'd vowed over and over that his intent was to protect her and yet he'd done the thing guaranteed to hurt her most. There wasn't any excuse he could make. No matter how much he'd worked on his people skills, he hadn't learned all the lessons he needed now.

She shrugged free of his hands. "That's what I thought. There's nothing left to say." She unhooked the diamond charm necklace and dropped it in his palm. "Please, just take me to Vermont and then get out of my life."

Twelve

She'd come full circle.

Locking her rental car, she strode up the flagstone walkway leading to her childhood home, her body more than a little weary from her day of travel, her argument with Troy. After they'd fought, he shut down. He'd offered her his plane to see her mother and then he'd disappeared into his computer-filled man cave.

And now she was home. The countryside was dark, other than lights on the house and barn and another marking the entrance to the dirt driveway.

But even in the dim light, she knew her way by heart. Her sister hadn't changed much on the two-story clapboard farmhouse, not even the black shutters. There were a few extra flowers in the garden and more toys in the yard—a bike lying on its side, tire swings spinning in the wind, and a fort built into the V of a sprawling oak tree. A sign hung on the front with *No Boys Allowed* painted in bright red letters.

Not a bad idea.

She couldn't get past feeling like a fool. After telling herself a million times Troy was a playboy and she had a radar finely tuned to find jerks, she'd still made the same mistake. She'd trusted the wrong guy.

But damn, he was so good at the game. He'd romanced her in a way no man had even thought of trying, dazzling her with contrasts. One day they were dining in France and another day picnicking off fresh fruit from the trees around his Costa Rican retreat. Who gave a woman a cowbell as well as a charm with exclusive black diamonds?

A genius playboy, that's who. He'd told her he'd studied how to be funny, how to charm and weave his way through society, yet somehow she'd never considered he was using those skills to manipulate her into going to bed with him in less than a week. She wanted to pound her head against a tree.

Or collapse on the front stoop and cry her eyes out.

Her older sister pushed through the front screen door, hinges creaking. They could have been twins born seven years apart, yet they'd taken two such different paths. As much as Hillary had scoffed at anyone staying on this farm, her sister definitely appeared to be the wiser one.

Claudia opened her arms and hugged her hard. They'd been close as kids, taking care of each other. What had changed? When had she quit helping her sister?

Hillary stepped back and hooked an arm with Claudia. "Where are the kids and hubby?"

"Asleep, but looking forward to seeing you in the morning. Where's your Robin Hood Hacker Hunk?"

"Long story. Can we save it for later?" When she could talk about him without crying? Like maybe sometime in the next decade. "I'm sorry to have kept you up so late… I'm sorry I left you to take care of everything with Mom and Dad."

"You don't have to apologize for anything." Claudia squeezed her sister's hand on their way up the steps they'd climbed countless times. "You're living your life. That's what grown-ups are supposed to do."

"Are you living yours the way you want? With Mom staying here?" She needed to hear that she hadn't totally wrecked her sister's life by bailing.

Claudia tugged open the creaky screen again. "No one wants to have an alcoholic mother in and out of rehab clinics. And I'm sure you don't want to have to keep footing the bill because I'm too cash-strapped with three kids to feed. We both do what we can."

"Writing the check is easy."

"Ha! So says the woman who doesn't have a kid in braces." Her sister guided her through the house, toward the back guest room. "Come on. Mom tried to stay awake to see you, but she's on a lot of pain medication. She drifted off about an hour ago."

Only a few more steps and they would be outside their mother's door, where she slept.

"I'll see her in the morning then. We could all use a good night's sleep." Hillary turned quickly, stopping in the kitchen, a traditional wide-open space with a six-seat oak table in the middle. "I appreciate your trying to make the distribution seem fair, but I still feel guilty. Like I've run away."

"We're both children of an alcoholic. That leaves a mark on the way we deal with things." Claudia snagged a caffeine-free Diet Coke off the counter, popped the top and passed it to her sister before getting one for herself. "I lean toward the whole codependent gig, and you lean toward avoidance. We're both trying to do better, to be better. I figure as long as we're both still trying, then there's nothing to be gained from beating up on ourselves."

Hillary leaned against the tile counter, sipping the Diet Coke. "It seems so strange that she came here to die when she always swore she hated this place, that the boredom drove her to drink."

"Honey," her sister crooned squeezing her arm, "you gotta know that was just an excuse."

Hillary looked around the kitchen with all its windows showcasing the wide-open space...much like Troy's place. "It's really pretty here."

"Yes, it is." Her sister smiled serenely, tipping back her can of soda.

"You can say 'I told you so' if you want." She deserved everything coming her way after she'd been all but snobby about the place. Until this moment, she'd never really seen her home without the dark filter of her mom's bitterness.

"I'm not a gloater. You should know that about me." Her sister tapped her can against Hillary's.

"I do, which is probably why I offered to let you lord it over me, since I knew you wouldn't."

"That's convoluted logic."

"I picked it up from the best." Another thing she'd learned from Troy this week. How could so much happiness and pain be mingled together?

Her sister cocked her head to the side, brow furrowed. "You can love here and love somewhere else, too. That's okay."

Hillary nodded. "I'm starting to understand that." She looked around at the children's art on the fridge, at the cow clock on the wall, and found the words falling from her mouth in spite of the burn of tears behind her eyes. "Troy has this place in Costa Rica, and it's amazing. But not because it's flashy. His home is actually very rustic—with a lot of high-tech gadgetry of course, but the look of the place is earthy. It's *real*."

"Sis, I gotta confess, this is a stretch. You're comparing Costa Rica with Vermont? No offense to my beloved home state, of course."

"I know, I know, I've thought the same thing." Her jumbled thoughts from this whole crazy week started coming together in her mind like puzzle pieces.... She'd been using the farm as an excuse for her own unhappiness. On some level, she must have known that or why else would she have insisted on carrying little cow talismans as reminders of home? Her childhood hadn't been perfect, but it hadn't been all bad. There were good memories, too. Life wasn't clear-cut or black-and-white like the spots on a cow.

Had she been missing the boat on her career, as well? Focusing on the glitz at the expense of depth? Did she really want to spend the rest of her life planning parties? Troy had found simplicity and meaning underneath all the wealth. She'd been so busy judging Troy, she hadn't considered her own superficial choices. Her narrow view of the world had likely led to her previous bad choices in men.

But she should have realized Troy was different. Special.

She set her soda on the counter. "I'm trying to say a place's beauty isn't about the trappings. It's about appreciating it exactly as it is."

"That's pretty profound, actually." Her sister stood beside her, leaning back against the counter, quietly waiting.

So much more effective than if her sister had pressed.

"The media paints Troy as this arrogant, urbane guy." She thought of that first time she'd seen him on the plane. "It's a face he puts on for the world, and honestly that persona is sexy as hell."

Her sister raised one eyebrow and waved for Hillary to keep talking.

"But the real person underneath it all is infinitely more fascinating." So much so, she didn't know how she would ever get over him.

"You're in love with him."

"Completely," she answered without hesitation.

"Then why isn't he here?"

Such a simple question.

He wasn't with her because…?

She'd pushed him away. Yes, he'd lied to her. He wasn't a perfect man. God knows, she wasn't perfect, either. Just because he'd screwed up, that didn't mean everything about their week together had been false.

Life wasn't all or nothing for either of them. They would need time together to build a relationship, to learn to trust each other. She understood that now.

But would Troy understand it, as well—if she got a second chance to tell him?

"You owe me for this, Colonel." Troy rocked back on his heels, jamming his fists in his tuxedo pockets to keep from punching a wall in frustration over having to hang out at a black-tie fundraiser.

Less than two weeks had passed since he and the colonel had come to Chicago, and already the man was calling again, asking him to show his face at this dinner dance for some reason he'd yet to disclose.

In D.C.

Which happened to be the last place on earth Troy wanted to be since it reminded him of Hillary. He just wanted to go back to Costa Rica and lock himself in his man cave for some serious alone time. Except he couldn't go back to Costa Rica, not when he'd made love to her in every corner of the place, his home so full of memories he'd been climbing the walls without her.

Salvatore clapped him on the back as the jazz band fired up a Broadway show tune. "Actually, I don't owe you a thing. The way I remember it, you owe me."

"Our agreement didn't include back-to-back gigs." Even if this one was a good cause, hosted by Senator Landis to raise money for the area Big Brother program for at-risk and foster kids. "In spite of my playboy rep, I do have to work."

"Just pretend for a couple of hours, then your time will be your own for at least…oh, let's say six months." Salvatore held up his hand. "I promise."

Troy angled to the side for a waiter carrying a silver tray of appetizers to pass before saying to the colonel, "With all due respect, you lie."

Salvatore adjusted his red tie. "I take offense at that. Lying is a very dishonorable trait."

Troy ground his teeth. Had the colonel been hired by Hillary to call attention to all his flaws?

Then as if conjured from his thoughts, he saw her across the room. *Hillary.* She wore a simple black dress with complete elegance, outshining every other woman in the room. His fist clenched the diamond pendant tighter—her necklace—that he'd been carrying around in his pocket since she left him on the island. What were the odds he would see her at the first place he went after leaving Costa Rica?

The odds were off the charts, in fact.

"Damn it, Colonel." He glared at Salvatore. "Did you set this up? You want me to crawl back to her? She made it clear she doesn't want me. She doesn't trust me. That's all there is to it."

"Bull."

His head snapped back. "What did you just say?"

"You heard me. You're a smart man. A genius, actually, part of why I work with you. But you're also manipulative. You use that brain to trick people into doing what you want, while making them think it was their idea. Another reason you're a great asset to my team. But that kind of game playing does not go over well in relationships."

"I have friends."

"Who play by your same convoluted—sometimes sketchy—rules." Salvatore gripped him on the shoulder in a move that was almost…fatherly? "Here with Hillary, you had a chance at a normal, healthy relationship, and you blew it. Any clue why?"

"You seem to have all the answers today. You tell me." And God, he actually meant it. He wanted help, to find a way to get her back because the past days without her had been pure hell.

"I can't give you all the answers. If you want her bad enough, you'll figure this one out on your own. Which you can do if you use that genius brain of yours and think." He tapped Troy's temple. "Why are you here when she's here?"

"Because you set us up."

Salvatore shook his head. "Think again."

With a final pat on Troy's shoulder, the colonel faded into the crowd.

Could Hillary have actually called the colonel and asked for his help? Why would she have reached out to Salvatore rather than him?

That answer was easy enough. He'd made himself inaccessible to everyone except Salvatore. He'd hidden away in his cave and used all his techie toys to make himself unreachable.

Hillary had told him from the start she had trust issues

and he'd pushed that one inexcusable button. It was almost like his subconscious had self-destructed the relationship. For a man of reason, that was tough to swallow.

But love wasn't about logic. Hell, his feelings for Hillary were definitely not anything rational. He just loved her, and he wanted her. And he intended to do everything in his power to win her back.

Click.

The cool metal wrapped around his wrist. He barely had time to register the sensation before he looked up and found Hillary standing beside him.

Click.

She locked the other handcuff around her wrist.

Hillary hoped the smile on Troy's face was for real and not an act for the crowd. A spotlight focused on them as she led him across the ballroom floor. The partiers applauded while the senator took the mic from the lead singer in the band to thank Troy Donavan for his very generous donation.

That part had been Salvatore's idea—when she'd contacted him begging for help in finding Troy. She'd been surprised to learn from Salvatore that he and Troy actually worked together on a more regular basis—but it made sense. She'd already realized there was more to the man she loved than the superficial. And even as a teen, he hadn't cared what the world thought of him. He'd been out there crusading in his own way. She was glad now that she hadn't known before about his work with Interpol. That would have made it too easy to trust him. She wouldn't have had to search her heart and open her eyes.

Salvatore had even made her a job offer she found more than a little tempting…leave her D.C. position and sign on to freelance with Interpol. She and Troy had a lot to talk about. Thank goodness Salvatore had worked out a plan for her to speak to him. Granted, something a little less high profile would have been easier on her nerves. But Salvatore had insisted this would work best.

Hillary searched for a private corner, but there were people everywhere. Finally, she tugged him down the corridor and into a powder room—and, as she'd hoped, the presence of a man chased both of the occupants out. She passed the bathroom attendant folded cash and said, "Could you give us ten minutes alone, please?"

Laughing under her breath, the attendant ducked out into the hall. Hillary locked the door after them and turned back to Troy only to find herself at a loss.

She'd been so focused on getting him alone and making her gesture meaningful. She'd even planned at least three speeches...all of which flew out of her head now that she was face-to-face with him. So she gave herself a moment to just soak in the beloved sight of him, here, with her again.

God, he knew how to wear a tuxedo, with the white silk scarf and fedora. He stole her breath as well as her thoughts.

Troy held up their wrists. "You sure do know how to make an impression."

"I wanted to make sure neither of us could run away this time."

"Good move." He stroked the inside of her wrist with his thumb. "How is your mother?"

The past couple of days had been hectic, getting her mom settled in with hospice home care, talking during her lucid moments. "She and I have done a lot of speaking again. We're finding a way to make peace." As much as was possible, but they were trying. "But that's not why I'm here tonight. Troy, I want to tell you—"

He pressed a finger to her lips.

"You know what? Hold that thought." He cupped her waist and lifted her onto the bathroom counter next to a basket of rolled-up hand towels. "I need to say some things to you first. Any objections?"

Smiling hopefully, she held up their cuffed wrists and jingled the cuffs. "You have my undivided attention."

"For starters, you left this." He pulled his free hand from his pocket. Her diamond cow necklace dangled from his fingertips. "It belongs to you."

A smile played with her lips and her heart. "I'm guessing there aren't a lot of women on the lookout for one of those."

"It's a one-of-a-kind, made for a one-of-a-kind woman." He reached behind her neck, taking her cuffed hand along as he latched her necklace in place again.

The charm still carried his heat as it rested against her chest.

He clasped their hands between them. "You've taught me a lot, Hillary Wright."

"What would that be?"

"I've prided myself on being fearless in business, fearless in standing up for a cause, even if it lands me in hot water." He linked hands with her. "But I botched things when it really counted. When it comes to relationships— when it came to the way I handled things with you—I haven't grown much beyond the kid who hid in his computer room rather than risk having people let him down. I betrayed your trust, and I'm so very sorry for that."

There hadn't been many people in his life teaching *him* how to trust when he was growing up. "The fact that I'm here should tell you something. I forgive you for not telling me right away, and I hope you'll forgive me for running rather than talking through things."

"Thank God." His throat moved in a long slow swallow.

His eyes slid closed, and she realized how, in spite of his grins and jokes, he really was sweating this every bit as much as she was. She mattered to him.

She rested her forehead against his.

Troy threaded his fingers through her hair. "You're a hundred percent right to demand I pony up my one hundred percent where you're concerned. You deserve it all, everything, and I want to be the man who makes that happen for you. I need to tell you something else, about Colonel Salvatore and—"

"Your freelance work with Interpol?"

"How did you…? He told you, didn't he?"

"Yes, he did, when I asked him to help me find you."

Troy eyed her warily. "And you're not upset with me for not explaining it myself? I know how important trust is to you."

"I'm assuming that kind of work isn't something you just go around sharing with people right away, but you'll have to clue me in on the nuances since it looks like I'll be signing on with the colonel, as well. He says his recruit list needs some estrogen."

For once, she'd stunned Troy into complete silence. His jaw went slack, and he started to talk at least twice, only to stop and shove his hand through his long hair. Finally, he just smiled and laughed. He wrapped his unshackled arm around her and spun her once before setting her on her feet again.

"God, I love you, Hillary. No questions or doubts in my mind, I am so in love with you." He kissed her once, twice then held on the third time until her knees went weak. "You know I'm going to want to be with you on any assignment so I don't go crazy worrying. Maybe I should be more laid-back, but when it comes to you—"

"You already are everything I could want, and of course we'll be together, always, so I can watch your back," she said against his mouth, her heart so full she could barely breathe. "I love you, too, Troy, my totally original man. Mine."

"Yes, ma'am, I am." He kissed her, firmly, intensely, holding for at least seven heartbeats. "I intend to work on being the best man possible for you each and every day." He sketched kisses over her forehead, along her eyes, finishing on the tip of her nose. "I'm a smart man, you know. I'll figure this one out if you'll give me the time."

"How much time were you thinking about?"

"A lifetime."

She took his hat and dropped it on her head. "It just so happens, that totally works for me."

* * * * *

A RULE WORTH BREAKING

MAGGIE COX

To Joy
You were and always will be one of
the true lights of my life.
With love and affection,
Maggie x

CHAPTER ONE

'WHAT DO YOU think?' Unable to suppress the disagreeable sense of disappointment that was churning in his gut, Jake Sorenson glanced up at the stage at Rick—his 'partner in crime'—who was all but wearing out the floor, pacing back and forth in his worn Cuban-heeled boots. *The auditions weren't exactly going well.*

Rick abruptly stopped pacing to spear an exasperated hand through his dull gold hair. Studying Jake, he snapped, 'What do I think? I think that Rosie Rhys-Jones, or whatever her name is, just isn't good enough. God knows Marcie is a hard act to follow, but *Rosie...*'

'Josie.'

'Josie. Whatever...' Scowling, Rick folded his muscular arms across his leather waistcoat and continued. 'The woman would be fine on a cruise ship, entertaining folk with more money than taste, but she's not lead vocalist material and that's a fact. Bottom line is, Jake, I can't see any of the singers we've heard so far fronting a potentially great band like Blue Sky—can you?'

In answer, Jake stared off into the distance. Mentally reviewing the past few auditions, he couldn't help but agree. He returned his arresting blue gaze to his friend and the characteristic dimple that highlighted a rare smile appeared at the side of his mouth.

'You're right, of course. We'll just have to keep on looking.'

Jake rarely elaborated. Not unless he absolutely had to.

But he knew that when it came to making a decision ultimately the final say would be his. Although Rick had been in the music business even longer than he had—at the height of his career Jake had been one of the most successful record producers in the business—he knew that the other man valued his expertise and judgement.

'Is there anyone left outside to see?' Yawning as he rose to his feet, Jake stretched his arms high above his head. The movement made his shirt ride up several inches to reveal a taut flat stomach tapering into lean hips and long-boned thighs, currently encased in faded dark blue denim.

At the same time Rick expertly jumped off the stage and ambled across the dusty wooden floor to join him. 'Not unless they're lurking in the graveyard out there' he joked.

He feigned an exaggerated shiver, his bemused expression conveying exactly what he thought about conducting auditions in an obscure village hall deep in the heart of rural England. But Jake knew that doing things this way at least afforded them a certain amount of privacy that wasn't always possible in London.

The music press and tabloids were always keen to know what he was up to. He was the man who had famously brought several acts from the UK to prominence. But at the height of his career he'd been caught up in a destructive scandal that had cut short his seemingly unstoppable rise to the top when it hit the headlines. After that Jake had dropped out of producing and promoting bands to lick his wounds, reassess his life and reflect on what he might do instead.

For a few years following his very public fall from grace he'd become a perpetual nomad, travelling the world. And while he'd thought he would never entertain the idea of working in the music industry again, when he'd been travelling he'd begun to listen to and study the ethnic music of other cultures and realised that he couldn't leave music alone. It had always been and still was his abiding interest—the thing that made life worth living. And when he'd finally brought his explorative sojourn to an end he'd returned to the UK and made the decision to go back to his roots.

He'd started out managing a band long before he'd become a producer and now, after fifteen years in the business, had come full circle to manage Blue Sky.

Glancing down at his watch, he grimaced. 'Anyway, I think I've heard enough to know that we haven't found our singer yet. Want to call it a day?'

Dropping his hands to his hips, Jake glanced across at the three band members who were waiting expectantly for him to make a decision about what they were going to do next.

'No doubt these guys have had enough, too. So let's go get a hot pie and a beer. We can make an early start in the morning. There's a girl from Birmingham that might be a possibility. She's lead vocalist in a band that have attracted quite a following in her home town'

Despite trying to sound hopeful, Jake knew his downbeat tone conveyed that the girl from Birmingham was more than likely another no. What he was looking for—what they were *all* looking for—was someone extraordinary, a girl who stood out from the crowd, who could hold her own fronting a band that had been on the brink of major success before Marcie's sudden and abrupt departure.

It was a crying shame that the woman should have decided at the eleventh hour that she'd rather marry her childhood sweetheart and go and cultivate grapes in the Dordogne than front a rock band. But that, as they said, was showbiz. Still, if anyone could work a miracle Jake knew that *he* could. All he needed to prove it was to find an amazing singer.

A door slammed loud and hard and the shock in the room was tangible. The sound reverberated round the vaulted high-ceilinged hall like a cannon exploding. *What the hell...?*

Jake was taken aback when he saw the perpetrator. Tall, slim and dark-haired, she was struggling with the belt of her raincoat, which he could see had become trapped between the hall's back doors when they'd slammed shut. His transfixed gaze worked its way up from long black suede boots to slim toned legs clad in sheer black hosiery. For a long moment he was fixated by a shapely knee, where its smooth flesh peeped intriguingly through a frayed tear the size of a small coin. As she struggled to free her belt the girl emitted a breathy little sound that might have been a curse.

Briefly turning his head, Jake found Rick grinning. *He knew it wasn't just because the girl had got herself in a fix.* When she finally extricated the belt and lifted her head to murmur a blushing apology he felt as though all the air had just been punched out of his lungs. *She was absolutely stunning.* Even at a distance he could see that her eyes were the most dazzling emerald-green he'd ever seen in his life. Add to that apple cheeks, and full, luscious lips stained the colour of ripe cherries, and Jake sensed all the testosterone in the room heave a collective sigh—his own included.

Rick was the first to recover. 'Hi. Can I help you?' he called out cheerfully.

'This is where the auditions are being held, isn't it?'

Glancing nervously round her, the girl took in the five men standing there, as well as the stacked plastic chairs lining the walls, the dusty floor and the lofty ceiling with its yellowing cracked plasterwork. Her expression was definitely bemused, as if she couldn't quite believe where she'd landed. She still hadn't moved any further away from the door.

'Am I too late? I'm sorry I couldn't get here a bit earlier but I've been stocktaking' Swiping a hand down her short black skirt, she tugged the edges of her raincoat together in front of it, as if she might have inadvertently displayed more than she wanted to.

'Stocktaking, you say?' Rick's wolfish grin grew even wider. 'You can check *my* stock any time you want to, honey.'

Time to take charge, Jake thought with a flash of irritation. The girl might be easy on the eye, but she was more than likely another time-waster or wannabe—and God knew he'd auditioned enough of them in the past four days to be honestly weary of hearing any more.

To make matters worse, he'd *lived* with a girl just like that and she'd all but broken him with her relentless desire for fame and fortune. Not to mention what she'd been prepared to do to get it. *In any case, the girl in front of him probably couldn't sing for toffee.*

But even as his cynical gaze surveyed her he felt a hot flash of desire throb through him. He was almost dizzy with the power of it, and in that moment he saw it as a warning to steer well clear—because something told him that, given the chance, the allure of this incredible beauty would be too hard to resist.

The realisation that he might be tempted honestly scared him. Temptation was never a simple option. In Jake's book it equalled weakness, and he was a man who liked to be in control. From a young age he'd quickly intuited that if he didn't take care of himself and instigate boundaries then he was damn sure no one else would.

'Actually, you're too late.'

But even as the words left his lips he immediately belied them. Helplessly drawn, he found himself moving towards the bewitching woman, and somehow the necessity to get her to leave…and *quick*…melted clean away. All his instincts told him to take the chance to admire her beauty while he could. After all, it wasn't every day that a veritable *angel* presented herself in front of him…

'What I mean to say is' he went on 'is that you're too late for the auditions today but you can come back tomorrow if you're serious. If not, then all I can do is thank you for your interest and wish you well.'

'You're questioning if I'm serious or not? If I'm not serious about auditioning then why do you think I'm here?'

Surprised that she would come back at him like that, Jake sighed. His innate instinct was for self-preservation, and his mind scrambled to give her a legitimate reason why he couldn't let her audition today.

'Well, if that's the case, then you won't mind coming back tomorrow, will you? We've been auditioning since early this morning and we could all use a break,'

Watching her wrestle with the emotion his words must have wrought, he saw her hand tuck her hair behind her ear, then free it again as if she wasn't quite sure what to do next.

'I was really hoping you could hear me tonight. The thing is, I won't be able to make it tomorrow'

'Then you can't be that serious about auditioning, can you?'

Hot colour suffused her apple cheeks—but not because of embarrassment, Jake guessed. His cutting rejoinder had infuriated her.

Not wanting to be swayed by her angelic face and big green eyes, he told himself to stand firm. Nonetheless, he heard himself ask, 'What's your name?'

'It's Caitlin. Caitlin Ryan.'

'Well, Caitlin…' Folding his arms across his chest, he let his light-coloured gaze flick an interested glance up and down her figure, simply because it was too irresistible to ignore. 'Like I said, if you're serious about auditioning then you'll come back tomorrow, when it's more convenient for us to hear you. Shall we say around eleven-thirty?'

'I'm sorry…' The woman's incandescent emerald gaze was immediately perturbed. 'I don't want to be a nuisance, but I honestly can't make it tomorrow. A close friend—the manager of the shop where I work—is having her wisdom teeth removed, and I'm the only one who can stand in for her while she's away'

Jake fought down a compelling urge to laugh out loud. Of all the answers he might have expected her to furnish him with, the imminent removal of a friend's wisdom teeth hadn't been one of them!

He could almost sense Rick's laughter bubbling up behind him. *Damn.* It was going to be pretty hard to refuse this beauty anything when she was staring back at him like some little girl lost, those big green eyes of hers reflecting equal measures of hope and disappointment.

'Give the girl a break, man.' As he planted himself beside Jake Rick's amiable features creased into a persuasive smile. 'The band is still set up, so what have we got to lose?'

My sanity, for one thing, thought Jake, with grave misgiving. If Caitlin Ryan looked like a little lost puppy now, before he had even heard her sing a note, God only knew what she was going to look like when he told her *Sorry... don't give up the day job.*

Expelling an aggrieved sigh, he dragged his fingers impatiently through his mane of dark hair and stared at her.

'Okay,' he drawled, his tone painfully resigned, 'I'll give you ten minutes to show me what you can do.' *Or, more to the point, what you can't.* He couldn't pretend he was expecting very much.

Caitlin's heart beat double-time. *Okay, I can do this, she told herself. Singing is second nature to me.*

But her morale-boosting self-talk didn't seem to be having a great deal of effect as she nervously made her way across to the stage. The three young men already there ambled casually back to their instruments and she wondered how many singers they'd already auditioned—because frankly they weren't looking too impressed.

Registering the band's name on the large bass drum in front of the drum kit, and privately acknowledging that she'd never heard of it, she somehow made her lips shape a smile. The lead guitarist introduced himself first. Telling Caitlin that his name was Mike, he extended his hand to help her as she negotiated the final step of the wooden staircase that led onto the stage. He had an open, friendly face she noted, unlike *Captain Ahab* down there, who looked as if he'd just as soon as take a bite out of her rather than throw away a smile on someone who was clearly a time-waster.

Why, oh, why had she thought this was a good idea? Just because she loved to sing, it didn't mean that she had anywhere *near* enough talent to make it her career...

'By the way, I'm Rick. The man who told you to come back tomorrow is the head honcho. Aren't you going to take off your coat?'

At the foot of the stage the fair-haired man who'd persuaded his boss to give her a chance grinned up at her, with a teasing twinkle in his dancing hazel eyes that was in complete contrast to the reception Caitlin had received from his stony-faced colleague.

As his dark, brooding friend stayed ominously at the back of the hall she noticed he was staring back at her, as if to say, *Your performance is going to have to be exceptional if you're going to impress me.* He was regarding her as if he fully expected her to disappoint him. *Who was he anyway? Caitlin wondered?* He might be the man in charge of the auditions, but although he'd asked for her name he hadn't volunteered his own.

In answer to Rick's comment about removing her coat, she answered, 'I'd rather keep it on, if you don't mind. I'm feeling a little bit chilly.'

Her hand curved round the mike stand as if to anchor her to something solid. *Oh, why had she worn this stupid short skirt?* Because her friend Lia had told her she should make an effort to 'look nice' for the audition, that was why. Caitlin should have stuck to her preference of wearing jeans and a T-shirt.

Raising his voice so that she could hear him clearly, Rick asked, 'So what are you going to sing for us?'

Caitlin told him. It was a song that was regarded as a classic in the annals of rock culture. Although it had a driving, pulsing beat, there was also great passion and pathos in the lyrics and she loved it.

'Good song choice.'

She couldn't help colouring at the approval in his voice and turned her head towards the band so that he wouldn't see he'd unsettled her. 'Is that okay with you?' she asked them.

The blond bearded drummer, who'd introduced himself as Steve Bridges, answered her with a precise drumroll, and to Caitlin's right the stocky Scottish bass player, whose name was Keith Ferguson, played a couple of chords on his guitar.

'Let's rock and roll, then, shall we?' Rick gave her a mock salute. 'It's all yours, honey. Take it away.'

I can do this, Caitlin told herself dry-mouthed as she waited for the band to play her in.

For a couple of seconds she squeezed her eyes shut tight. If she wanted to stay strong she wouldn't glance at Mr Tall, Dark and Foreboding, lest one disapproving look from those strangely light blue eyes of his smothered the small vestige of courage she had left. But as the music struck up around her fear helpfully receded, replaced by her desire to sing.

She knew this particular number inside out. What she *wouldn't* admit to the present company was that she'd only sung it in the bath or in the privacy of her bedroom. *Oh, and once to Lia.* Her lack of experience would really freak them out if they knew about it before they heard her. Suppressing a suddenly uncharacteristic urge to grin, she listened for her cue, then opened her mouth and launched into the vocal.

Electricity shot through Jake's system with all the power of a lightning bolt. His stomach muscles clenched hard as excitement and shock suffused him. As he listened to the honey-eyed, sexy vocal emanating from the raven-haired beauty onstage he knew they'd struck gold. He didn't even have to let her finish the song to know it, but of course he would.

Caitlin's classy vocals melded with the rich, tight sound the band had worked so hard to attain as though they'd been made for each other. Her performance was stand-out amazing…knee-buckling.

Catching sight of the exchanged grins between the band members, he also saw Rick's silently mouthed '*Eureka*' as he turned round to give Jake the thumbs-up. There wasn't one girl Jake had heard sing in the past four days who came even remotely close to the talent of Caitlin Ryan. Hell…there wasn't one girl he'd heard sing in the past couple of *years* who was even in her league. The woman delivered a song as if she was born to it. *Damn.*

He moved his head in wonder as he watched her, her body moving in a naturally sexy sway to the beat of the music, her shapely legs drawing his appreciative gaze despite her strange insistence on keeping her coat on. With the right clothes and make-up this girl would be sit up and beg gorgeous. As good a singer as Marcie had been, she couldn't hold a candle to Caitlin Ryan in the looks department. He didn't wholly go along with the idea that a singer needed to be attractive, but good looks certainly didn't hurt in this business.

Suddenly his desire for sustenance at the local pub dissipated like snow in the desert. Jake was excited again. Enthused. When the mood was on him he could work twenty-four hours a day without a break if he wanted to, and he would willingly do so to get this band on the road again, expecting nothing less than the same commitment from everyone else.

As the last chords of the music died away Caitlin inhaled a relieved breath to steady herself. Then she reluctantly released the microphone.

Behind her, Steve Bridges blew an appreciative whistle. 'That was incredible. You absolutely killed it.'

Feeling her face grow warm at the compliment, she was taken aback when the two men who had been watching her vaulted onto the stage.

'What other bands have you been in?' Jake demanded.

Glancing back into his mesmerising eyes—eyes the colour of blue ice melting under steam—Caitlin's heart bungee-jumped to her toes. 'I—I haven't been in any other bands,' she admitted softly.

'You're kidding me.' Rick looked completely nonplussed.

Startled that he didn't believe her, she widened her eyes in surprise.

'I wouldn't pretend about something like that. The truth is I've only ever sung for my own amusement and because I'm compelled to. I just love music. I'm passionate about it.'

The rock-hard muscles in Jake's stomach compressed tightly. *He could tell she had passion...had it in spades, he thought.* That was the major difference between her and the instantly forgettable *wannabes* he'd recently auditioned.

'So you've never sung professionally before?' he queried.

'No. I haven't.' Her huge green eyes were absolutely guileless. Gazing back into their depths was like looking down to the bottom of a clear unsullied lake on a hot summer's day.

'So, what do you do to keep body and soul together?'

'You mean for a living?' Caitlin sighed. 'I'm a shop assistant. Remember I told you I had to stand in for the manager earlier today?'

'And where is the shop?'

'It's here in the village, of course.'

Jake was honestly stunned. They'd been auditioning girls from as far afield as Scotland, and this girl—this incredible find of theirs—came from the very village they were auditioning in. It was altogether ludicrous.

Laughing out loud, Rick slapped his leather-clad thigh. 'Well, if that doesn't beat it all! You mean for the past four days now we've been tearing our hair out trying to find a singer and you've been here all the time?'

'I only found out about the auditions when I saw the ad in the post office. I couldn't believe it. Nothing as exciting as that ever happens in the village. It seemed...' she flushed a little '...it seemed like a sign.' Tucking some silky strands of ebony hair behind an ear, Caitlin smiled self-consciously. 'Anyway…thanks for hearing me and giving me the chance to sing for you. Whatever happens, I really enjoyed it.'

She turned away to climb back down from the stage and leave, but was taken aback when Jake held up his hand, a distinctly puzzled crease straining his handsome brow.

'Where do you think you're going?'

'I've got to get back to work. I—I told you…we're stock-taking. I don't suppose we'll finish until late tonight.'

'Do you want to sing with this band or not?' he demanded, hardly able to believe what he was hearing.

'Do you mean…? Are you saying…?'

The stunned look on her face would be almost comical if Jake had a mind to laugh—which he absolutely *didn't*.

'On the strength of the performance we've just heard, I think I'd be a fool not to offer you the chance of singing with the band. I think we're all in agreement that you're just what we're looking for.'

Even though he directed a meaningful glance towards Rick and the others, Jake barely needed confirmation of his decision. Not when the final say categorically rested with him.

Eyes narrowing, he continued, 'But if we take you on you do realise that there's a hell of a lot of work ahead of you? You may be able to sing, Miss Ryan, but there's a lot to learn before we let you loose onstage in public. Have you honestly never sung professionally before?'

He didn't believe her. As exciting as the prospect of singing with the band was, Caitlin knew instinctively that if she accepted the job her relationship with this man was never going to be one made in heaven.

She nervously cleared her throat. 'I was in a school band from fifteen to eighteen, but I've done nothing since then. We only played local functions. Events like Christmas parties, special birthdays and anniversaries…stuff like that'

'And you were the lead singer?'

'No. That is…we all sang. There were six of us altogether. But I occasionally played piano and guitar.'

Rick's eyebrows flew up to his hairline. 'You're a musician as well?'

'Yes. That is, I read music and play a little. I practise whenever I can…at least on my guitar. I no longer have a piano.'

No wonder she knew instinctively exactly where to come in with the vocal, Jake mused. Only someone who was a competent musician or had a natural ear for music could pull that off without rehearsal.

He saw his astonishment reflected back at him when his glance collided with Rick's.

'Sweetheart, as far as I'm concerned there's not the slightest doubt in my mind that you're the right singer for this band.' The American smiled, his hand enthusiastically shaking Caitlin's. 'By the way, my full name is Rick Young—I'm Blue Sky's official dogsbody and general "helper-outer". That means I organise the gigs, make sure the band shows up on time, and most importantly collect the fee at the end of the show. The man standing beside you with the poker face is Jake Sorenson—well-known record producer and the band's manager. You must have heard of him? Anyway, he's going to make us all rich one day, like him. You can count on it. If anyone can work miracles round here, Jake can. He's been in the business so long he's probably due for a plaque in the Rock and Roll Hall of Fame.'

'Very funny.'

Jake didn't put out his hand for Caitlin to shake. *Right then he had the strangest feeling that if he did he wouldn't want to let it go.* If this venture was going to work at all then he needed to maintain the requisite professionalism at all times. The last thing he needed was to get personally involved with Little Miss Hole in her Stocking. The band had been through enough upheaval and disappointment with Marcie walking out. No… If they were going to work together then he was going to play strictly by the rules. He *had* to, no matter how irresistible the temptation. And if he should at any time forget that vow then all he had to do was remember the scandal that had near crushed him and killed his career.

Taking a sidelong glance at Rick, and seeing that his friend's avidly appreciative gaze was all but glued to Caitlin, as if only a madman would want to look anywhere else, Jake firmed his resolve. 'Strictly by the rules' went for Rick and the guys, too. And, by God, he'd make sure that they knew it.

As the band welcomed Caitlin he saw that their pleasure was absolutely sincere. He also saw how her lovely face lit up at their enthusiastic welcome, how a faint flush of pink stained her cheeks as she strove to handle it, and something told Jake she was definitely an innocent compared to the rest of them. *That too could be a sticking point, he reflected*...especially in the dog-eat-dog world that was the music business. But, that said, it made a refreshing change to meet someone with hope and enthusiasm in their eyes— someone who wasn't old and jaded before their time as he probably was...

'Come into my office, Miss Ryan,' he invited her. 'We need to talk in private.'

Vaulting off the stage, Jake strode to the end of the hall, the sound of his boot heels echoing loudly in his wake.

After eagerly helping Caitlin down from the stage, Rick hurried to catch up to his enigmatic boss. 'Hey, don't you want me there too?' he called.

Turning, Jake shook his head, a muscle flexing in the side of his hollowed cheek. 'Not at the moment, my friend. There'll be time enough to go over the timetable for rehearsals when we talk later. We'll have a group meeting tomorrow afternoon so that we can discuss everything. Right now I just want to have a private chat with Miss Ryan'

'Miss Ryan?' Rick frowned. 'What's wrong with Caitlin?'

Ignoring the comment, Jake turned and opened his office door.

Her trepidation mingling with excitement, Caitlin followed him. The whole experience felt strangely surreal to her. The office that Blue Sky's charismatic manager was using was a room not much bigger than a generously-sized broom cupboard, she saw. All it contained were two grey plastic chairs and an upturned orange box masquerading as a table. One small window allowed just a paltry glimpse of sky.

Moistening her lips, Caitlin sucked in a breath. Somehow being in such close proximity to Jake Sorenson was ten times more testing than any audition she could imagine. He had the kind of highly charged aura round him that would stir the senses of a blind woman, she mused nervously.

'Take a seat,' he instructed.

Feeling undeniably overwhelmed, she complied. When she sat, her knees unavoidably pressed up against the rough wood of the orange box as she strove to make herself more comfortable. Adjusting her coat as she waited for Jake to carry on speaking, she felt her anxiety definitely intensify.

'You've already told me that you have a job. I presume that's full-time?' Flipping open the black notebook on top of the box, he started writing inside it.

'That's right.'

'You said you work in a shop? What kind of shop?' Lifting his head, Jake pinned her to the seat with his pale blue eyes.

'It's a shop called Morgana,' she told him. 'It specialises in esoteric and personal development books, but we also sell things like incense, Native American jewellery, ambient music and crystals.'

And I love working there, she silently reflected. She shifted in the hard plastic chair. It would be a real wrench to leave that job, but what was the point in having a passion in life if you weren't planning on doing anything about it? Her friend Lia knew just how much Caitlin loved music, how she loved to sing. And then Caitlin had told her that she'd seen an ad in the post office

Versatile female singer aged twenty to thirty wanted to front established band specialising in soft rock.

Auditions were being held in St Joseph's church hall, in the very village where they lived, and Lia had encouraged her to go for it.

'It must be clear to you that if you want to sing with this band you can't work full-time in a shop as well?'

Jake didn't take his eyes off of her as he addressed Caitlin, and the blatant directness of his unsettling blue gaze made her feel as if someone had just curtailed her oxygen supply.

'Rehearsals start tomorrow afternoon and will continue every day after that for the next three weeks before the band performs in public. After that we'll be all over the country for an initial three-week tour. Are you ready to commit to such a schedule, Miss Ryan?'

'I hadn't really thought about much beyond the audition,' she confessed honestly, 'but I realise whoever gets the job will have to be prepared to do regular gigs and eventually tour. So, yes, I am ready to commit, Mr Sorenson. I've never wanted anything more.'

'And you know that means giving up your present job to do so?'

'Of course.'

Although she hadn't hesitated to answer in the affirmative Jake didn't miss the slightly perturbed frown between her elegant brows, and once again he had the distinct impression that Caitlin was a relative innocent when it came to the type of worldly experience that the rest of them had.

'Does that worry you?' he asked.

Lifting her chin, she was intent on holding his gaze and not shying away from it, he saw.

'I'd be a liar if I said it wasn't daunting to leave something I'm so familiar with for something much more challenging, but I want to rise to that challenge. Especially if it's going to help me realise my dream of becoming a professional singer. Besides…change is inevitable, isn't it? Nothing stays the same.'

'You don't have to make it sound like it's something to fear. There's many a singer who'd give their eye-teeth to have the opportunity I'm offering you. Blue Sky may have lost their lead vocalist but they're still an established band. Just before Marcie left they were invited to play on one of the top music shows on television.'

And the guys had been gutted when they'd had to cancel the engagement. It might have been the big break they'd been praying for…

'Please don't think that I'm ungrateful.'

Shifting self-consciously in her seat, Caitlin snagged her stocking on a splinter from the orange box. As she picked at it to free herself she blushed scarlet, because Jake's gaze was suddenly focused on her knee instead of on her face. The very air between them seemed to throb with heat and a disturbing prickle of perspiration slid worryingly down her spine.

'I think I'm still in shock,' she admitted, 'I didn't expect to get as far as this. I'm still trying to take it all in.'

'Well…' Reluctantly withdrawing his glance from her knee, Jake strove to remain businesslike. 'I'm not asking you to sign on the dotted line tonight. But that doesn't mean I'm giving you the chance to change your mind. When I've decided that I want something, Caitlin, I won't rest until I get it. So be here tomorrow at five. We'll be rehearsing until late in the evening. Do we have a deal?'

She bit down on her lip. 'Yes—yes, we do. But can I make it five-forty-five instead? I have to close the shop at five-thirty. I won't be any later. I can be here in just ten minutes if I drive.'

'Five-forty-five it is, then. And before you leave you'd

better give me your address and mobile phone number, just in case.'

Caitlin gave him the information and watched warily as Jake scribbled it down in his black notebook. Then he threw down his pen and got to his feet. She followed suit, her heart racing as he towered over her. She was five foot seven in her bare feet, but his physical domination of the tiny space seemed to make the already diminutive room even smaller.

Her fingers shaking, she fastened a couple of her coat buttons and managed a tentative smile. 'I'll see you tomorrow then, Mr…?' She had a moment of panic because she'd somehow forgotten his surname.

'You can call me Jake.'

To her utter surprise and secret delight a dimple appeared as if by magic at the corner of his very sexy mouth. Caitlin's insides knotted painfully.

'Right.'

'There's just one more thing before you go.'

'What's that?'

'I'd better explain one of the most important house rules, and that is there's to be no fraternising after hours with members of the band—and I'm not talking about a few drinks backstage after a gig. Am I making myself clear?'

Now Caitlin's face really *did* burn. She tried to look anywhere but straight at Jake. If he seriously thought she would—that she might— Of course he could have no idea that she'd sworn off men for good, she realised. But after what she'd been through with her ex-boyfriend Sean she'd rather trek through the Sahara Desert with a fur coat on than risk another soul-destroying relationship with a man… however brief.

'All I want to do is sing. I'm not interested in anything else. I can positively assure you of that.'

Jake couldn't help wondering why. He'd glimpsed pain and fury in those pretty green eyes of hers just now, as if even the suggestion that she might find herself attracted to a member of the opposite sex was tantamount to contemplating suicide.

He sighed. 'Okay, then. There's just one other thing.'

'What's that?'

This time Caitlin's wary gaze met his in pure defiance, as though she dared him to transgress one more inch into her private life.

Jake ventured a teasing smile. 'I'd seriously think about investing in a new pair of stockings, if I were you'

'How did you know they were—?'

'How did I know that they were stockings and not tights?' He gave her a shameless grin. 'Put it down to long experience...' he drawled, pretty sure that if he told her he'd had a tantalising glimpse of her stocking-tops when she'd first sat down she'd exit so fast he wouldn't see her for dust. 'You can't beat the genuine article.'

'Is that so? Well, anyway...I didn't know you could tell.' With a disturbed frown Caitlin tried to remember to breathe. Sheer embarrassment made her babble. 'The trouble is I seem to have an unhappy knack of snagging them whenever I wear them. They're not really practical. I normally wear jeans.'

'Take it from me...' Jake's voice dropped down a discernible notch or two, making his tone arrestingly smoky '...stockings are better...'

CHAPTER TWO

THE DOORBELL JANGLED and the wind chimes that hung liberally from the lilac-painted ceiling tinkled prettily in the ensuing draught. As far as Caitlin knew, Nicky, their part-time help, was around somewhere, and should have registered the fact that they had customers, but she must have absented herself to go to the bathroom.

Sighing softly, she didn't look round, in the belief that the other girl would appear any minute now, and instead continued to scrub at the particularly stubborn patch of dirt she'd found on the lowest shelf of the temporarily emptied bookshelf. When the stain didn't respond to her increased scrubbing with a damp cloth Caitlin scratched at it with her fingernail, a spurt of annoyance shooting through her when she realised it was the horrid remains of someone's chewing gum.

Of all the... She was immediately affronted on Lia's behalf. How dared someone come into this beautiful space and foul it with chewing gum? Some people just didn't have any respect. Some people just—

'Hi, there.'

Caitlin froze at the sound of that smoky bass voice. Still tense, she turned her head and glanced up to meet Jake Sorenson's indisputably amused glance. Had it really been just a day since she'd last seen him? Was it possible she could have so easily forgotten how dangerously attractive the man was, or that his mere presence had the power to erase anything else from her mind?

Irritated by her purely female response to his tall, dark good looks, she realised she was gaping up at him. What was even worse, he'd caught her wearing an old and tatty pair of jeans that had shrunk in the wash and now adhered to her thighs like a second skin. Caitlin had opted to wear them because she knew she'd be undertaking some general cleaning that day and hadn't wanted to risk ruining any of her good clothes. What made things worse was that she'd also elected to don a favourite old red T-shirt that had also seen better days, and it clung where it didn't ought to cling, possibly inviting too much unwanted attention…like *now*, when Jake's disturbing light blue eyes were making a slow and deliberate inventory of her body.

Heat crawled up her spine…*sexual* heat. It completely undid her. Just what was he *doing* here? Couldn't he have telephoned if he'd needed to speak to her? He had an unfair advantage, taking her by surprise like this.

Leaving her cloth on the bookshelf, she abruptly turned and got to her feet. Long strands of glossy black hair escaped her loosely tied ponytail to drift down gently over her flushed cheeks, and there was a smudge of dust on her nose. She struggled to get her greeting past her lips.

'Hi. I'm sorry, but you've caught me at a rather awkward moment. I was…'

'Let me guess…stocktaking?' Jake drawled softly.

She swallowed hard. The man could read a technical pamphlet on assembling flat-pack furniture out loud and it would still make her hot. 'Cleaning. I was just cleaning. Stocktaking was yesterday.'

'It's nice to see such dedication to the task. You looked like you were giving it your all.' Smiling faintly, he glanced round him. 'Interesting shop,' he remarked, sliding his hands into the back pockets of his jeans and nodding to himself as his gaze made another leisurely reconnaissance.

The heady scent of sandalwood incense perfumed the air and Caitlin wondered for the first time ever if it wasn't just a tad overpowering. Why she should suddenly be concerned about such an inconsequential thing, she didn't know. All she knew was that she wanted Jake to get a good impression of her workplace and not judge it adversely.

Jake's interested glance narrowed as he examined some of the titles on the bookshelves either side of the ones Caitlin had been cleaning. He glimpsed *Living Your Destiny* and other esoteric titles and permitted himself a smile. He'd known many hippies in his time, who had loved this kind of stuff. He looked up. From the painted ceiling dangled a myriad of wind chimes and crystals, and the music of some Native American drums pulsed gently. But, as eye-catching and diverting as the room furnishings were, he had no trouble bringing his gaze straight back to Caitlin.

He hadn't forgotten how pretty she was, and he was certain that the shape that had been intriguingly hidden behind her coat yesterday would be equally arresting…especially as he'd already been treated to the sight of her long slim legs in those tantalising black stockings. But nothing had quite prepared him for the mouth-wateringly feminine curves that he was looking at now.

Her scarlet T-shirt was at least one size smaller than she needed and it clung sexily to her voluptuous breasts, with the light stretchy fabric hugging her delectable shape like a second skin. Hell, he was on fire—uncharacteristically caught off-guard by his acute reaction to the green-eyed temptress in front of him. There was a tense knot in the pit of his stomach as he tried to tamp down the forceful desire that gripped him.

As he stared helplessly he registered the distinct outline of Caitlin's nipples beneath her bra—and was it his fevered imagination or had they just puckered a little tighter? He'd already been treated to the tempting sight of her delightful derriere as she'd crouched down, cleaning the bookshelf, and God help him, why did he have the distinct feeling that Christmas had arrived early? Because it wasn't just Caitlin's vocal talent that would put Blue Sky on the map. The woman's stunning beauty would put some serious icing on the Christmas cake too.

'My friend Lia owns the shop.'

Folding her arms protectively across her chest, because she'd mortifyingly caught Jake's gaze straying there, Caitlin silently berated herself for wearing that particular shirt today of all days. But then how was she to have known that Jake would pay an impromptu visit?

'As I told you, she's at the dental hospital today, otherwise I'd introduce you.' Her gaze automatically gravitated to the counter, missing the familiar sight of a diminutive slim blonde with elfin features and soft brown eyes.

Nicky must be taking a bathroom break. Caitlin couldn't help wishing that the girl's timing had been better. Just my luck, she thought. If Nicky had been around she could have somehow diverted Jake's attention. But he surely hadn't visited the shop to browse…

'Anyway, what can I do for you?' she asked.

Jake stared at her in bemusement. *You wouldn't believe how creative I could get about that,* he thought, and then gave himself a harsh mental shake. Where were his brains, for goodness' sake? He had a perfectly legitimate reason for seeking out their new vocalist and yet he was standing there gawping at her like some horny teenager hoping to get laid. The realisation was sobering.

'About the rehearsals this afternoon,' he started, 'I just wanted to let you know that we'll be working quite late tonight—perhaps into the early hours of the morning. If you have a boyfriend I hope he's the understanding type. If not, we're all in trouble.'

'There's no boyfriend.'

'Good.'

Caitlin frowned. Rubbing her hands briefly up and down her bare arms, she glanced back into Jake's arresting blue gaze. The man had the kind of reined-in sexuality and physicality that couldn't help but put her on her guard. It didn't help matters that he had a 'bad boy' smile that was surely reserved for a woman's wildest fantasy...*if* she was in the market for such a fantasy—which she most definitely wasn't.

Still, the hard honed body outlined by his black T-shirt, jeans and fashionably battered leather jacket would surely be a thing of beauty without clothes. There was not so much as a hint of surplus flesh on that taut, streamlined physique. The man clearly kept himself in good shape. She couldn't prevent the small shiver of appreciation that ran up her spine. But it wasn't just the commanding, easy-on-the-eye physique that made Caitlin so intimately aware of him. Something told her that Jake Sorenson didn't take any prisoners. When he told her that they would be working late tonight she was certain he meant it in the fullest sense of the word.

What if I've made a terrible mistake? she fretted. *It's the thing I want to do more than anything else in the world, but what if I'm really not cut out to be a singer in a band?*

Her mind slipped into panic mode, as it was apt to do when she was hit by a sudden attack of self-doubt.

He must have read her mind just then. 'Don't look so terrified,' he cautioned, amusement lurking in the steamy blue depths of his mesmerising eyes. 'I promise not to drive you too hard on your first night. But after that I'm afraid you'll just have to roll with the punches like everybody else. Anyone who wants to pursue a dream has to make sacrifices, and the music business is a hard game, Caitlin. It's notoriously competitive and cut-throat, and that's an almost conservative description. If you want to be a success in this game you have to grow a fairly thick skin. Blue Sky have played all over the country in the past two years, trying to establish themselves, and they've gained a loyal following. When their lead singer Marcie walked out it was a huge shock. More than that it was a betrayal. But I owe it to the rest of the band to make good on my promise to take them to the top—and, trust me, I'm going to do exactly that. Failure is just not an option in my book. Do you understand what I'm saying?'

Caitlin did. *Signing up for commando training with the SAS would probably be easier.* She tried for a smile but couldn't help the nervous little quiver that hijacked her lips instead. Was the man always so serious, she wondered?

'I'll try my best not to let you down…Jake.' She added his name because she reasoned she should start being less formal, and couldn't help savouring the taste of it on her tongue— like an enticing new flavour she'd never sampled before.

He scowled.

'That's not good enough. Say, *I won't let you down, Jake.* Not, *I'll try.*'

Flustered, Caitlin pushed a stray strand of hair away from her suddenly burning cheek. 'I *won't* let you down, Jake.'

'That's better. Now, come here.'

Before she'd gleaned what he intended he firmly drew her towards himthen gently erased the smudge of dust she'd inadvertently acquired on her nose. Her senses were immediately bombarded by the warm sexy tang of leather mixing provocatively with the alluring masculine scent of the man himself.

If someone could bottle it, they'd make a fortune, Caitlin thought. She felt more than a little off-centre as she stepped away, especially when she saw that he was smiling. A deep, sensual tug registered low in her belly.

'Thanks. I'm probably covered in dust and looking a right mess, aren't I?' she remarked nervously.

The words were out before she could check them. She could have kicked herself, because now Jake would think she was fishing for a compliment—which was absurd when she did honestly believe she must resemble something the cat had dragged in.

But with a charismatic quirk at a corner of his lips Jake elected not to comment. Instead he walked to the door, opened it and gave her a brief salute. 'I'll see you tonight. Five-forty-five. Don't be late.'

As he stepped out onto the pavement Caitlin had a distinct sense of being dismissed. More to the point, she felt bereft, as if he'd somehow taken a part of her with him. The bell jangled as the door swung back on its hinges and she released a long slow breath, as though she'd been holding on to it for nothing less than a lifetime.

The realisation that she was late, even though she had a perfectly legitimate reason, made Caitlin furious with herself. Parking her car on the gravel drive that led up to the sombre-looking Victorian church hall, she bit back a ripe curse, fumbling to organise her car keys and purse as she shut the car door behind her. To add insult to injury, a light rain had started to fall.

She glanced down at her watch and her anxious gaze once more registered the time. *Six-fifteen...* She wasn't just late—she was *very* late. But how was she to have known that a customer would walk in the door at exactly a minute before five-thirty? She could hardly turn the girl away—especially when she'd tearfully told Caitlin that she'd just broken up with her boyfriend and someone had recommended she get some rose quartz to help her.

Lia had often teased her friend that she was a magnet for the heartsick, but Caitlin's naturally compassionate nature wouldn't allow her to stand back and do nothing when someone was hurting. When push came to shove, though, however she explained her tardiness to Jake Sorenson something told her it wasn't going to cut any ice.

Summoning every scrap of courage she could muster, she pushed open the creaky wooden door that led into the porch, wrinkling her nose at the pall of mustiness and damp that clung to the air, her heart bumping against her ribs at the sound of instruments tuning up.

Behind the door that led into the cavernous hall Jake was testing the microphone in the familiar time-honoured way of performers the world over: '*One two, one two...*'

Murmuring a briefly fervent prayer, Caitlin pushed open the door. The overhead lights were dimmed, she noticed, and the three members of the band on stage continued to play as Rick Young melted out of the shadows to position himself in front of her. Despite his serious expression, at least his hazel eyes were twinkling, she saw.

'You're late, pretty lady. Not a good start, just thought I'd warn you.'

He jerked his chin towards Jake as Blue Sky's enigmatic manager jumped off the stage, his long jeans-clad legs carrying him purposefully towards Caitlin. It didn't take a genius to deduce that he wasn't happy. *Blast!*

Her chilled fingers curled over the car keys in her pocket and held them tight. It wasn't as if she was late deliberately. She honestly wanted to take this amazing opportunity they were offering her. But right now, judging by the fierce scowl on Jake's handsome face, it might just be about to be taken away from her.

'I'm sorry I'm late. I just—'

'What was the last thing I said to you?' he barked.

Startled, Caitlin glanced across at Rick. His expression conveyed that he'd witnessed similar scenarios too many times before to be at all perturbed.

'Don't be late?' she ventured, her teeth anxiously clamping down on her lip.

'And didn't I also tell you to be here at five-forty-five? It's now twenty past six. You're thirty-five minutes late. That's not acceptable, Miss Ryan. It's not acceptable at all.'

Jake was shifting restlessly from one black-booted foot to the other, a muscle ominously flinching in the side of his lean, unshaven jaw. Caitlin didn't dare quip that his watch must be fast, even though it clearly *was*. The fact that he was unshaven made him look edgy and dangerous—as if anything could happen and probably would.

'A customer came into the shop just as I was getting

ready to leave—' the words came out in a heated rush as she gripped even more tightly onto her car keys.

'Couldn't you have turned whoever it was away and told them to come back tomorrow?' he snapped.

Affronted, Caitlin widened her eyes.

'I *never* turn customers away. People don't just come into our shop to buy things, Mr Sorenson. Many of them come in for healing of one kind or another. The girl that I saw was distraught. She'd just broken up with her long-term boyfriend and was looking for something that might help ease her distress. I'm not so cold-hearted that I would tell her in her hour of need to come back tomorrow.'

Jake was so taken aback by this answer that the red mist of anger that had threatened when Caitlin had walked in late dissipated like ice beneath the sun. Sucking in his cheeks, he blew out a long, slow breath, shaking his head and taking a moment to compose himself. *I must be losing my grip*, he thought irritably.

Caitlin proffered a hesitant smile. Jake's bemused glance collided with hers just as one corner of her pretty mouth nudged a very sexy dimple. Something hitched in his heart… not to mention below his navel.

'Well, we've wasted enough time as it is,' he growled. 'Take off your coat and get yourself up on stage. We've got a hell of a lot to get through tonight and we may well be here until breakfast—so be warned.'

After making her apologies to the other band members, seeing that Jake's attention had suddenly been claimed by Rick, Caitlin fell into animated conversation with them about music. Did they write all their own songs? Did they ever do any covers? And, finally, did they have a playlist for tonight's rehearsals that she could look at?

The young men were only too pleased to answer her questions, interspersing their answers with jokes and anecdotes and generally going out of their way to help put her at ease. Mike Casey, the lead guitarist, with his tousled dark hair and rather serious brown eyes, explained that he added the harmonies to several of the songs and he and Caitlin would need to spend some time together working on them. Then he told her that he and the others had rented a house in the village for the duration of their stay and she'd be more than welcome to come over and work on them there.

'Caitlin?'

She spun round at the sound of her name, folding her arms across the blue chambray man's shirt that she'd thrown over the too-revealing red T-shirt she'd been wearing earlier. The long shirt-tails skimmed her bottom in her tight jeans and helped her feel a little less vulnerable than she had done in the shop, when Jake's toe-curling glance had all but consumed her with its frank and hungry intensity.

She was staring into the same hauntingly blue depths now as he looked up at her from the foot of the stage. Her mouth dried. He handed her a sheet of paper with music and lyrics on. Accepting it without comment, she let her gaze fall eagerly on the title. It was another great rock standard that she knew by heart.

The lyrics were passionate and heart-rending, and she'd sung it with genuine feeling when she'd first learned it because she'd empathised with the sentiment of the song only too well. It was about a girl whose dreams had been cruelly shattered when the man she loved had used her and ill-treated her and had consequently robbed her of every bit of self-confidence she had...

But now... Her glance quickly perused the musical arrangement and her heart skipped a nervous beat, because the time had come for her to really prove to both the band and their enigmatic manager that she could deliver what they hoped she could. It was one thing to conquer her fear of an audition—quite another to front a band for the first time ever and do it well. This was where things started to get serious.

'You know the tune? We can choose something more contemporary if you prefer?'

Jake's blue eyes honed in on the roomy chambray shirt Caitlin had donned over the sexy red T-shirt and once again he sensed that she wasn't at all at ease with her body. *Why else had she covered up?* And how would she cope when she had to perform on stage in front of a crowd he wondered?Would she be self-conscious then?

She was a naturally beautiful woman, and the sensual aura she exuded when she walked into a room was a killer. It was a given that her looks would be a big asset to the band, and he didn't want her to try and hide that sensational body behind oversized clothing. Still, there was plenty of time for that particular discussion. Right now Caitlin had to prove to them that she was a worthy replacement for Marcie.

'The song is fine' she told him. 'I know it well.'

'Good. Take it away, guys.'

As the band started to play the introduction Caitlin listened carefully, curving her hands round the microphone stand in readiness and staring towards the back of the hall rather than at Jake. Her body was tense as a sprinter's at the start of the most important race of her life, but she didn't need to glance at the lyrics as she waited for her cue to come in. The words were etched on her soul.

There was no need for her to imagine that she was the woman she was singing about because she *was*. She'd been used, hurt and scorned by a man she'd once loved and trusted, and the devastating experience had taught her to keep her guard up. Adversity had taught her a huge lesson and, hard as it was, it had helped her to grow stronger.

I'll put steel round my heart that your poison arrows can't dent
And I'll be the phoenix rising that you never saw coming...

Those were the lyrics.

Suddenly her eyes flew open and Caitlin's glance fell on

Jake. He was attired from head to toe in black, and his concentrated expression was utterly serious as he watched her performance. Minutes later, when she came to the end of the song, she was glad, because she desperately needed to suck in a steadying breath. Her heart was thumping hard at the painful memories the words had evoked. *Yet, meeting Jake's gaze once again, she didn't immediately withdraw when it hit her that he had seriously begun to fascinate her.*

It was probably just hormones, she thought irritably. She certainly wasn't looking to take things further than a working relationship. Apart from it being against the rules, she wasn't looking for a man. Just like in the song, Caitlin had had the relationship from *hell* with one particular man and it had nearly destroyed her. She certainly wasn't going to entertain the idea of being with someone who could twist her insides into knots merely by looking at her.

'Not bad,' he said grudgingly.

Her fervent hope had been that she'd done much better than just 'not bad', and Caitlin's heart plummeted. Still, Jake was the boss, and she wasn't there simply in search of praise. Her ambition was to earn her living as a bona fide singer—never to be dependent on anyone either for love, self-esteem or security.

That was why seeing the ad for the auditions had excited her. It really had seemed like a sign that she should step up to the plate and start to fulfil her destiny. Staying at the shop and 'playing safe' just didn't feel like the right option any more. Her family had moved on and so should she. *It wasn't the possibility of fame that interested her...far from it.* Her passion was the music itself—the potential to experience joy in doing what she loved to do and to share it with anyone who cared to listen.

So she would bow to the man's far greater experience in such matters and give her all to improve. She prayed her efforts would be enough.

'Wow! Honey, you'll never be poor with a voice like that,' Rick told her as he went to stand next to his friend.

The contrast between the two men was striking. Rick's longish tousled hair was tinted a sun-kissed blond, while Jake's was a dark chestnut-brown, and their physiques were markedly different too. Jake was broad-shouldered and lean, his body supremely fit and toned, while Rick was shorter and more muscular. But, whatever the contrast in appearance, Caitlin sensed the two men were firm friends. There was a definite camaraderie between them that suggested their association had been born out of knowing each other for a very long time.

'She was fantastic,' Rick commented, turning towards Jake. 'I felt every ounce of emotion she put into the song… she made it her own.'

'That may be true,' Jake responded, his cool glance deliberately sliding away from Caitlin's. 'But it won't belong to her until she knows it intimately, inside and out. Let's do it again, guys. Then you can do some of your own material.'

It was three hours later when Caitlin was finally able to take a breather. Perched on the edge of the stage, with her long slender legs dangling over the side, she was attempting to eat her portion of the Chinese take-away that Rick had ordered. Her throat ached, her head throbbed and she could have fallen asleep standing up.

The band's charismatic manager hadn't let up for one minute in his efforts to get the best out of her vocal performance and she felt as if she'd done twelve rounds with a prize fighter. Whilst she was perfectly aware that singing was a very physical occupation, even if a person was blessed with a good voice, nothing could have prepared Caitlin for the sheer effort that Jake demanded.

During the past three hours she'd survived admonition after admonition to, 'Try again!' 'Put your heart into it, woman!' 'Hold back a little on that note…drop down a

key…' *'Damn it, Caitlin! You're just not trying hard enough!'*
Now she could barely summon up the energy to eat, despite
the fact that the shrimp chop suey and bamboo shoots with
Chinese mushrooms looked and smelled delicious.

'Not hungry?'

Her tired glance fell on Jake's long jeans-clad legs as he
dropped down beside her. Her heart skipped a beat. Lifting
her gaze, she looked up into the hauntingly misty depths of
his soulful blue eyes. It struck her as unfair that a man should
possess such enviably long black lashes, but then she mused
that Jake must have been at the head of the line when God
was dishing out extraordinary good looks…not to mention
sheer animal magnetism.

Caitlin sucked in a less than steady breath when the
scent of his cologne forged another assault on her belea-
guered senses. In answer to his question, she responded, 'I
thought I was.' Shrugging, she put her carton of food aside
and touched a paper napkin delicately to her lips. 'I only
had a sandwich at lunchtime…it wasn't very nice either.'

'You must have known this wasn't going to be easy. Still
sure you want to go through with it?' Jake challenged. 'You
need more than just talent in this game, Caitlin. You need
equal measures of grit and stamina too.'

'I can summon up plenty of grit and stamina when I need
it. Just try me.'

A flash of defiance lit up her defensive green eyes and
Jake chuckled softly. She'd freed her lustrous long hair from
its ponytail and now it flowed down her back like shining
black silk. Examining it more closely, he detected flashes
of mahogany within the darker strands. His fingers were
itching to touch it and he closed his hands into fists to stop
himself from reaching out to do just that.

'It's obviously going to take me a little while to learn all
the new songs,' she breathed, 'but I'll take a copy of the music
and lyrics home with me and practise them on my guitar.'

Jake had almost forgotten that Caitlin was a guitarist as

well. How good he didn't yet know, but judging by her vocal talent he guessed it wouldn't be far behind.

'Good move,' he commented, 'but the first thing you're going to have to do is to hand in your notice at the shop. There's no way you can have a full-time job there outside of singing with the band. In just three weeks' time we'll be on the road and you'll have to kiss this sleepy little village goodbye.'

The words sounded so *final* that Caitlin couldn't help shivering. But she immediately reminded herself that the most amazing opportunity had come her way, and she should take it with open arms and think herself blessed. No one got anywhere in life without taking risks. God knew she should have absorbed that fact by now, with all the New Age reading she'd done since working for Lia.

She'd lived in the village for most of her life, having moved from London with her family when she was just a toddler. When her parents had decided to join her brother Phil and his wife in California three years ago Caitlin had opted to stay put. She wasn't ready to leave the country, she'd argued. There was still a lot to experience living in the UK.

But most of all she'd stayed because she'd needed time to forge her own identity—the chance to bring her own dreams into fruition, not just tag along on someone else's. *She'd even needed to make colossal mistakes, like her relationship with Sean.* None of those things would have been possible surrounded by her well-meaning but highly controlling family.

She swallowed hard.

'So…does that mean you're offering me a full-time position with the band?' she asked.

Her stomach churned as she waited for Jake's reply.

'Looks that way doesn't it?' He smiled. Then, agile as a cat, he leapt to his feet and crossed the stage to join Rick and the others.

CHAPTER THREE

'WE'RE ALL GOING back to the Pilgrim's Inn for a few drinks—want to join us?'

Mike Casey stood waiting as Caitlin shrugged into her raincoat. Everyone else was outside. Steve and Keith were loading the van with the equipment and Jake and Rick were deep in discussion. Rick had extended the same invitation to her earlier, and Caitlin had told him she'd think about it. But the very idea of going into that particular pub again, after what had happened between her and Sean on her last visit, made her feel faintly ill.

Sean had been so bad that night—out of his head on a cocktail of drink and drugs—and she'd feared the worst. She had been right to. The cruel words and jibes that he'd taunted her with had just got worse and worse as the evening progressed. . *The sharpest knife couldn't have cut her more deeply.* Add to that the humiliation of his verbal attack being witnessed by a pub full of people before the landlord threw him out—well, it had been enough to make her want to give the place a wide berth for ever.

Lifting her gaze to Mike's, she said, 'It's kind of you to ask me, but I think I'll have to say no. It's already quite late.'

Stealing a quick glance at her watch, she saw that it was ten-thirty-five, and they'd been rehearsing since three o'clock that afternoon. Her throat was parched and her body ached from the sheer effort that Jake had demanded. The man apparently had endless reserves of energy that made

Caitlin feel as if she was the slowest runner on the track in comparison. No. She'd much prefer to go home, shower, get into her pyjamas and put her feet up with a glass of wine and a bowl of crisps at her elbow.

'You call ten-thirty in the evening *late*? We're talking Saturday night, here. Don't tell me the whole village goes to bed early?' Mike's dark eyebrows flew up to the tips of his tousled fringe. 'You must have led a sheltered life, if that's normal for you.'

At his disbelieving grin, Caitlin conceded a shy smile. 'You must think I'm pretty boring, right? No way could I ever claim to be a typical rock chick, that's for sure. But I realise my early nights will have to come to an end when the band goes on the road.'

'You two ready?' Rick appeared at the door, his hazel eyes appraising Caitlin and Mike with interest. 'I have to lock up. Caitlin? Jake would like a word.'

What now? ow? Caitlin groaned inwardly at the prospect.

Jake hadn't lied when he'd said he would go easy with her on the first night but that after that she'd have to roll with punches like everyone else. He'd been harder on her than on any of the guys in the band. Maybe that was because they already knew what was required and she didn't? But somehow Caitlin didn't think that was the only reason Jake had been yelling at her all night.

Maybe he didn't like her. Maybe he was already regretting taking her on due to her lack of experience. She could speculate until night turned into day but she'd be none the wiser until they had a conversation.

Wearing his familiar black leather jacket over a sweatshirt and jeans, Jake was leaning against his Jeep. He straightened as Caitlin walked towards him, and even at the distance that separated them she sensed an undeniable magnetic charge that put her on her guard. It had started to rain, and the sound of the other band members' voices floated on the air as they huddled round the big white transit van they transported their equipment in.

As Jake continued to hold her gaze Caitlin sensed something register low in her belly—*a combination of fear, apprehension and irrefutable sexual attraction.* She didn't know whether to smile or run.

A fierce gust of wind just then almost tore her open raincoat from her shoulders, revealing her curvaceous figure in perhaps more detail than she wanted him to see. She felt alternately hot and cold all over as her boots crunched across the gravel.

'Rick said you wanted to speak to me?' She was slightly breathless as she presented herself, her long black hair lashing across her face in the wind and rain.

Straight away Jake noticed Caitlin shiver in her insubstantial raincoat. *He knew a way to warm her up.* Another place, another time, he might have given into such an urge. God knew Caitlin Ryan had been testing all his powers of self-control from the very first moment he'd set eyes on her.

'So, are you going to join us for a drink or what?' he asked tersely.

'That's what you wanted to talk to me about?'

Catching the ends of her raincoat belt, she twisted it tightly round her waist. In vain she tried to shove her long hair out of her eyes and noticed her hands were trembling. *What was it about this man that could unravel her so easily?*

'I already told Mike that I wasn't coming. I'm going home to get an early night.' she said. 'Don't worry I'll make sure I'm here at three o'clock on the dot for rehearsals tomorrow.'

'I want you to come for a drink.'

The pupils of Jake's eyes had turned unsettlingly dark… so dark that there was just the palest blue circle ringed round them.

'It's a good opportunity for us to get to know each other. Tomorrow's Sunday. You can have a lie-in.'

Caitlin could hardly argue with his reasoning, even if her

heart *was* fluttering madly at the very idea of spending the rest of the evening in the company of the charismatic band manager. But there was also the not exactly small matter of her showing up at the Pilgrim's Inn. There was always a small influx of visitors from outside the village, but generally customers were mostly a local crowd, and there were bound to be people there who remembered how Sean had humiliated her.

'I—I'd rather not come, if you don't mind.'

'The invitation was an order, not a choice. You're going to have to get used to late nights if you're going to sing with this band. Get in the car. You can ride with me and Rick'

So that was how Caitlin found herself squeezed into a worn red velvet corner seat in the pub, with Rick on one side and Jake on the other, as the band members stood round the cosy fire in the iron grate, hogging the heat and nursing their pints of beer.

From the jukebox Sting's voice boomed out: something about not standing so close... *Caitlin could easily have echoed the sentiment.* Rick had hung her raincoat over the back of a chair but she wasn't bereft of warmth—not when Jake's hard-muscled thigh was pressed against hers. A full-on radiator couldn't have made her hotter. Every time he shifted even slightly the renewed contact made Caitlin's heart miss a beat.

'So tell me, Cait. What music do you like to listen to?'

Rick had been shortening her name ever since they'd arrived at the pub and she tried not to flinch, because her ex, Sean, had always called her that. Her gaze anxiously swept the room. There were several groups of young people seated around the tables, clearly enjoying themselves. Thankfully nobody had paid her any particular attention. Behind the bar two barmaids were busily serving customers, and one of them, a voluptuous blonde named Tina Stevens, was wearing a neckline so low that if she wasn't careful she'd be arrested for indecency.

Bringing her attention back to Rick, Caitlin answered. 'Oh, I have such a wide taste you wouldn't believe it. If I had to sum it up I'd say I love music with a good beat and great songs with good lyrics. How about you? What do you enjoy listening to?'

Shrugging, Rick took a sip of his beer then put it carefully back down on the cork beer mat. 'My taste is very similar to yours, honey. It's clear that you and I have a lot in common, a *hell* of a lot in common, in fact.'

'That's the beer talking,' Jake observed wryly.

The gravelled intonation of his deep voice made all the hairs stand up at the back of Caitlin's neck. *Was it her imagination or had his thigh moved even closer to hers?*

'He's just trying to get into your good books.'

'That's unfair. A man like me doesn't have to *try* to get into any woman's good books. They naturally gravitate towards me. I'm gifted like that. Talking of which…'

Suddenly getting to his feet, Rick carefully eased his way round the table so as not to dislodge their drinks. Caitlin saw that his avid glance was focused determinedly on a smiling Tina Stevens behind the bar, who at that very moment was leaning dangerously across the counter in her figure-hugging red top, chatting to yet another appreciative male customer.

'Excuse me, guys, but I can see a maiden's honour is at stake if I don't go and rescue her…' Rick headed purposefully towards the bar.

Breathing out a relieved sigh, Caitlin was glad to have a little more room to manoeuvre, but she was still dizzy at the thought of having to deal with Jake on her own. As discreetly as she was able, she moved her leg away from the hot press of his jean-clad thigh.

'She'll have him for breakfast,' he said, and grinned.

The shock of suddenly meeting his steamy blue glance at such close quarters trapped Caitlin's breath somewhere between her throat and her mouth. She found herself a little too intimately aware of the faint shadow of beard across his top lip and jaw, his long straight nose and the sexy indentation in his sculpted chin. Most of all she was aware of the provocative message his hypnotic blue gaze seemed to be conveying to her. It was indisputably sexual. And it made every muscle in her body tighten and clench.

The whole room diminished down to just that look.

'He looks like he can take care of himself,' she murmured, hardly aware of moving her lips.

'So...' Taking a leisurely sip of his beer and studying her at the same time, Jake asked casually, 'Why no boyfriend?'

Hypnotised by the long fingers that curled round his glass, Caitlin found herself envying it his touch, wondering what it would be like to feel those same long fingers intimately touching *her*. The very notion made her *burn*, and she took a hurried sip of her dry white wine, deliberately focusing her gaze on the drink instead of him.

'I didn't know it was compulsory.'

'Did I imply it was?'

She didn't answer. Thinking about Sean and how she had let him come *that* close to wrecking her life was not something she wanted to revisit...certainly not in casual conversation.

The flash of pain he witnessed in Caitlin's eyes just then took Jake by surprise. As defensive as she undoubtedly was, she hadn't been quick enough to hide it. There were also faint lines of hurt round her mouth that betrayed her. *Clearly she had let someone get too close and got herself burned in the process.*

Even though he'd experienced a similar painful scenario in a relationship, something inside him said he should be careful not to let empathy lower his defences. Relationships by their nature were always going to be challenging, no matter what the situation. But Jake wasn't such a bastard that he couldn't find it in him to be concerned.

'So, what happened?'

'What do you mean?'

'You got hurt by a man,' he said thoughtfully. 'Who was he?'

'Do you mind if we don't talk about this?'

Jake's question was definitely too close for comfort. Taking another sip of wine, she felt her cheeks burn as she sensed the alcohol take effect.

'We're going to be spending a lot of time together over the next few weeks—the next few months, even. Things are bound to come out. Why not tell me now and get it over with?'

Inadvertently glancing down at her purple T-shirt, at the scooped neckline that revealed a tantalising glimpse of her cleavage, Jake felt the muscles in the pit of his belly clench. He shifted in his seat.

'That might be the case, but my personal life is not up for discussion. Please don't press me on this.'

There was a tremulous hitch in her voice that made Jake feel like the most insensitive oaf on earth. On impulse, he reached across and covered her hand with his own—even if he *did* risk going up in flames at the contact.

'I'm sorry...' he murmured.

Caitlin didn't know whether he meant he was sorry for putting pressure on her or whether he was sorry for what he guessed might have happened in her relationship. *Either way, she didn't welcome his sympathy.* It was easier to deal with his irritation. At least it stopped her feeling sorry for herself. In any case, she'd done enough wallowing in despair to last a lifetime.

But it was impossible not to stare down at the strong, capable hand covering hers. As she did so, she examined the unique silver and jet ring that he wore. It comprised two black stones in a figure of eight setting and didn't detract from his masculinity one iota... In fact it *enhanced* it. She found herself strangely reluctant to extricate herself.

Speaking her thoughts out loud, she commented, 'That's a beautiful ring.'

'Yes, it is. It was a gift.'

He probably should have got rid of the thing, come to think of it, because it certainly wasn't for sentimental reasons that he still wore it. But Jake wasn't about to tell Caitlin that the jewellery had been given to him by his ex-wife Jodie a year and a day after they were married and six months before they divorced.

It suddenly occurred to him to wonder if she'd read the sordid little story of their break-up in the newspapers at the time. But, as she hadn't even indicated that she knew who he was when they'd first met, Jake took refuge in the thought that perhaps the scandal had somehow passed her by.

Withdrawing his hand abruptly from hers, he glanced across the now slowly emptying pub at Rick, who was still engaged in conversation with the buxom Tina Stevens. There was no sign of the blonde's previous admirer, Jake saw.

Turning back to Caitlin, he asked, 'Have you had enough?' His glance fell on her barely drunk glass of wine.

'Is that a hint you want to leave?'

'I think I should take you home. You look done in.'

'You don't need to take me. I'm quite capable—'

'Why don't you just put your coat on?'

Outside the wind was fierce as Caitlin walked along the deserted pavement with Jake. He walked with eyes front, one hand jammed into the back pocket of his jeans, his handsome profile ominously unsmiling as his dark hair blew across his face.

'How far do you live from here?' he asked, 'We can take my car if you're tired. I've barely drunk anything at all.'

'I'm only ten minutes up the road and I prefer to walk. But I don't expect you to walk with me.'

Caitlin couldn't help feeling tense. It was near impossible to guess what he was thinking or feeling. The man was a law unto himself. And the tension between them hadn't eased one iota. If anything it was *worse*.

'So, how do you feel about the way things are going?'

Taking her by surprise, Jake turned his head to examine her as they walked. It took a few seconds for her to get her thoughts together.

'You mean the rehearsals? I think they're going well. I mean, I know I've still got a lot to learn, but as well as learning the songs when I'm with the band I'm working on them at home whenever I get the time.'

She tucked her flying hair behind her ear and tried to relax, but it was hard when her companion's enigmatic expression hardly revealed what he might be feeling.

He sighed. 'You're doing just fine, Caitlin. I have no doubt that you're the perfect singer for Blue Sky. You're got a great voice, you're beautiful and sexy…you're the whole package. But even great talent can't make it work on its own. Blue Sky isn't some five-minute wonder, like some of these manufactured bands that litter the charts. A lot of those bands are the product of slick marketing, purely designed to make money. They're not about real, dedicated musicians who get together because they're passionate about music. I told you it wasn't going to be easy. If anything, it's going to get harder. There's still a lot of work ahead before we start touring, and then the pressure really will be on. I suppose I just want to know whether your commitment is total, or whether you wouldn't prefer staying here in the village, working in your little book store? Don't get me wrong—I can see how that must have its appeal for a girl like you.'

'What do you mean, a girl like me?' Already bristling at what she perceived as Jake's patronising tone, Caitlin glared at him in the lamplight. 'You don't even *know* me.'

Raising a dark eyebrow, he smiled. 'I know you like to pretend you're tougher than you look, that you can handle anything I throw at you, but—'

'Stop right there!' Her hackles were really up now. '*Pretend* I'm tough? Do you think I'm such a wilting flower I'll break at the first sign of pressure? For your information, I survived two years of hell with a man who was a drug addict and alcoholic who took me for every penny I had. I even had to sell my piano, and it was my dearest possession. As well as that I lost my home, my car and my dignity. I lost it all just to pay for his drug habit. Yes, I was a fool—but one day I woke up and found the strength to tell him enough was enough. Then I picked up the broken pieces of what was left of my life and started over. I've survived hardship and pain and I'm all the stronger for it—so don't you dare tell me I *pretend* I'm tough!'

She paused to take a breath.

'As for wanting to be in the band—singing *is* and always was my greatest passion and I'll do whatever I can to make it my career. I sing because I'm compelled to—not because I want to be famous or have my picture in the papers. All I want to do…all I've *ever* wanted to do…is sing. So when you ask me if my commitment is total, my answer is categorically *yes*!'

By the time she'd finished her impassioned speech Caitlin found herself on the brink of tears. She'd blurted out all the things she'd never meant to reveal—things about her past that she really would have preferred to have kept hidden…especially from a man like Jake Sorenson, who probably thought she was an idiot for falling for a loser like Sean Gates.

But Sean hadn't always been a loser. Once upon a time he had been the sweetest man in the world, and Caitlin had believed that she loved him…

'Hey…' Reaching out his hand, Jake gently stroked the tips of his fingers down her cheek. 'I wasn't casting aspersions on your character. I'm sorry if it came out that way.'

The surprisingly feather-light touch made something clench deep inside her. Recognising it as a hungry need to be held, she immediately stiffened.

'I'm sorry, too.'

Shaking her head, she automatically moved away in a bid to resurrect her defences. But as she started walking again Jake caught up to her, grabbing her arm to make her stop. This time his hold was deliberately firm...*possessive*, almost.

'Don't run away from me. I only want to help you.'

As his intense gaze shot arrows of living blue flame into hers she caught her breath.

'Help me...*how*?'

Bending his head, Jake delivered his answer with a hard, hot kiss that was nothing less than volcanic.

As his lips moved rapaciously over hers, even though she was shocked to her core, Caitlin found herself kissing him back as if her very life depended on it. She even drove her hands through his hair to anchor him to her.

Instinct was like a wild river that had burst its banks and it was near impossible to think about anything above the untamed ferocious beat of her heart...except perhaps to realise that the man kisses were as good as he looked and even *better* than the most erotic fantasy she could imagine...

The delicious sensation of his velvet-textured lips against hers and the warm glide of his tongue in her mouth stirred feelings inside her that she'd never before experienced so wantonly or intensely. *It was during those explosive few moments that Caitlin knew the barriers of safety she'd erected so painstakingly round her heart had come under serious threat...*

Even as she had the realisation Jake brought the kiss to a reluctant end, examining her with a gaze that was more than a little stunned but still very much aroused.

In a low voice he murmured, 'Don't be ashamed because you told me your story. The music business is littered with casualties like your ex-boyfriend. I don't believe that they're bad people. Serious addiction is an illness, not a weakness. Don't shut me out because you've revealed something you wished you hadn't, Caitlin.'

She inhaled sharply and withdrew her hands from his hair. It had started to rain again, and droplets of moisture were settling in quick succession on the silken dark strands that she'd so hungrily slid her fingers into, sparkling there like morning dew.

He sounded so kind and concerned—as if he intimately understood every lash of hurt she had ever suffered and sincerely empathised. Everything about him was almost unbearably seductive, and it made Caitlin ache to lean into him, to perhaps invite another kiss and even ask him to come in for a cup of coffee… But she quickly came to her senses when it hit her just what she was contemplating—and the likely consequences of such a reckless act. *Hadn't she endured enough pain without inviting more?*

She shook her arm free.

'To shut you out I'd first have to let you in, Jake, and I'm not going to do that. Not even if you promised me the earth.'

'Now that it's come to it I don't want to let you go' Lia asserted.

Finishing stirring the mug of coffee she'd made, she brought it over to the small wrought-iron table where the girls sat for lunch. There wasn't a lot of room in the basement, where all the stock was kept, but Lia had had a worktop and sink put in, as well as installing a fridge and a microwave oven, so that the girls could have some hot food from time to time.

Lost in thought, Caitlin was jolted back to the present as the petite blonde pulled out the chair opposite and sat down.

'Sorry, what did you say?'

'I said I don't want to let you go.' Lia breathed out a heavy sigh as she curled her hands round the steaming mug of coffee, her pretty brown eyes not bothering to try and hide her emotion.

Caitlin was genuinely touched. The girls had been friends for a long time now, seeing each other through good times and bad, and it was going to be as much a wrench for Caitlin to relinquish her job as it was for Lia to lose her. She'd always considered the esoteric bookshop to be the best place in the world to work in. Not only was she surrounded by books that had the potential to heal and uplift, but many like-minded people came into the store—and the fact that she worked with her best friend was a blessing.

But for the past week and a half Blue Sky had become more than just a wonderful opportunity to realise a long-held dream. It had become *personal*. Not only had Caitlin grown to respect and admire her fellow musicians, she was also starting to really care about them too. They worked so hard, were passionate about their music, talented and dedicated to their craft, and when Marcie Wallace had walked out they'd been understandably devastated. Caitlin wanted to help put things right…she wanted to help them realise *their* dreams too.

'It's not going to be easy for either of us,' she agreed now, sliding her hand across Lia's. 'But I'm not leaving for good. I might not be working in the shop any more, but that doesn't mean I won't be around. I'll still live here in the village, and when I come home after touring we'll see each other every day because I'll come in and chat and have coffee with you.'

'I know all that.' Lia freed her hand and drove her fingers anxiously through her short blonde hair. 'But if you want to know the truth I've been worrying myself sick about you.'

'Why?' Caitlin was astonished.

'Well…going off with a bunch of strangers to God only knows where. How do you know you can trust these people?'

'Lia, I've got to know them. They're not strangers any more. They're professional musicians. Jake Sorenson, their manager, is—'

'Jake is who I wanted to talk to you about.' The blonde drew a deep breath in. 'Didn't you recognise who he was when you first saw him? Don't you remember there was a "kiss and tell" scandal about him in the papers a few years ago? His wife left him for one of the biggest rock musicians in the world then spilled the beans about their marriage in an article in the papers.'

Lia's words started to ring a bell. As memory presented a helpful picture of the artist her friend had referred to Caitlin stared at the other girl in shock.

'I remember. She left him for Mel Justice…the lead singer with the band Heart and Soul. I didn't realise the record producer she was married to, was Jake.'

'Well, it was. And the picture she painted of her life with him wasn't exactly flattering. Did you know she was a model? Not high-profile, but a familiar face in the magazines just the same. The main reason for the exposé was that Jake had promised to make her a star and he didn't. Apparently she wanted to give up modelling to become a singer. But when they got married and he didn't come up with the goods she had an affair with Mel Justice and eventually divorced Jake to be with him.'

'Then she sold her story to the newspaper,' Caitlin said quietly.

It jolted her to realise that he'd been married. She hadn't read the story, but just before Lia had nudged her memory about what had happened she'd been about to comment that Jake Sorenson was a true professional—a man who elicited respect and admiration from his peers—and that she felt very fortunate to have him as a mentor. *But even as the thought occurred accompanying it was the stirring memory of last night when Jake had kissed her…*

'Anyway, what has any of what you've just said got to do with what *I'm* doing, Lia? Why are you digging up old news about Jake Sorenson?'

'Why? Because I want you to know what you're getting yourself into that's why'

Lifting her mug of coffee to her lips, her friend agitatedly put it down again without taking so much as a sip.

'As your best friend, I can't help feeling responsible. The people in the business you're getting into are open to all kinds of temptations and bad behaviour. They certainly don't seem to exhibit much loyalty towards each other. I'd hate for you to be associated with the band and have it all backfire on you if the press decide to dig up that kiss and tell story and speculate over if you'll do the same, should anything go wrong.'

'But I'm not having a personal relationship with Jake, am I? I'm only singing with the band he's managing. Plus, I wouldn't dream of selling my story to the press even if I had one! I'm twenty-six, remember? Not some gullible teenager. I can absolutely take care of myself.'

But Caitlin's heart still raced. Nothing Lia had said before had remotely indicated what her friend really felt about her decision to join the band. Up until now she'd been so positive…so encouraging. *'Follow your passion,' she'd said. 'Don't let anything get in your way.'* Now Caitlin didn't know what to think.

It wasn't any of her business what had or hadn't happened in Jake's marriage. In fact it explained why he sometimes seemed a little aloof. As well as destroying any trust you'd once had for a person, to have your spouse sell their story about your marriage to the papers must have been truly demoralising. But at the end of the day Jake's personal life was nothing remotely to do with her.

'Okay, so if it's true that you can take care of yourself then what about Sean?' Lia's brown eyes sparkled.

Caitlin could hardly believe what she was hearing.

'That was below the belt, Lia,' she murmured. 'Okay, so I've made some wrong turns in my life. Haven't you? Hasn't everyone? It doesn't mean that everything I do is doomed to failure or disaster, does it?'

'I shouldn't have said that. About Sean, I mean.' Lia sniffed. 'I'm sorry, Caitlin. I should know better, considering the business I'm in, shouldn't I? It's just that sometimes it's hard to put wisdom into practice when it comes to someone you care about. You know what men can be like.

They've got a one-track mind when it comes to women like you, and I mean that as a compliment. You're beautiful and talented, with a sweet and trusting nature. They're bound to try and take advantage and here you are—going off into the wide blue yonder with five of them!'

'Well, you've got to try and stop worrying, Lia. I'm going to be just fine. I'm doing what I want to do, right? Nobody is forcing me. If I can trust that everything will be okay, then why can't you?'

Abruptly rising to her feet, Caitlin carried her empty mug over to the sink. Then she rinsed it out and turned it upside down on the drainer.

'I'd better get back upstairs and relieve Nicky so that she can have her lunch. Today's my last day at the shop, so let's not spoil it by having an argument.'

'I'm sorry. I'm just feeling a bit on edge because you're going. Don't be mad at me?' Lia pleaded as she got to her feet.

'Don't be silly!' Grinning, Caitlin fondly ruffled her hair. 'How on earth could I be mad at you for caring? Since that particular commodity has been sadly lacking in my life for quite some time, I can assure you I'm open to all the TLC I can get!'

But even as she laughed off her friend's concern Caitlin couldn't help dwelling on what she'd said about Jake. The revelation about Jake's former marriage perturbed her. She didn't often read the celebrity gossip that littered the newspapers and social media, and right now she was glad that she didn't. Whatever had happened between Jake and his ex-wife, it must have been painful for both of them, she reasoned. She should just focus on singing with the band and not concern herself with how Blue Sky's manager might or might not conduct himself in private.

CHAPTER FOUR

AT THE END of an emotionally fraught day, Caitlin sank back into a hot steamy bath and exhaled a heartfelt sigh. Flickering candles cast dancing shadows on the walls of the small, once shabby bathroom she'd sought to transform with some pink paint, pale blue curtains and accessories. She was genuinely pleased with what she'd achieved.

Closing her eyes, she breathed in the exotic perfume that filled the air from the scented candles and her favourite aromatic bath oil. Trailing her fingers idly in the water, she let her thoughts whirl. Electing to leave her job, she hadn't exactly burnt her bridges, she reflected, because Lia had promised she could have a job with her any day. But it was still a scary thought to realise that she was giving up something relatively stable and secure for something that was its direct antithesis.

Splashing a handful of water across her shoulders, Caitlin opened her eyes and absently watched the droplets roll down her warm, scented skin. Frowning, she thought about the afternoon's rehearsals and how Jake had regularly berated her for lack of concentration—not to mention for pretty much everything else. He'd yelled at her so often that the rest of the crew had cast each other quizzical glances, as if to ask, *what's going on?*

Was he behaving like that because he regretted kissing her? She hadn't *asked* him to kiss her! Her concentration might well not have been what it should, but despite the rights or wrongs of that inflammatory kiss how did the man *expect* her to react when she'd just left the job that she'd been devoted to for the past five years? It just wasn't that easy to detach herself from a person or a place she cared about.

At least Rick and the others had been more understanding. They had even brought along a bottle of champagne to celebrate her 'release', although Jake had declined to join them in their impromptu toast during the break. Instead, he'd collected his leather jacket and gone out for a while… 'To get some fresh air,' he'd tersely explained.

'Blast you, Jake Sorenson! I'm doing my best here. Give me a break, can't you?'

Grabbing the innocent plastic yellow duck bobbing about on the water, she flung it down in temper. It made a very sad little splash. Not nearly enough impact to vent the anger that was bubbling up inside her.

Then, as if on cue, the doorbell rang.

Caitlin cursed out loud, determined to ignore it. But when it rang for a second and then a third time her resolve crumbled and she hauled herself out of the bath, grabbed the blue terry robe off the peg behind the door and struggled into it, littering the air with vague mutterings of irritation as she did so…

Stomping through the living room, then down the cold linoleum-covered stairs, she wondered who could be so inconsiderate and foolhardy enough to disrupt one of her favourite pastimes.

'Jake.'

All the strength seemed to drain from her limbs as she came face to face with her unexpected visitor. His lean, athletic frame was clothed entirely in black, and his long legs and broad shoulders were outlined by the filtered orange glow of a nearby street lamp. No other man had the power to disturb her as much. Jake had a presence that scrambled her thoughts into a muddled tangle and almost made it hard to breathe. All compelling lean angles and shadows, his gorgeous cheekbones were almost impossibly perfect.

Meeting his bold gaze, she asked, 'What is it? Is something wrong?'

'Can I come in?'

Because the request had caught her off guard, Caitlin found herself nodding. Then she stepped back into the dimly lit hallway, with its unfortunate flocked gold wallpaper and worn red carpet, to let him enter. The damp hair that she'd screwed up so carelessly into an improvised knot hung loose and heavy behind her head and several long ebony strands had worked free to glance against her cheek. Beneath her robe her body was still slick with moisture because she hadn't had time to dry herself. And she was stark naked beneath that robe...

It was a fact that did little to add to her confidence. Not when Jake edged past her with an enigmatic little smile that made all the strength ooze out of her limbs like sherbet through a straw.

'Up the stairs,' she instructed weakly as he turned and waited while she closed the front door.

Glancing briefly up the narrow staircase that led to her flat, he said, 'You go first.'

Caitlin had been afraid he might say that. With her face burning she squeezed past him, inadvertently inhaling the heady scents of cedarwood and leather and the fresh smell of the outdoors that clung to him as her body brushed briefly against his. It was like coming into contact with a power supply, she thought as she began to ascend the stairs. There wasn't a cell in her body that hadn't felt the effect.

Every step she took in her slim bare feet with their scarlet-painted toenails was pure *agony* because she was acutely aware of Jake, just inches behind her. The belt round her waist had been fastened so tightly he couldn't fail to be apprised of her shape beneath the perfectly innocent terry robe, and Caitlin squirmed inwardly all the way up into her living room.

'Come in,' she invited.

His heart thudding, because his senses were still infused with the memory of their kiss the other night, Jake trained his gaze on his surroundings in a bid to divert his aroused recollection.

He immediately registered what had once been an ornate Victorian fireplace that was now home to a small electric heater that surely wasn't big enough to heat the whole room. There was a large pink ceramic vase with palm fronds in it just to the side of the hearth, and a large squashy red sofa with multi-coloured cushions arranged against the wall. Above it was a large gold-framed print of *Flaming June* by Frederic Leighton. The vivid orange of the lady's dress was clinging like a sunburst to her pale reposing figure.

Jake absorbed all of this in just a few short seconds, but inevitably his gaze was helplessly drawn back to Caitlin. In her charming state of *dishabille*, how could it not be? What *was* that scent she was wearing?

With her face scrubbed clean of make-up, her silky black hair escaping all attempts at confinement, and wearing nothing but a plain terry robe, to Jake she was temptation personified. If she had the power to make him hot when she was dressed in tight jeans and a T-shirt it was nothing compared to the effect she was having on him in her present get-up. He just prayed that her pretty green eyes wouldn't stray far south of his stomach, because right then he was fighting a losing battle to keep his lustful stirrings to himself.

So much for his promise to maintain a professional distance. He'd already broken that vow by stealing that incendiary kiss the other night. One taste of pure, unadulterated heaven had ensured that sooner or later he would be back for more. He'd already had to make himself scarce once this afternoon, because two hours of Caitlin up on the stage wiggling her hips as she sang, her breasts bouncing ever so slightly in her hot pink T-shirt, had almost made him crazy with want. Professing a need for some fresh air had just been a handy euphemism for what he really needed...a cold shower so icy it would freeze an ordinary mortal into a cryogenic trance.

When Jake didn't immediately speak, Caitlin nervously wiped her hands down her robe and motioned vaguely towards the sofa. 'Why don't you sit down? I just need to go and dress. I was having a bath when you rang the bell.'

'Don't get dressed on my account,' her visitor drawled, making no discernible move to sit down.

Her face flamed red.

'I'm still wet,' she gulped, immediately wishing she could take back her innocently meant remark, because Jake's glance was all but stripping her naked. Want, need and lust swirled between them. 'I mean I need...'

Caitlin's hand trembled as she saw Jake's eyes grow tellingly dark. Now his glance was focused on her mouth, on the soft, plump lower lip that her tongue had just innocently dampened.

'What are we going to do, Caitlin?' he asked softly, his gravelly voice reeling her in with its disturbing undisguised intonation of heat and sex.

'Do about what?'

'About *us*. Don't pretend you don't know what I mean. For God's sake, the kiss we shared the other night when I walked you home was no innocent kiss goodnight. I got the distinct impression that you enjoyed it as much as I did. Was I wrong?'

'Look, I really need to go and put some clothes on. If you wait here I'll make us some coffee once I'm dressed and then we can talk.'

Jake smiled. She was gazing at him as though hypnotised. As she studied him her bewitching emerald eyes were dazzled—*glazed*, almost. Whatever she felt about him, she couldn't deny there was a combustible attraction between them. And he couldn't think of another woman who had the ability to send his pulse sky-rocketing and his libido raging with just a simple glance.

It wasn't just her beauty that drew him to her. There was a refreshing innocence about Caitlin. Having met so many women whose hunger for fame and success made them employ any means possible to get what they wanted—*his ex-wife being a case in point*—he found Caitlin was like a breath of fresh air. Jake had never wanted a woman more in his life…wanted her with an ache that was the sweetest agony from the moment he woke up in the morning to when he lay down to sleep at night.

'Good. Because it won't go away,' he continued. 'Sooner or later we're going to have to deal with it.'

Caitlin's already pink cheeks flushed even pinker. Then she turned and fled into the bedroom to get dressed.

Sighing, Jake dropped down onto the squashy red sofa, picked up a cushion, then angrily jettisoned it onto the floor. *Just what the hell did he think he was doing?* He'd called in on her because he'd wanted to apologise for being so uncompromising at rehearsals, but as soon as he'd set eyes on her in that innocent terry robe of hers he'd known immediately that she wasn't wearing anything underneath it. Somehow his rigidly imposed self-control had gone out of the window and all he'd been able to think about was how soon he could get her into bed.

He wanted to bury himself so deep inside her he'd assuage every ache he'd ever had…*hers* too. Yes, he'd had the odd one-night stand since Jodie had done the dirty on him—how else could he satisfy a healthy libido—but nothing could have prepared him for a hunger so primal, so insatiable, that it threatened to consume him body and soul if it wasn't satisfied.

Dragging his fingers through his hair, Jake slowly shook his head. To add to his frustration Caitlin's provocative scent lingered in the room, tormenting him. Where was she, for goodness' sake? How long did it take to throw some clothes on? *Longer than it would take him to tear them off that was for sure...*

Restless, he got to his feet, his long legs taking him to the other side of the room and back again as he paced the floor. The living room was ridiculously small—almost oppressively so. A few family photos sat on the mantelpiece, along with a small glass jar full of assorted coloured crystals.

Jake was far too distracted to examine the photographs more closely, so he turned away to survey the rest of the room. A large pine bookcase dominated an entire wall, and there wasn't a shelf on it that wasn't crammed to bursting point with books. He barely stole a glance at the titles he was so keyed up, but he couldn't fail to notice that most of the literature dwelt on self-development or philosophy.

Had Caitlin been interested in those subjects before or *after* her catastrophic relationship with the drug addict? Jake was curious. Clearly she must have been driven to seek out some sort of guidance after such an ordeal. Somehow he felt chastened. Living with a drug addict and alcoholic would certainly be no picnic. He himself had had friends and associates who'd been drawn down a similar destructive route. He'd told Caitlin that the music business was full of such casualties.

But she'd confessed to him that she'd lost everything, including her home. That must surely be the reason why she was living in this *rabbit hutch*. Jake would go stir crazy, living in such a confined space. Being the grateful owner of spacious homes in London, New York and LA—which were admittedly empty most of the time, due to his peripatetic lifestyle—he doubted he would manage even half as well if he had to live the way Caitlin did. Even his room at the quaint Pilgrim's Inn was three times the size of this one.

Without realising it, his hands had curled into fists down by his sides.

He'd remarked to her that addiction was a disease, not

a weakness, but by God he'd like just ten minutes with the jerk who'd ripped her off so badly that she was reduced to living in two shabby rented rooms.

'What would you like to drink? Tea or coffee?'

Caitlin's voice took Jake by surprise. Turning round, he avidly noted her long shapely legs, which were encased in soft worn denim, and the pretty pink top she'd donned, which was fastened at the front with little pearl buttons. In her apparent haste to get dressed the top two buttons had been left undone, inadvertently revealing the creamy cleft between her breasts, and the arresting sight made him catch his breath.

But she might not have left the buttons undone deliberately—she hardly needed to resort to feminine wiles to get his attention. All the woman had to do was glance at him with those bewitching emerald eyes and Jake was all hers.

'Neither,' he answered. 'Why don't you just come and sit down so we can talk?'

Caitlin acquiesced, her brows puckering when she noticed that one of her multi-coloured cushions was lying on the floor. Inside her chest, her heart was galloping at what felt like a worrying breakneck speed.

When Jake had asserted that sooner or later they would have to 'deal with it', had he been saying that it was inevitable that they had an affair? Because if he had then he hadn't reckoned with her iron will. It didn't matter how attracted she was to the man, she wasn't the type to jump thoughtlessly into bed with him. Sean was the only man she'd ever been intimate with, and to be honest it hadn't been anything to write home about even when she'd foolishly imagined herself in love with him.

Being a singer and a member of Blue Sky was far more important than having a hot little affair with the band's manager, she told herself.

'I was rough on you today.' Still standing in the centre

of the room, Jake rubbed a hand round his beard-darkened jaw. 'I feel like I owe you an apology.'

'Why?'

'Because I pushed you too hard.' He flinched as though genuinely regretting it.

'You don't have to apologise. I know I've still got a long way to go and I need all the help and guidance I can get. Rick says that you're the best, and so do the others. I'm hungry to learn, Jake. You shouldn't lose any sleep over the fact that you had to yell at me a few times.'

Gritting his teeth, he silently cursed the ache in his groin that refused to be tamped. *It wasn't the fact that he'd lost his temper a few times that he was losing sleep over.* She was sitting on her sofa, looking about as tempting as Eve in the Garden of Eden, and her soothing velvet voice rolled over him like honey. She might not know it but she was seducing him as thoroughly as if she sat there naked, beckoning him to come to her.

'Are you always this reasonable?' He quirked an eyebrow.

Although he'd apologised, he was still spoiling for an argument—*anything* to defuse the sexually charged tension between them.

'No.' An amused smile played at the corners of her mouth. 'Sean used to accuse me of being unreasonable all the time.'

'Sean?'

'My ex-boyfriend.'

'The drug addict.' Jake hadn't meant to sound cruel, but the fact was he wasn't in the mood to be magnanimous. A stab of jealousy had sliced through his insides at Caitlin's reference to the man she'd previously been in a relationship with.

Suddenly rising to her feet, she let her fingers toy restlessly with the little pearl buttons on her blouse. The gesture inevitably drew his gaze.

'Amongst other things he was a painter and decorator by trade. Not that he was in work very often…For obvious reasons.' Her expression was briefly pained. 'But, like you said, just because he was an addict, it didn't mean he was a bad person. He was easily led by some unsavoury friends, that was the trouble.'

Caitlin dipped her head and Jake found himself automatically taking a step towards her.

'So, you were "unreasonable" because you tried to warn him off those so-called friends?'

'Yes… That and because I didn't give him money as often as he liked to buy his drugs. I was struggling to keep the roof over our heads as it was. I had a lovely flat that I'd bought with a legacy my grandmother had left me and I was eventually forced to sell it because of Sean. He was in so much debt due to his drug habit.'

'And where is he now?' he asked. *A million miles away, he hoped.* Outer Mongolia wouldn't be far enough.

'When we broke up he said he was going to London. His brother lives there and he was going to stay with him to try and straighten himself out. I hope for his sake he was able to. But, that said, I'm just so glad he's out of my life. Being with him had me fearing for my sanity. I hardly knew who I was any more. Sometimes I can't believe what a fool I was to trust him and believe that he would change. One thing's for sure…I'll never give my trust so easily to a man again.'

Her emerald eyes glistened briefly and Jake swallowed hard. He hated the idea that she wasted even a *second* of her time thinking about her ex and what he had put her through.

'Anyway, I don't know why I'm standing here telling you all this,' she finished.

'I asked you to. What about your family? Were they supportive when they found out what was going on?'

'My parents and my brother are in America. He moved out there first and they followed. They've started up a business out there. Anyway…'

With a shrug Caitlin briefly met his eyes and then looked quickly away again.

'I didn't want them to worry about me so I didn't tell them. I made my bed and I had to lie in it. They gave me the chance of going with them when they left but I opted not to take it. Besides, they always taught me it was important to stand on my own two feet, and I wasn't going to go running to them the moment I was in trouble. I wanted to prove to myself and to them that I could turn my life around and be proud of myself.'

'Whilst that's commendable, I thought families were supposed to help each other out when one of them was in trouble?'

'Do yours? Help you when you're in trouble I mean?'

Jake hadn't expected her to turn the question on him. For a dizzying moment he found himself awash in a sea of feelings that he usually tried to submerge…feelings of pain, confusion and a sickening sense of being abandoned by life.

His mouth drying, he answered, 'No… They don't. They *can't*. I don't know who they are. I was raised in a children's home.'

Caitlin's bewitching green eyes immediately softened. 'Oh, Jake…I'm so sorry.'

The suggestion of concerned sympathy in her voice was like a gun pointed straight at his heart. He immediately sought to deflect it.

'Don't be. I learned very quickly not to depend on anyone else for either my happiness or my wellbeing. I survived the experience—that's all you need to know. That's all *anyone* needs to know.'

Twisting her hands together, she took a few moments before commenting, 'You've done more than just survive, Jake. You've made an amazing success of your life.'

'Is that how it looks to you?' The question was painfully ironic.

'Anyway, regarding my own family, we're…let's just say we respect our differences. They have their life and I have mine.'

'You mean you haven't told them that you've joined the band?'

'I will tell them…eventually. But, just not right now.'

Jake shrugged. 'It's your call.'

'You said that you learned not to depend on anyone else to make you happy. What about romantic relationships, Jake? Have you had maybe one or two that haven't worked out?'

'Who *hasn't*?'

A reticent smile suggested that discussing his own experiences was the last thing he wanted to do. It wasn't hard to understand why he should feel that way. Nobody welcomed talking about the things that had hurt them. Yet Caitlin couldn't help wanting to know more. *Despite her vow never to easily trust another man, the idea of perhaps trusting Jake was strangely compelling.* After all, he knew what it was like to have been badly hurt by someone and wouldn't knowingly inflict similar hurt on someone else…would he?

Drawing in a deep breath for courage, she asked the question she'd been longing to hear the answer to since talking to Lia.

'My friend Lia—the manager of the shop where I worked—she told me that she once read in the papers that you'd been married.'

As Caitlin had expected, Jake's guard slammed down like a portcullis. 'Then why ask if I've had any relationships that haven't worked out? It must be obvious that my marriage didn't, if your friend read about it.'

He let loose an irritated sigh, but Caitlin detected weariness in the sound, as if he was well and truly sick of the subject.

'Presumably she also told you that my wife left me and then sold a sordid little tale to the press?'

She flushed, feeling uncomfortably guilty. 'Yes…she did.'

'Then that should tell you it was hardly a match made in heaven. My ex was a manipulative little liar…what else do you want to know?'

'Please don't be so defensive. I was hoping you might tell me your side of the story. I never read any details myself. To be honest, I didn't even recognise you when we first met. I don't often read the newspapers, and neither do I use social media very much. I honestly won't breathe a word of this conversation to anyone…not even to my friend.'

'I take it I have your word on that?' Jake's blue eyes were momentarily fierce.

With her heart thudding, Caitlin nodded. 'Of course.'

'Her name was Jodie and she was a model who wanted to become a pop singer. I had no idea of her ambition at the time. Anyway, we met at a party and had a few dates. She was pretty and engaging enough to capture my attention, and on a weekend break to Rome I foolishly asked her to marry me.'

He shook his head in mocking disbelief.

'Practically as soon as we were married she started to put pressure on me to help her get a record deal…all the while telling me I was the best thing that had ever happened to her and that she was madly in love with me, of course. You'd think I would have known better.'

He gave a harsh self-deprecating laugh before continuing.

'She couldn't sing, and when she realised I wasn't going to help further her career she started an affair with Mel Justice—the lead guitarist of the bestselling rock band on the planet. I was travelling in South America on business when she moved in with him and on my return she told me she was filing for divorce. Then, when the case came to court, she cited mental cruelty because I'd allegedly promised to help make her a star and I hadn't…'

The way Jake shook his head told Caitlin everything she needed to know about how he'd felt about that.

'In the story she portrayed me as some kind of Svengali who'd preyed on her naïvety and led her astray. If it hadn't been so painful and hadn't ruined my reputation it would have been funny. Anyway, with the help of a high-profile

American lawyer, courtesy of her new boyfriend, she got her divorce and was awarded a ridiculous sum of money from me for so-called damages. Then she married her lover and became Mrs Justice.'

Jake's telling of the painful events was succinct and to the point. But to have had his reputation sullied by Jodie's lies and for her to have sold her story to the newspapers because she hadn't got what she wanted out of him must have seriously shattered his belief in relationships. Sighing, Caitlin tucked some drifting strands of hair behind her ear.

Relieved to have done with his story, Jake moved across to the sofa to join her. Breathing out on a sigh, he gently touched his knuckles to the side of her cheek. *As soon as he'd done it he knew he was lost.*

Even though he'd kissed her, touching Caitlin was still a revelation. Her skin had the texture of the purest silk. An erotic image of her lying naked in his bed, her slender limbs tangled in black satin sheets, her eyes dark with desire and her skin flushed pink with arousal, slipped easily into his mind to taunt him even more. He wanted to touch her everywhere. He wouldn't rush. He'd take his time and savour every inch of her beautiful body, every flavour. Was she uninhibitedly vocal? Or would she whimper gently when he brought her to climax?

'Anyway, I think I've said enough. Thanks for telling me about Sean. I hope it hasn't upset you too much?' It didn't surprise him when his voice sounded less than steady.

'It hasn't. I'm fine.' Caitlin willed herself to move, to put herself out of reach of his seductive touch and wrest her gaze from the haunting blue eyes that made her feel so restless and hungry.

She burned for him. Could Jake see that? Could he tell? If she was going to make her dream come true she couldn't afford to let him know just how much she desired him. Becoming intimately involved with Jake Sorenson would be a disaster personally *and* professionally. Somehow she had to play it cool…for *both* their sakes. They were both recovering from seriously hurtful relationships and, if nothing else, they should exercise some common sense.

'I'm just very tired.' Faking a yawn, Caitlin surprised herself by following it up with a genuine one.

Jake immediately got to his feet. Planting his hands either side of his straight lean hips, he nodded. 'I almost forgot how late it was.'

He should be glad of the excuse to leave. *He didn't dare risk staying for much longer because being with Caitlin was putting an impossible strain on him to stick to his vow to leave well alone.*

'I know we haven't discussed the situation we've got but that will have to wait. At the end of the day, the band is the first priority. I'll see you tomorrow at rehearsals. Three o'clock, usual place.'

'I'll be there.' Caitlin pushed to her feet.

'Good. I'll see myself out. Don't come down.'

Following him onto the landing, Caitlin felt every muscle in her body tense as she stared at his back, at the soft leather jacket that accommodated his broad shoulders to perfection, at his long, hard-muscled legs and taut, lean behind. A wave of heat rolled over her and almost made her lose her balance. She'd never ogled a man in her life before, but there was something about Jake Sorenson that made her behave out of character…something wild and untamed.

She'd stared down into a yawning abyss of darkness many times during those two hellish years with Sean, and had lost count of the times she'd prayed for her life to be 'normal'. But, in truth, she'd always known that she could never be content with a conventional nine-to-five existence. She needed more than that…*much* more. That was why she'd shown up for the audition with Blue Sky. That was why she was willing to kiss goodbye to the sleepy little village that had been her home and that was why she wanted to take her chances with Jake and the others…

'Jake?'

Coming to a standstill at the bottom of the stairs, he glanced up at her. As she stared back into his fathomless blue eyes Caitlin mused that it was like falling into the sky.

'Thanks for dropping by and for…for our little chat.'

'No problem.'

Conveying that he was in a hurry, Jake abruptly opened the door and slammed it shut behind him.

CHAPTER FIVE

THE BLAST OF a car horn sounding right outside her front door made Caitlin jump. In the throes of getting ready for her evening out, she glanced at the clock on the mantel and saw that it was later than she'd thought.

Softly cursing, she yanked her hairbrush roughly through her sable hair, then quickly painted her lips with the new plum shade of lipstick she'd bought. Her hand was a little unsteady as she applied it and, to make matters even worse, she decided that the colour was a little too dramatic for her liking. But she was just going to have to grin and bear it. She was already feeling tense at the distinct possibility of being chastised yet again for lateness. That would make it the third time this week and it might just be the straw that broke the camel's back as far as Jake was concerned.

Hurriedly snatching her leather jacket off the couch and pulling it on, she grabbed her purse, shoved it into a pocket and flew down the steep, narrow staircase as if the hounds of hell themselves were after her. Her breath hitched as she hurried towards the ominous-looking black Jeep, its engine running.

Jake leaned across and pushed open the passenger door. 'Hi,' he greeted her.

His expression didn't give much away, and it couldn't help but increase the overall sense of trepidation that Caitlin was feeling. They were going to see a band tonight and would be spending a large amount of time together...*alone*.

She didn't doubt the experience was going to be a real test for them both.

'Hi.' There were three seats in the front of the vehicle and she automatically sat next to the window and slammed the door shut.

'I want you next to me.'

'What?'

The slow burning heat from Jake's gaze almost scorched Caitlin where she sat. He didn't embellish the comment. He didn't *have* to. They both knew only too well why he wanted her to sit closer to him. *Could day resist following night?* She'd have loved to have had a handy reason with which to refuse him, but her mind was worryingly bereft of anything helpful as his arresting blue eyes entrapped hers.

With thumping heart she murmured, 'Feeling lonely, are we?' Then, before he could reply, she somehow found herself sitting in the luxuriously upholstered leather seat next to his.

His lips lifted in a grin.

'Not any more.'

'Well, I'm glad that I've made you happy.' Her dark hair brushed against her reddened cheekbone as she bent to buckle her seatbelt. 'For *once*.'

Chuckling, Jake put the car into gear and steered it smoothly away from the kerb. It should have reassured her that he seemed to be in a particularly good mood tonight, but it didn't make things any easier. *Not when she was already gripped by the familiar disturbing waves of disorientation and desire that seemed to be inevitable whenever they were together.* And all day that combustible kiss they'd shared when he'd walked her home from the pub had played over and over in her mind.

Their attraction for each other had been growing stronger and stronger. It only needed the tiniest spark to turn it into a conflagration. It was made even more acute now, by the intimate space they shared in the car.

Caitlin couldn't help stealing a covetous glance at Jake

as he drove. True to form, he was clothed in his habitual black, with no apparent concessions to dressing up for their night out—although he didn't need to wear fancy clothes to draw a woman's eye. *Not when he exuded charisma simply by breathing.* Add to that, he had the intriguing persona of a man who'd been around musicians for most of his life and had seen it all…group bust-ups, wrecked hotel rooms, drink, drugs, groupies and corrupt management…and had lived to tell the tale. Jake had been there, done that, and worn the T-shirt.

Sighing, Caitlin smoothed her hand down over her jeans and couldn't help wondering what people would see in her when she finally took to the stage to sing. Would they quickly categorise her as just another starstruck wannabe? A wide-eyed innocent without much experience of anything at all? *If they did, then they couldn't be more wrong.* How could they know the narrow escape she'd had from the kind of destructive relationship that most mothers of daughters had nightmares about? Consequently, she was far from ignorant about the pitfalls that awaited girls who were too trusting, who kidded themselves that they could 'fix' a partner's problems simply by loving them enough. *Caitlin had found to her cost that that was one of the biggest lies believed by women.*

Jake must have sensed her shudder and he turned his head in surprise. 'Are you okay?'

'Yes, I'm fine.'

Obviously deciding not to pander to any sense of insecurity she might be feeling, he drawled, 'I trust your clothes aren't going to turn into rags if I don't get you home by midnight?'

He was, of course, referring to her habit of turning in early if she could. Caitlin's cheeks seared pink with embarrassment. Early nights free from anxiety had been denied her in the days when she'd waited up for Sean, praying he hadn't got himself into more trouble. If she'd had a pound for every prayer she'd uttered in those two harsh, unhappy years she'd be a rich woman.

When he hadn't come home when expected Caitlin had hoped the police hadn't got him in a cell somewhere, or that some drug dealer he owed money to hadn't beaten him up, or worse. When he'd lied to her yet again, let her down or stolen money from her, she'd prayed hard for the strength to cope—still foolishly believing that she could somehow rescue him from the dark road he'd been intent on travelling down. But when he'd started to bully her, threaten her and finally *hit* her, she'd dug deep for the strength to end the relationship before it ended *her*.

The bottom line was she wasn't about to apologise to Jake for something that had been an important part of her emotional recovery, no matter how much he scorned her early nights.

'There's about as much likelihood of that as you turning into Prince Charming any time soon,' she muttered.

To her astonishment, she actually detected a smile on Jake's lips. It was only slight, and a less sensitive person might have missed it, but she was so intimately attuned to the man's every unconscious gesture and nuance she couldn't help but be aware of it. It did funny things to her insides that 'almost' smile of his, not to mention other sensitive areas of her body…

Pursing her lips, she stared determinedly ahead of her as a sudden fierce shower of rain sheeted the windscreen's glass, temporarily obliterating the view until Jake switched on the wipers.

'And there was I, hoping we'd get a clear night with a romantic moon and starlight,' he quipped.

'Is that really what you were hoping for?'

Lifting a shoulder, he smiled again, this time more freely. 'Why? You don't think I have it in me to be romantic?'

The remark immediately threw her.

'How would I know? I don't know you well enough.'

'Then it's clearly time for me to do something about that, don't you think?'

He didn't turn his head to look at her. The provocative words were simply left hanging in the air between them, like a small but lethal incendiary device.

Urgently feeling the need to change the conversation to something far less dangerous, Caitlin asked, 'So, who's the band we're going to see tonight? You didn't tell me.'

'They're called Ace of Hearts. The lead singer is Nikki Drake and I'd really like you to see her. She isn't what you might call the best singer in the world, but what she lacks in vocal range she more than makes up for in her performance. It's electrifying. She lives and breathes the band and it shows.'

'And you're hoping that I might pick up a few tips?'

The rain ceased as suddenly as it had started, and as the wipers squeaked redundantly across the screen Jake's brief azure glance at Caitlin was like a heat-seeking missile that went straight to her womb.

'Sure,' he answered.

Jake was amazed that he'd even got the word out. Whenever he caught sight of Caitlin's bewitching face—whether by design or by accident—he was all but struck dumb. Ever since he'd kissed her he'd been filled with an insatiable desire to know her intimately. As far as he was concerned, not having to share her company with anyone else tonight was like being given the keys to heaven.

For a man that prided himself on always being in control of situations, his feelings for this woman were unravelling him. If he didn't act soon to counteract the danger then the walls he'd built around his heart, brick by brick, would come crashing down and render him helpless. Whilst he would do everything in his power not to let that happen, there was no reason why he shouldn't take Caitlin to bed to help get her out of his system...*was there?*

'Do you know her well? Nikki Drake, I mean?' she probed.

Hearing the curiosity in her voice, Jake smiled. He smiled because he detected the unspoken question that she *really* wanted to ask, which was *How well do you know her?* Although he'd never been remotely attracted to Nikki, he couldn't help but experience a certain male satisfaction at the idea that Caitlin might be a little jealous.

'I know her well enough. But then, I know a lot of people in my business,' he drawled.

Not for the first time Caitlin realised that Jake was a man of few words. But, whatever he said, there was always a wealth of meaning behind it that often required some serious detective work. Then again, perhaps she should just go with the flow and not worry too much about what he meant. Jake was Jake: enigmatic, taciturn, not giving an inch. She'd better get used to it if she was going to make a half decent job of working with him.

But what she wouldn't give for him to one day speak about *her* in the same admiring way that he spoke about Nikki Drake... She was feeling ridiculously jealous of the woman when she hadn't even seen her or heard her sing yet.

'Then I can't wait to see her,' she remarked, hoping that the amiable smile she gave would convince him that she meant it.

There wasn't a single gaze in the room that wasn't trained on the sexy strutting singer onstage. A small shapely blonde, her blue eyes heavily outlined with thick black liner, her generous mouth painted with bold red lipstick, Nikki Drake held the mike as if she owned it and commanded the small raised stage with every sexy thrust of her hips, every husky note that she sang.

Her slender body was encased in tight black satin and a wide scarlet belt was cinched tightly round her impossibly tiny waist. Her creamy breasts were clearly enhanced by the loving support of a daring uplift bra *Sex on legs,* as her friend Lia might say.

The performance was riveting. While the music throbbed around them Caitlin experienced an adrenaline rush like nothing she'd ever experienced before at a live concert. Was this how Jake wanted her to look? Commanding, sexy, wearing tight, hard-to-breathe-in clothing specifically designed to highlight every curve, every undulation? Unashamedly putting everything she had on show?

Her throat was dry from the combined heat of wall-to-wall people crammed into a space not much bigger than a living room. Taking a hasty sip of her rum and Coke, with the ice in the glass already melted to slivers, Caitlin almost jumped out of her skin when Jake moved up behind her. Her senses reeled with shock when his lean, hard body was all of a sudden on intimate terms with her back, his denim-clad thighs carelessly brushing the backs of hers as his warm, bourbon-laced breath drifted tantalisingly over her hair. Caitlin went rigid.

'What do you think?' he asked, and the husky timbre of his voice did seriously X-rated things to her body, draining her limbs of all their strength in the process.

'About—about what?' She could barely squeeze the words past her throat.

'About Nikki and the band of course. What did you think I meant?'

Jake's amused smile was almost tangible. She didn't need to see it to know that he was taking great pleasure in teasing her. She was suddenly grateful for the dim lighting and the intimate proximity of the other bodies around her, because she didn't want him to see that her face was burning.

'She's very good. They're all very talented. I'm really enjoying the music,' she told him.

'Without a doubt you're a better singer,' Jake responded. 'All we have to do now is find the right image for you.'

'As long as you don't expect me to pour myself into tight black satin. I'll definitely draw the line at *that*.'

To bolster her flagging courage, Caitlin tipped up her glass and drained the entire contents of the drink that remained. Her head swam a little as the alcohol hit home, but it was as nothing compared to the dizziness she was already experiencing with Jake getting closer by the second.

'I think we should go for something more classy. *Sexy...* but classy.'

His hand drifted over her hip to settle on her waist, his fingers deliberately sliding across the thin silk of the white camisole she wore beneath her jacket. Caitlin almost stopped breathing.

When she lifted her hand, ostensibly to move his away, his fingers caught hers and trapped them possessively. The words she'd started to form were suddenly obliterated as she closed her mouth, shut her eyes and sensed Jake press even closer. A tremulous shudder went through her as he brushed her hair aside and planted a devastatingly erotic kiss on the sensitive juncture between her shoulder and neck.

The unexpected caress went straight to her core and almost made her whimper with pleasure. *It was as though he had branded her.* Beneath the flimsy fabric of her strapless bra her nipples turned rigid and achy and her legs turned seriously weak. Thank God for the music and the crowd, because if they'd been alone right then Caitlin was certain her defences against such a passionate assault on her senses would have been zero.

Desperately needing to regain her composure, she straightened and turned round to face Jake. But the message his compelling blue eyes were conveying drove every coherent thought in her head straight out again.

'Don't. Please don't.'

Even as she softly uttered the words she thought they didn't make sense. *She* made no sense. Half plea, half whisper, they were carried away by the hypnotic beat of the music, by the laughter of the couple standing next to them, a young man with his arms firmly round his pretty Titian-haired girlfriend as they swayed together to the music.

'Please don't what?' Jake caught her hand and unhesitatingly drew her in tight to his chest.

Such eyes he had, Caitlin thought feverishly…piercing blue-grey, like mist swirling over a storm-ravaged sea…

Holding Caitlin against him was the most exquisite pleasure bordering on pain that Jake had ever experienced. Her soft yet slender curves fitted his embrace as though she'd been made for just that purpose.

The sound of the throbbing music, the approving cheers of the audience, the chink of glasses from the bar and the soporific scent of incense that hung over them like a heady cloud—they all faded away, leaving Jake with nothing but his overwhelming need for the woman in front of him.

His desire to make Caitlin his own in the most primal way a man and a woman could consummate their lust was testing him to the very limit. Already he was hurtling close to the edge of that self-imposed control. He knew he shouldn't want her so much. Professionally, it had disaster written all over it, and personally he wasn't ready to trust a woman. After what Jodie had done trust didn't come easily. Both those reasons should make him stay well clear.

With a supreme test of will, Jake slid his hands up to Caitlin's shoulders, where he briefly let them linger. Then he gently but firmly moved her away. Her eyes instantly registered surprise and confusion and Jake cursed himself for torturing them both.

'I don't want to hurt you,' he murmured.

Caitlin bit her lip and inclined her head in a brief nod. Then she turned back to watch the band, crossing her arms over her chest as if to protect herself. Her beautiful hair cascaded down her back like the most luxurious black silk and Jake ached with every fibre of his being to reach out and touch it. He had been captivated by women before, but not like this—*never* like this.

What he needed right now was another drink. He'd have to be careful not to exceed the limit, because he was driving, and even another drink would be no consolation for his present sexual frustration. Sensibly, he decided against it. Instead, he stayed put to watch the band and decide which elements of the performance he could point out to Caitlin that might help her when the time came for her to make her debut with Blue Sky.

'Hey, that was good. Where did you learn to play guitar like that?'

Mike Casey sat cross-legged on the living room floor, barefooted and tousled-haired, his guitar resting easily against his thighs. His brown eyes regarded Caitlin in admiration. She'd just given him a personal rendition of a well-known singer's most iconic track, with all its attendant complicated chord changes and a few innovative ones of her own. He wondered if Jake or Rick had heard her play yet, because Caitlin didn't just play a 'little', as she'd modestly confessed at her audition. The woman knew her way round a guitar as if the instrument were a natural extension of her own graceful hands.

Setting down her guitar to take a sip from the soft drink Mike had given her, she answered, 'I had lessons when I was younger. I pestered my mum for them until she got sick of me asking and conceded. She really wanted me to learn the piano, so I made a compromise and agreed to learn that too.' She grinned. 'After a while I stopped having the lessons and basically taught myself.'

She shrugged, not wanting to make a big deal about her ability. Her reasons for learning to play both instruments had always been purely self-motivated. The plain truth of the matter was that her music and her books had kept her sane whenever life had threatened to get a little less dependable and reliable—like when her parents had announced they were leaving the country to join her brother Phil in America.

Phil was the 'blue-eyed boy' who, in their eyes, could do no wrong. An old familiar twinge of resentment surfaced but Caitlin quickly squashed it. At the time her sense of abandonment had been acute and music had been her only solace—an anchor in a world where nothing had made sense any more. She'd often wondered if that was why she had hooked up with someone like Sean. He'd entered her life when she'd been feeling especially low and he'd charmed her with his boyish smile, amusing jokes and the sense that he was a bit of rebel. She, poor fool, had lapped up his attention as though she'd been marooned on a desert island for years without seeing a single soul.

Mike was thoughtful. There was a real buzz of excitement in the pit of his belly when he thought about Caitlin and what she could potentially bring to the table for the band. Not only had they found themselves an amazing singer, but he'd discovered another musician he could harmonise with as well. There was no doubt in his mind that they could be a great team. The girl was worth her weight in gold.

'What you did just now was more than "good", Caitlin. You really know how to play.'

'Thanks.' Her smile was shy, but appreciative. After last night's humiliating little encounter with Jake as they were watching the band she definitely welcomed a boost to her morale this morning.

God, she'd made such a fool of herself. Her heart thudded and slowed at the memory. It had been a bad mistake to let him see how much she wanted him. *Not that she'd had much choice in the matter, when her body had seemed to have an agenda all of its own...*

But then afterwards, when he had dropped her home to her flat after a near silent car journey filled with the most electrifying tension, Jake had confused her yet again when he'd insisted on accompanying her to her door and waiting until she'd got safely inside. There had been no sign of his earlier rejection at the concert.

The man was a genuine enigma and no mistake. Yet Caitlin understood why he had to put the band first. He wouldn't jeopardise Blue Sky's chances by having a meaningless fling with their new lead singer. *Not that any association with Jake, however brief, could ever be meaningless...*

'Have you had the chance to learn the two new songs I gave you?' Mike asked, his glance flicking interestedly over the pretty white gypsy-style blouse she was wearing with faded blue jeans.

'After I got home from the gig I was up most of last night working on them,' Caitlin told him, suppressing a yawn. She carefully withdrew a folded sheet of paper from her jeans pocket. 'Do you want to give them a try?'

'Sure. That would be great.' Picking up his guitar again, Mike started to tune it.

The unexpected sound of a ring on the doorbell interrupted him and he broke off to spring nimbly to his feet. During his absence Caitlin took the opportunity to lean back against the edge of the pink velour couch behind her, stretch out her legs and idly finger her guitar strings. As much as she wanted and needed to learn the songs, it had probably not been the most sensible thing to do to stay up long into the early hours trying to master them. *What she wouldn't give for a long lie-down...*

Her eyes drifting closed, she was just wondering how on earth she was going to get through the rest of the day when the sense that she had company alerted her. She looked up to find Jake staring down at her. He had a disconcerting glint in his eye that made Caitlin shiver helplessly, and she hastily sat up to drape her arm protectively across her guitar. *What had she done wrong now?*

'Hi.' It wasn't easy to sound casual when all she could think about was what had happened between them at the gig. But straight away Jake was all business.

'You're giving rehearsals a miss this afternoon. We're going out,' he declared.

Dazedly, she answered, 'We are?'

Mike had come back into the room behind him and her gaze swung from his to Mike's and back again.

'Not Mike,' Jake qualified firmly. 'Just you and me. I'm taking you shopping.'

'But I don't want to go shopping.' Caitlin didn't even pause to wonder what for. All she knew was that she was in no fit condition to trudge round some overheated shopping mall—with or *without* Jake.

'This has got to be a first. A woman who doesn't like shopping? Where have you been all my life?' Mike joked.

But Jake didn't look remotely amused. His handsome countenance was as implacable as usual. In his black leather coat and blue jeans, his square jaw fashionably unshaven, he looked as if he was in no mood to entertain an argument, no matter how convincing or passionate. Caitlin tensed.

'Get your coat,' he ordered.

'But Mike and I were just—'

'I'm not interested. I just want you to get your coat and be quick about it. I don't want this to take any longer than it has to.'

He had a nerve! It was at Jake's suggestion the previous night that Caitlin had come round to Mike's to get some guitar practice in.

'You can't just walk in here and tell me what to do.' She defiantly stayed where she was, even though her heart was beating like a jackhammer. Blue Sky's lead guitarist was staring down at his feet as if they were suddenly the most interesting sight in the world. *No moral support there, she thought irritably.*

'I thought I'd just done exactly that.' Lifting a mocking eyebrow, Jake was unimpressed. 'Now, if you want to continue to be a member of this band, I'd seriously consider doing what you're told and being quick about it. We're driving to London, and at this rate we won't get there before one o'clock. That hardly gives us enough time.'

'Enough time for *what*?'

Clearly mad at him, Caitlin finally got to her feet, gripping her precious guitar by its neck as if it was Jake's neck she'd like to throttle. Her pretty face was flushed with emotion, her bewitching emerald eyes spitting fire, and in that instant Jake experienced a longing for her so deep that it hurt.

He knew he was only being short-tempered because he was furious with himself for wanting her so badly. Tough. Life could be unfair like that. If there had been the remotest possibility that they could find another singer even half as good as Caitlin, then he would seriously have considered letting her go. The band and Rick would undoubtedly give him hell but, damn it, if it was a choice between confronting their rage and losing his sanity then he knew which one he'd plump for.

The sheets on his bed had been a crumpled mess when he'd woken this morning. If he'd slept two hours he'd be surprised. It had been a hell of a long time since any woman had got Jake in such a stew—not since Jodie, and that had been six years ago. But even at the height of his attraction to Jodie it had never been like this. This mindless, helpless, heated longing that he felt for Caitlin was driving him slowly crazy.

If she had been any other woman but Blue Sky's new lead singer he wouldn't have hesitated in succumbing to his carnal desires. But Caitlin Ryan was strictly off-limits. *Hadn't he said so to himself when he'd first heard her sing?*

'Jake?' When he didn't immediately reply, but levelled his compelling blue gaze straight at her in warning, Caitlin had to suppress the worrying impulse to leave, to put herself out of the line of fire. Why was he so furious with her? What had she done to make him so disagreeable?

'You need some clothes,' he explained grudgingly. 'Working clothes. The band plays its first date in London next week and we need to kit you out. I've arranged to meet a stylist I've worked with for years…someone I trust who will help guide you. Her name is Ronnie. Rick has had to drive up north on business, so today's a good opportunity to sort things out. Now, go and get your coat…*please.*'

Driving a weary hand through his tousled mane, Jake looked as if his patience was being sorely tested. In the meantime, Caitlin's mind was racing. *He was taking her to buy clothes?* That would mean she'd have to parade herself in front of him, not to mention this stylist, whilst getting hot and bothered, trying on garments in cramped changing rooms and no doubt feeling woefully inadequate when something didn't look right or didn't fit.

Was it really necessary that he go with her? And did she really need a professional stylist to help her choose the right clothes? Couldn't Jake simply trust her own judgement as far as dressing herself went?

One look into that arrogant male visage and she had her answer. She could stand there and argue until they got old and Jake would still insist on going with her.

'I hate and detest shopping,' she said, before turning on her heel and grabbing her coat off the back of the pink velour armchair. 'And if you think for one second that I'm pouring myself into some horrible skin-tight catsuit for the sake of this band then you've got another think coming!'

And with that she shouldered angrily past Jake out into the hallway—but not before suffering the added indignity of hearing the two men she'd left behind chuckling between them in some ancient patronising ritual of amused male bonding.

CHAPTER SIX

JAKE COULDN'T REMEMBER the last time he'd had so much fun. Nor could he remember his inflamed libido being put under such torturous conditions in an even longer time. An obliging assistant—a skinny little redhead, with pansy-blue eyes and freckles—had thoughtfully supplied him with a comfy chair while Ronnie, the dependable stylist, selected several items of clothing from the rails and at regular intervals handed them to Caitlin to try on.

As she disappeared in and out of the changing room, trying on various different outfits, her expression veered alternately from plain put upon to seriously contemplating doing him some damage. The funny thing was, even when she was scowling at him, Caitlin was prettier and sexier than any other woman he could think of. So, although their little shopping trip had a serious purpose, it was also providing Jake with some royal entertainment.

'You didn't tell me this would be one of the easiest assignments you've ever given me, Jake. This girl is an absolute dream to dress!' The fashionable and gamine stylist curved her scarlet-painted lips with pleasure as she dropped down beside Jake. 'I mean, I've dressed some of the best female recording artists in the world, and all I can tell you is if she sings as good as she looks…'

'She does,' he assured her laconically. Then, with a sigh, he added, 'Whether you're a record producer or the manager of a band, singers like Caitlin come along once in a lifetime…*if* you're lucky.'

'Then one thing's for sure, my friend,' Ronnie said, knowingly patting his knee. 'The rest of the music industry will be quaking in their boots—because without a doubt this amazing find of yours is definitely going to put you back in the game...with bells on!'

And on that note, as if on cue, with an impatient swish of the changing room curtain Caitlin suddenly appeared before them wearing red faux leather jeans cut low on the hip and a sheer white chiffon blouse that had a lacy frill edging the cuffs. And, because the diaphanous blouse revealed so much more than it concealed, Jake was treated to the captivating sight of her luscious breasts crammed into a flimsy white lace bra that appeared barely equipped to contain them. He also saw that she had a deeply sexy belly button that put him in mind of a harem and long, hot desert nights...

With her arms akimbo, she glanced first at Ronnie, then at him, and her bewitching green eyes clearly proclaimed her disdain.

'I hope you're both satisfied. In my opinion, I look utterly ridiculous in this outfit.' Flicking back her shining dark hair in a huff, Caitlin flushed, her apple cheeks growing even pinker.

When Ronnie would have gone across to reassure her, Jake immediately rose to his feet to take charge.

'Let *me*,' he told her meaningfully, lowering his voice.

He made his way over to his new protégée.

'Believe me, you look anything *but* ridiculous.'

A heated injection of pure carnal pleasure pulsed through him as he came face to face with Caitlin's arrestingly beautiful gaze. His blood had been simmering since she had got into the car with him outside Mike's place and, as entertaining and necessary as it was, this little fashion parade wasn't helping.

Everything about the woman was driving him wild...her scent, her beautiful emerald eyes, that gorgeous long black hair of hers, and even the endearing little habit she had of chewing down on her lower lip when she was feeling over-whelmed or anxious. *As for her figure... Ever since he had seen it he'd been thanking God he was born a man.* It was a shame they were in one of his stylist's favourite fashion houses or he might have demonstrated his appreciation a little more graphically.

'Well, I'm not going on stage looking like this. I haven't become a singer for people to ogle me. If you like the outfit so much, why don't *you* wear it and be done with it!'

Caitlin stepped towards Jake as if she'd like to wipe the smile right off his face with a slap. Towering over her, he immediately closed the gap between them and made him-self slowly breathe out.

'Calm down. You're getting all hot and bothered for noth-ing.'

Hot and bothered didn't begin to describe how Jake was feeling. God knew he was making a supreme effort to cor-ral his aroused feelings, but it was damn near impossible with Caitlin huffing and pink-cheeked in front of him, her luscious breasts rising and falling with every breath that she took.

'Ronnie and I just wanted you to try a few different looks. It doesn't mean you have to go with anything that doesn't feel right. Ultimately it's your decision.'

Jake's reassurance effectively took the wind out of Cait-lin's sails. She hadn't meant to be deliberately obstructive, but appearing in revealing clothing in front of *anyone,* let alone Jake, wasn't something that came remotely easy to her. It wasn't anyone's fault that she was so insecure about her body, but she *was*. She'd often been teased as a child for being 'chubby', and even though she knew rationally that she was in good shape now she guessed that the hurt of being picked on and singled out because of her appearance had never quite left her.

But maybe this was her chance to overcome her insecu-rities and act differently for once. In any case, the least she could do was have a sense of humour about the proceedings. The fact was, she was a singer in a rock band and people would expect her to look the part...even to look *sexy*.

Cringing at the thought, she suddenly found herself unable to meet Jake's glance directly. He was so arresting, from the top of his tousled dark hair and the haunting chiselled perfection of his face to the tips of his feet in his stylish worn leather boots. In his long leather coat, with tight jeans and a midnight-blue shirt opened casually at the neck, he wore his clothes as if he didn't give a damn...which made it all the more challenging for Caitlin, knowing she regularly had to face him.

'I don't like wearing this kind of revealing clothing. I'm just not comfortable dressing to show off my body,' she admitted quietly. And because she was feeling vulnerable, every cell vibrating with the tension of being so intimately scrutinised, she folded her arms across her chest, only too aware that Jake's heated blue gaze kept dipping helplessly to that area.

'Why?' Nonplussed, he shook his head. 'Tell me what's going on in your head that makes you feel embarrassed about revealing such a God-given asset? Because that's what it is, Caitlin.'

His glance momentarily flicked towards the elegant and manicured Ronnie, who sat waiting patiently for him to finish before coming over to join them and give her opinion.

'It's not easy to explain,' Caitlin answered.

Jake turned back to her to give her his full attention. Taking up where he'd left off, he remarked, 'You're beautiful, Caitlin. If I gave you a bin liner to wear you'd still look stunning. Why don't you just enjoy being young, having the freedom to dress a little outrageously?'

'It's all right for a man to come out with that, isn't it?' Furiously twining her hair behind her ear, Caitlin glared. 'Women don't leave men just because they get older. Even nowadays, when you'd think we would have got a little bit more enlightened, older men are labelled "interesting" or "experienced" while the complete reverse is applied to women.'

An amused smile twitched at the corners of Jake's lips.

Caitlin paused. Maybe she was overreacting. After all, surely he had a point—she should take advantage of being young and free and go wild. Still, his sentiment had struck a nerve. Was Jake the kind of man who would leave a woman just because she was getting older or had put on weight? The music industry was hardly known for nurturing healthy relationships, was it? Not when everything seemed to be dominated by image these days.

The pop charts were littered with pretty young things with average talent and attractive bodies who had their five minutes of fame and then disappeared. But, as far as relationships went, it didn't mean that she couldn't fantasise about one day finding a man who wanted to stay with her come what may. It was just a shame that Jake Sorenson clearly *wasn't* and never could be that man. He might be attracted to her because he admired the 'packaging', but that was all it was: a passing meaningless attraction that would no doubt blow itself out as soon as he'd taken her to bed... *if she let him.*

The thought made her heart slam against her ribs.

'Don't paint all us men with the same brush.' Reaching out his hand, Jake gently loosed the glossy strand of hair that Caitlin had tucked behind her ear and watched it glance against her cheek as it fell silkily down to her shoulder. 'I sincerely hope I'm not as shallow as you seem to think I am. When you get past the physical attraction, I'm quite aware there's got to be something deeper and more compelling to keep both parties in a relationship interested. If I found a woman I wanted to spend the rest of my life with I'd never let her go...no matter what happened.'

Jake's arresting blue eyes were regarding her so intently that Caitlin felt the imprint of his gaze resonate deep inside her. Along with the heartfelt words he'd expressed, his intensely examining glance shook and unravelled her. It made her body burn and her heart race. It stirred a longing in her for things that she knew could never be.

'This is the last outfit Ronnie gave me to try on. I think I'll go and get changed now. I suddenly feel quite cold.'

Despite the intimacy that Jake had woven round them, the harsh cold reality of the situation suddenly doused the heat that had all but drowned her just a moment ago. *Caitlin was beginning to care too much for Jake and that was dangerous.*

Turning away, she rubbed briskly at the chilled flesh on her arms in the diaphanous blouse, and was taken aback when he moved swiftly behind her and turned her firmly back round to face him.

'That first outfit you tried on…the purple velvet top and the long black skirt with the chain belt? That looked great. Shall we go with that for starters?'

A muscle flexed in the side of his lean jaw. The outfit he'd described was one of her favourites, too. *It seemed that they agreed on something after all.*

'Okay.'

'And, by the way, we're not going straight home after this. We're going back to Ronnie's place for a while, then I'm taking you to a club. We'll eat dinner there and enjoy some entertainment.'

He was taking her to a club? What was that all about?

'Why didn't you mention this before? What kind of club?'

Jake's expression remained as inscrutable as ever, yet he definitely had a twinkle in his eye. Caitlin frowned. *What on earth was the man up to?*

'I wanted it to be a surprise,' he drawled. 'Hopefully an enjoyable one.'

'I've hardly got the right clothes with me to go out for the evening…especially to a club. Can't we leave it for another night?'

Ignoring her hopeful plea, he clenched his jaw and firmly shook his head.

'Sorry, but you're not going to wriggle out of this one. Trust me. Tonight will be just what you need. As for not having the right clothes—why don't you pick out one of the outfits you were looking at to wear? You can get ready at Ronnie's.'

'Those outfits are ludicrously expensive, Jake! I can't afford—'

'I'm footing the bill. You can have anything you like—and I mean anything. Think of it as a gift.'

More than a little overwhelmed by his unexpected generosity, she was almost lost for words. 'Well...I mean, that's very kind of you, but just what kind of place is this club you're taking me to?'

He smiled one of his maddening sexy smiles that could stop a woman in her tracks in less than a heartbeat and said, 'It's classy...very classy. That's all you need to know.'

'Let me help you to choose something. Jake has told me where you'll be going and I know the perfect outfit. We'll also need to accessorise you with shoes and jewellery to complete the look.'

The fragrant Ronnie was suddenly at her side and, whilst Caitlin had plenty of reservations about being kitted out for an evening out with Jake somewhere 'classy', she sensed that any more attempts at wriggling out of the night's events would be a waste of energy.

In the sumptuous mirrored enclave of the exclusive members-only jazz club, frequented not just by aficionados but by many well-known celebrities from the worlds of music and film, Jake sat opposite Caitlin at a beautifully laid dining table and thanked the gods for giving him a legitimate excuse simply to sit and gaze at her.

Ronnie had helped select the perfect outfit for her tonight. The powers of the 'little black dress' should never be underestimated, she'd told him knowledgeably, and she'd been right. The slinky little number she'd come up with had taken his breath away when he'd seen Caitlin wearing it. It had a daringly low-cut neckline that immediately drew the eye to her sensational cleavage, and the fitted black satin clung to her body in all the right places. The voluptuous curves that she contrived to keep hidden from the world were tonight displayed in all their glory.

Add to that some sexy red lipstick and the sultry, alluring perfume that Jake had chosen especially for her—*he'd slipped out to purchase it as Caitlin had got dressed*—and he doubted there was a single male in the vicinity who would ever forget seeing her.

He sucked in some air and breathed it out again slowly. An unexpected need to protect her had crept into his blood and he couldn't help now and again surveying the other diners in case they looked a little *too* interested in her. He knew it was crazy when very soon Caitlin would be appearing with the band and from then on would be in the public domain. But in light of his protective feelings and undeniable need to keep her to himself, how was he going to handle it? he wondered. *It was a dilemma that had never affected him before...*

The manager of the venue—an immaculately dressed Frenchman called Dion, who famously took great pride in entertaining an elite clientele—had expressed delight at seeing Jake. It had been a long time since the two men had met. The last occasion had been just before his ex had written that dreadful exposé about him. After that Jake had retreated to lick his wounds and kept a deliberately low profile. Even so, the Frenchman had recognised Jake straight away.

'It's so nice to see you back in public again, Mr Sorenson,' he'd told him. 'It's been too long.' Then he'd turned to Caitlin and commented, 'Many beautiful women come to this establishment, but *you ma chère*...you take my breath away!'

In truth, Jake had almost been readying himself for a small stampede when he'd walked in with Caitlin on his arm. He'd honestly sensed the moment when the other stylishly attired patrons seated at the tables had drawn in a collective awed breath. They might be surprised at seeing him out in public again, but he doubted their interest was solely in him. The woman by his side was the main reason they glanced their way, and Jake would be a liar if he didn't admit to feeling both pride and pleasure at the realisation. After all, he was only human.

Although the club featured predominantly jazz, and there was a smoky-sounding sax playing in the background, tonight was Burlesque night,—and that was what he'd brought Caitlin to see.

'This is some place,' she commented shyly.

'And you've just elevated it to a whole other class,' he said, and smiled.

Delicately sipping her Margarita, she added, 'I feel so guilty drinking this when you're just drinking soda and lime.'

'There's no need. I'm quite happy being teetotal tonight. Especially when I have a very precious cargo to drive home,' he teased.

Jake supposed it was inevitable that the compliment would make her cheeks turn pink, but he loved to see her blush. It reminded him that she was still relatively innocent…*quite a rarity in his world.*

'I've heard of Burlesque, but I don't know very much about it. Isn't it some kind of variety show?' she enquired.

Even before he told her the answer Jake sensed the muscles in his belly clench hard in anticipation of her reaction.

'It can be that. But Burlesque is really an art form…it's about celebrating the beauty of the female form.'

'Oh…? You mean it involves things like striptease?'

'It's much more than women simply taking their clothes off. Sometimes all a girl might remove are her gloves. But it's the way they do it that makes it an art form. Plus the costumes the girls wear and the way they move is part of the spectacle. I just want you to sit back and enjoy it…to feel proud of being a woman.'

'Is that why you brought me here? To show me how women can be confident about displaying their bodies when they perform? So I won't be self-conscious when I perform with the band?'

'Yes. You're already going to command the stage with that incredible voice of yours, but I don't want any doubts about your body to hold you back. I want you to enjoy every second you're on that stage when you perform.'

To his surprise, Caitlin downed what was left of her cocktail with a flourish, licked her lips and declared, 'In that case I think I'd like another drink…a little Dutch courage wouldn't go amiss. Do you mind?'

'Are you serious?' Leaning over to her, Jake tenderly stroked the pad of his thumb down over her cheek and said huskily, 'Baby, do you have *any* idea how dangerously alluring you are in that dress? If you asked me to get you the moon I'd do my damnedest to get it for you.'

'Oh, I wouldn't expect you to go *that* far,' she said, and grinned.

His lips twitching in amusement and delight, because Caitlin was clearly starting to enjoy herself, Jake signalled for a waitress to take his order just as the sultry sax in the background came to a sudden halt, the lights dimmed and all eyes turned expectantly towards the stage…

The show was spectacular. Caitlin was swept away by the sumptuous display of dance and movement from the predominantly 'Rubenesque' women who took to the stage in their stunning costumes and exaggerated make-up. At no point did she feel remotely embarrassed or self-conscious at all the comely flesh on display. For perhaps the very first time she felt proud to be a woman and unashamed of her own voluptuous curves.

Jake had been right. It had been a good idea to bring her to a Burlesque night. *But her companion hadn't reserved all his attention for the show.* More than once throughout the evening she'd caught him looking at her as though mesmerised, despite having a bevy of stunning women on the stage in front of them.

That brooding glance of his had made Caitlin feel more than a little aroused. In fact it had made her long for him to take her somewhere private so that she could demonstrate exactly just how excited he made her feel... And Jake wasn't the only one who was enjoying the view. Dressed in the flawless single-breasted Armani suit that unbeknownst to her he'd brought with him to change into for their visit to the club, with his incredible blue eyes glinting like diamonds and his chiselled jaw dusted with late-night shadow, he looked expensive and assured, and he exuded the kind of charisma usually attributed to A-list movie stars.

Caitlin wanted to pinch herself to make sure she wasn't dreaming that he was solely hers for the evening. Who would have guessed that a man who famously adopted a 'don't give a damn' attitude about what he was wearing could wear a tux with such effortless panache?

Later that night, as Jake turned the Jeep onto the motorway to head home, he wondered wryly if Caitlin had any idea what a test it was for him to concentrate on his driving when she was snuggled in the seat next to him wearing that alluring black dress. The 'LBD', as Ronnie had called it, had put him in a state of highly charged sexual tension for the whole evening, and he knew it wasn't going to dissipate easily.

By the time they'd reached the village and Jake had pulled up outside Caitlin's flat he was honestly glad of the opportunity to get a breath of fresh air to help him think straight. But first he had to wake her and help her to the door, because she'd fallen asleep as soon as they'd got into the car. It was inevitable she would be a little drowsy.

'Hey, sleepyhead, we're home.'

Curling his hand round her slim upper arm, Jake shook

her gently. The second she opened her big green eyes the tension that already gripped him mercilessly doubled.

'Have I been asleep? I must have been, because that journey went in a blink.'

Shaking her head, Caitlin undid her seatbelt and sat up. Her lustrous dark hair spilled down over her shoulders and the air was suddenly provocatively imbued with the sultry scent Jake had bought her. *What had he been trying to do? Make her even more irresistible than she was already?*

'Well, we're home now, and you need to get straight to bed,' he stated, almost groaning out loud at his ill thought out choice of words—because that was *exactly* where he'd like to go with her. 'Give me your key. I'll open the door for you,' he added.

The cold night air hit him as soon as he stepped out of the car and proved to be just the tonic he needed to cool his blood. Quickly inserting Caitlin's key into the lock, he opened the door onto the hallway and waited for her to step over the threshold in front of him. As soon as she did Jake's blood was stirred all over again when she turned back towards him. She'd draped her jacket over her shoulders and now tugged the sides more closely over her chest, but not before he had a glimpse of her delectable cleavage. *For both their sakes he should say goodnight and leave her.* His usually dependable sense of control was rapidly deserting him.

But his decision was immediately compromised when Caitlin narrowed the gap between them and said softly, 'Thanks for a really wonderful evening, Jake, and also for the lovely clothes and everything. You made me feel like a princess, and no one's ever done that for me before.'

'It wasn't difficult, Caitlin. In my eyes you *are* a princess.'

It was then that Jake thought, *To hell with self-control* and pulled her into his arms. He kissed her with a hunger he could no longer deny, and the desire that was always just a breath away whenever they were together flared beyond control. But when Caitlin carefully freed her lips and he saw the longing in her eyes—*the kind of longing that went way beyond a desire simply to make lov*e—the immensity of what he was contemplating and the possible consequences hit him like a brick dropped from a great height.

With his heart thundering, Jake moved out of their embrace. 'I think it's time we said goodnight, don't you? It's been a long day for both of us and we're just a couple of days away from the band's first live performance. We need to get some rest to make sure we're fit for what's to come.'

'I know you're right, but—'

Even before Caitlin had finished what she was saying Jake was out through the door and walking towards the car.

Two days of intense rehearsal followed Caitlin's magical night out with Jake. And, although she'd had a wonderful time, she couldn't forget how quickly he'd distanced himself from her after he'd dropped her home—even though just before he'd left, his lips had passionately claimed hers as if he really meant it. Now he was acting as if the kiss had never even happened. It was easy to sense that his focus was back on the band and what lay ahead of them, but Caitlin couldn't help feeling he was somehow abandoning her.

A couple of evenings later Jake surprised them all by giving them a day off. They'd had two more gruelling days of rehearsal and they more than welcomed the unexpected opportunity for a bit of 'R&R'. But, although Caitlin appreciated being able to rest and have a day to herself, she started to fret about the upcoming live shows. The new-found confidence she'd experienced after seeing the Burlesque seemed to be rapidly diminishing.

Having the day off hadn't helped. All it had done was to make her worry even more. That was why she found herself making her way to the Pilgrim's Inn that night, hopefully to see Jake and express her concerns. Just a few dedicated patrons occupied the cosily lit lounge bar and Caitlin was grateful, because it had taken every ounce of courage she could muster to make this eleventh hour trip to speak with Jake.

As far as Blue Sky's enigmatic manager was concerned his new lead singer would be having an early night and dreaming about what a resounding success she was going to be when she debuted with the band—because tomorrow was the big day: the day when Blue Sky introduced their new female vocalist to the world…or at least to the audience at the famous rock café in London where they were playing.

But Caitlin wasn't just apprehensive about what lay ahead, she was plain *petrified*—so petrified that she was suddenly having some serious doubts.

I'm sorry but I've made a terrible mistake. She heard the words go round and round in her head and imagined the confusion and then anger in Jake's eyes when she said them.

She sighed. *She didn't really want to quit.* All she was looking for was a little reassurance. If Jake couldn't give it to her, after all his years of experience in working with singers and musicians, she didn't have a prayer.

Tina Stevens was busy polishing the bar, her jaw working overtime as she chewed on some gum, her long red nails clicking against the varnished wood as she ran a duster over the already shiny surface of the counter. The brown eyes that were heavily outlined with kohl gave Caitlin a cool once-over as she approached, but she continued to polish as though her life depended on it.

'Excuse me, I—'

'What can I get you, love? Are you on your own or are you meeting somebody?'

There was a distinct note of disapproval in the blonde's voice, as if she believed that women who came into bars on their own somehow spelt trouble.

For a disconcerting moment Caitlin wondered if Tina had been working that night when Sean had turned particularly nasty. But, unable to remember very much other than the soul-destroying humiliation of being insulted by her boyfriend in public, she opted not to dwell on it. *Goodness knew she had enough on her mind without fretting about the past.* All she wanted—all she needed—was for Jake to tell her that everything would be all right, that she wasn't about to suffer another humiliation tomorrow night when she sang.

'I'm not meeting anybody.' Pushing her rain-dampened fringe out of her eyes, she squared her shoulders in her long charcoal-coloured raincoat. 'I wondered if I could have a word with Jake Sorenson? He's staying here, isn't he?'

Immediately Tina stopped polishing, and her expression was far from convivial. As the two women faced each other the record that was playing on the juke box suddenly changed and a song that Caitlin remembered from her childhood replaced it. *It was her mother's favourite song.*

An avid music fan, Terry Ryan had played the tune to death when Caitlin was little. She would enfold her little daughter in her arms and dance round the room with her, crooning gently against her cheek as she softly sang the words, whilst Phil—Caitlin's older brother—who was disdainful of anything remotely 'girly' would groan in mockery.

'Typical boy!' her mother would say, and laugh, instantly forgiving him as though it was his birthright.

Memories... Caitlin suddenly found herself pole-axed by them. Treacherously, her eyes filled with tears. What was *wrong* with her?

She was missing her family—that was what was wrong. Here she was, on the eve of what could be one of the most important nights of her life, and where were her parents and brother? On the other side of the world! They were completely oblivious to the fact that Caitlin had resigned from her job, never mind joined a rock band as their lead singer!

She had never felt as alone or as afraid as she did right then. She was twenty-six years old, about to embark on the biggest challenge she could imagine, with nothing but her dreams, her wits and her talent to help see her through.

'You must be Cait...the singer.'

As if it had suddenly dawned on her who Caitlin was, Tina stopped chewing her gum and crossed her arms in front of her chest. The sudden movement jiggled her ample breasts in the red V-necked angora sweater she wore. Well... *nearly* wore.

'It's Caitlin.' The correction of her name was automatic. She remembered that Rick had been using the shortened version of it since he'd met her, and that he apparently had a real soft spot for the buxom Miss Stevens.

'Yeah...right. All set for tomorrow, then?' the other girl asked.

Not really.

'I hope so. Could I see Jake?' Caitlin's lip quivered a little as she made an attempt at a friendly smile.

'Room Three. Turn left at the top of the stairs.'

'Thanks.'

'Nice talking to you.'

Could have fooled me, Caitlin thought.

Making her way up the thickly carpeted staircase, with its faded floral tread, she focused her gaze on the landing at the top, on the ponderous oak sideboard with its gaudy Victorian lamp and the sepia-toned photographs of the village that were displayed on the wall behind it.

The dark old-fashioned surroundings seemed incongruous when she thought of Jake. She wondered why he hadn't rented a house in the village, like the other band members had. But then it occurred to her that maybe Rick had something to do with his decision to stay at the Pilgrim's Inn. Perhaps the voluptuous Tina Stevens had an equally arresting friend he wanted to introduce to Jake, for instance?

Disliking that particular train of thought, Caitlin arrived at the top of the stairs and glanced anxiously round her. Two doors faced each other across the landing. Before she could talk herself out of it she rapped briskly on number three. She immediately registered the sound of male voices coming from the room and realised that Jake and Rick must be in conference about the concert tomorrow.

She didn't know whether to stay put or turn around and leave. But the decision was made for her when the door suddenly opened and Rick appeared. Untypically, when his usual mode of dress was more extrovert, he was wearing a pair of ordinary faded Levi's and a plain white T-shirt.

He gave Caitlin his trademark roguish smile when he saw that it was her. 'Hello, gorgeous. Come to join the party?'

His candid gaze moved over her figure in her buttoned-up raincoat—possibly the most unsexy item of clothing she possessed. But Caitlin didn't give the thought much attention.

'No. I mean, I just came to see Jake…if I could?'

Her mouth suddenly drying, she stared across the top of Rick's hard-muscled shoulder and found the man she was looking for. His long-legged form was lounging in an over-stuffed green and gold striped armchair and his glance met hers, a knowing smile curving his lips. *He looked as if he'd been expecting her visit.*

Her feverish thoughts went into overdrive. He'd given them all the day off and advised them to get an early night in preparation for the following day, but he clearly didn't apply the advice to himself. Did the man *ever* get an early night in his business? Caitlin somehow doubted it.

'If I've come at a bad time—' she started, suddenly embarrassed. Had any of his other artists ever sought him out the night before a debut concert to seek his reassurance she wondered? Would her sudden attack of nerves disturb him and make him doubt his decision to hire her as Marcie's replacement?

He must have intuited that she was on the point of changing her mind about talking to him because he said suddenly, 'Stay right where you are.'

The words were uttered like a command from on high and Caitlin immediately froze. Rick sighed and moved away as Jake took a couple of leisurely strides towards her. As he drew near she saw that his hard, lean jaw was dark with late-night shadow and his slightly cool stare put her on her guard. That less than friendly glance hardly invited a frank admission about her doubts and feelings concerning the gig tomorrow, she thought anxiously.

'I thought you might come to see me tonight,' he drawled.

'Did you?' Caitlin heard the strength in her voice desert her.

'Yes, I did' He turned round to find Rick. 'Give us a few minutes, will you? Come to think of it, we'll probably need a little longer than that. Go and have a drink with Tina.'

Looking doubtful, his colleague shrugged. 'I'd really like to oblige, Jake, but whether Miss Cold-as-Ice down there will even serve me is another matter. We've had a bit of a falling out.'

'You brought it on yourself, Rick. Sort it out.'

'Sure. You're the boss.'

Clearly unhappy, Rick didn't say another word. But he still found a smile for Caitlin as he passed her. Then he left the room, shutting the door firmly behind him. She shivered. She suddenly didn't feel at all easy about finding herself alone with Jake.

'Can I get you a drink?' The charismatic manager strolled across to another ponderous Victorian sideboard and, opening a door, extracted a bottle of Bourbon along with two glasses.

'No. Not for me, thanks.'

When Caitlin declined his offer without further ado he poured himself a conservative amount of alcohol into a shot glass and advanced slowly towards her. Not for a second did he take his glance off her. His blue eyes glinted dangerously, just like a shaft of sunlight catching the burnished blade of a sword. She couldn't help tensing. *The charming man in the Armani tux who had taken her to the Burlesque had apparently disappeared.*

Tipping back his glass, Jake swallowed down the drink

before saying, 'So...care to tell me why you've come to see me tonight, Caitlin? It certainly isn't to make small talk, is it? What's on your mind? In my experience there's only *one* reason a woman comes to a man's hotel room late at night.'

As if to illustrate what he meant, he flicked his intense gaze over her as if he'd like to strip every stitch from her body and devour her, and then take his slow, sweet time doing it all over again.

Caitlin tried desperately to calm the rioting sensations he was stirring inside her.

'Well, that's not the reason I came to see you, Jake... as hard as that might be for your ego to take. My visit is a purely practical one.'

'Is it?' His expression doubtful, he put his glass down on a nearby side table and turned back to give her a deliberately lazy smile. 'You break my heart, Caitlin Ryan...but I think you know that, don't you?'

'What do you mean?'

Her mind was in a complete spin, and if she hadn't backed herself up against the door just then there was a distinct danger that she might simply have crumpled to the floor. Her legs were trembling so hard they hardly seemed to have the strength to keep her upright.

'What you do to me with those slow, hot looks of yours is nothing less than criminal.'

His voice a low, grating rasp, Jake yanked her away from the door and pulled her roughly into his arms.

CHAPTER SEVEN

CRIMINAL... CAITLIN COULD have used the same adjective to describe Jake's kiss. The way he took her mouth was near savage, and it almost knocked her off of her feet. This was no inept fumbling, no tentative exploration, but a devastating passionate assault on the senses.

With a hungry groan that seemed to emanate from the depths of his soul, he swept his tongue over the warm recesses of her surprised mouth as one firm hand possessively anchored itself in the long thick strands of her hair to render the contact between them even more intimate.

As his tongue thrust deeper, harder, mimicking the ultimate sexual coupling between a man and a woman, Caitlin swallowed her breath, tasting him, her senses intoxicated by the dark sultry flavours of bourbon and avaricious heat. She gripped onto the sensuous silk of his shirt with all the strength and tenacity of someone hanging from a precipice by their fingertips...as if she dangled into empty space and could fall at any moment.

But from the instant Jake had captured her mouth there had been no thought to deny him. Not when everything in her clamoured wildly for more of the same. Only a frigid woman could not want what Jake was giving her right now, and Caitlin was anything but that. She was a living, breathing, loving human being, and it was too long since she'd been held and desired—too long since she'd been loved like a woman longed to be loved by a man.

Oh God...how did I survive without this? she thought.

All she knew was that her legs suddenly didn't have a hope of holding her up for very much longer. Not when the equivalent of a hundred volts of pure unadulterated pleasure was pulsating through her as though she were plugged in to her own personal ecstasy machine.

Almost mindlessly driving her hips against Jake's, she heard herself moaning urgent little sounds of want and need—sounds that were as alien to her as this wild, savage joy that was pouring through her veins. Sean had never taken her anywhere *near* close to the kind of heights Jake was taking her to now. Never before had passion come at her like a wild, untamed river, bursting its banks, sweeping everything that stood in its way to exciting uncharted shores that left her dazed and trembling.

Hungrily she acquiesced as he alternately nipped and grazed at her mouth, every now and then her tongue meeting and dancing with his, her breasts burning into the hard granite wall of his chest. She was certain of one thing and one thing only...that she never wanted this sweet, irresistible agony to end.

Unbelievably, Jake turned up the heat. Now their invisible passion dial hovered somewhere between boiling and the point of no return. As he rocked his hips deep into hers the solid ridge of his button fly was testimony to his driving, hungry need, and when he suddenly broke contact to look down at her Caitlin glanced back at him in surprise.

It was a shock to witness the depth and strength of desire contained in that blistering gaze. His pupils were almost totally black, ringed with just the slimmest band of devastating blue. From his lips his breath issued hard and fast, and there was a thin sheen of sweat on his ridged brow.

'I don't want our first time to be up against a door. You've got to tell me what you want, baby.'

As he finished speaking he reached behind him and shot

the bolt, enveloping her in a dizzying cloak of heat and his disturbing, sensuous male essence.

'Do you want to stay with me tonight? We can go to bed now and finish what we started. I can keep you up all night and give you pleasure like you've never dreamed. Is that what you want?'

With deft fingers Jake freed the top three buttons on her coat and jerked the material aside to cup her breast through the thin material of her T-shirt. Her nipple, already rigid and tingling with need, pressed helplessly, wantonly into his palm.

Why did he have to stop and ask what she wanted? Caitlin thought. Why couldn't he just carry on the way they were going and take what she was so ready to give him?

She was shocked at the desperation of her wild thoughts. What he was doing—his long fingers now circling the nipple of her other breast, alternately nipping and squeezing—was making her womb throb with an almost unholy ache. If he took her right now she'd welcome the possession and count herself blessed. *That was how much she wanted him.* She was hungry to feel his sex deep inside her, to complete the electrifying bond that had been slowly and devastatingly drawing them together since the very first moment they had met.

But this was crazy—and not just crazy, but completely and utterly reckless. Jake must surely know that? He was the one who'd sternly advised Caitlin against 'fraternising' with the band out of hours, and as he was their manager he had to include himself in that warning. The potential pitfalls of turning a working relationship into a personal one could only spell disaster.

And, anyway, it was wrong to assume that Jake even *wanted* a personal relationship with her. A hot and fast seduction in a hotel room didn't usually pave the way to something deeper and more meaningful, did it? Was sex all that he wanted from her? If it was, then it was nothing less than an insult—because she was sure he could get that from any woman.

Realising how close she had come to throwing away something precious—namely her self-respect—Caitlin flung Jake's hand away and straightened her T-shirt. As she did so her heartbeat accelerated so hard she was momentarily dizzy. Seeing the spasm of confusion in his eyes, she sensed tension of another kind radiating from his body.

'What's wrong?' he ground out.

'I'm not going to sleep with you, Jake.'

'Sleeping isn't exactly what I had in mind.'

His words made her flinch. Her body hadn't stopped aching for him, and her mouth throbbed and burned from his unbelievably passionate kisses, but the idea that he would bed her simply just to 'scratch an itch' hurt her deeply. Having already had the soul-destroying experience of being used by a man, she wasn't about to set herself up to play the same old destructive tape again...

'All right, then, let me put it this way.' Impatiently she pushed back a drifting strand of hair from the side of her face to unwaveringly meet his gaze. 'I'm not going to have sex with you. I won't jeopardise my relationship with the band and neither will I be used by you because I happen to be "convenient". And, contrary to what you might believe, I didn't come here tonight because I had something personal in mind. All I wanted was a little reassurance because I was nervous about the performance tomorrow.'

Jake cursed softly beneath his breath. His disturbing blue eyes raked over her features, pinning her to the spot. It was clear to Caitlin that he was immersed in a deep inner tussle between utilising his common sense and trying to curtail his desire. Like her, he was still reeling from the throes of the incendiary passion they'd ignited. There was a thin film of sweat on his brow and it was evident he was still turned on. With the fulfilment of his desire evidently thwarted, now he was frustrated and angry as well as aroused.

'Is that what you think? That I'd take advantage and use you just because I wanted sex?' A muscle flexed warningly in the side of his exquisitely carved cheekbone. 'If you think that then I seriously underestimated you, Caitlin. You've listened to all the less than flattering stories about me, bought them as fact, and condemned me even though I told you the truth about what happened between me and my ex. Don't you remember that it was *my* reputation that got dragged through the mud because of the lies she wrote in that blasted article? *Not* hers?'

Caitlin hardly knew what to say. Was she guilty of judging Jake without trial? Without even giving him the chance to prove his character? After all, it wasn't just him that had suddenly found himself driven by the libidinous desires of the body. She was in exactly the same position!

Sighing, he agitatedly drove through his fingers through his already mussed hair.

'Anyway, perhaps you'd better just leave before my "questionable" character contaminates you even more. You'd better get home and get some rest. You know what's ahead of you tomorrow and I want you to be at your best.'

Her heart almost thudded to a stop. Tomorrow *would* be a big day…perhaps the most important one of her life so far. It was a shame that she'd spoiled things by coming over to Jake's and starting something she couldn't finish.

'I'm sorry that I—that I…'

'Don't beat yourself up about it. You're going to be just fine, Caitlin. That's what you want to know, isn't it? All you have to do is concentrate on the songs, the music. Blue Sky is a great band and they'll be helping you every step of the way. It's not going to be as hard as you imagine. Trust me. You've got a great voice and you're a stunning-looking girl. In terms of fulfilling the criteria for success in this business, you've got it all. You can't fail.'

If Jake had meant to reassure her he'd done it in a strangely reticent way. Caitlin still felt ill at ease. Plus she could easily sense the anger that simmered beneath his thin veneer of civility.

'I was going to say that I was sorry for—' Blushing, she was unable to complete the sentence when he was all but eating her up with his eyes.

'Turning me on?'

'I think I should go.'

'As much as it pains me to agree with you, you're probably right. Though that doesn't mean I wish you weren't.'

His words taunted her as Caitlin turned and fumbled with the bolt on the door. Then she fled from the room with a breathless 'goodnight' before she could change her mind.

Right then it was tempting for Jake to search for solace in the bottle of bourbon he had opened, but he couldn't fool himself that it would help. He'd been through enough heartache in his life already to think that it would.

His ex's wasn't the only betrayal he had endured. His mother had given him up for adoption when she'd found herself pregnant at just sixteen, and the home where she had placed Jake hadn't been able to find him adoptive parents due to his having a heart murmur. He had been in and out of hospital from birth up until he was eight years old for regular check-ups, by which time he had become quite used to being a bit of a loner. As he'd grown up and become stronger physically the heart murmur had corrected itself and he had resigned himself to living in the children's home until he reached sixteen.

Jake hadn't viewed it as a negative thing because by necessity it had taught him to be self-reliant. *The only friends he had depended on had been his books.* He had developed an insatiable curiosity about the world and had genuinely enjoyed reading and studying. Having done well in his exams, he'd managed to get himself a place at college, and then he'd found himself at university, studying cultural anthropology.

It was during that time that he had also developed an abiding interest in music. Jake's time at college and university had been his saving grace—along with a couple of genuinely caring and interested tutors who had encouraged him to go for his dreams and never to give them up.

Now, he stalked across the thickly carpeted floor and threw open the window onto the night. He was definitely in need of some fresh air. A fierce gust of wind hit him straight in the face, startling him, but it didn't remotely leech any of the heat from his body. *He knew himself to be too far gone for that.*

Even though Caitlin had left, he still burned from their passionate embrace. It was as though every nerve in his body throbbed with electricity and tension. Taking a cold shower was the obvious answer to try and ease his discomfort—but, frankly, it would be like putting a plaster on a third-degree burn. No…Jake would just have to wait it out. At least that or wait for some degree of common sense to return.

Caitlin Ryan had turned his whole world upside down. Here they were, at the start of the band's tour, and he had fallen like a ton of bricks for their new lead singer. He wouldn't go so far as to fool himself that he was in love with her—more *in lust*—but he was aware that one or two quick hot tumbles in bed were never going to be enough to satisfy the bone-deep yearning he had developed for her. Not for one moment had he meant for such a thing to happen, but somehow, in some way, Caitlin had got into Jake's blood and there wasn't much he could do about it.

How in hell was he supposed to keep a clear head and do all the things he normally had to do to help support and motivate the band? Get them out on the road with all guns blazing? Just seeing her every night for the next six weeks up on stage was going to be the sweetest torture. He already had to feel sorry for Rick and the others, because his mood sure as hell wasn't going to improve if he couldn't touch Caitlin in the way he ached to touch her. He'd either end up

having to take religious vows or quit managing the band.
Either way, his libido was definitely going to come under
some serious duress.

The first shock Caitlin had received on reaching London was
the discovery that she was going to be put up in Jake's flat
in Chelsea for the two nights they were there. It had turned
out that the rest of the band all had homes in the capital, including Rick. But Jake had quickly vetoed his friend's suggestion that Caitlin stay with him.

It had been too late for her to protest at the arrangement
and organise an alternative, so she'd kept her doubts to herself and agreed. The most important thing was the coming
performance, and she absolutely had to make a good impression…for *all* their sakes. But when they'd arrived at the fairly
compact popular West London venue, Caitlin had found herself having to change into her stage gear in the ladies' room,
because by the time they'd rehearsed, done a sound-check
and had a meeting with the venue manager there had been
no time to go back to Jake's place and get ready.

Frowning into one of the less than pristine mirrors, she
had applied her make-up with a thumping heart and trembling hand, inadvertently spilling the contents of her make-
up bag into the porcelain sink when she'd yanked out a tissue
too hard to pat her lipstick dry with.

Now she stood in the wings with the rest of the band,
feeling a bit like a little girl playing dress-up in her mother's best clothes, only partially tuning in to Rick's animated
pep talk as he paced up and down in front of them, like an
army sergeant pumping up his platoon for battle. In front
of the small raised stage the crowd had swelled and the anticipation that crackled in the air was not dissimilar to the
lightning strike before a torrential downpour.

There was a rumour going round that many of Blue Sky's
fans who had supported them from the beginning with Marcie had turned up to support the band's return, in spite of

their disappointment that she had walked out. Naturally Caitlin fretted that she would never pass muster.

Rick had told her that her style was quite different from Marcie's but that that was a *good* thing. Her strong vocal suited the band's music perfectly. *Like a match made in heaven,* he had assured her with a smile. But, while she welcomed the compliment, and was glad that the relative intimacy of the venue was perhaps not as intimidating as a much larger one might have been, her stomach was sick with nerves at the thought of being put through the ultimate baptism of fire for a new singer.

And where was Jake? He had been with them up until about half an hour ago, when he'd murmured something about 'last-minute arrangements' then disappeared. Caitlin found that now, when it came to the crunch, she needed his assurance more than ever.

'Is everyone okay?'

And suddenly he was there, his grin lighting up the dim little space to the side of the stage like a beacon shining in the dark, his misty blue eyes immediately seeking her out as though it was implicitly understood that she was the one who needed his assurance the most.

'You look terrific,' he told her.

Even as he spoke, Jake was thinking that she looked much better than that. *She looked nothing less than drop-dead gorgeous.* The purple velvet top she had selected on their shopping trip clung to her body in all the right places and her long black skirt skimmed the flat plane of her stomach and the soft swell of her hips as though it had been exclusively designed for her shape and her shape alone. Inevitably, his blood headed immediately south. Even if Caitlin couldn't sing a note, the men in the crowd were going to give her a lot of rope and that was a fact. It heartened him to know that they were all going to be pleasantly surprised.

'Trust me. You haven't got a thing to worry about. Just go out there and sing like you do in rehearsals, but even better.

If you get nervous, then just focus on me…I'll be out front as soon as you get onstage.'

'Okay. I'll do that… I can do that.' Caitlin managed to summon up a smile from only God knew where.

Eager to add his own brand of reassurance, Rick ran his hands up and down the sides of her slim arms and planted a sound kiss on her cheek. 'Just for luck, beautiful…not that you're going to need it.'

She barely opened her eyes during the first few bars of the opening number. It was much easier to simply shut out the sight of the crowd so that she could sing. She had been taken aback by the vociferous welcome they'd received from the fans when they walked onto the stage, somehow not expecting it to be quite as effusive as it had been. They didn't know her yet, and Caitlin had a lot to prove…

However, she was quickly swept away by the music and the need to sing, and as the wall of sound crashed over her she patted her thigh in time with the beat and started to enjoy herself. She was sure that performing in front of an audience must be an even bigger adrenaline rush than shooting rapids, and nothing had ever felt so right or so perfect.

That was when she finally opened her eyes. *That was when she saw Jake…*

He was clapping along with the rest of the crowd, watchful and silently assessing, his features so handsome and compelling that several women in the audience furtively glanced his way whether they were with someone or not. Releasing a long breath, Caitlin gave him a brief smile, then turned her attention back to the avid sea of faces in front of her.

Many people were capturing her and the band with their mobile phone cameras. She could almost feel the tangible sense of surprise in the air, the pleasure—and beneath the cool black satin of her long flowing skirt her legs couldn't help trembling. Steve Bridges gave her an extra drumroll to indicate his approval, and to her left Mike Casey muttered low, for her ears only, 'You're going to have them eating out of your hands, Cait.'

And she *did*. By the time they'd finished the final number of the night the crowd was with her all the way, cheering and clapping and stamping their feet for more. As baptisms of fire went, Caitlin couldn't have wished for a more favourable flame.

Backstage, she ran the gauntlet of well-wishers, road crew and fans alike, arriving in the small room the band had been allocated to more back-slapping, applause and champagne…courtesy of Jake. She barely registered the burst of bubbles on her tongue because everything felt so surreal. However, she *did* register the satisfying feel of Jake's strong arm wound possessively round her waist.

If anybody speculated on the 'extra-special' attention she was getting, no one dared voice it—least of all Rick, who was watching them with a stern 'headmaster' scowl as he bellowed to no one in particular that he needed another beer and *fast*.

Outside, as the venue emptied and the road crew loaded the van with Blue Sky's equipment—'Tank' and Dave, stalwarts of the industry, who had worked with Jake many times before—Rick pulled Caitlin aside as she was about to step up and get into Jake's familiar black car.

Jake had given her his keys and told her he wouldn't be long. He was still inside, checking arrangements for the following night when they would play their second and final London gig. There would be an even bigger crowd the next night, he'd told her, because the press would have got wind of her performance via the comments posted on social media sites and would come to check it out.

As Caitlin stood waiting to hear what Rick had to say, right on cue it started to rain.

'Is something the matter?' she asked warily.

'I don't know. You tell me.'

'Now you're being cryptic.' She started to smile, but straight away saw Rick wasn't in the mood to be placated.

'Is something going on between you and Jake?' he demanded.

Her stomach plummeted to her boots.

'And don't tell me you don't know what I mean.'

His hazel eyes were accusing and his shaggy blond hair was beginning to wave even more in the rain. Tugging up the collar of her raincoat, Caitlin shuddered.

It had been an amazing night. She had not only overcome her trepidation at singing in public, she had really begun to live her dream. She was bursting to talk to Lia and tell her all about it. Up until just a moment ago she'd wanted to shout out her news to the whole world. *I did it! I really am a singer in a bona fide rock band!* But now, as she gazed anxiously back at Rick, she felt as though someone had got a pin and deliberately popped her balloon.

'There's nothing going on between me and Jake other than him looking out for me and helping me settle in…with the band, I mean.'

'We can't afford another screw-up after the Marcie debacle. If you end up walking out on everyone because you got too involved with Jake then it will have serious implications for the band. I don't think they deserve that after all their hard work…do you?'

'No. Of course I don't.'

Caitlin knew what Rick was saying was only right, and she had no intention of letting anyone down. Just because Jake had put his arm round her when she'd come off stage and bought champagne to celebrate it didn't mean that the man was any more trustworthy than Sean. She had already intuited that f she had a physical relationship with him then her heart would seriously be at risk—because any woman with an ounce of common sense could easily see that he wasn't the type of man to commit to anything more meaningful. And Caitlin wasn't the type of woman to be intimate with a man and then forget it…as if were no more important than a trip to the hairdresser…

She lifted her chin. 'Don't worry, Rick. I promise you that the band comes first. Besides, I'm not looking to get personally involved with anyone.'

Liar. Nobody wanted to be alone for ever. And she wasn't the only girl in the world who hoped to find love again after the heartache of a failed relationship.

'Then we understand each other?' Rick reached out his hand to wipe away a raindrop glistening on her cheek.

'Understand what, exactly?' a deep male voice intoned.

CHAPTER EIGHT

JAKE HAD WALKED up behind them. Straight away you could have cut the tension with a knife. Caitlin found herself wishing she hadn't agreed to stay the night at his flat. If it was going to make things this awkward between the two men, then she'd see if she could locate a cheap hotel for herself.

When neither she nor Rick rushed to answer his question, the glance he gave them was searing.

'I said, *understand what*, exactly? We'll stand here all night in the rain if we have to, until I get an answer.'

Rick hefted a sigh. 'Okay, Jake, if you really want to know then I'll tell you. I was warning Cait about getting personally involved with you. Just a few weeks ago Marcie walked out, leaving us high and dry. By great good fortune and the gods of rock and roll we found Caitlin. The last thing we need is to screw up the band's chances because she might get hurt by you and end up leaving the band.'

'I won't leave the band—I told you!'

Exasperated and embarrassed, Caitlin wanted to shake Rick. Did he really think she was so naïve that she'd risk the fantastic opportunity she'd been given to sing with the band in favour of a fleeting romance with Jake? As far as she was concerned she was in Blue Sky for the long haul, whatever happened.

Jake also looked exasperated. 'If there's anything personal between me and Caitlin then that's where it stays… between the *two* of us. We're both agreed that the welfare of the band comes first. I've been in this business long enough to know where my priorities lie. Now, it's been a long night, and Caitlin ought to get some rest if she's going to give another good performance tomorrow.'

'Under the circumstances, perhaps she'd better stay at my place instead?' His jaw clenched, Rick defied the taller man to give him an argument.

But Jake wasn't having any of it.

'I've given you my decision, and as far as I'm concerned it doesn't need debating.' With a ferocious scowl he grabbed the car keys out of Caitlin's hand and shouldered past her.

She stared at the other man. 'Why did you have to go and say that?'

'Because somebody has to look out for you, sweetheart. Jake is my best buddy, as well as my boss, but the truth is he doesn't have the best track record where women are concerned. Apart from with his ex—a relationship which probably scarred him for life—he doesn't go in for long relationships. I'm sure you know what I mean? And you're not like any of the other girls he's been with. You're sensitive, for a start. If you get too involved with him and he dumps you, you won't be able to take it on the chin and simply put it down to experience.'

'And what about you, Rick? Have *you* got a better track record? Anyway, contrary to opinion, I'm quite capable of taking care of myself. This is like a dream come true for me, to sing with this band, and I don't intend to mess it up, believe me.'

Behind them Jake started up the car's engine. Glancing round, Caitlin found his unsettling blue gaze blazing back at her through the windscreen.

She turned back to Rick. 'I've got to go.'

Saying no more, she walked to the car and got in without a word. She was still fumbling with her seatbelt when the vehicle pulled away from the kerb with a loud squeal of rubber on Tarmac.

* * *

Jake made a final check on Caitlin where she slept in his bedroom…*in his bed*…and then quietly closed the door behind him. In the large and airy living room, with the blinds pulled down and the blond oak floor cool beneath his feet, he dropped down onto a futon-style armchair. Then he leaned back to stare broodingly up at the ceiling.

Rick had no right, warning Caitlin not to get involved with him. What the hell did his friend think he was doing? Had Jake ever interfered in Rick's many and varied 'relationships'? No—he'd stood back and watched the fall out so many times it wasn't funny. *But then Rick wasn't contemplating having a hot, steamy affair with the band's gorgeous new singer, was he?*

Jake was only too aware that if he went ahead and had an affair with Caitlin it would be an extremely foolish and risky thing to do, with perhaps irreparable consequences. If he had any respect for the guys in the band—*and he had that in spades*—he shouldn't even be considering it. But then he hadn't achieved the success he had enjoyed by *not* taking risks. He wasn't setting out to break Caitlin's heart, but if they did get involved for a while he'd make it clear that he was only responding to an undeniable physical attraction that he couldn't resist.

If she felt the same then there wouldn't be a problem. If she *didn't* then Jake would simply have to put the whole thing down to experience and do his best to turn away from her in that department. Although God knew it wouldn't be easy.

Maybe once upon a time he'd nurtured a secret hope that he'd find a girl, settle down and eventually raise a family, but that hope hadn't survived for long. *Jodie had seen to that.* He didn't know if he would ever trust another woman again.

Having had a mother who had abandoned him was bad enough. Discovering that his wife had been having an affair—and with someone who had such a high profile that the press would have a field-day—Jake hadn't had a prayer of protecting himself. Especially not when, in typically mercenary fashion, Jodie had concocted a vindictive story about their marriage and given the media carte blanche to say what the hell they liked about him. *He wasn't in a hurry to get burned a second time.*

Blowing out a breath, he let his jaded gaze take inventory of his surroundings. The fashionable and expensive apartment might be just a stone's throw from the King's Road in Chelsea, but its distinctly minimalist decor and general air of emptiness were testament to the fact that he was hardly ever there. Since leaving the children's home all those years ago he'd been regularly on the move—never staying in one place for any notable length of time.

Helplessly, he found his thoughts returning to Caitlin. If he was frank with her—made it clear that he was one of life's gypsies and wasn't looking for anything long-term or permanent—would she yield her body and a little of her time until the flames of desire they ignited together burned themselves out? And afterwards would they still be able to maintain a working relationship, see each other every day and have no regrets?

'You're a real prize, Jake Sorenson. You know that?'

Despising himself, because what he was prepared to offer her wasn't really very much at all, he pushed to his feet and paced the floor, restless and on edge because the woman he was crazy about was sleeping just a few feet away from him in the next room…in *his* bed…*alone*.

She had barely said a word to him when he'd brought her back to the flat. She had simply looked at him with those soulful green eyes of hers and made a polite comment that the flat was 'really beautiful', then walked round the living room examining every single print that decorated the walls as if fascinated.

They were mostly artistic photographic prints of well-known music artists Jake had worked with, along with one or two high-profile fashion models who had worked on video shoots. As Caitlin had studied them it had become eminently clear to him that not one of them could hold a candle to her.

He should have told her how beautiful she'd looked tonight, how great she'd done, that she'd made them all proud. But he had been too keyed up because he'd been fighting to keep the lid on his attraction. And Rick's warning had kept going round and round in his head like a mantra that was hard to shut out. So they'd had a cup of coffee, some brief conversation about nothing very much, and then he'd shown her into the bedroom.

It hadn't just been him and the band who had loved her performance tonight. The audience had loved her too. But, drawing on his extensive experience, Jake knew it wasn't all going to be plain sailing. Audiences were notoriously fickle until they really got to know a band, and they'd encounter all sorts on this tour before it was finished. *There would be criticisms, too.* Jake just hoped that Caitlin could handle them.

But there was no doubt in his mind that, with her talent and beauty, Blue Sky could win themselves a prestigious recording contract. As long as they were consistently able to come up with the goods he had the contacts and the know-how to help make all their dreams come true. *Except maybe his own...*

Once again his thoughts turned to the beautiful girl asleep in his bed. She was a dark-haired enchantress, with a face and a body that could enslave *any* man, and Jake had undoubtedly fallen under her spell. Cursing beneath his breath, he headed determinedly towards the bathroom and a long, cold, hopefully passion-killing shower.

The distinct sound of music playing disturbed him. For a few moments Jake just lay still, staring up at the ceiling. He was lying on the rarely used spare bed in the flat's guest room, but he'd phoned ahead to the caretaking agency he used for someone to come in and tidy the place and make up the beds with fresh sheets before they arrived.

Blinking away his disorientation as he properly came to, he realised that the radio was playing in the kitchen. *Caitlin.* She must be up and about. At the thought of the woman who had given him yet another sleepless night he groaned and propped himself up on his elbow. Then he dragged the fingers of his free hand through his tousled dark hair.

Glancing down at the distinctive bulge beneath the sheet, Jake released a long, slow breath. Jumping out of bed straight away wasn't an option when he was so heavily and obviously aroused. Better that he wait for a few minutes and concentrate his thoughts on something either mundane or unpleasant to help dispel the heat in his groin. But that was no easy task, with Caitlin beginning to join in the chorus of the song on the radio, her sexy tones making him tingle all over just as if she were lying next to him, crooning softly into his ear.

A few moments later she was knocking at his door. 'Jake, are you up yet? I've made you a cup of tea.'

Caitlin sounded so damn cheerful that he wanted to get up, drag her inside, throw her down on the bed and have his wicked way with her without further ado.

He released another heartfelt groan.

'That word doesn't get mentioned round here in the morning. I'm strictly a coffee man,' he grumbled, plumping up his pillow and jamming it behind his back.

'No problem. I can just as easily make you some coffee. How do you like it?'

'Hot, dark and sultry, with a little bit of sugar...just like my women.'

'I see you've recovered your sense of humour...'

'Apparently I have.'

Jake couldn't believe he was having this conversation through a closed door. He glared at the offending wood panel as if his gaze had the power to burn a hole through it.

From the other side Caitlin remarked brightly, 'By the way, thanks for giving up your bed to me. I hope you were comfortable too. Did you sleep all right?'

What a question!

He rubbed a hand round his beard-roughened jaw. Rocks on the desert floor couldn't have been more uncomfortable. He'd tossed and turned so much that he felt every single day of his thirty-six years this morning. *And little Miss Hole-in-her-Stocking wasn't helping, with her cheery wide-awake tone that conveyed she'd slept like a baby...*

'No, I didn't,' he growled.

There was no response.

For a few moments Jake thought his guest had returned to the kitchen. Then, to his surprise, the door opened and she walked into the bedroom. Wearing tight faded jeans, and a loose-fitting white T-shirt with clearly no bra underneath it, Caitlin fixed him with a tentative gaze. A soft flush suffused her cheeks when the corners of his mouth crooked upwards in a smile.

'Something wrong?' he asked huskily.

'You said that you didn't sleep?'

The way she said it let him know she was concerned, guilty, or both. It was too good an opportunity to waste and Jake wasn't a man who ever let a good opportunity sail by without grabbing onto it.

'Yeah...I might just stay put for a while longer and catch up a little.'

Caitlin couldn't take her eyes off Jake's heavenly chest. He was all lean, rippling muscle, rock-hard stomach and tanned flesh. With his sexy tousled hair and sleepy-eyed expression, the man was as handsome and seductive as a mythical warrior. And what did she think she was doing, daring to come into his room and stare at him as if she'd come to pay homage to one of the gods?

It was perhaps inevitable that he should pat the space

next to him in the luxurious bed and suggest, 'Why don't you come and join me?'

'I slept well. I don't need any more rest.'

'Did I mention rest?'

Caitlin swallowed hard. 'No, but…it doesn't look like there's a lot of room,' she said nervously.

Suddenly she was so aroused that it was impossible to pretend indifference. Jake was one sexy, charismatic specimen and she was only human. Could she help it if her neglected libido was nearing boiling point and needing resolution? Heat was already seeping up her thighs, between her legs, making her moist, while the sensitive tips of her nipples tingled painfully against her shirt.

'You underneath, me on top…how much room do we need?' Jake parried seductively, his blue eyes drowsy with desire. 'We can make it work.'

It was an outrageous suggestion and Caitlin didn't dare take him up on it…*did she?*

Glancing up at the faint morning light filtering through the slats of the rolled-down blinds, she was suddenly consumed by an avalanche of doubt. And not just doubt at her ability to get herself out of trouble when the situation demanded it, but at putting her common sense versus a desire so red-hot it was already burning her.

The sheer, unmitigated sensual tug of Jake sitting up in bed, with his chest bared and his eyes goading her towards something so deliciously sinful that it made her weak just thinking about it, was in the end too hard to resist.

With her heart thudding, she replied, 'I've never…I've never gone in for casual sex. I just wanted you to know that. Do you have some protection?'

He stared. 'I've got everything we need right here.'

Jake had known he'd finally lost his battle against temptation as soon as Caitlin had walked into the room. The longing to hold her in his arms and to know her intimately had finally overridden all sense of right and wrong.

He wasn't aiming to hurt either her or the band. He had too much respect for all of them for that. He was merely following an irresistible impulse that wouldn't be denied. That said, there would be nothing casual about sex between him and Caitlin. Even though she was gorgeous—the ultimate male fantasy come to life—Jake admired her for the courageous woman she was.

He sighed with pleasure. Beneath the thin protection of her virginal white shirt her aroused nipples were practically drilling a hole thought the material, and he knew that if he touched her at the apex between her delectable thighs she would be hot and ready for him straight away. The thought slowed and thickened the blood coursing through his veins. It was like being drip-fed with unadulterated honey. And he was so desperate for her, so hungry, that if she didn't soon join him he seriously thought he might explode.

Her hands were shaking as Caitlin undid the zipper on her jeans and stepped out of them. Then she nervously moved towards the edge of the bed, dressed in nothing but the T-shirt and white cotton panties. The scalding, hungry gaze that Jake pinned her with was so blatantly carnal she thought she would melt. No man had ever looked at her with such unfettered desire in his eyes before, with such wild, primitive heat.

Low-voiced, he murmured, 'Why don't you take off your shirt'

What's a girl to do? Caitlin thought wildly. Then simply did as he asked.

A carnal whirlpool had rolled over her, snatching her up in its maelstrom so completely that there was nothing she could do but give up struggling and let it carry her where it would.

Her movements were unknowingly sensual and provocative as she pulled her shirt over her head to remove it. Her full, perfectly rounded breasts with their dusky dark nipples jutted towards him and every delectable line and curve of her sexy body was revealed in all its glory. Her small, slender waist, the voluptuous swell of her hips and her smooth, shapely thighs all came under his hungry scrutiny as he gazed his fill.

When she finally removed the shirt and let it fall to the floor her flowing dark hair drifted silkily across her breasts and partially hid them from view.

'Shall I take these off too?' she asked shyly, indicating the white panties.

'No.' Jake reached towards her and pulled her firmly down onto the bed. 'That particular pleasure is going to be mine.'

With her hair spilling wildly across her face, Caitlin gulped down a shocked breath as he slid expert hands down over her hips and practically ripped off the flimsy underwear.

'Jake, I—' But whatever she'd intended saying next was cut off by the hot press of his mouth and the skilful invasion of his tongue seeking hers as his heavily aroused manhood pressed deeply into her soft belly.

Her senses were all but overwhelmed by his intoxicating heat and the erotic masculine scents of his body. One of his hands slid across her breast, rubbing and kneading the already inflamed nipple, nipping and squeezing until she gasped her pleasure into his mouth and bucked her hips against his. *It was clear they were singing from the same song-sheet.* His mouth closing over her nipple, Jake suckled hard and Caitlin whimpered her delight.

Lifting his head, he breathed, 'I've got to take care of something…'

Reaching across to a nearby chair, where he'd left his jeans, he delved into a pocket and withdrew a foil packet. He wasted no time in expertly tearing it open. Sheathed in the protection, Jake turned his attention back to Caitlin, kneeing her slim thighs apart to insert an explorative finger into her moist heat.

Even as she gasped, she knew she was more than ready for him, and was gratified when he positioned his sex and thrust assuredly inside her. Her thoughts utterly deserted her as she drowned in an ecstatic pleasure like no other she'd ever experienced. The sheer emotion she felt at the wonder of it caused her eyes to fill with tears. Then she cried out as Jake's mouth found the hollow between her neck and shoulder and bit her there.

His lips sought hers again and his kiss was deep and hard as he thrust into her mouth with his tongue even as his sex filled her and he felt her scalding satin heat engulf him. If he died right now he'd die happy. He'd never experienced pleasure or desire like it. Beneath him, Caitlin writhed and moaned, her breath released in hot little gasps that seared his skin, and when she raised her hips to welcome him even more deeply, and suddenly convulsed round him, she cried out for a second time and he saw that her beautiful emerald eyes were moist with tears. Her expression was stunned. She looked like a woman who had never experienced the full orgasmic impact of climax before.

The mere thought undid Jake. Within seconds he was thrusting even deeper, whispering against her ear how beautiful she was, how perfect. Then his own desire and need reached its crescendo and he was swept away on a cascade of a joy so fierce and so perfect that he had no words to describe it. In fact it stunned him to silence.

His blue eyes glittering with feeling, he manoeuvred himself carefully to lie down beside her and with his fingers gently traced the exquisite line of her jaw. 'Caitlin?'

'What?'

Jake was stroking her ear, securing a silken strand of long ebony hair behind it. Gazing back into the incandescent eyes that looked like bewitching green fire, he silently acknowledged that he'd never experienced such depth and strength of emotion lying with a woman before. He only knew that he had the sense of feeling strangely privileged.

'I think you're the most beautiful woman I've ever known.'

Even as his words lifted her spirits higher than they'd ever been lifted before, Caitlin was already missing the warm heavy press of his body. She wanted to tell him to come back, to love her again and never stop... Only the icy fronds of harsh reality swept through her like winter just then.

She thought, *But he doesn't love me, does he? All we enjoyed together just now was great sex.*

The fact that she'd never even got close to orgasm with Sean, and that more often than not she'd seen to her own needs after the event, would hardly register with Jake. Besides, a properly committed relationship wasn't what he was looking for, was it? They both knew that. When he stopped desiring her body Caitlin would just have to learn to concentrate all her energies on her singing and view him solely as Blue Sky's manager.

Could she do that? Could she cut off her emotions so easily when what had just taken place between her and Jake had been nothing less than earth-shattering? *Her whole world had been utterly changed forever.* Did he realise that just the merest touch from him was enough to set her on fire, to make her need him as much as she needed to breathe?

Glancing back into his steady blue gaze, she wondered how it was possible for a man to have such luxuriant long lashes and still be so incredibly masculine. Perhaps it was the hard, lean jaw, with that slight indentation in the chin, or was it the exquisitely shaped mouth with the slightly fuller lower lip? A mouth made for passion...for the erotic pleasures only shared by lovers.

Of course it went without saying that Jake must have had a few of those...perhaps more than Caitlin cared to know about. Right now the thought of even *one* was enough to make her heart jolt sickeningly.

'That's high praise, coming from a man like you,' she

answered, affecting a light, breezy tone to shield her true feelings from him.

He frowned. 'What do you mean, a man like me?'

'I just mean you must have known many beautiful women. I won't kid myself that I'm particularly special.'

Now his handsome visage looked perturbed. 'Hey. Why say that? Don't you know how much pleasure you've just given me? You mesmerise and intoxicate me, Caitlin. Sharing what we just shared was beyond wonderful.'

Caitlin couldn't help but smile—even as she came to a distressing conclusion about what she had to do for *both* their sakes.

'Thank you. I'm glad you think that. I thought so too. But now I think we should both come back down to earth, don't you?'

Lightly removing Jake's hand from where it lay across her stomach, she rolled over and leant down to pick up the clothes she'd discarded on the floor.

'Where do you think you're going?'

He sounded surprised, upset. Not immediately answering, Caitlin stepped into her panties, then got to her feet. She hurriedly pulled on her T-shirt and quickly got into her jeans, sensing him watching her broodingly.

'Are you going to tell me what's going on? Why the sudden urgency to get up when we can take our time? We can stay here all day if we want. There's no hurry.'

Combing back her hair with trembling fingers, she turned to face him.

'I suddenly came to my senses, that's all. Hopefully, now that we've got this out of our system, we can get back to normal and concentrate on work. I think we should both ensure that what happened between us won't happen again, Jake. From now on our relationship should be strictly about the band. Now that I'm clear about our priorities I'll go and get a quick shower and then make some coffee.' She started to move towards the door.

'Forget the damn coffee, woman!' Jake threw back the covers on the bed, to all intents and purposes coming after her. 'Come back here and get into bed.'

'Why?' Despite her resolution not to let herself down by crying, Caitlin knew her eyes were already filling with tears. 'So that I can be even more reckless and stupid than I've been already?'

When he didn't answer but instead shook his head, as if her outburst was totally incomprehensible, she flew out through the door without another word and headed determinedly for the bathroom.

CHAPTER NINE

I'M SORRY I didn't talk to you a bit more about how I felt. Silently rehearsing the words, Caitlin wished she'd said them out loud to Jake before he'd abruptly left the flat that morning to go God only knew where.

He'd barely acknowledged her when he got up, and when he'd emerged from the bathroom he'd simply told her he was going out for a while and slammed the door. His cold manner had made her want to curl up into a little ball and disappear. Even as he'd moved towards the door Caitlin had wanted to plead with him to stay.

It was evident that she'd soured things by getting out of bed and declaring that they should come back down to earth and concentrate on the band. Even though it was the sensible thing to do, the *right* thing, she knew it wouldn't make either of them happy. How could it, when the intensity of their lovemaking had clearly demonstrated how strong their attraction was? Would doing the right thing help them to deny it?

Weary with going over the same ground over and over again without resolution, she diverted her restless energy with undertaking a little light cleaning round the flat. Although it was obvious that the fashionably minimalist living quarters barely needed it, to Caitlin's mind it was better to do *something* rather than sit there twiddling her thumbs and worrying herself sick about what had happened.

She would never regret their lovemaking. How could she ever regret revelling in the joy of being a woman, in the power of her body to give and receive such mind-blowing pleasure as she had done with Jake? Their brief union had stirred feelings and emotions long buried, and she couldn't be angry about that. Not when her body still glowed and throbbed with the attention he'd given her.

And even if he hadn't been motivated by love, the truth was…Caitlin *had*. There was no longer any point in denying it.

Locating a vacuum cleaner and duster, she cleaned the flat to within an inch of its life. When all the surfaces gleamed to her satisfaction, and the living room sang with the scent of beeswax, she opened the windows to allow fresh air to circulate. Then she went into the kitchen to make herself some toast and coffee.

Her appetite taken care of, she retreated to the living room to browse a lone copy of a glossy music magazine. Her attention was immediately caught by an interesting little snippet ringed in red. It was all about Jake.

What's former music promoter and artist supremo Jake Sorenson up to these days? Rumour has it he's gone back to his roots and is managing a tight little foursome called Blue Sky. After the lead songstress Marcie Wallace recently walked out, a little bird told yours truly that the search is on for a dazzling new diva to replace her.

All we know is that she'll have to be pretty exceptional to meet Jake's well-known exacting standards. Remember that this is the man who made his fortune bringing world-class bands Soft Rain and The Butterfly Net to prominence, then dropped out into self-imposed obscurity for five years after a vindictive exposé by his ex, Jodie Parks.

Knowing Mr Sorenson's famed proclivity for discovering matchless talent, we'd seriously advise watching this space…

'"Dazzling diva"? Are they serious?'

Chewing anxiously on the inside of her cheek, Caitlin dropped the magazine onto the small mahogany table as though she'd suddenly been burnt. Because the idea of her being a diva in any shape or form was preposterous.

She leant back into the cream-coloured futon and gathered a cushion close to try and absorb the shock and disbelief that rolled through her. Yes, she'd made a good start with the band—she'd dipped her toe in the water and got her feet wet, and the enthusiastic reception from the audience last night had been more, *much* more than she'd hoped for. But could she come up with the goods night after night for the next three weeks without letting herself and the others down?

Her fingers tentatively stroked down the sensitive skin of her throat. She'd have to seriously think about taking better care of her voice, for one thing. That aside, her most pressing thought right now was Jake. Where on earth had he got to? Was he still mad at her for deserting him so abruptly this morning?

It stunned her to realise that she was in love with him. She hadn't been in the market for a relationship and hadn't intended to be for a very long time. But then she'd never dreamed fate would bring a man like Jake into her life. A man who one minute wanted her as much as he wanted to take his next breath and the next…

Her insides knotted anxiously, and because the feeling so unsettled her she jumped up and went in search of some window cleaner and a cloth and started to clean the windows.

'What the hell do you think you're doing?'

Caitlin nearly fell off the chair she was precariously balanced on. Even with its aid, the glass corners of the window frame were particularly tricky to get to. But it was hard to believe she'd been so absorbed that she'd somehow blotted out the sound of Jake's key in the door and had therefore been unprepared for his appearance.

She turned to observe him. 'What does it look like I'm doing?'

'You'd better get down from there before you break your neck!'

Before she could react Jake had moved across to her and caught her by the waist. Then he unceremoniously hoisted her off the chair. Caitlin felt her face flame red.

'Stop treating me like a child, will you? I'm perfectly capable of cleaning a few windows without supervision.'

'That might be the case, but who in hell asked you to clean the windows in the first place? I hire someone from a cleaning firm to do that. I hired *you* to sing in a band, not become my domestic.'

Jake glanced impatiently around him and Caitlin saw him register the spotless parquet floor, the plumped-up cushions on his easy chairs and futon, the shining glass on his framed prints. Aware that his hands still lingered at the sides of her waist, she wished her heart wouldn't beat quite so fast—because his touch was already making her feel weak.

'I can't help it' She shrugged, 'I always clean when I get tense. I can't stand inactivity…not having something to do.' Her teeth clamped down on her lip.

'I see.'

Beneath his impenetrable glare, she felt like a small child being told off by her parent.

Because she was nervous, she remarked thoughtlessly, 'By the way, I notice that you don't have many personal photos around?'

As soon as the words were out Caitlin wanted the floor to open up and swallow her.

Jake's expression was immediately dismayed. 'If by "personal photos" you mean of family, then you know very well that I don't have any.'

Her insides turned over. 'I…I'm so sorry I said that. I was just nervous. But personal photos could equally mean friends. Didn't you have any close pals when you were young?'

When he didn't immediately comment, she felt as if the hole she'd just dug herself had got even deeper.

'You mean at the children's home? Not really.'

His tone was chillingly matter-of-fact. Caitlin knew she should steer the conversation away from his heartbreaking childhood as quickly as possible, but care and concern for him made her not want to shy away from it.

'Do you mind if I ask how you came to grow up in a children's home, Jake?'

'My mother gave me up because she was just sixteen when she fell pregnant with me and in her wisdom decided to have me adopted. Only I *wasn't* adopted. I was hard to place because I was born with a heart murmur. The people at the children's home told me that most interested adoptive parents were wary of taking on a sick baby.' Shrugging, he shaped his lips into a sardonic smile. 'Not that I minded… it was their loss. As I grew older I realised what an asset it was to be left alone by people. I learned to enjoy my own company, to pursue my own interests without interference.'

Caitlin stared, trying hard to assimilate everything she'd heard. 'And what about the heart murmur? Do you still see a doctor or specialist?'

'No. I grew out of it. It got better all by itself. It hasn't been an issue since I was young. Anyway, are you going to tell me what's making you so tense, or do I have to guess?'

Suddenly impatient, he relieved her of the scrunched-up cleaning rag she was still holding onto and threw it onto the window ledge.

As Caitlin fought hard to marshal her thoughts, Jake sucked in a breath and let it out again slowly. 'I don't want you to worry about what happened between us.'

'I'm not. I mean, I was just…I was just…'

He held up his hand to indicate she should stop talking. His blue eyes glittered. 'Hear me out. I don't want you to worry about it because I don't regret a damn thing. And, contrary to what you might think, I'm not going to pretend it never happened.'

A warm rush climbed into her chest. The anxiety that had propelled her into her frenetic cleaning bout slowly subsided, leaving her with a sense of joy so acute she couldn't resist the smile that tugged at her lips.

He didn't regret it... That surely had to signify something, didn't it?

'However,' he continued, 'even though I won't pretend it never happened, I agree we can't risk a repeat performance. You were right when you said we should concentrate on the band.'

Caitlin's brief joy was quickly replaced by crushing disappointment. It was so intense that it was as though all the breath had been brutally sucked from her lungs.

'You think that's the best idea?' she murmured.

'It's not because I don't want us to be together again like we were this morning...'

Capturing her wrist, Jake firmly wove his fingers through her own. His misty blue eyes mesmerised her, and she saw that he was hungry for her again—and yet it was clear he was furious with himself. She suddenly realised that he didn't *want* to desire her so much, and was furious because she was hardly helping him to resist.

'You got into this because you wanted to realise a dream,' he went on. 'One day soon this band is going to be very successful...that is if we're all committed to the same goal. If you and I don't maintain a professional relationship then the whole thing could fall apart. I think that would be a great shame, don't you?'

She wasn't going to disagree. With a brief nod she dropped her gaze. To her surprise, Jake released her hand, slid his fingers beneath her jaw and lifted her chin.

'I've been to see Rick and I've arranged to stay over at his place tonight. You can stay here. Treat the place as if it was your own. I'll be over to pick you up at about six. We'll do a sound-check and run through the playlist. Tomorrow, when we go to Brighton, I've booked you into a separate hotel from the rest of us—a much nicer hotel, because you deserve a little luxury. All in all, I think the arrangement is for the best.'

Caitlin swallowed hard.

'Why? Don't you trust me, Jake? I'd much rather be in the same hotel as everyone else. Do you think that because we made love I'm going to make a nuisance of myself?'

Hurt cramping her throat, she pulled out of his grasp and strode across to the other side of the room. Folding her arms, she stared blankly up at a large photographic print of a beautiful redhead. The sight of it made her even sadder when she remembered that there weren't any more personal photos around because Jake had no family. It broke her heart to think that he'd grown up without someone to love him.

'Are you crazy?' he ground out. 'It's *me* I don't trust. It's like I told you before—I have a job to do and a little bit of distance wouldn't be a bad thing right now…at least when we're not working together.'

Everything he said made the utmost sense, but it didn't prevent Caitlin from feeling desperately disappointed. Hope was futile, she realised. She didn't have a right to hope for anything as far as Jake Sorenson was concerned. And thank goodness at least one of them was taking charge of the situation. Of *course* it was right that the band should come first.

Wasn't her passion for music and singing the reason she had auditioned in the first place? It certainly hadn't been because she was looking for another relationship. And she was sure she wasn't looking for some 'on-off' hot little liaison with Blue Sky's charismatic manager. The sooner she let Jake see that she wasn't going to waste her time crying over spilt milk, the better.

'It sounds like you've taken care of everything. Good. I

can't say I'm not glad about that. Rick was right when he said it would a bad idea, making things personal between us.'

'Leave Rick out of this' with a grim scowl Jake walked angrily towards her. 'What's between you and me is nobody's business but our own. You got that?'

What could Caitlin do beneath that frosty glare but acquiesce? Even if what he had just said contradicted everything he'd said previously. Their relationship *wasn't* just their own business—wasn't that the point? Blue Sky had a vested interest in her not having a personal relationship with their manager. They were probably concerned that Jake would break her heart and she would end up leaving the band…just as Marcie had.

Perhaps it really *was* for the best if Caitlin and Jake pretended that their passionate liaison hadn't happened after all. If Jake could be cool about it then she would just have to learn to do the same.

That night, having heard positive feedback about Blue Sky's performance the previous night, the music press turned out in force. Onstage, determinedly giving her all, Caitlin had had to contend with flashbulbs popping in her face at regular intervals and backstage afterwards it was even worse.

A huge number of people had squeezed into a room not much bigger than a cloakroom. The atmosphere was hot, stuffy and claustrophobic, and the smell of alcohol mingled liberally with the accumulated heat of bodies pressing in too close. All she really wanted to do was to get back to Jake's flat and escape.

The sense of panic that gripped her had taken her by surprise, and she'd more or less clammed up when too many questions had been catapulted her way by over-zealous reporters who barely gave her even a second to answer them. If it hadn't been for Jake, dealing with their questions with cool professionalism, as well as Rick protecting her from the crush, Caitlin would have fled in a heartbeat—never mind that publicity *any* publicity…was meant to be good.

Mid-morning the next day found her sitting in the foyer of the old-fashioned seafront hotel in Brighton that Jake had booked the band into, delicately hiding a yawn behind her hand as Rick and Jake conversed with the desk clerk. The rest of the band members were out on the small square patio, chatting. Caitlin stifled another guilty yawn as she watched them.

'Are we keeping you awake, Cait?'

Taking her by surprise, Rick gave her shoulder an affectionate squeeze, then dropped down beside her on the padded seat, stirring the air around them with the musky scent of his cologne.

'I couldn't sleep last night.' Shrugging her shoulders in the faded denim jacket she wore over a blue maxi-dress, she attempted a smile.

'Excitement keeping you up, huh?'

Rick was grinning, and she saw her companion's astute hazel eyes were curious. 'Something like that,' Caitlin replied.

Let him think that, she decided. It was a lot less complicated than confessing that she'd been missing Jake. That her body had been aching for him all night.

She would swear that she'd tossed and turned from midnight to dawn because she needed him so much. No wonder she felt as if she could sleep for England this morning!

Jake had bunked down over at Rick's, and the Chelsea flat had been soulless and empty without him. Even last night's undoubted success and the ensuing interest from the press hadn't been able to console her.

Was it really so wrong that she should want Jake as badly as she did? Her gaze helplessly gravitated towards him as he leant casually back against the reception desk, his glance sweeping thoughtfully over her and Rick. Today, his long legs were encased in faded black denim, a leather belt with a buckle was slung low on his tight, lean hips and his leather jacket was folded casually across one arm. His expression made her heart turn over. She wondered if he'd had similar trouble getting to sleep last night.

As his searching glance deliberately sought hers Caitlin sensed the hot sizzle from the contact erupt in her belly like a flare.

'We've got a few things lined up for today, but perhaps you can catch up on some rest later on, before the gig tonight.'

With her face warmly glowing, Caitlin guiltily turned her attention back to Rick.

'Sounds good to me...what things?'

'You mean you don't know?'

'No, I don't.'

'Didn't Jake tell you about the photographs?'

'What photographs?'

'We're booked into a studio in a couple of hours.'

Jake was suddenly there in front of them.

'We're getting some promotional shots of the band.'

Caitlin refrained from commenting. She was wondering if a couple of hours would be enough to transform her sleepy-eyed expression into something half resembling awake. Aside from that, she *hated* having her photograph taken. Next to eating beetroot, it was right up there on the list of things that made her squirm.

'So be sure to wear something sexy,' Rick piped up with a grin. 'You're bound to give the current babes in the charts a run for their money!'

Caitlin immediately rounded on him with an affronted glare. 'The campaign for equal rights for women clearly just passed you by, didn't it? Why strive for intelligent observation when you can just go for the lowest common denominator?'

In his usual incorrigible fashion he returned, 'Because life is complicated enough, without trying to be clever. I'm a simple guy. Can I help it if I have an eye for beauty?'

'You've made your point, Rick.' Jake's blue eyes were icy as he flashed him a warning glare. 'Now, why don't you just leave it there?'

'Can I check into my hotel now?' Caitlin interjected quickly. 'If these photos are strictly necessary then I'd like to get a shower and make myself presentable before we go.'

Rising abruptly to her feet, she pulled the edges of her denim jacket more closely across her dress's scooped neckline. All the testosterone flying around was making her nervous.

'Sure—I'll take you. Let's go back to the car.' Jake handed Rick a bunch of key cards. 'You guys go and sort yourselves out. I'll make sure Caitlin is okay and catch up with you in about half an hour.'

Getting to his feet, Rick frowned. 'Gee, I wish taking care of our "best asset" was part of *my* job description. It can hardly seem like work, can it?' he quipped.

Almost imperceptibly Jake's shoulders stiffened. Feigning indifference to the undoubted tension between the two men, Caitlin started to walk away. But Jake caught hold of her elbow and led them across the shiny parquet floor towards the exit.

She shook off his hold. 'I'm quite capable of—'

'Not now, Caitlin.'

Without even sparing her a glance, he conveyed the fact that his temper was on a very short fuse. Only a fool would seek to ignite it, so she swallowed down her indignation and turned her attention to keeping pace with his long-legged stride.

Flipping off the top of a bottle of beer from the mini-bar in his room, Jake imbibed a generous draught of the ice-cold contents and then dropped back down onto the bed. Sounds of the city permeated the forest-green curtains he'd drawn to shut out the night, and inside the images on the television screen silently flickered.

He'd deliberately muted the sound, but for a moment or two his attention was caught by the intense expressions of two lovers bidding each other goodbye at a railway station. The corners of his mouth lifted in a smile and a warm feeling climbed steadily into his chest—but it wasn't just because of the touching scene. *The sight of the lovers had inevitably made him think of Caitlin.*

Her name alone had the power to convey feelings inside him that he scarcely knew what to do with. Watching her pose with the rest of the band that afternoon for photographs had been both heaven and hell. She'd worn fitted black jeans with a virginal white stretch top that had clung lovingly to her breasts, and at the photographer's behest had taken off her boots and socks to leave her feet sexily bare. With her river of ebony hair, sparkling green eyes and naturally beautiful smile, Jake's hadn't been the only jaw to hit the floor when she'd stood as instructed with the other band members to pose for the camera.

'Anyone need some ice to help them cool down?' Rick had quipped as they'd stood together, observing the proceedings, and the comment had made Jake feel far from friendly as he thought of his colleague fantasising about the woman who had so recently become his lover...the woman he was trying desperately hard not to want because protocol demanded he abstain.

Dismayed by the violence of his feelings, he'd taken a couple of steps back to compose himself as he'd wrestled with a near overwhelming urge to kidnap Caitlin after the shoot and take her back to his hotel room. That was when his imagination had gone into overdrive.

Groaning, he took another swig of beer and glared at the television as the thought of yet another cold shower made him want to grab the offending equipment and throw it out the window. *That would be a coup for the press*...the band manager at the centre of a scandal with his model ex-wife a

few years ago drawing attention once again with a demon-
stration of typically 'rock star' behaviour in a hotel room.

Irritably dismissing the thought, Jake brought his attention back to Caitlin. She had yet again done them proud that
night, her sexy, heaven-sent voice alternately whipping up
the crowd or innocently seducing them, her vocals meld-
ing perfectly with the band's tight, rich sound. In just three
short weeks she'd learned more, given more, and was shap-
ing up into more of a professional than some people in the
business he'd known for years. He might be biased, but Jake
knew they were onto something good.

But if he didn't touch her again soon he would lose his
mind. That was if he hadn't lost it already.

He stretched out his hand for the telephone next to the
bed. He could at least talk to her, tell her... Tell her *what*,
exactly? That he was going crazy just thinking about her?
That he was desperate to hold her and demonstrate in no
uncertain terms just how much he desired her?

He let the receiver clatter noisily back onto its rest. He
couldn't do it. He wouldn't put Caitlin in such an untenable
position. He'd just have to find some other way of working
off all his nervous energy. *Was that the correct term for a
raging libido these days?*

With a humourless smile, he drained the bottle of beer
dry, then stood up and threw it into a nearby wastepaper bin.
Then he reached for his jacket and slammed out through the
door without even pausing to switch off the TV.

The jarring sound of a bell ringing right next to her ear
had Caitlin burying her face into her lilac-coloured pillow in a bid to shut the noise out. *It must be someone's car
alarm going off down the street—or a fire drill, perhaps.*
Her mind played games with the sound, encouraging her
to carry on sleeping. Someone would see to it soon, she
thought vaguely.

Only all of a sudden she was wide awake and scrambling to sit up as it finally registered that it was the phone beside her bed that was ringing. Clamping the receiver to her ear, she impatiently pushed her hair away from her face and squinted at the glowing green digits blinking back at her from the alarm clock…

Two-thirty a.m.? What the…?

'Hello?'

'Caitlin. Were you asleep?'

Jake. At the sound of that gravelly bass voice her heart-beat accelerated like a rabbit being chased by a fox.

'What's the matter? Is anything wrong?'

Had something happened to him? Was he hurt? In trouble? Caitlin's fertile imagination went into overdrive.

'Nothing's wrong. I'm downstairs in the lobby. Can you come down?'

'It's half past two in the morning!'

'I'm quite aware of the time.'

God, it was so good to hear his voice.

'Why? I mean, why do you want me to come downstairs at this time of night?' Even as she asked the question she was swinging her legs out of bed and seeking out the jeans and warm red sweater she'd folded onto a chair.

'Because I want to see you.'

His tone immediately conveyed his impatience, making his statement sound more like an order than a request.

Caitlin frowned, 'You could see me in the morning after breakfast. I don't make much sense until I've had my cup of tea.'

'Damn it, Caitlin! Just put some clothes on and get down here, will you?'

Jake hung up on her, leaving her staring at the telephone as though it had suddenly sprouted a beak and a couple of wings.

Shaking herself out of the daze she was in, she hurried into the bathroom. Splashing her face with some cold water, she quickly brushed her teeth, then combed her dishevelled hair with her fingers. There was no time to even think about applying some make-up. At any rate, what did he expect? It was two-thirty in the morning, she was tired and dazed—and…if she admitted it…more hopeful than she had a right to be considering he'd kept her at a deliberate distance for the past two days.

Crossing her arms over her soft woollen sweater, she stepped warily out of the lift to find him waiting by the doors, his lean jaw dark with night-time shadow, his hair mussed and his piercing blue eyes preternaturally bright. Desire for him was like a flash flood, fierce and elemental, and it rendered her immediately weak.

'Jake…' His name on her lips was little more than a murmur.

'Come for a walk' he said, catching hold of her hand and urging her towards the rotating glass doors of the exit.

Mid-stride, Caitlin ground to a halt to stare at him. 'You want to go for a walk? Are you crazy? It's two-thirty in the morning.'

A muscle tensed visibly in his jaw and Caitlin allowed him to guide her outside. The wind cut through her like an icy blade and, catching her shiver, Jake immediately shrugged off his jacket and draped it around her shoulders.

Her eyes wide, she glanced up at him. 'What's all this about, Jake?'

'Come on—let's walk. It's too cold to stand around.'

They headed out towards the pier, Jake catching hold of her hand again as if it was the most natural thing in the world for him to do. The night sky was almost black, but there was still plenty of light. Aside from the stars and the curved sliver of moon that permeated the velvet blanket there was plenty of neon to light up the streets, and even the occasional car's headlamp as it flew past.

For most of the way Jake had stayed silent. Now he stopped, drawing Caitlin close against him before staring out to sea.

'You were amazing tonight.'

He turned back to survey her. Heat slid down her spine and radiated down into her pelvis. The unexpected compliment took her by surprise.

'Thanks…I really enjoyed myself. The band were great, weren't they? I particularly liked—'

Jake silenced her with a hard, hot kiss that made her stumble against him.

Her lips were like soft satin pillows that couldn't help but invite him to keep tasting them. But he didn't just want to kiss her. He wanted to do so much more… The very idea made him tighten. Then it made him hard.

Lifting his head, he examined the dazed expression she wore—the moist, softly opened mouth that he'd so spontaneously and heatedly ravished, and the shining green eyes that he defied any man not to lose his soul to.

'I'll go crazy if I can't make love to you soon,' he confessed.

'We can't. Remember, we agreed…?'

Emitting a curse, Jake stared at Caitlin and drove his hands through his already windblown hair in frustration.

'I know what we agreed. I know what we *should* do. But the truth is that when you were posing with the others today at the photo shoot I hated every single one of them for looking at you…for no doubt imagining what it would be like to make love to you… No one has a right to look at you like that but *me*.'

Nervously, Caitlin slid her tongue over her lips. 'What's the meaning of all this, Jake? What are you telling me?'

'I'm telling you that I want us to be lovers. I'm not saying I expect it to be forever but I want us to be together.'

'What you're saying is that if we get together you don't expect it to be a permanent arrangement?'

'Yes.'

The expression in his eyes looked haunted for a moment.

'The idea scares you?'

'I just don't trust that long-term commitment can ever really work. Look at the examples I've had.'

'You mean there's no chance you might be able to change that view? We've all been hurt, Jake…including me. After what Sean did to me it was never going to be easy to trust another man. If I can open my mind to the idea…can't you?'

He sighed. 'I'd like to tell you I could…but in all honesty I don't hold out much hope. I know myself too well.' He shook his head in frustration. 'Look, do things have to be so serious? Can't we just have some fun together?'

'I take it you're talking about sex? Is that how you see relationships, Jake as a chance to indulge in a little light-hearted sex with no commitment whatsoever?'

'No! You're taking everything the wrong way. Look, Caitlin, I'll respect you and take care of you for however long our relationship lasts…we'll enjoy whatever time we have together—that's all I meant. I only know that I want us to be up-front about things to everyone—not play cloak and dagger and pretend we aren't an item. After all, we're adults, aren't we?'

He seemed quite certain that their relationship couldn't last. Yes, his past had made him wary, and perhaps even *scornful* of any kind of commitment, but didn't he want to change that belief to something better? As much as she loved him, if Jake didn't have any faith that things could be different Caitlin wasn't going to settle. Her self-respect was paramount, and she wasn't about to risk losing it for even a second…not even for the man she loved.

'I'm sorry, Jake.' Pulling his jacket from her shoulders, she pushed it into his hands. 'If all you're offering me is some temporary little affair—some supposed "fun" until you grow tired of me and move on to somebody else—then I'm going to have to say no. You once asked me if I was sure I was committed to this band and I told you categorically *yes*. Right now that's all I'm interested in—the *band*. Now, if you'll excuse me, I really need to get back to my bed. If I don't get at least six hours' sleep then I won't be fit for anything tomorrow. Goodnight, Jake.'

Just before she turned and walked away Caitlin had the bittersweet satisfaction of seeing the bewilderment and hurt in Jake's eyes. But as she put more and more distance between them the pain she felt at knowing they would never be lovers again was so intense that she felt as if it drilled a hole right through her heart and out the other side.

Jake stayed where he was, staring out at the frigid sea for what seemed like an eternity. It was hard to take that Caitlin had turned him down. But then everything he'd wanted to say to her had somehow come out wrong.

His heart had leapt at her soft-voiced confession that she'd found it hard to trust another man after what her ex had done to her, and she'd given him a genuine opportunity to meet her halfway when she'd said that if she could open her mind to the idea of learning to trust again, why couldn't he? But he'd completely messed it up when he'd let fear take over instead. She'd been insulted that all he seemed to be offering her was a temporary affair.

Did she really believe that, given time, their association could become more permanent? Was she perhaps hoping for marriage?

He couldn't help it, but the idea of marriage made Jake's blood run cold when he recalled what Jodie had put him through. Caitlin was nothing like his mercenary ex-wife, but if she became well known, with all the temptations that fame would undoubtedly bring to a beautiful girl like her, wasn't it possible that *she* would be the one who grew tired of the relationship and wanted to move on to a better prospect? It would kill him to have to go through another bitter court battle if his new wife treated him in the same heartless way his ex had.

As he dug his now freezing hands into his jacket pockets and moved back down the pier Jake knew that as much as he cared for Caitlin, as much as he *desired* her and yearned to protect her, he couldn't risk losing his heart to her and having to endure the consequent fall-out should things go wrong.

Because if that happened, this time he really would be a broken man.

CHAPTER TEN

PLANTING HIMSELF AT the back of the crowd that night, Jake sensed the familiar zig-zag of electricity shoot through him—as he always did before a band walked onto the stage…especially a band he was managing.

The day he stopped being excited about his work was the day he stopped living. He'd witnessed too many managers in the business become lazy or complacent when they got rich, content just to milk the financial rewards without actively contributing to a band's or a singer's success. Jake was scathing about such behaviour. For himself, music was its own reward—and if he could help a band attain success, then every sleepless night and grey hair was worth it.

Blue Sky was a week into their tour and the venue that night was a noisy and popular music pub on the Kent coast. The band were booked to play there from eight-thirty onwards. At Jake's suggestion they had made some last-minute alterations to the playlist, taking out a couple of the original tunes and replacing them with two slower numbers that Mike had written and that in Jake's opinion were outstandingly good. He was also showcasing Caitlin's skills as a vocalist.

On a more personal note, he loved to hear her sing those love songs—loved to hear the emotion in her voice that made all the hairs on the back of his neck stand up. Those performances sent shivers down his spine. *Not that he'd admit it to anyone—least of all to Rick, who seemed to be watching him like a hawk these days.* He couldn't exactly blame him. He was so sure that if Caitlin and Jake got together the result would be the break-up of the band.

Folding his arms across his chest, he released a frustrated sigh. He hated being in such a bind. But what the hell was he supposed to do? *Ignore* the feelings he had for her? The woman had got so deep into his blood that if he didn't get his daily fix of her he felt as if someone had died. If Jake hadn't know better he'd have sworn he was in—

Whoa. He reined in the thought with an accompanying sense of genuine panic.

'Good crowd tonight.'

Suddenly Rick appeared beside him, depositing a dark pint of real ale into Jake's hands with relish. Taking a deep draught of his own drink, he exhaled with pleasure, wiping the froth from his top lip with a grin.

'I've been told by the barman that this stuff is like nectar. It certainly beats that pint of warm dishwater masquerading as alcohol that I had last night.'

'I'll take your word for it.' Warily, Jake raised his glass to sample some of the dark brew for himself. As it slid down his throat the bitter taste of hops lingered unpleasantly in his mouth, confirming what he already knew to be true… he was no real ale aficionado. Give him a bourbon and Coke any day.

'So, how do you think things are going?' Rick asked, turning briefly to flash an irrepressible grin at a shapely blonde who'd walked by.

'So far so good,' Jake answered, his glance instinctively guarded. 'The band sounds great, and Caitlin's singing just gets better and better. We're going to be getting more great reviews…it's a given.'

'Man, I bless the day she walked into that musty old church hall and her voice blew us away. The gods were smiling on us that day, that's for sure.'

'I agree.'

'Hey, Jake, I hope you didn't take my advice about not getting involved with Cait too personally. I mean, we've been friends for a long time. We've never let a woman come between us before.'

'It was sound advice,' Jake replied soberly.

'Not that I blame you for being attracted to her. She sure is one beautiful woman, isn't she?'

Taking another reluctant sip of his beer, Jake remarked, 'You won't get an argument from me.'

The lights suddenly dimmed, and amid the tangible air of expectation that rippled round the audience the band walked onto the stage.

Jake's excitement was heightened along with everyone else's, but the smile on his face quickly turned into a frown when he saw what Caitlin was wearing. In place of the long skirts and silky tops she'd been favouring since they'd started the tour she was dressed in black bootcut jeans that hugged her hips like a second skin and a stretchy little white top that emphasised her eye-catching chest.

The males in the crowd weren't slow in demonstrating their appreciation. Jake did his best to try and shut out some of the more ribald comments. But with her flowing black hair, smiling green eyes and long legs, Caitlin was doing serious things to his blood pressure. He knew it was crazy, but he hated the mere idea that every red-blooded man in the room was fantasising about her. And underneath the hot, swift stab of jealousy that assailed him Jake felt a growing admiration for her daring. It seemed that Little Miss Hole-in-Her-Stocking was finally coming out of her shell.

Registering the looks of delight on the faces of the other band members as well as the crowd's, Caitlin launched into a mesmerising rendition of an iconic blues number and Jake silently acknowledged that her talent was astounding. As he watched her hips sway sexily to the music, her little white top riding up almost to waist level, he didn't think he'd ever felt so aroused or more hungry for a woman in his life.

* * *

Caitlin was quickly learning that after the almighty adrenaline rush of a live performance it was easy to crash down to the absolute depths shortly after. Now, alone in yet another hotel room—albeit a very luxurious one—with her room service supper left untouched on a tray, she sat in her pyjamas and robe with her head in her hands, feeling lonely and depressed.

An attack of the blues was the last thing she needed. But, as well as missing Jake's touch, the truth was that she was missing Lia—missing the easy camaraderie they shared. She also missed the buzz of working with her in the bookshop. Caitlin wasn't ungrateful for the privileged position she found herself in—actually living her dream of being a singer—but she'd be lying if she said she didn't miss the people and the place that she thought of as home.

Sighing, she reached for a magazine that was lying on the coffee table and decided to take it to bed with her. She was heading towards the prettily covered divan when there was a soft knock on the door. She opened it to Jake.

'Hi,' he greeted her. 'Can we talk?'

With her heart skipping a beat, she automatically stepped aside to let him enter. Her whole world immediately narrowed down to the force of his presence, her senses registering sensation overload with just one whiff of that sexy cologne he wore and one scorching glance from those extraordinary blue eyes of his.

Jake was a big part of the reason that Caitlin had crashed so low after tonight's performance. She still didn't really know where she stood with him, and the situation was making her as jumpy as if she was walking barefoot on tin tacks. One minute he was scowling at her and the next he was eating her up with his eyes. No wonder her nerves were stretched tight to the point of snapping.

Tonight he'd been very cool again, addressing her only when he had to, while in contrast Rick and the guys in the band had been elated with her performance and hadn't hesitated to show it. She was seriously perturbed that Jake seemed intent on giving her the cold shoulder. Had he decided that she was right about keeping their relationship a purely business one?

'You didn't eat your supper.' He glanced at the untouched tray of food balanced on the coffee table..

'I wasn't very hungry.'

'You have to eat to keep your strength up. Performing night after night can really take it out of you.'

'Thanks for your concern.' Making no attempt to couch the sarcasm in her tone, Caitlin raked her fingers through her recently washed hair, then caught the belt on her robe and wound it round her hand.

'Your performance tonight was wonderful. Anyone would think you'd been doing this for years. The others can't sing your praises enough.'

'And you?'

She barely managed to get the words past the ache in her throat. She ached to touch him, to drive that too serious expression from his haunting eyes and make him smile.

'If I started to tell you what I really think about you I wouldn't get back to my room tonight.'

His voice was huskily low, and every word he uttered sent inflammatory arrows of desire scudding crazily all over her body. Grabbing for a lifeline, Caitlin's gaze found and settled on the bottle of mineral water she'd ordered with her meal.

'Would you like a drink? It's only water, but—'

'I don't want a drink. I know I'm breaking all the rules here, but the truth is, Caitlin, I just can't stay away.'

His glance never leaving her face, he shrugged off his leather jacket and threw it onto a chair. Her mouth went dry at the sight of the hard, lean biceps that defined his upper arms in his black short-sleeved T-shirt. Startled, she focused on the dimple right in the centre of his chin—as usual his firm jaw was fashionably unshaven—but the dark shadow of beard didn't detract one jot from his heartbreakingly good looks. If anything, it simply added to the 'bad boy' persona he seemed to project without even trying.

'Well, you should,' she snapped. Turning on her heel, she unscrewed the top of the bottle of mineral water and took a swig. When she'd finished she turned back again and said, 'Because I don't want you here.'

Not commenting, Jake strolled across to the light switch and dimmed the overhead lights to a softly seductive glow.

Barely aware of what she was doing, Caitlin placed the water bottle back down on the tray. 'What are you doing?'

'I want you to come over here.'

'No.' But even as she answered in the negative she moved slowly towards him, as if she didn't have a will of her own…

When she was almost there she stopped and stared at him with desperation in her eyes. Jake opened his arms. In less than a second she'd closed the space between them to bury her face in the warm, musky scent of his T-shirt, registering the strong, steady throb of his heartbeat beneath the steely hardness of his chest. His hands fisted into her hair and he pressed her even closer against his body. Her heart was racing harder than it had ever raced before.

'Jake? Jake, I—' Raising her head, Caitlin stared into his smouldering gaze, want and need clawing at her as she registered the pure raw desire in his eyes.

Planting his palms either side of her face, he slanted his mouth hotly across hers to steal a hungry kiss that left them both stunned. With a groan she invited another kiss, her tongue intimately dancing with his, savouring the seductive flavours of bourbon and coffee and the hot, drugging sensuality that was uniquely *Jake*. Her hands slid down his back and lifted his T-shirt eagerly to trace the hard ridge of his spine with her fingertips. She was weak with wanting him, and when he backed up against the wall and deftly turned her in his arms, so that she took over his position, she allowed him to do it without so much as a murmur of protest.

'You know what I want to do?'

Her eyes widened in shock as well as anticipation as he expertly relieved her of her robe, then started to undo the buttons on her pyjama top.

'What?' Caitlin's voice was a barely-there bedroom rasp, because what Jake was already doing to her with his strong, sure touch and his drugging, sexy voice was nothing less than X-rated.

So much for years of trying to convince herself that her sex drive was low! Right now she didn't know how she wasn't just ripping his clothes off and taking what she wanted without hesitation. With a soft whimper, she briefly closed her eyes as he divested her of her top and feasted his hungry glance on her bared caramel-tipped breasts.

'I want to take you right here…and I want it to be hot and slow and deep…until we both go out of our minds with the pleasure.'

Even as Caitlin's heart beat wildly in her chest Jake lowered his head to claim her breast, drawing it deeply into his mouth. Bucking against him, she drove her fingers into the silky strands of his hair, crying out as ravenous need spiralled from her breast to her womb. He suckled and laved, teasing her rigid nipple with his tongue, then took her deep into his mouth again, his unshaven jaw sliding roughly cross her more tender skin, abrading her, marking her with his brand, leaving the trail of his scent all over her. Then he applied the same treatment to her other breast.

She was still quivering when Jake released her throbbing wet nipple and moved back up her body, with the wickedest smile she had ever seen. His pupils darkened to black as he settled his hands on the waist of her pyjama bottoms. With a firm tug, the silky fall of material shimmied down to her ankles. Her cheeks flushing heatedly, Caitlin watched him retrieve the protection he'd brought from his back pocket.

Her gaze immediately gravitated to his belt. He opened it to let his trousers slide down over his thighs and reveal his boxers. He loosened them, then ripped open the foil packet that contained the protection. He sheathed himself and Caitlin released a long, slow breath. Sliding her slender arms round Jake's neck, she pressed her body ardently against his. Immediately his hands moved to settle on the silky curve of her bottom, skimming her flesh and then pressing and kneading it until she was weak with want—until she thought she might die if he didn't take her soon.

Then he ravished her mouth again, before trailing hot damp kisses across her cheeks, her forehead, her eyelids, his clever hands stroking her body well past the point of no return, moving deftly to cup her in her most feminine place. Caitlin couldn't help but whimper his name, her lips pressing into the juncture between his neck and shoulder, kissing the warm masculine flesh with growing desire, taking lascivious little nips with her teeth...

Her body was primed to accept him. She knew she could no more prevent this act from reaching its logical conclusion than deny herself breath. Jake might be wary of commitment and find it hard to trust, but right then she impatiently pushed the thought aside—because she was greedy for his loving and would take anything she could get...*rightly or wrongly.* She would enjoy this time with him and revel in it. Revel in the fact that she was a sensual, desirable woman and that Jake was the only man in the world she wanted as her lover.

'Open your mouth,' he instructed, gravel-voiced and when she did he kissed her hard, sliding his hand beneath her bottom and raising her hips to the level of his. As her long, slender legs easily straddled him he plunged inside her with one sure, firm thrust, sending her world spinning off into another galaxy.

'Oh, Jake!'

Caitlin held on tight as he filled her again and again, each thrust more sure, more urgent, deeper than she could imagine, stealing kisses from her lips, her throat, her earlobe, until she thought she might die from the sheer dizzying pleasure of it.

'This is what I've been fantasising about doing all day,' he breathed against her neck, and at the same moment her world really did spin off its axis.

Jake quickly followed her. At the moment of climax he bucked hard against her, raggedly saying her name, the muscles in his toned hard body quivering like ropes of steel in the aftermath.

As his head fell forward onto her chest Caitlin drove her fingers through his tousled dark hair and had to bite her lip hard to stop herself from confessing that she loved him. *More than that, she wanted to marry him and one day have his children.*

Her certainty was so all-consuming that she thought surely Jake must sense it. But fear that all she would achieve by making such a confession might be to scare him away forever stopped her telling him. Jake had been a gypsy all his life, Rick had said, and probably always would be. What made her dare to hope for even a second that *she* could change his mind about that and help him see that they could still enjoy the pleasures of home and family?

'All right, everybody, time out. Cait? I'd like a word.'

Vaulting nimbly onto the small raised stage, Rick couldn't hide his exasperation as yet again Caitlin failed to come in at the right time on the intro.

Flushing a mortified pink, she turned round to shrug an apology to the rest of the band. To give them credit, they unanimously agreed that everyone was entitled to an off day now and then, and discreetly left the stage to her and Rick.

'What's going on with you this morning?' Rick didn't shy away from expressing his irritation. 'Didn't you get much sleep last night?'

She sighed. Sensing her cheeks burning at the accuracy

of Rick's innocent statement, she frantically thought of what she could say in answer.

To her surprise and delight Jake had spent the night. He had only returned to his room just as the sun came up—and then only reluctantly. Consequently neither of them had had much sleep…not when there had been far more exhilarating pleasures to occupy them. Caitlin knew she must have the dazed look of someone who'd burnt the candle at both ends. Her body still ached from Jake's passionate attentions and her concentration was all but shot to pieces.

Arriving for rehearsals at the intimate jazz club where they were appearing this evening, Rick had announced that Jake wouldn't be joining them until later and that until then he would be looking after things.

'I never sleep well in a strange bed,' she mumbled.

Rick's hazel eyes narrowed. 'You sure that's the reason?'

Agitatedly spearing her fingers through her hair, Caitlin sensed them tremble. Then she winced as she accidentally yanked out the silver hoop in her earlobe.

'What other reason would there be?'

'I don't know, babe…you tell me.'

She felt besieged—not to mention guilty…*guilty as hell.* Why couldn't Jake be around when she needed him? He would have taken charge of the situation in a second. She wasn't happy about lying to Rick about their relationship. With all her heart she wished they could be totally up-front about it, just as Jake had said he wanted to be.

'I don't know what you're getting at, Rick. I told you it would take me a while to get used to the change of lifestyle. It's hardly a crime that I'm feeling tired, is it?'

'No, it isn't.' Sighing heavily, Rick moved behind Caitlin and started kneading her shoulders. 'You're too tense. That's the trouble. Relax, can't you? Drop those shoulders. C'mon…listen to Uncle Rick.'

As jumpy as she was, she had to admit that what Rick was doing felt good…fantastically good. Right now her spine might have been made of concrete, she was so on edge, and anything to alleviate the tension had to be a step in the right direction. If she could only grab a couple of hours' sleep before the gig tonight she would be back on track again.

Dropping her head, she groaned as Rick's fingers applied some deeper pressure at a particularly tender spot between her shoulderblades. 'You're good at this, aren't you?' she murmured. 'You could have a whole new career, you know.'

'I must confess I've been told that before.'

Caitlin heard the smile in his voice.

'By one or two very grateful ladies who've succumbed to the pleasures of these hands.'

'You're quite the Casanova, aren't you?'

'Yes, well…if the cap fits.'

Her masseur halted his ministrations to drop a brief teasing kiss at the side of her neck… Unfortunately at the very same moment that Jake walked into the room.

The band's charismatic manager stopped dead in his tracks.

'Is this how you rehearse the band, Rick? Because if it is then we've got a serious problem on our hands…wouldn't you say?'

CHAPTER ELEVEN

WITHOUT REALISING IT Jake had clenched his hands into fists down by his sides. As he fought to corral his steadily growing temper his blazing blue eyes burned back at them both, his gut swirling with jealousy. *What the hell did Caitlin think she was playing at, allowing his best friend to fool around with her like that?*

Pink-cheeked and embarrassed, she stepped towards the edge of the stage. He wasn't surprised she was defensive.

'We *were* rehearsing, Jake. I just had a couple of problems Rick was helping me with.'

'Oh?' Jake's lip curled scathingly. 'Since when did I employ Rick as the group's masseur? Clearly I missed that.'

'For goodness' sake—the girl is tired! Tired and tense… I was just helping her iron out some of the kinks so that we could get on. The guys have gone outside for a break. I think I'll go call them back in.'

'No. Stay right where you are.'

His boot heels ringing ominously on the wooden floor, Jake strode towards the stage.

'We don't do anything else until I get to the bottom of this.'

With a horrible sinking feeling in the pit of her stomach, Caitlin jammed her hands into her jeans pockets and took a deep breath in. Was he jealous? Was that why he was so angry?

Her heart beat double-time, because she couldn't help noticing how gorgeous he looked. Dressed in fitted black jeans, a maroon shirt and a dark pin-striped suit jacket that flowed over his lean hard body as if it was tailor-made, he resembled one of those seriously unapproachable Italian models that featured in glossy magazines. His dark tousled hair and glittering blue eyes gave him a dangerous sexy edge and ensured there was nowhere else she'd rather look than at him.

'What are you talking about, Jake?' Rick jumped off the stage to confront the other man. 'You'd better explain.'

'I'm talking about you kissing her!' Jake glared at his friend.

Rick was bemused. 'I was just fooling around. You know me…I never could resist a pretty face.'

'That's a poor excuse for fondling my—'

'Go on… Your *what*, Jake?'

He'd been about to say my woman.

The realisation hit him hard—like a brick dropped on his head from a great height. As statements of ownership went, he couldn't have put it much more clearly. Here he was, standing head to head with his best friend and long-time associate, the pair of them like a couple of prize-fighters about to go into the ring. Jake cursed under his breath. He couldn't keep a lid on his temper, could he? He'd just had to let it out. Now he'd blown the whole situation wide open.

Rick's hazel eyes narrowed. 'You're sleeping with her, aren't you?'

Caitlin bristled indignantly. She most definitely didn't appreciate being discussed as if she wasn't there…as if she was some inconsequential possession rather than a human being. But as Jake glanced up and his heated glance locked onto hers it was as though he'd reached out and touched her. For a few debilitating seconds, her head swam.

'You just couldn't keep your hands off her, could you?' Rick's tone was scathing.

'Isn't that supposed to be *my* line?'

'Don't get cute with me, Jake! Just answer the damn question.'

With a terse shrug, the other man folded his arms. 'Yes. Caitlin and I are having a relationship. But don't start jumping to conclusions. It doesn't mean it's going to impact negatively on the band.'

'Is that right? Then how come we're at loggerheads? Answer me that. How long have we worked together? It's been a long time, Jake. In all that time we've barely had an angry word—and that's something in this business. Damn shame it has to happen now…and all because of a woman!'

'And just what's *that* supposed to mean?' Stooping down to climb off the stage, Caitlin dusted her hands and wiped them shakily on her jeans. 'In case you hadn't noticed I'm a person—just like you are. What is it with you and women, Rick? You like us well enough when it suits you, but something tells me you're deeply suspicious of our motives. Just to reassure you—I have no hidden agenda, and neither have I any intention of leaving the band. That being the case, you have no reason to doubt me. When I give my word, I keep it.'

'Right now, honey, it's not *your* word that I'm concerned about.'

'Okay, Rick… If you want to discuss this any further then you'd better meet me back at the hotel when we're finished here. I'm not prepared to stand around and lock horns with you when we're already eating into valuable rehearsal time. The band has a performance to give tonight and that's priority number one.'

With a brief glance down at his watch, Jake turned his attention to Caitlin.

'I want you to pull out all the stops tonight,' he told her. 'I didn't tell you before, because I didn't want to make you nervous, but there's going to be an A&R man from one of the big labels watching the show tonight. I can't make any promises, but if you and the band impress him enough there's a real possibility of getting a record deal. Kenny Swan knows that I don't back losers, and his interest has been snared by footage of you and the guys on social media over the past few nights. I'm counting on you—so don't let me down.'

Dumbly, Caitlin nodded. The possibility of the band gaining a recording contract so soon into their tour was nothing short of amazing. Yet right at that moment it paled into insignificance next to her unquenchable longing to be in Jake's arms.

She was relieved that he'd openly admitted to Rick that they were intimate, and she wanted the chance to show him that what they felt for each other could indeed flourish into something meaningful and lasting if they trusted their feelings and gave it a chance. At least now there would be no need to hide the fact that they wanted to be together, and she could really put her heart and soul into her singing.

Jake smiled. 'Work hard and I'll see you both later. I have a couple of important calls to make.'

'Jake?'

Suddenly finding her voice again, Caitlin stopped him in his tracks as he strode towards the back of the venue. Her anxious glance encompassed a scowling Rick as he leant back against the edge of the stage.

'I don't want you and Rick to fall out over this. My commitment is first and foremost to the band. I know you know that, but I just wanted to reiterate it.'

Jake's expression was as implacable as ever. 'I'm glad to hear it. Just concentrate on giving your best performance tonight and we might all come out on top.'

And with that he walked away.

He had the worst headache in living memory. The pain was so intense it had sent him hurrying down the narrow streets at half past five in the afternoon in search of a chemist.

Holding the packet of painkillers just a few minutes later, Jake ripped out two white tablets from the foil strip and swallowed them down with a warm can of cola. Grimacing, he threw the barely touched drink into a nearby wastebin and, biting his lip against the merciless throb in his temple, returned to his hotel.

Bolting his room door, he drew the curtains shut tight to blot out what was left of the daylight, then threw himself down on the bed and stared contemptuously up at the ceiling. *One thing was certain...he couldn't go on like this.* He only suffered migraines this bad when he was pushed into a corner, and his head was letting him know that right now he was probably jammed into the tightest corner he'd ever encountered.

There was no question that he wanted Caitlin. The situation between them wouldn't have developed if he hadn't. The electricity they generated between them could turn on the Christmas lights in Oxford Street without a power socket in sight. But lust was one thing and—dared he say it?—*love* was something else entirely.

He caught his breath, mulling the thought over.

Was love what he felt for Caitlin? If it was, then where did he go from here? In most people's books love meant commitment...the one thing he had always shied away from.

Jake was pretty sure now that what he'd felt for Jodie definitely *hadn't* been love. His decision to marry the woman had been crazy and it had cost him dearly. The truth was he had never committed himself properly to her. Wasn't that why he'd taken every opportunity to distance himself by travelling so often? She'd probably sensed his reticence at being with her long before she'd had her affair.

But what if the desire to escape reared its head again when he was with Caitlin? *He couldn't bear the thought that he might break her heart.* After the hell her ex had put her through she deserved someone who wouldn't cut and run. Someone who would support her journey as a singer. Someone who would be there when she needed them. Someone she could count on to stay around for more than just a few short weeks or months… In fact *someone the complete antithesis of himself.*

And now, to make matters worse, he had Rick on his case. When all was said and done his friend had every right to be furious with him. Jake had broken his own unwritten code about fraternising with band members and he'd potentially put the band at risk because of his fascination for Caitlin.

He would endeavour to put things right as soon as Kenny Swan from Lightning Records had seen the band perform tonight. If the man gave them a recording contract then hopefully it would help Jake decide what he needed to do, and maybe then—*and it was a big maybe*—he would finally be able to have some peace.

'You can come? Lia, that's fantastic!'

Dropping down onto the bed, with its prettily embroidered quilt, Caitlin clamped her mobile firmly against her ear. To hear that her best friend was at last able to get away and come and hear her sing was the best news she'd had all day…next to the chance of Blue Sky getting a record deal, of course. But ever since that uncomfortable exchange between Jake, Rick and her at rehearsals that morning she hadn't been able to help worrying about what might happen next.

Rick's mood hadn't improved since Jake had left him in charge, and Caitlin feared for their friendship. *Was she to blame for their falling out?* If she was, then she would do her utmost to put things right. But in less than a couple of sentences Lia's cheery voice had managed to dispel her worry and doubt and replace it with a sudden rush of optimism and hope.

If Caitlin gave a good performance tonight—the *best* performance she'd ever given—the band might get that record deal, Jake and Rick's friendship might return to its previous status, and Jake might start to see that he and Caitlin had a future together outside of the band.

'I might be a little late if the traffic is bad,' Lia was say-

ing, 'but I'll definitely be there. I've booked a room at that
bed and breakfast you're staying at, like you suggested, so
we'll be able to have a good old natter when we get back
from the club. I'm so excited I can't wait! Hey—and you
know what else?'

'What?'

Holding her hand out in front of her, Caitlin frowned at
her chipped purple nail polish, wondering if she'd have time
to repaint her nails before the gig tonight. It had to be right.
Everything had to be right or it would be *her* fault if things
went wrong. She was suspicious like that, and she wasn't
taking any chances.

'I took a peek at your horoscope today,' her friend continued. 'Do you know what it said?'

'Go on.' There wasn't a muscle in Caitlin's body that
didn't clench tight.

Lia took a deep breath in. 'Well, Saturn is meeting Venus
today, and I'm sure you know that Venus is the planet of love
and money? The timing is perfect. Saturn meets Venus beneath the auspices of the Mars/Jupiter rendezvous, so if you
long for something in the money or romance stakes today's
probably the time to ask for it. What do you think of that?'

Caitlin couldn't help but concentrate on the romance as-
pect. What would it take for Jake to see that she was serious about him? That she wanted to spend the rest of her life
with him? That she'd go anywhere at any time with him and
wouldn't regret a thing just so long as they could be together?

'Well, I've just been paid, so I'm okay for cash. As for
romance, I...' She fell silent.

'Has something been going on?'

'What do you mean?' Leaning back against the plump
pillows stacked against the padded headboard, Caitlin nervously wound a silken strand of burnished dark hair round
her finger.

'Are you having an affair with someone in the band? Wait

a minute… I bet it's with the manager, Jake Sorenson.' Lia sounded emphatic. 'It's *him*, isn't it?'

'Next you'll be telling me that you're psychic.'

Smiling grimly at her own bad joke, Caitlin deliberately stalled for time. She had the beginnings of a headache and prayed that her friend wouldn't start giving her a lecture on the wisdom—or *lack* of it—in pursuing a relationship with Jake. Besides, it was far too late for her to start taking advice on *that* particular subject.

'That's not good news. It may or may not be deserved, but the man has a certain reputation after that scandal with his ex. Are you looking for trouble, or what? You're in a vulnerable situation as it is, and now you've gone and done possibly the worst thing you could do by getting involved with him! Oh, Cait…how *could* you?'

Shutting her eyes briefly tight, Caitlin slackened her hold on the phone, thought of Jake and the damage he could do to her heart with just a smile, and mused silently, *How could I not?*

'I've been looking for you.'

Jake.

At the sound of that familiar low-pitched voice Caitlin almost broke out in a sweat. Hanging her coat more securely on the old-fashioned peg in the dressing room, from which the garment had just slipped for the third time, she turned slowly round to face him. Her gaze made electrically charged contact with his.

'I popped out for some fresh air, but I've been here for about half of an hour,' she told him.

With its gilded French-style furnishings, including a sumptuous gold couch, a chaise-longue, two matching armchairs and a chic glass-topped coffee table, the room that had been designated for the band was full of old-style glamour, making it quirkily appealing and atmospheric. The walls were covered in photographs and posters of the bands and musicians who had played there over the years—some extremely well known—and Caitlin had already spent several minutes studying them and marvelling at how fate had brought her there to perform.

But her attention was no longer on the room. Jake's brooding presence was already making her feel feverish with need, and she didn't think she could be any more intimately aware of him if she tried.

'Rick's just gone to the bar to get you a drink.'

'Thanks.' She agitatedly twisted the silver bangle she was wearing, then pushed her fingers through her hair. 'It's far too hot in here...don't you think?'

He was smiling that roguish smile of his that could scramble her brain in a second and turn her limbs to damp strands of spaghetti.

'It's always hot when we're in a room together, Caitlin... Don't tell me you've never noticed?'

'Yes. Well...'

'By the way, you look sensational tonight.'

Jake's glance couldn't help but avidly home in on Caitlin's figure. She was dressed from top to toe in black—bootcut jeans that clung lovingly to her slender thighs and a slim-fitting shirt cut high on the waist that dipped just low enough to give him a tantalising glimpse of her delectable cleavage.

Just thinking about the taste of that satin-smooth flesh when he kissed her, he had to suppress the compelling urge to lock the door behind them and keep her captive. He hoped that Kenny Swan would appreciate the supreme sacrifice he was making in letting Caitlin go out there to sing tonight.

'I really hope there are no hard feelings between you and Rick.'

Jake shrugged. 'Rick and I will sort things out. We always do.'

A moment later he had shortened the distance between them. Reaching out, he laid his palm over her cheek. Soft as a newly opened petal, it beckoned him to touch again. As if anticipating the event, her plump lower lip quivered and the sight inevitably made his blood slow and thicken. Now he wanted to taste her, to plunder, to *brand*...

But he was swiftly denied the pleasure when Caitlin caught hold of his hand and lifted it firmly away.

'I need to talk to you, Jake.'

'After the gig tonight. We'll have a proper conversation then.'

'No. I need to tell you something now. I've got a friend coming back with me tonight. A friend from home.'

Disappointment, heavy and crushing, cramped his chest. 'Male or female?' he quipped jealously, straight away knowing that as a matter of principle he disliked the person already. *It didn't matter about the decision he ultimately had to make for both their sakes.* Right then, Jake wanted the dark-haired beauty in front of him exclusively for himself.

'It's Lia.' She shrugged a shoulder. 'The owner of the shop where I worked.'

'I remember...the one who had to have some wisdom teeth removed?'

Smiling wryly, Jake lifted a strand of Caitlin's hair and stared down at it, transfixed. Her green eyes widened.

'Jake? Is everything all right?'

Even as she asked the question dread coiled in the pit of her stomach. Somehow she knew that everything *wasn't* all right. There was something he wasn't telling her...something she was certain would cause her untold hurt...something she didn't want to know until she absolutely *had* to—because right then all she wanted to do was keep this man in her company until the last possible second...

'Stop worrying. Everything's fine.'

Jake had just bent his head to kiss her when Rick pushed opened the door and strode in. Depositing the tray of drinks he carried down onto the coffee table, his hazel eyes locked accusingly onto them both.

'Still taking care of business, Jake?' he commented sarcastically.

Even before Jake stepped out of their embrace Caitlin sensed his anger and irritation. Once again she put the blame for helping to create animosity between the two men squarely on her own shoulders.

'Don't blame Jake.' Lifting her chin, she unwaveringly met Rick's glance. 'It's my fault. I was the one who—'

'Save it, sweetheart.' His smile was resigned, but not unkind. 'You wouldn't be the first woman to become infatuated with Jake, and if I'm not mistaken you won't be the last.'

'I'd stop right there if I were you.' The cold glare that Jake directed at his colleague glittered like the sparkle of ice in a glacier.

'Why?' Rick demanded. 'Because you don't want her to hear the truth?'

'What truth?' Caitlin's mouth had already gone dry as sand.

'Jake doesn't have a particularly good track record with women. In this business not many men do…the temptations are often too great to resist. But, to be fair…' His glance focused even more intently on Jake. 'He *was* burned badly by his ex, and after that he swore never to commit to another woman again. I'd be very surprised if that view had changed. In any case, whatever he's told you, I wouldn't take it too seriously, Cait.'

The tension that rebounded between them deepened. In the pit of her stomach Caitlin felt sick, cold dread. Was he telling the truth? Was Jake intending to end their relationship before it had even really got started? Had she been painfully naïve in thinking that their passionate lovemaking really mattered to him? Jake had already made it clear that he wasn't offering her anything more meaningful.

What an idiot she was! When was she going to learn that some men were in the business of *taking*, not giving? Every time her ex Sean had told her that things would be different, that he would change, that they had a bright future together, she had believed him. Yes, she had even believed him when she'd bailed him out with the last five hundred pounds in her savings account, because he'd sworn to pay it back with interest. *Of course he never had.*

This wouldn't be the first time she'd been deceived by a man. But then, maybe *she* had done some of the deceiving. Hadn't she deceived herself when she'd believed that, given time and the chance to really get to know her, Jake might want to take their relationship more seriously? Her heart ached with renewed hurt when she realised finally that it wasn't true…could *never* be true.

'It's all right, Jake.' Even though her eyes had filled with tears, Caitlin faced him with an unflinching stare. 'Whatever you might think, I'm not as naïve as you imagine. We slept together, we made love…but deep down I never thought you intended to take things further. Don't worry. I'm not going to make a scene. And, despite what *you* might think, Rick, I'm not going to go to pieces because it's over between Jake and me. We'll still have a professional relationship…a good one, I hope. And now that that's clear I think I'll go and find the others and check in with them.'

She made a move to turn away.

'No—not like this, Caitlin.'

Jake scraped a frustrated hand through his hair. He was furious with Rick for putting him in such an untenable position. But he was also furious with himself—because now it looked as if he'd deliberately used Caitlin. *Nothing could be further from the truth.* He was crazy about her. Thinking of her practically consumed his every waking moment. What he felt for her was like nothing he'd ever experienced before, and the power of it took his breath away. And if he had trouble telling her that, then it was surely down to an inherent lack of trust that anything good could ever last?

Never in his life had he experienced feeling safe. Even as a small boy in the children's home he'd known that when he fell he fell alone. There would be no loving parent to pick him up and reassure him that everything would be all right.

Jake swallowed hard. Caitlin's beautiful emerald eyes were glistening with tears and in those few heartrending seconds he had never felt lower.

'I never meant to hurt you,' he breathed, lifting his hand to dry the moisture that tracked down her cheek.

She immediately backed away. 'Forget it.' Not giving him even the merest glance, instead she looked at Rick and enquired, 'Are the boys in the bar?' He nodded. 'Then I'll go and join them.'

She headed towards the door—but not before she heard him say to Jake, 'Just as well I'm around to pick up the pieces.'

CHAPTER TWELVE

JAKE COULDN'T BELIEVE that Caitlin had accepted a lift back to her guesthouse from Kenny Swan. The man was a smooth-talking Lothario, old enough to be her father. What on earth had possessed her? He had been all over her like a cheap suit, and if it hadn't been for the fact that Rick had pleaded with Jake not to make a fuss, because at the end of the gig Swan had offered them a lucrative contract, Jake would have put him straight about a few things.

As far as he was concerned a deal wasn't a deal until all the 'i's had been dotted and the 't's crossed, and he wasn't agreeing to a damn thing until he examined the details for himself...*preferably* under a microscope. He hadn't spent fifteen years working in the industry for nothing.

But right then, even though Blue Sky's good fortune should have been uppermost in his mind, it wasn't. *Caitlin* was. He could have strangled Rick for forcing the issue be-tween them out into the open like that, without any regard for their feelings. No wonder Caitlin was mad at Jake. She had every right to be. And now he was suffering all kinds of agony, wondering if Kenny Swan had taken her straight back to her guesthouse or whether he had persuaded her to go home with him to his penthouse in Mayfair.

As far as pretty women went, rumour had it that the man had very few scruples. And it was little consolation to Jake to recall that Caitlin's friend Lia had been with her. He'd in-tuited that the blonde could easily take care of herself, and

Kenny wouldn't have hesitated to drop her off at the guest-house and then continue on to London with Caitlin, should she agree to the arrangement.

But even as he had the thought Jake knew that she *wouldn't*. She would never abandon her friend...she was far too loyal for that.

If only Jake hadn't been waylaid by the rest of the band, wanting to discuss the record deal, at the same time that Caitlin had been ensnared by Kenny at the bar, he would have persuaded her to go outside with him and get some fresh air. By the time he'd been able to return his attention to them Jake had seen that they were gone. He'd dashed outside, only to see the tail-end of Kenny's gleaming sedan with its tinted windows disappearing into the night—no doubt with Caitlin seated snugly beside him while her little blonde girlfriend sat in the back.

'I thought you could probably use this.' Rick placed a steaming cup of black coffee on the bar and pulled up a stool next to Jake.

The venue was slowly emptying of late-night revellers who'd watched the band and were clearly reluctant to go home. Behind the two men bar staff were methodically clearing tables and stacking chairs. A mournful-sounding love song was playing softly in the background, and Jake couldn't help but feel despondent. The relentless longing for Caitlin that had taken up residence in his heart didn't abate, and he knew it was serious. The mere idea that she might walk away and find somebody else was simply not to be tolerated. *It dawned on him then that he'd move heaven and earth just to be with her...*

'Thanks.'

'I scrounged it off a pretty barmaid...charmed her with my good looks and irresistible wit.'

'Now, there's a surprise,' Jake commented drolly.

The two men fell silent for a while.

As if disturbed by the gloomy expression that flitted across his friend's features, Rick remarked consolingly, 'Kenny's probably just dropped her off at the guesthouse. Cait's a clever girl. If he tries anything she'll soon put him straight.'

'You think? But I could hardly blame her if she *did* go home with him, could I?' Jake stared grimly down into his coffee.

'You really care about her, don't you?'

There was a tone of genuine surprise in the other man's voice.

'Is that so hard to believe?'

'I'm sorry, buddy. I just—'

Jake sighed. 'What I felt for Jodie all those years ago wasn't love, Rick. I was just tired of being alone and I kidded myself she was important to me in the ridiculous hope that my feelings might grow fonder. Needless to say, when I realised she only wanted me for what she could get, they *didn't*. As things turned out…I'm glad about that. I'd rather she took my money and everything I possessed than broke my heart. That's a pain I couldn't get over so easily.' Grimacing, he shook his head. 'But what I feel for Caitlin is… Well, it's like nothing I've ever experienced before. I already know she's got the power to break my heart.'

'Sounds to me like it's love, Jake.'

He didn't dispute the fact. For a few heartfelt moments he let the thought settle.

'Look, I know I should put the band first, but to tell you the truth I've been thinking about resigning as manager and asking you to take over. I was thinking I should get out while the going's good and limit any disappointment and ill feeling it might cause. Things are really starting to take off for Blue Sky, and you know exactly what to do to maximise their potential and take them right to the top. They trust you, Rick. You'll all be just fine without me.'

'Why would you want to resign, Jake? Is it because you're afraid of hurting Cait?'

'She deserves this chance just as much as the others do. What she *doesn't* deserve is for me to screw it up because I've become personally involved with her. I don't know if I'm capable of maintaining the necessary professional detachment any more. I feel like a house of cards that's been knocked down. It's not like me to lose my head over a woman. But since falling for Caitlin I can't eat, I can't sleep, and my concentration feels like it's been blown apart by a scatter gun. At this rate I'm not going to be much use to anyone—let alone myself.'

With a rueful grin, Jake raised his coffee to his lips.

It was Rick's turn to sigh. 'Trust me, resigning isn't the answer. Cait wouldn't want that, and nor would the guys. And *nor*, for that matter, would I. If you want her then go after her, man! What are you sitting here for? If she *has* gone back to Kenny's—'

'I thought you said that wasn't likely?'

Jake's cup clattered against the saucer and hot black coffee sloshed messily over the side. He was suddenly seized by the most terrible doubt. *Would* Caitlin have been persuaded by Kenny to go home with him? What if she had agreed in order to teach Jake a lesson?

'Hey, slow down. Of course it's not.' Rick said. 'Look, I'm sorry if I haven't been as supportive as I could have been. I guess I'm just very protective of the band. I'll just have to accept the fact that you and Cait are an item now. Having got to know her a little, and knowing you like I do, I'm sure you won't let your relationship damage the band in any way. To tell you the truth, I'm glad you've finally found someone you really care about. In my opinion, you couldn't have found anyone better than Caitlin. She's pretty special. If you really want to check that she's okay why don't you drive over to the guesthouse and see if you can talk to her?' he exhorted.

Moved by his friend's support, and clutching at a ray of hope he perhaps had no right to cling to, Jake glanced down at his watch.

'It's two in the morning, Rick. I booked her into a guest-house because she said she didn't want to stay in another soulless swanky hotel, and the place is run by a landlady who's about as friendly as Attila the Hun. When I booked the place that reassured me. She keeps strict hours and she likes her guests to be back before midnight. The prospect of banging on her door at this hour of the night just so that I can tell Caitlin I—'

'Love her?'

The grin hijacking his friend's face was wide. Jake scowled. Then he drove his hands agitatedly through his hair.

'Is that what you call this perpetual longing and needing and climbing the walls when I can't be with her?'

The other man nodded knowingly.

Inside Jake's chest his heartbeat stumbled at the realisation that he'd allowed Caitlin to believe that his attraction to her was purely physical. *He'd been seriously kidding himself.* Now he knew that he'd put her happiness and wellbeing way above his own. That was why he'd told Rick he was willing to resign as the group's manager.

He blew out a long, slow breath. 'Then I guess you're right. But if she thinks that means us moving in together into some detached mock-Georgian in the suburbs then we're likely to have our first real fight. I couldn't do it. That's why I've never settled anywhere. I'm a born gypsy. I get too restless to stay in one place for long…you know that.'

'Yeah, and I also know that you haven't even asked the lady what she wants yet. First you need to tell her that you love her. Caitlin's a great girl, Jake. She's as passionate as you are and she loves the band. She loves singing. Do you think she would have auditioned if she'd wanted to settle for some safe little existence in the suburbs? I hardly think so.'

Glancing back at Rick, he felt the ray of hope that had surfaced earlier suddenly grow much brighter.

'Hey, if you ever get tired of being on the road I could see you winding up as some sort of relationship counsellor.'

'You think so?'

'No, I don't.' To Rick's consternation, Jake lightly punched him on the shoulder and laughed. 'Not in a million years.'

'That aside, what are you going to do about Cait? Are you going to try and see her tonight?'

'No… Not tonight. It's been a tough few days and she needs her rest. I'll just have to trust she went back to the guesthouse with Lia and go and see her in the morning. In the meantime…' He reached into his back pocket to retrieve his mobile, 'I'll send her a text…just to check.'

'Sounds like a plan. Now that's settled, how about a *real* drink?'

Signalling to one of the barmaids, Rick gave her one of his incorrigible smiles and looked hopeful.

Having ordered a latte and a blueberry muffin, Caitlin stared out through the café window at the frigid purple and grey sky that definitely heralded rain. It didn't particularly disturb her. She couldn't feel much gloomier than she did already.

The impersonal little text she'd received last night from Jake had hardly been reassuring.

Hope you enjoyed last night's gig and got back to the guesthouse OK. I'll catch up with you in the morning.

He hadn't even included an 'x' to denote a kiss.

But then she knew she had played her part when she'd stupidly accepted a lift from Kenny Swan without even telling him. She'd done it because Jake had been busy talking to the rest of the band and she had felt inexplicably jealous. *Ignored.* She knew it was ridiculous, because he *was* the group's manager, but right then she hadn't wanted to share him with anyone. Even Lia's reassuring presence hadn't consoled her.

The news about the recording contract was wonderful, but her pleasure was sadly tainted by the hurtful realisation that the man she loved didn't love her back.

'Cheer up, love, it may never happen.' The handsome young assistant who had taken her order returned with her coffee and cake.

'What did you say?' She glanced up at him, not comprehending.

'You looked sad…I was just trying to cheer you up. Anyway, enjoy your coffee.' With a cheeky wink and a tuneless whistle, he returned behind the counter.

Discovering that she'd suddenly lost all desire for cake, and after taking just a few sips of her coffee, Caitlin scraped back her chair, left the money for her bill on the table and hurriedly left. *How could she possibly eat when all she could think about was Jake?*

'Where have you been?'

He was waiting outside the guesthouse when she returned and the expression on his face was as implacable as ever. Steeling herself against the blast of icy wind that suddenly hit her, Caitlin shoved her long hair out of her eyes and stared.

'It's nice to see you, too,' she murmured..

'I was worried about you. I even got your landlady to check your room—which was no easy feat, I can tell you. She told me that your bed was made but she couldn't tell whether you'd slept in it or not.' Stepping towards her, he frowned. 'What's going on, Caitlin?'

'Nothing… I just went for a cup of coffee, that's all.'

'So you *did* sleep in your bed last night?'

'Of course I did.'

'Why didn't you reply to my message asking if you were Okay?'

'It was two o'clock in the morning when you sent it—that's why. I was tired and I fell back to sleep. Wait a minute…where did you think I'd slept if it wasn't in my bed at the guesthouse?'

'You were eager enough to go off with Kenny.'

'The man offered us a lift, and because you seemed busy talking to Rick and the others I accepted. I was tired, Jake. I'm still a novice at this game and I expend a lot of energy trying to get it right.'

'You're doing just fine, Caitlin. In fact you never cease to amaze me with how dedicated you are in giving a great performance. Last night you were flawless. You knocked it out of the park!'

'Thanks.'

Her smile was guarded and a flash of pain squeezed at Jake's heart. *Had he pushed her too hard?* He'd hate to think she wasn't deriving any pleasure from singing with the band any more.

Making a concerned examination of her features, he noticed for the first time that she was unusually pale, and beneath her lovely green eyes he could see bruising shadows.

'We should talk,' he said quietly.

'Not right now. I need to go inside and pack and say goodbye to my friend. She'll be wondering where I am. I didn't wake her to let her know I was going out.'

She moved towards the steps that led up to the house's front door. Jake stared in disbelief. Then he came to his senses and caught hold of her arm.

'Are you trying to hide something from me, Caitlin?'

'What do you mean?'

'Tell me the truth. *Did* you stay at Kenny's place last night?' He was unable to hold back his fury at the thought.

Her green eyes flashed.

'I already told you that I didn't. The man is a snake. I

know he wants to sign us, but if the agreement means he has some unspoken right to make suggestive remarks to me whenever he gets the chance then you can find another singer—and I don't say that lightly. I love this band, and I want it to do well. But I've played the part of sacrificial lamb before, and I'm damn sure I'm not going to play it again. Not for anybody!'

'Did he insult you? Hurt you?' Jake's voice was a gravelly undertone.

He could hardly believe that he'd put Caitlin in such a vulnerable position. When he saw Kenny Swan again he'd have to be physically restrained from connecting his fist to his jaw…contract or no contract. And he was pretty sure the rest of the crew would feel the same.

'Of course he didn't. Apart from making me cringe at some of the comments he made about his sexual prowess and inviting me to join him in his hot tub he didn't try anything. Anyway, Lia was with me,' she answered. 'Plus, like I told you before, I'm tougher than I look. Lucky for me I wear any bruises I acquire on the *inside*.'

The idea that he might be responsible for some of those invisible bruises affected Jake more deeply than he could say.

'I'm sorry. But you should never have agreed to let him drive you home. You should have come to get me and I would have taken you and Lia back to the guesthouse straight away. Now, why don't you go and say goodbye to Lia, then come back to my hotel with me?'

Caitlin couldn't easily hide the resentment that flashed through her. She pulled her arm free and rubbed it.

'What would be the point, Jake? If you want to talk about our relationship then there's really not much to discuss, is there? Why prolong the agony? We had an affair…a meaningless affair. It happens all the time—especially in this business. You of all people should know that.'

'Meaningless? Is that what you think this is?'

Jake hated hearing her talk like that…as if he made a habit of sleeping with different women just because he could. He'd never been a saint, but neither was he promiscuous—despite what the gossip columns might have suggested over the years.

For the first time since he'd acknowledged his feelings about Caitlin to himself Jake was forced to consider that perhaps she didn't feel as intensely as he did. The thought was so unpalatable that it hit him with all the force of an express train travelling at full speed. Suddenly being uncertain of his ground shook him badly.

'Like I said, you've made your feelings about me pretty clear.' She sighed. 'It was me that clouded things with my stupid hopes and dreams. You'd think I would have learned after Sean, wouldn't you? Anyway, the band is the most important thing…not whatever's going on between you and me. At least we're agreed on that.'

Twisting her hands together, Caitlin managed a tremulous smile just before she turned away.

If I can just hold it together until he goes, she thought, then I might…just might…get through this with my pride and dignity intact. And I might stop him from ever finding out that he's the only man who has my heart and always will…

'You're wrong, you know.'

Still with her back to Jake, Caitlin released a weary sigh. 'Wrong about what?'

'The band *isn't* the most important thing to me.'

She froze. Then she slowly turned round to find him wearing a smile that was uninhibitedly warm and sexy, and it drove every single thought out of her head. His twinkling glance fused to hers and she couldn't have looked away even if she'd wanted to. As her body was suffused with unexpected heat even the icy wind swirling round them seemed suddenly to grow less frigid.

Her mouth drying, she asked, 'It isn't?'

'No, it isn't. *You* are, Caitlin. You're the most important thing in my life. I'm not proud of the way I've handled things between us, but to say I've never felt like this before would be the understatement of the century. An earthquake couldn't have shaken me up more.'

'I wondered where you'd got to, Cait. Now I see what's delayed you.'

The front door opened to reveal the diminutive Lia, dressed in pink sweatshirt and jeans, her brown eyes alighting on Jake as if she'd inadvertently stumbled upon the devil incarnate.

'What's *he* doing here? Unless he's come to talk to you about work then I think you should tell him to go. He'll only upset you, and you've had enough grief from him already to last you a lifetime.'

'Hang on a minute, Lia, I—'

Caitlin was cut short when the blonde hurried down the steps and pushed her aside to plant herself in front of Jake. With her hands on her hips, she proceeded to tell him exactly how she felt.

'She broke her heart over you last night, Jake Sorenson. She cried like the rain. I've never seen her cry like that since she was with Sean—and he took her for a ride too, making promises he never intended to keep. I *told* her you'd break her heart. Well, I hope you're feeling proud of yourself. And then, if your own conduct wasn't bad enough, you go and leave her in the clutches of that middle-aged Lothario, reeking of enough cologne to sink a battleship! Thank heaven I was with her last night or God only knows what might have happened. If you and he are an example of the kind of people in the music industry then Caitlin would be better off singing at our local pub on a Saturday night. At least she'd be safe.'

Shock jack-knifed roughly through Jake at the thought that he hadn't protected Caitlin when he should have, and regret that he'd caused her even a moment's pain. He could see how the situation must appear to Lia, and he'd be the first to admit it didn't look good. It was a crying shame that his reputation preceded him, because no matter how he behaved he was damned—in the blonde's eyes at least And Kenny Swan's conduct didn't exactly create the best of impressions either.

He fixed the girl with a steely glare.

'Please don't slot me into the same category as Kenny Swan. At least spare me *that* particular insult. I assure you that Blue Sky won't be dealing with him again. More to the point, I'll ensure that Caitlin deals with someone else at the record company. There are plenty of genuinely good people who work there. As for the rest—I think that's between Caitlin and me…don't you?'

'Caitlin?' Her brown eyes glinting like a protective mama bear's, Lia folded her arms and looked round at her friend for confirmation.

Caitlin nodded. 'I'd like to have a few minutes alone with Jake. I think it's needed.'

'Just as long as you don't let him persuade you to do anything you don't want to do. You've got free will, remember? You got over Sean and you can get over *him* too.'

With a warning glance at a bemused Jake, Lia sprinted back up the stairs and went inside the house.

'Does she always behave like an aggrieved matador about to pick a fight with a bull?' he asked dryly.

Caitlin's smile was tentative. 'For some reason she's very protective of me.'

'I'm glad.'

Although in future Jake wanted to be the one doing all the protecting. He knew that now—knew it without a single doubt. The thought was exhilarating…like a hang glider hitting a warm air thermal. All he had to do now was convince her that he was in earnest.

'Will you come back with me to the hotel for a while? I'd really like to say what I have to say to you in private.'

Smoothing her hand down the front of her raincoat, Caitlin sucked in a steadying breath.

'I have something I want to say to you too, Jake. But I'm not waiting until we get back to your hotel. It's better said out here, in the open. You've told me that I'm important to you, but the truth is…the truth is I don't know if I can be enough for you.'

She swallowed hard, her cheeks glowing a little with embarrassment.

'What about the next pretty girl who becomes infatuated with you? You like your lifestyle just the way it is. You don't want to commit yourself to one person and I don't want anything less.'

There…she'd finally said it. She'd put her cards on the table and the consequences be damned.

'Is that what you think? That you're not enough for me?'

To Caitlin's consternation, he laughed out loud.

'I don't know if I could handle you if you were any more woman than you are already, but I'd willingly die trying! What's all this talk about not being enough? Caitlin, you're my fantasy come to life—my most heartfelt dream come true. Why would I be remotely interested in any other woman? It's true that there will always be pretty women in this business, but that doesn't mean I'll be remotely interested. Why would I if I have you? In any case, most of my time and energy goes into my work, and that's the way I've wanted it…up until now, that is.'

With a meaningful pause Jake allowed his gorgeous blue eyes to reflect a promise that Caitlin hardly dared believe.

He continued. 'And now I'm planning on using some of that time and energy in keeping you one very happy and contented woman, Caitlin Ryan…for the rest of your life.'

'What are you telling me, Jake?' She still wasn't convinced of the startling equation her fevered brain had helplessly arrived at.

'Is it really so hard to comprehend?' He smiled, 'I'm asking you to marry me.'

'You're serious?'

Her breath caught on a gasp. She was giddy and light-headed at the same time, just as if she'd been spinning on a carousel.

'I'm perfectly serious.'

Jake purposefully covered the short distance between them and took hold of Caitlin's hands in earnest.

'Don't you get it? I love you and I want you to be my wife. I think you already know what a nomadic life this is, being on the road with a band…it's never going to be a con-ventional lifestyle. I'd be lying to you if I said it would be.'

'That's a relief, because that wouldn't suit me at all. I'm a bona fide rock chick now, remember? I have my reputation to consider.' Caitlin's smile was uninhibitedly warm. 'Home will always be wherever we are together, Jake. There's a big wide world out there and I want to see some of it. If you're willing, you could show me, couldn't you?'

'I can't think of anything I'd like more.'

Suddenly impatient, Jake pulled her into his arms and planted a hot, hungry kiss on her mouth. He heard the soft helpless moan she breathed as he gently withdrew. Drawing the pad of his thumb down over her cheek, he was deeply satisfied to see the mutual desire and longing that her pretty green eyes reflected back at him.

'But I don't want you to think that I'm not open to com-promise regarding a more permanent home,' he told her. 'Eventually I'd like us to have children…buy a place in the country, maybe? A place where they'll have plenty of space to play and grow up.'

Caitlin couldn't help but be moved by his heartfelt dec-laration. To hear Jake say that he wanted them to have chil-dren, that he was more than willing to embrace the prospect and ensure that his own children did not have a lonely child-hood bereft of family or siblings like he had done… Well, it was *beyond* wonderful.

She sighed. 'I love you, Jake…I love you with all my

heart. There's no one I'd want to be the father of my children but you. Do you really want to marry me?'

'Right now I can't think of anything I want more than for you to be my wife. Except perhaps to have you naked in my bed.'

'And us being married—it won't cramp your famous rock and roll lifestyle?'

Jake grimaced. 'The so-called rock and roll lifestyle isn't all it's cracked up to be. For one, it's bloody lonely out on the road for weeks at a time, and after a while one hotel room looks much the same as another…whether it's in Islington or Istanbul. I'm never going to be a conventional nine-to-five husband, Caitlin, but I'll always be there for you when you need me. That's a promise.'

'Then I suppose my answer to such a sincere and heartfelt proposal has to be yes.'

'Yes, what?'

Lia put her head impatiently round the door, her chin jutted warningly towards Jake.

Grinning, Caitlin told her. 'Jake has just asked me to marry him.'

Lia's face was a picture. Tussling between giving them both a lecture and fighting the urge to smile, because of the way Jake's twinkling blue eyes were all but devouring her friend, she concluded that it would be a crime against passion for the two of them *not* to get married.

'Oh. I suppose that's all right, then.'

Jake's eyebrows flew up. 'You mean we have your permission?'

'You know very well that Caitlin doesn't need my permission.' With an irritated huff, Lia stepped out to survey them properly. 'But when you care about people you naturally want what's best for them.'

'I agree.' Glancing towards her, he said clearly, 'I love your friend, Lia. And, if you'd be so kind as to leave us alone together for a while, I won't hesitate to demonstrate the fact.'

The neatly painted front door of the guesthouse closed behind Lia with an obliging click.

As Jake's mouth descended avariciously on Caitlin's lips a profound sense of coming home rolled over her. The sensation was so powerful and so warm that she knew to the depths of her soul that there was no more room for doubt or mistrust. She was no longer a displaced person, aching for someone to love who would unreservedly love her back.

She'd grown in confidence since joining Blue Sky, and wherever her journey as a singer took her everything would be all right—because Jake would be there with her, loving her and rooting for her all the way…her husband, her manager, her friend—and, one day, the beloved father of her children.

Long seconds later Jake broke off their kiss to gaze deeply into Caitlin's eyes. 'There's just one small snag,' he said seriously.

'Oh? What's that?'

'You *do* know that we're probably going to have to contend with Rick singing a solo at the wedding?'

'Is there any way we can divert him?'

'We can always ask Tina, the barmaid at the Pilgrim's Inn, if she'd help us out.'

'Do you think that she would?'

'How could she *resist?*'

They were still laughing as they ascended the guesthouse steps, intent on sharing a celebratory drink with Lia.

* * * * *

LET'S TALK

Romance

For exclusive extracts, competitions
and special offers, find us online:

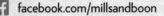

- facebook.com/millsandboon
- @MillsandBoon
- @MillsandBoonUK

Get in touch on 01413 063232

For all the latest titles coming soon, visit
millsandboon.co.uk/nextmonth